The Trickster's Song

Samantha MacLeod

Published by Samantha MacLeod, 2018.

THE TRICKSTER'S SONG

First edition. August 17, 2018.

Written by Samantha MacLeod.

To Jayne, who read the first version and said it should be longer.

You were right.

FAIR WARNING

Welcome, reader.

You've picked up the third book in a series. You are, of course, quite welcome to read this series out of order. Most of this particular book takes place in the distant past, and you don't need to read the previous books in order to follow Loki's story.

However, if you're wondering how the Norse god Loki came to marry the mortal woman Caroline, you can find that story in *The Trickster's Lover*[1]. If you'd like to read about the circumstances surrounding the birth of their daughter Adelina, those events take place in *The Wolf's Lover*[2].

Also, please be warned.

This story is not tame. There are graphic depictions of sexual encounters, violence, sexual assault, and the death of major characters.

Still interested?

Good. Then move a little closer to the fire, my friend, and let's begin.

---

1.   https://www.amazon.com/Tricksters-Lover-Erotic-Loki-Romance-ebook/dp/
       B01K352QNA/ref=sr_1_1?ie=UTF8&qid=1498491200&sr=8-
       1&keywords=trickster's+lover

2.   https://www.amazon.com/dp/B078VNWKT3/
       ref=sr_1_7?s=books&ie=UTF8&qid=1515327655&sr=1-7

CHAPTER ONE

"Do you really think she'll be all right?"

I glanced up from the mirror in our bedroom, where I was fumbling to jab a sparkly earring into my earlobe, and saw Loki's shoulders straighten. If I had to guess, I'd say the Norse god of fire and lies was stifling a sigh.

He turned and gave me a glorious smile. "Yes, darling. I think she'll be fine."

"But we've never left her alone before..."

I glanced toward the closed door of the nursery where Adelina was sleeping, for now, and fought the urge to check on her just one more time.

"You leave her with me every day when you go to work, do you not?"

"Well, that's different," I protested. "You're her dad. And you're a god."

"You did interview twelve candidates for this babysitting position, my darling."

I sighed. "I know. But—"

"And Stephanie was here for two hours yesterday. I think you showed her how to operate the Diaper Genie at least five times." Loki looked like he was struggling to suppress a smile.

"But what if—"

He wrapped his arm around my waist and pressed a finger to my lips. "Wife, when was the last time we went out?"

"Uh—" I stammered. "Before the semester started?"

He shook his head, and I tried to think. It was difficult to remember what life had been like before Adelina was born. And it had only been— Wait, how long had it been?

"Four months," I said. "Didn't we go out to dinner just before she was born?"

His arm tightened around my waist. "Five."

"Really?"

"Five."

Loki started to nibble my ear. I almost pushed him away, but his lips actually felt...*good*. I leaned against him and tried to remember what it felt like to be turned on, to crave the sensation of his body pressed against mine.

"I took you to Bali," he whispered. "We had dinner on the beach."

"Oh!"

Heat raced to my cheeks. I remembered that dinner. I also remembered what we'd done afterward, on an isolated stretch of white beach, as the moon rose over the gently phosphorescing waves. I'd been supremely, hugely pregnant. Everything about me had been round and swollen, from my cheeks to my ankles. I felt revolting.

But my husband made me feel like a goddess.

I had so many orgasms under that tropical moon I thought I'd pass out. In fact, I must have passed out, because the last thing I remembered about that night was waking up naked in our bedroom, in sheets filled with the fine, white sand of Bali's beaches.

And then Adelina showed up, two weeks earlier than anticipated. And things had—

Well, they had changed, of course. What did I expect?

The doorbell rang, and I jumped out of Loki's arms. A second later Adelina's shrieking cry pierced the air, slicing through my chest like a cold knife. My brief flicker of arousal vanished with my Bali memories, and I rushed to her bedroom.

My daughter was red-faced and wailing in her crib. She'd broken free of her careful swaddle wrap, and her tiny fists railed at the world. Her face was a contortion of rage beneath her flaming hair.

I loved her so much it hurt, like a kick to the gut.

"Shhhhh, Mommy's here," I whispered as I wrapped her in my arms.

Adelina arched her back in response to my pathetic attempts at comforting. Like she always did. A month ago, Dr. Singh diagnosed her with colic, shrugged, and told me some children are just more difficult than others.

Lucky me, I'd thought. I couldn't just have a nice, normal baby.

And then I'd felt so guilty for that horrible thought I had cried in the parked car for twenty minutes after the appointment while Adelina shrieked in the backseat.

I heard Loki chatting with Stephanie in the living room as I rocked Adelina, trying to find the right position. In my three months of motherhood, I'd discovered you can still hear a lot, once you get the hang of filtering out all the screaming. I changed Adelina's diaper, offered her a breast, and rubbed her back while I listened to the innocuous chatter in the living room. Adelina was still wailing when Loki entered the nursery.

And then she stopped, as abruptly as she'd begun. Her huge, blue eyes focused on Loki's face, and her mouth arched into a smile. She was so beautiful, so tiny and vulnerable and absolutely perfect, that I suddenly wanted to cry.

"Oh, honey, I don't think we should leave her," I whispered.

Loki took Adelina from me and kissed her forehead. "Be good," he whispered.

I could have sworn she nodded.

He shifted the newly changed Adelina to rest against his shoulder and reached for me. "We are leaving," he said. "Mortal woman, it has been four months."

I sighed. Loki tugged me toward his body, and I fell into his arms. I closed my eyes against his neck, breathing him in, salt and wood smoke and the milky warmth of Adelina. Damn, I was so tired I could probably fall asleep like this, propped up by his strong chest. I couldn't remember the last time I'd slept through the night; right after Bali, perhaps. And Loki slept even less. He claimed he didn't need sleep, but I wondered about that when I woke at two in the morning to see him leaning against the wall, our daughter nestled in his arms, his face pale and solemn in the moonlight filtering through our window.

Loki shifted, kissed the top of my head, and then kissed Adelina until she giggled. He stepped out of our embrace, lifting Adelina's little body in front of him.

"Look at your mother," he whispered into her tiny shell-shaped ear. "Doesn't she look delicious tonight?"

His hungry eyes traveled the curves of my black dress, and something hot flared deep inside me. Something I hadn't felt in a very long time.

"Okay," I said, smoothing my hair. "Okay. She'll be fine. Right?"

Loki grinned and twirled with Adelina in the hallway. "She'll be fine," he sang as they danced to the living room.

Stephanie, our new babysitter, was the model of professionalism. She had a master's degree in child development and worked as a nanny during the day. By the time I interviewed her, a cold desperation had taken root in my gut; I'd gone through so many sitters and nannies who looked great on paper only to panic at the thought of actually leaving my defenseless newborn baby with them. When Loki finally convinced me Stephanie wasn't hiding any dark secrets, I offered to pay her double what we'd advertised.

No wonder she was smiling.

Or perhaps her warm smile had something to do with Loki. His black suit clung to his body in all the right places, showing off his lean muscles. His pale eyes danced above his high cheekbones and soft lips. And when he smiled—

I shook my head, trying to convince myself that sudden pang of jealousy was totally irrational. He was a Norse god, after all. Of course he's attractive. To young, unattached babysitters. Young, unattached, blonde babysitters.

"Thank you so much for having me," Stephanie gushed.

My chest tightened as I watched them together. Did Stephanie's finger just linger on Loki's arm?

"Oh, thank you," he said, dismissively. There was a ragged edge to his voice, and his eyes were examining the low neckline of my black dress.

The house suddenly felt a few degrees warmer. Shit, I thought, maybe I did remember what it was like to be turned on.

"We'll be back soon," I stammered, tearing my gaze away from the obvious intent in Loki's.

"In a few hours," Loki added. His hand touched the small of my back and sparks scattered across my skin. "We're not going far."

By that he meant we were staying on this continent. In San Francisco, even, barely an hour's drive. I'd insisted we travel like normal people, in a normal taxi, just this once. Sometimes things went wrong with Loki's teleportation magic, occasionally very badly wrong, and I didn't want an ocean between me and my child.

I checked Adelina's diaper one last time before we left, kissed her, and barely restrained myself from bursting into tears at the front door. It was basically the same routine I went through every morning when I left to teach at Stanford.

The cab was already waiting for us when Loki stepped through the front door. Loki opened the cab for me and I climbed in, my heart churning with a heady mixture of guilt, relief, and anticipation. Loki's hand was up my skirt before we'd gone a block.

"Honey," I whispered, gesturing frantically with my eyebrows at the cab driver.

Loki put his finger over my lips, a gesture that turned me on much more than it should have. He leaned over to me, his lips brushing my neck. "He can't see us," he whispered.

"Really?"

"When he looks back here, all he sees are two respectable parents chatting about their jobs." Loki's lips brushed my earlobe and my body released a wave of heat, flooding the space between my legs. "I'm an accountant."

I would have giggled, but by then his lips were on mine. Oh, he felt good. His kisses were so hungry, forcing my lips apart, making me moan into his mouth. How long had it been since my body burned like this? I couldn't remember, couldn't even think—

Loki's hands traced the black fabric of my dress, circling my breasts. My nipples jutted to attention, responding to his every move. His hand slipped around my neck and I heard the purr of my zipper as Loki pulled it down. He slipped the dress off my shoulders, exposing my lacy red bra.

"In the cab?" I gasped. "Really?"

"Oh, yes," he said.

My bra came apart with a twang, and his lips were on my nipples, kissing them gently while his hand eased between my thighs. I shot a panicked glance at the rearview mirror; we'd stopped at a red light, and the cab driver looked like he was texting someone. Loki's fingers traced my clit and my head rolled back. Oh, fuck it, I thought.

Loki leaned away from me, and my eyes fluttered open. He gave me a slow, incendiary smile as he licked his fingers. Arousal shot through me like a flame devouring dry kindling. Every part of my body ached for his touch. I yanked my dress up over my thighs and climbed onto his lap.

"Here?" he growled against my neck. "In the cab?"

Heat poured off me in waves. I felt the hot length of his erection through his pants and moved against it, digging my nails into his shoulder. "Oh, fuck, yes," I panted. "Lose the pants."

He laughed and shifted his weight. His pants vanished. For a heartbeat his cock pressed against my entrance and I moaned, wordlessly begging for him. Then his hips thrust against mine, and he entered me.

I gasped. Oh, oh damn, had he always been so big? He filled me so completely it almost hurt. His forehead rested against mine and, for a moment, we were both still, our breath commingling, our bodies wrapped within each other.

When we moved, at first, it was almost as though we moved together, in rhythm, our bodies mirroring each other. Then the cab jolted forward, and Loki's thrusts grew more urgent. The speed felt good, echoing the rocking of his body against mine as the car hummed along the road. I raised my hands, bracing myself against the ceiling of the cab, pushing him further into me. His hips thrust beneath me, faster and less rhythmic, and I thought *oh damn, oh yes, I'm going to make him come for me, I'm going to make him—*

His body shuddered beneath me, and I came hard, screaming his name. My orgasm swept over me for a long time, erasing the world, erasing everything but the pleasure his body brought me.

When my mind finally staggered back to reality, Loki's arms were wrapped around my shoulders. "I believe we're almost there," he whispered.

I jumped. "Shit!"

Loki grinned as I pushed myself off his lap, trying to fasten my bra and smooth my dress as the cab slowed to a stop. My body tingled slightly when the driver knocked on the plexiglass window, a feeling I'd learned to recognize as Loki's illusions dispersing. I hoped I didn't look half as flustered and red-faced as I felt when I climbed out of the cab.

The restaurant Loki had chosen was one of those trendy Bay Area hotspots, all white and chrome with a menu that listed what farms the ingredients came from. It didn't seem like Loki's style, and I raised an eyebrow as we settled into our table near the window.

"Best wine list in town," he said, giving me a smile that made me ache for him all over again.

"Great," I stammered. "Bring on the wine."

CHAPTER TWO

After two unreasonably expensive glasses of wines whose names I could barely pronounce, and a first course of what I thought were steamed dandelion leaves, Loki leaned across the table. His lips touched my ear.

"There's quite a nice room directly upstairs," he whispered. "And it just happens to be completely empty."

His hand traced my thigh, moving upward. I glanced around the restaurant as my cheeks burned.

"Really?" I squeaked.

"Oh, you'd love it." His hand reached further. Heat smoldered in my core as his fingers brushed the edge of my sexiest black undies.

The waiter cleared his throat. I pulled away from Loki's touch as the waiter set a plate of smoked fish in front of me. He said something about how it was caught and prepared, but I wasn't listening. I was too busy watching Loki's eyes undress me from across the table.

"Yeah, let's go," I whispered, once the waiter finally left.

My husband's eyes sparkled. "Don't you want to eat first?"

"No." I reached under the table and caressed his thigh. "Just... you know, leave a placeholder or something—"

—And Loki's arms were around my waist, pushing me backward. I had a moment of vertigo as a patterned beige ceiling spun above me, and I caught a glimpse of dark windows filled with twinkling lights. Then Loki pressed me against something cool and hard, his lips were on mine, and I lost myself in our kiss. Loki's lips and tongue explored me slowly, teasing me, reigniting the same fire he'd kindled in the taxi on the way here. For a moment, I wondered how I could possibly be turned on again, after months of wanting nothing more than to sleep without being interrupted, when Loki pulled away.

I gasped when his lips left mine. The air felt colder without his body pressed against mine. My eyes slowly adjusted to the dimly lit and expansive room around us. An entire wall of windows showed the dazzling lights of downtown San Francisco silhouetted by the dark waters of the bay. The room's pale green walls were decorated with enormous, dark paintings, some sort of modern art that was vaguely disquieting, and the room was lit with a low, golden glow from lights embedded in the ceiling. Clearly, this room was closed for business.

The cold, hard surface below me appeared to be a desk. I pushed myself up to sitting, trying not to knock an elegant, abstract glass sculpture off the edge of the desk's dark wooden surface. It looked very expensive.

"Where are we?" I asked.

Loki's smile widened as he stepped backward. "A few stories up."

I twisted to look out the windows again. Yes, that sounded about right. The lights of 555 California Tower flickered in the darkness a few blocks off, and I could see the distant glow of the Golden Gate Bridge.

"And don't worry," Loki added. "I left an illusion in the restaurant."

His back was turned to me, and he seemed to be examining the wall opposite the windows. It was the only surface in the room that didn't feature an enormous and expensive-looking canvas. In fact, the only thing on the entire wall was what looked like a small, black keypad.

"For all intents and purposes, my love," Loki continued, "we appear to be a perfectly normal couple."

My laugh echoed through the room as I imagined us in the restaurant downstairs, Loki pretending to be an accountant and me pretending to be interested.

"Is this an...office?" I asked.

He nodded.

"Whose office?"

Loki's pale eyes flickered at me in the low light. "A merciless warlord. You'd like him, I bet. I'll have to invite him over one of these days."

He turned toward me with a half-smile so damn seductive it made my cheeks flush with heat. I dropped my eyes, only to notice how his tight black pants revealed the curving bulge of his formidable erection.

Oh. A familiar heat spiraled through my abdomen, and my throat suddenly felt tight. We used to fuck all night, Loki and I. There were times we'd drink wine and trade orgasms until the sun came up.

But everything changed when Adelina was born. At first, my body was so shredded from the birth I didn't even want to contemplate using toilet paper, let alone making love. And then, once my wounds had healed, I was so exhausted I could hardly think straight. For the first time since Loki appeared in my life, all I wanted to do with him was sleep.

I hadn't wanted to admit how terrified I'd been that my sex life was over, and I was doomed to live with the most attractive god in the Norse pantheon and an MIA libido. But now the slow burn of my arousal was building again, and the space between my legs was slick in anticipation and relief.

Yes, what happened in the taxi felt amazing. But no, it wasn't nearly enough.

I slipped out of my heels and slid off the desk, padding across the thick carpet to my husband. I embraced him from behind, pressing my cheek against his back until I could smell him, that cold salt and wood smoke scent that felt so much like home.

"Date night was a good idea," I sighed.

"I know," he replied.

Loki shifted slightly under my touch, raising his hand until it hovered over the black keypad on the wall. A heartbeat later, bright yellow sparks flew from the keypad in front of Loki's open palm. I yelped and jumped backward. A moment later, the entire wall slid open, revealing shelves stacked to the ceiling with the largest collection of wine bottles I'd ever seen.

"The best wine selection in town..." I muttered.

"Oh, you didn't think I meant the restaurant, did you?" Loki asked, raising an eyebrow.

"Very funny."

Loki flashed me a grin before turning to examine the shelves. The dark bottles nestled inside the wooden wine racks gleamed faintly under the golden glow of the recessed lights. Loki ran his fingers over several of the labels, clicking his tongue in appreciation.

"He's always had excellent taste, I must admit," he murmured.

Another shower of sparks flew from the keypad, and the wine racks slid sideways with a low mechanical hum. A shiver danced along my spine as new rows of bottles slid into place with a delicate click.

"And how will he feel? About us, uh, showing up?" I asked.

Loki pulled an elegant emerald bottle from the shelves and turned to me. "He'll be delighted, my darling."

He pressed the bottle into my hands. It felt smooth and cool, with a wide bottom and a graceful, slender neck.

"Although I suppose he may also be jealous," Loki whispered. "You are unusually beautiful, my wife."

My cheeks burned, and I opened my mouth to disagree. No one but Loki ever called me unusually beautiful.

"Shhhhhh," Loki said, pressing his finger to my lips. "Tell me. What do you think of the wine?"

I lifted the bottle and examined the label. I knew absolutely nothing about wine. I hadn't bought a bottle since I was in graduate school, and back then the only thing I looked at was the price tag.

But I recognized this name, written in a heavy, elegant serif font. Dom Pérignon. The faded brown label read 1959. My hands trembled.

"Shit," I said. "Isn't this, like, a thousand dollars a bottle?"

"More than that. Significantly more."

Loki's delicate fingers wrapped around the green bottle's thin neck. "Do you know how you open the world's most expensive bottle of champagne?"

I shook my head.

His smile widened as he tore the thin golden foil off the top. "The same way you open anything else."

Loki shook the bottle, then slipped his hands up the neck. A moment later the room resounded with an explosive pop, and I shrieked as cold bubbles poured over my fingers. Loki's laugh filled the room, making it feel warmer.

He raised the bottle to my mouth, and I caught the foaming stream between my lips. I've always loved champagne, and this was good; the carbonation sparkled across my tongue, and the dry sweetness made me think of summer sunlight.

Loki tilted his head to the side. "You know what would improve this?"

I knew better than to answer. A moment later something cold tickled the back of my neck, like a melting snowflake. I glanced down and was not entirely surprised to realize I was now standing totally naked in the middle of some stranger's very elegant office, holding an overflowing bottle of world's most expensive champagne.

"Better," Loki purred. He looked at me like he fully intended to devour me.

I lifted the champagne bottle to my lips, already feeling warm and happy from the two glasses of wine I'd had in the restaurant.

"You try it," I said, holding the bottle out to him.

Loki took it, his eyes flashing. Then he pressed his body against mine, and his clothes vanished. The feel of his cool skin against me made my throat contract until I gasped for breath. He lifted the bottle and drank deeply.

"Not bad," he said. "But—"

He wrapped his hands around my waist and pushed me backward until the hard surface of the desk jutted into my thigh. His lips met mine again, kissing me deeply. He tasted like champagne, sparkling and warm. My body thrummed with heat, a deep, red pulse surging from between my legs and filling every cell of my body. Damn, I wanted him. It didn't matter that we were in the middle of someone else's office, naked, drinking stolen champagne. Nothing was as important, as urgent and desperate, as the pull of his sex, the pleasure we made together.

Loki brought the thick, green bottle to his chest, pressing it between my heavy breasts before he raised it to trail the smooth glass over my collarbone and along my neck. I shivered; his touch on my neck always made me weak with lust.

He bent over my chest, bringing his lips to my jawbone. The bottle tilted in his hands, parting my hair around its smooth, round surface. I had just enough time to wonder what the hell he was doing when the cold splash of champagne trickled past my ear.

I yelped, but Loki held me still. He dropped his lips to my chest, licking the sparkling champagne from my collarbone and neck. My cry of surprise turned into a low whimper of longing.

"It's much better that way," Loki growled.

The bottle pressed against my back, its neck running along my skin, tracing the same path Loki's tongue had just blazed. He tilted the bottle again, and champagne poured across my shoulders and down my breasts. I gasped at the cold but, before I could speak, Loki's lips were on me again. He sucked the foaming liquid from my nipples, groaning with pleasure.

My milk-heavy breasts tingled with his touch. I sank my fingers into his thick, red hair, letting the pleasure of his touch swell through my body. The room spun around me, making me feel like I'd had much more than a few swallows of champagne and a half bottle of wine.

Loki's mouth dropped to suck champagne from the curve of my stomach, tracing my stretch marks with his soft lips. He poured another flood of champagne over my body, and I cried out as the cool liquid raced over my skin. My clit pulsed with a steady, needy throb, but Loki hesitated just above my thighs, his tongue lapping at the champagne beading across my skin.

"Loki," I gasped. "Damn, Loki, please!"

In answer, he pulled the bottle from around my back and poured a stream directly over my breasts. My nipples tightened and ached under the bubbling froth. The liquid splattered across the desk with a soft tinkling sound, like breaking crystal. Champagne foamed between my legs, cool against the heat of my arousal. My hips thrust up as I moaned wordlessly, begging him for release.

With a low, animal groan, Loki's head dropped between my legs. The heat of his lips chased away the cool rush of champagne. I braced myself against the hard surface of the desk as my body rocked against his mouth. I was whimpering now, and the throbbing between my legs was almost unbearable. Loki's tongue snaked across my sex, licking champagne from everything but my clit.

"Oh, champagne is much better this way," Loki purred. I felt his voice as much I heard it, and my body reverberated with waves of desire.

The bottle slipped down my naked chest, sliding over my wet and sticky skin. Loki tipped its green neck between my legs, emptying what was left of the Dom Pérignon over my thighs. I heard it splash against the desk and drip into the carpet.

With another moan of pleasure, Loki descended and began sucking champagne bubbles from my sex. My back arched, and my eyes fluttered shut. I dimly realized I was moaning, whimpering his name over and over.

Something smooth and cool pressed against the wet heat of my sex. Loki's tongue flicked my clit, unleashing a jolt of ecstasy so intense I thought for a minute I'd come right there. Then, as I gasped for breath, Loki slid the neck of the champagne bottle inside me. I had enough time to cry out before his lips returned to my clit, sucking hard this time. I rocked against him as the champagne bottle hit some deep, hidden pleasure center.

"Oh, yes," I cried as my body started to crest. "Yes! Yes! Yes!"

My screams echoed off the enormous windows and the still, silent rows of wine bottles. With Loki's lips on my clit and the champagne bottle buried deep inside me, I came so hard my vision went black. My entire body tensed and then went limp, sinking back against the desk as the dimly lit room swam around me.

Slowly, Loki eased the graceful bottle out of me. He leaned over my chest, slowly licked the green neck, gave me a very predatory smile, and set the empty bottle of Dom Pérignon down gently on the desk next to me.

"I think I'll get another," he said.

My body still hummed with pleasure as I twisted my neck to watch his slender, muscular body cross the room. The sight of his stiff cock made something deep inside me clench with hunger, despite the intensity of the orgasm that had just burned through my body.

Loki lifted another bottle from the shelves. This time, he pulled the cork with his teeth. Another hollow pop echoed through the room, and foaming bubbles surged over his fingers. He brought the bottle to his lips, and I watched the pale flash of his neck as he drank.

"Not bad," Loki said, wiping his mouth with the back of his hand. "Try it."

He crossed the vast room silently and held out another bottle. I sat up to take it, sliding forward in the pool of spilled Dom Pérignon. My naked skin prickled as I swung my legs over the edge of the desk. We'd made quite a mess of this office.

The bottle Loki handed me was darker, and it felt heavier. The name etched in black across the pale brown label, Krug, seemed a bit crude for an elegant champagne. The year read 1924. I giggled.

"I've heard that was a good year," I said, raising the bottle to my lips.

This champagne tasted sharper, with a stronger bite and less fermentation. I put the bottle down to tell Loki what I thought, but his lips met mine before I could speak. He tasted like champagne and the wild, salty tang of my sex. I opened for him, giving him everything, and he moaned into my mouth, still hungry.

Loki's hands tightened around my waist as he pulled me forward. I slid through the pool of champagne and wrapped my legs around his narrow waist. His cock slid inside me without hesitation, without even breaking our deep kiss. His lips caught my moan of pleasure; he was so much bigger than the neck of the champagne bottle. And, damn, he felt so right between my legs, his stiff cock buried deep inside me, as though I'd found a part of myself I hadn't even realized I'd been missing.

He raised the second bottle and splashed a thin stream of foam between our bodies, the liquid slipping between our bodies, making my breasts slide across the solid muscles of his chest.

I didn't think I could possibly come again, but Loki's hips curved into mine, rocking my body against his, and my breath stuttered. My skin felt too hot and too cold at the same time, as though my nerve endings had frayed. The fizzing liquid between us heated with our bodies. Loki's breath came in short gasps above me, but his body moved fluidly, thrusting into me slowly and deeply, rubbing my clit as we came together.

I let my head fall back. Behind me, the lights of San Francisco sparkled against the darkness, their orange and red and white flashes blurring as the ebb and surge of another orgasm teased me, approaching with Loki's deep thrusts, then retreating with his slow, measured pace. I dropped my hand, bracing myself against the champagne-soaked desk, lifting my hips to him.

"Harder," I gasped. "More!"

Loki curled his fingers in my hair, clinging to me. "Yes," he growled.

His back tightened under my legs, and his hips moved faster. It still wasn't enough; I drove my ankles into his thighs, trying to pull him into me. Loki groaned, thrusting into me so hard the heavy desk beneath me squeaked in protest. I sank my fingers into his shoulders, clinging to his writhing body as the red swell of another climax moved closer and closer.

Loki screamed my name, throwing his head back as his cock pulsed inside me. A heartbeat later my own orgasm crashed through me. I held onto him long enough to cry his name before I collapsed against his chest, panting, covered with a mixture of sweat and champagne.

CHAPTER THREE

Music. Somewhere, soft, instrumental music was playing. I blinked as my mind struggled to return from the obliteration of that last orgasm. Loki smiled at me, his eyes flashing. We were sitting across from one another in the restaurant. I took a deep breath and glanced down to see if I was still naked.

No. Thankfully, I was wearing my black dress. And it still looked okay, if a little wrinkled and damp around the hem. I shifted a bit in the seat. My chest and stomach felt sticky from the champagne, and yeah, I'd definitely lost my underwear somewhere along the way. I met Loki's dancing eyes across the table. Worth it, I thought.

I was hungry, too. An artistic-looking white plate sat untouched in front of me, and I tried to remember what I'd ordered. The chicken sous-whatever, maybe? I carved out an enormous bite and brought it to my lips. I don't know if it was the multiple orgasms upstairs or the restaurant's locally sourced ingredients, but whatever it was on my plate tasted freaking delicious.

"What about the..." I asked, glancing up at the faux metal tiles of the restaurant's ceiling once I finished my dinner. We'd left a mess of empty bottles and spilled champagne in that elegant, darkened office. Not to mention my red silk undies. "Is that going to be a problem?"

Loki looked upward, as if he were following my gaze. "Oh, that. Don't give it a second thought."

I lowered my voice. "Whose office is it?"

"Shall we go dancing?" Loki asked, ignoring my question.

I decided I didn't want to push him on date night. "Yes. I'd love to go dancing."

Loki smiled, but a shiver of apprehension traced its way down my spine. I glanced at the slim black watch on my wrist. "I mean, I don't know. We've been gone a couple of hours. Do you think—"

There was a gust of air on the back of my neck, like a melting snowflake, and Loki vanished. The seat across from me was empty. I blinked and stared for a minute, wondering if anyone else just saw that.

He reappeared just as I finished my glass of wine. "She's asleep," Loki said as he carefully re-folded the napkin in his lap. "Swaddled, with a clean diaper, and sleeping peacefully."

My heart felt like it might explode. "I love you," I whispered.

"So... dancing?"

"Please."

TO MY SURPRISE, WE walked to the club. I had no idea where we were going, of course, and Loki took the lead. I wrapped my arm around his waist. My head felt like it was floating from the wine and the sex, and it felt so good to be out of the house, with my arm wrapped around my husband's lean, muscular body.

Loki pulled me down an alley and pushed open a battered green door. Arm in arm, we entered a small, intimate club with faded couches and a strong smell of marijuana in the air. On stage, a collection of aging hippies played a sort of jazzed-up alternative folk music.

"Good?" Loki asked.

I smiled. In my sleep-deprived, alcohol-buzzed state, this place felt as comfortable as a warm blanket. "Perfect. It's perfect."

I sank into one of the red velvet couches as Loki ordered drinks. We sat with our legs intertwined, sharing something that sparkled and burned on the way down. And then we stood, and we danced.

The band played songs that tugged at my memory in strange ways, like echoes of something I'd heard a long time ago. I pressed my cheek against Loki's chest and closed my eyes, trying to remember where I'd heard the current melody before. Something about a rose, I thought, trying to follow the singer's beautifully warbling voice.

It took me a minute to realize Loki had stopped dancing. I stepped back and looked up.

He was crying.

My husband, the Norse god of fire and lies, was crying.

I didn't know what to do. I'd hardly ever seen him cry. After I almost died, for one. When he told me how he lost his son Nari and his first wife Sigyn, and then again when Adelina was born. That was it. In all the years we'd been married, and all the years before that, I'd only ever seen him cry three times.

I reached up, brushing his cheek with my fingertips, and his back stiffened. His tears vanished as though they'd never existed.

"I apologize," he said. "It's...an old song."

"Do you want to talk about it?"

He shook his head. "Not here."

I leaned against his chest again, but he didn't sway with the music. He didn't move at all. I heard his heart racing under his breastbone.

"I'm ready to go whenever you are," I said—

—And I blinked in a flood of sudden, harsh light. It took me a second to realize we were sitting at another table, on a white couch. Then recognition hit me, and my heart seized. The Holy Brew. Loki had taken us to the coffee shop down the street from our house. The one we went to on the weekends, carrying Adelina in the Moby wrap, sometimes even walking hand in hand. Loki had taken me to the most mundane, ordinary place I could image.

Shit. Was he all right?

Loki slumped in the couch, his legs crossed, his eyes unfocused. He hardly seemed aware of me. I tried to remember the last time I'd seen him sleep, and I drew a blank. He said Adelina preferred to sleep in his arms while he rocked her, and I was always too exhausted to argue.

"I'll get us drinks?" I offered.

He barely nodded. I watched him as I ordered, almost as if I were afraid he was going to vanish. But that would be ridiculous. Right?

"Yeah, what'll it be?" The cashier had blue hair and huge gauges in her ears, making her look aggressively hip.

"Uh, one latte, please. Decaf," I added, with a sigh. Sleeping was hard enough without any extra caffeine running through my system. "And a large mocha."

I glanced at Loki.

"With whipped cream," I added. He looked like he could use it.

I went back to the couch and sat next to Loki, resting my hand on his knee until the silence between us became too uncomfortable to bear.

"I'm here," I said. "If you want to talk."

He sighed and ran his hand through his hair. "I'm...not eager to discuss this."

The waitress brought us our drinks. I wrapped my fingers around the bright red mug of my latte, grateful for some distraction. We were the only people in the coffee shop. I felt awkward in my tight black dress with no underwear. And my totally silent husband.

Loki shifted on the couch, staring into the swirl of whipped cream atop his drink. "You will think less of me, mortal woman."

"Oh, Loki..."

My mind raced through all the myths and legends I'd heard about Loki, all the rumors and insinuations. Some of it was already pretty bad.

Actually, most of it was pretty bad.

He finally met my eyes and gave me a small, sad smile. "You will. Didn't you know I once slaughtered an entire town?"

I gripped my mug so tightly my knuckles turned white. "I don't—I don't know that one."

He laughed, harsh and bitter. "Of course. There was no one left to tell the story."

I took a deep breath and covered his hand with mine. His skin was cold. "I love you," I whispered. "Nothing will change that."

He dropped his head and looked at the floor.

"It was a very long time ago," he said.

CHAPTER FOUR

I t was a very long time ago.

I suppose it would now be called the Iron Age, although at the time it was, of course, the very pinnacle of human civilization. The amber trade was thriving, King Eadgils was brave and wise enough to rule justly, the fish were plentiful, and the harvests did not fail. It was good time to walk Asgard, a time when guests were greeted with requisite hospitality.

She was picking lingonberries when I first saw her. Oh, she could have been one of the Æsir, with her flaxen hair drifting down the generous curves of her hips. She was a tall woman, solidly built, with a chest that curved like the prow of a ship. I actually thought she might have been one of the Æsir, at first, which is why I approached her so boldly. I was only a few steps away when I realized my mistake, but by then I was close enough to hear her singing. The lyrics have changed with the fickle ravages of time, but the tune was close enough.

The Briar and the Rose.

It's a stupid bit of sentimental claptrap I've always enjoyed. I began to sing it too as I walked alongside her. Her basket was almost full, and she balanced it against her round hips. She only glanced at me, refusing even to smile, but her voice matched my harmony. We sang together as we followed the wide curves of the Dalälven River until the thatched longhouses of her town came into view, and her pace quickened.

"What's your name?" I asked as she stepped ahead of me.

She turned to me and smiled.

Lingonberries ripen in midsummer, when the lazy, burning sun lingers in the sky and time can be deceptive. I hadn't realized how long we'd been walking together and singing. The sun lolled against the horizon, as close as it would come to setting. It was midnight, near midsummer. A powerful, potent time. The long rays of the midnight sun caught her golden hair as it drifted about her face, turning each strand to flame. The light fell across her full lips and the generous swell of her breasts pressing against the straps of her dress. By the time I remembered I'd asked her a question, she'd turned to descend the steps to her village.

I could have left. Perhaps I should have left, all things considered. But the wind shifted as she sank down the rough stone steps to her village. Woven into the heavy brine of the ocean and the stink of human habitation, was the soft tang of her scent, the warmth and the sweetness of the beautiful woman who had spent the day with me, singing *The Briar and the Rose*.

Although it was past midnight, the swollen midsummer's sun gave me plenty of light for my project. A simple illusion allowed me to walk into her village unseen and collect a dozen of the empty baskets which were stacked among the longhouses and boat houses. I pulled them together and retraced my steps, walking away from the jagged coastline and toward the lingonberry fields.

Humming to myself, I slid the empty containers along the ground, tugging hundreds of the sweet, red berries from their stems with latent magical energy and letting them tumble into the baskets. It was almost hypnotically easy to wrap thin strands of magic around the tiny crimson globes and guide them home, handfuls at a time.

By the time the sun roused itself and crawled higher into the sky, I'd filled all of the baskets with sweet berries. I found a rock near the village and wrapped myself in an illusion, making sure the overflowing berry baskets and I both blended in to the horizon.

Until I saw her.

She crested the hill above the village, shining like the sun. But she wasn't alone, and disappointment cut through my chest with a surprisingly sharp edge. A crowd of girls milled around her, fluttering like moths dancing along the edge of a candle's flame. I shifted on the hard rock, trying to imagine how I could separate her from the others.

She glanced in my direction, frowned, and shaded her eyes with her hand. The other girls drifted away, bidding her an easy farewell with smiles and waves. My heart clattered against my breastbone as they left.

When she was alone, silhouetted against the brilliant blue sky and slowly churning ocean, I began to sing. Softly at first, then with gathering strength, I let the illusions bleed away. The beautiful woman stood stock-still, as if she'd been carved from ash wood, until I appeared before her with the dozen baskets of berries overflowing at my feet. Her cheeks colored, and her chest rose and fell as she took several quick breaths.

"For you," I said, gesturing at the berries I'd spent the night collecting.

She glanced down, then raised her hand to cover the smile spreading across her rose-colored lips.

"Now, whatever will you do with the rest of your day?" I asked, as innocently as I could manage.

She cleared her throat delicately as she glanced across the ocean. "Such a pity I'm not collecting berries today."

Only then did I noticed the wicker basket slung over her shoulder. Damn. I should have spotted this immediately; it was the kind of basket the women used to collect eels from the long, thin nets they staked in the muddy flats of the estuary. And the tide was now at its lowest ebb. I could smell the thick odor of the mud flats even this high above the village.

She took a step past me, then another, drifting toward the wide mouth of the Dalälven River. I bit my lip behind her back. Women didn't usually refuse me; neither did men. I was finding her delicate flirtation and subtle teasing damn near impossible to resist.

Her wide hips and long, golden hair were a pace away when the thin strands of her music lilted through the air. *The Briar and the Rose.* Grinning, I picked up the melody and followed her, the baskets of plump lingonberries abandoned on the crag above her village. She ignored me entirely as we traveled the wide banks of the river. But she sang with me, our voices rising and intertwining in the briny air and strong Nordic sunlight.

By the time I caught her, she'd already reached the muddy fields of the river and pulled her heavy skirts up to her thighs. Oh, the sight of her long, pale legs nearly undid me! Arousal rose in me like the tide, swallowing whatever clever flirtations I'd been planning. Her golden hair snared the sunlight as her scent filled the air between us, making my pulse race. Perhaps she wasn't one of the Æsir or the Vanir, but she had to be the most gorgeous woman Midgard had ever produced.

Her song faltered when she glanced backward and saw me standing on the shore. Once again, her hand moved to cover her smile as her eyes slid to the distant horizon. She hesitated, with one delicate, bare foot above the mud flats and one foot still planted on the thick, green grass of the shore.

"What's your name?" I asked, as softly as I could manage.

Someone called from the hills above us, and she jumped. Her foot sank into the mud up to her ankle. She met my eyes for a heartbeat.

"Perhaps you'll come tomorrow," she whispered as her cheeks reddened.

Cursing my lack of vigilance, I pulled a quick illusion around myself, rendering my body invisible. A heartbeat later a dozen girls came down the hill, burdened with similar wicker baskets and chattering incessantly.

I yanked on Midgard's magic and traveled the aether to Asgard, unseen and unheard, my recklessly demanding cock throbbing painfully against the confines of my armor.

I WAS BACK A DAY LATER, more determined than ever to at least learn her name, if not to savor the taste and texture of those hypnotically full lips. This time I waited until the tide was high and the fat summer sun had sunk low against the burnished gold of the ocean. She could have been sleeping, of course, but some deep instinct told me she was not.

Instead of following the river, I turned this time to the rise above her village and navigated the grassy hollows until I stood next to cliffs, which echoed with the pounding surf. Closing my eyes, I opened myself to the water, the shore, the distant cries of birds above the throbbing of the waves. Somewhere nearby, someone was singing.

She was hidden behind a rocky stretch of boulders, almost invisible from the shoreline. I might never have found her, if her beautiful voice hadn't carried past the stones to reach my ears. She was sitting by herself, protected by a rocky outcropping, spreading the lingonberries I'd collected for her on woven mats to dry in the sun.

I sang as I walked toward her, matching her tune. She had such a perfect voice; it put mine to shame. Our melodies entwined, spinning around each other as they drifted past the broken stones and out across the wide, cold ocean. She did not speak, but neither did she move away when I crouched next to her.

She finished spreading the berries just as we reached the last stanza of the song. My hand brushed hers when she lifted her empty basket. She turned away, but the air thickened with the tang of her arousal.

So, she did find me attractive, after all.

"You're very beautiful," I said, filling the silence created by the end of our song.

She smiled. That smile poured through me like molten heat. She'd been eating the berries. Her lips were stained red, and I could imagine how sweet she would taste. All my blood drained downward; I spun an illusion to hide the sudden erection pressing against the inside of my armor.

"Perhaps you'll come tomorrow," she said.

Another clear voice ran out through the air, and she stood, dusting off her skirts. Damn! I clenched my hands into fists. Of course they wouldn't leave this beautiful woman unguarded, any more than they'd leave the berries unguarded.

I stood, somewhat painfully as my cock strained against my armor, and faded into the shadows. An older woman reached the stones, greeting the beautiful woman with smiles and laughter. Hidden behind the rocks as they exchanged a few pleasantries, I shifted into my sparrow shape and took to the skies, trying to shake the heat of my arousal in the cool wind off the ocean.

I SPENT ALL NIGHT PACING that stretch of beach, humming to myself. Waiting. She finally came over the hills in late afternoon, a basket on her hip, her hair pulled back in a demure sprang. My heartbeat thundered in my ears. This time, she was alone.

I fell into step behind her, humming her tune in delicate counterpoint. As I watched, a flush spread over her chest and cheeks. She turned away from me, toward the distant undulations of the ocean, but not before I saw her eyes widen.

After a few verses, I touched her wrist. Not enough to slow her pace, but enough to feel her pulse fluttering beneath my fingers like a hummingbird's wings.

"What is your name?" I whispered.

Her footsteps faltered. She looked at me from beneath thick lashes and smiled, a secret half-smile. We stood halfway between the longhouses of her village and the loose collection of stones where she'd laid the berries out to dry, where another group of women would no doubt be awaiting her arrival.

"I know who you are," she said, her voice low and soft.

Of course. Sometimes mortals did. It was more common in those days.

"And who am I?" I asked, testing her.

"You're Fire-hair," she said, but she did not pull away from my touch. "The Jötunn who vowed blood-brotherhood with the All-father, and became one of the Æsir."

I said nothing, silently debating if it would be more advantageous to claim it or to deny it.

"You seduced Thor's wife," she said, "and cut off her hair."

Deny it. Definitely deny it.

"Me? I'm merely a humble fisherman from the neighboring village."

Her laugh echoed off the rocks. "If any of the fisherman in that village were so handsome, believe me, I'd have heard it."

Our eyes met. The briny air surged with the sweet tang of her sex, wet with anticipation. Her pulse raced beneath my hand. I dared to step closer, so close I almost brushed the full swell of her breasts.

"What do you want from me?" she asked. For the first time her voice carried a hint of hesitation.

"Nothing you'd miss."

My hand traced her wrist and traveled up her arm. She shivered under my touch.

"And when my belly swells with child? What then?"

My fingers reached the gentle curve of her neck. "Then you'll flash an ankle at some villager's respectable son and be cheerfully wed before anyone's the wiser."

"You must think quite highly of my charms." Her voice was steady, but her neck and cheeks flushed a deep scarlet.

"Why, yes, I do."

Her mouth opened, and I took the gasp from her lips. Her body pressed against mine, soft and sweet. The kiss was every bit as delicious as I'd imagined.

She pulled away from my arms, gasping. "Someone will see us!"

I lifted her into my arms like a child and carried her to the soft grass, casting a small illusion to make us both invisible. Then I unfurled my cloak and laid her upon it.

"No one can see us," I whispered.

Oh, I was careful, so careful and so painfully slow! I'd seduced women before, mortal women, women of the Æsir, women of the Vanir. I seduced Angrboða, one of the most powerful and highly-ranked Jötunn in Útgarðar, when I was barely out of adolescence. But I'd never before moved so slowly, or been so delicate.

I kissed her sweet lips for what felt like a lifetime before I reached to release her hair sprang. Her soft, long hair tumbled over her shoulders like molten gold. It would put Sif's to shame, I realized, as I breathed in the sweet tang of her scent. It would even put Sif's dwarven-crafted golden hair to shame.

Running my lips along her neck, I unlatched her brooch and slipped the folds of her dress over her shoulders, freeing her perfect bosom. Her nipples were flushed and hard, the soft skin of her breasts so pale I could trace the paths of her blue veins. Her breath caught in her throat as I ran my fingers over the pink nubs of her nipples. I grinned, bending to taste them.

She moaned and arched her back as I took her breast between my lips. The sea air filled with the tang of her arousal and the sound of her soft whimpers, like the splash of the waves against the rocks. I closed my teeth gently around the hard bud of her nipple, flicking it with my tongue until she was panting and arching her back.

Only then did I slip my hand up her skirt and between her legs, feeling her warmth, the slippery wetness that already coated her thighs. I teased her with my fingers as I licked and kissed those perfect breasts. When I finally brushed the hard nub of her clit, her entire body went rigid. I pressed into her gently, running my thumb in circles over that soft, swollen bud. She moaned, soft and low, as her thighs began to tremble. I dropped my lips back to her breasts, kissing her pale skin and sucking those perfect nipples while I caressed her nub. I tried to move slowly, but it wasn't long before she screamed and shuddered beneath me.

She was still gasping for breath when I shoved the heavy folds of her skirt to her waist and dipped my head between her legs. Oh, her taste! It was like drinking the summer sun. I almost came myself when I dipped my tongue into her velvet folds, and again when her thighs closed around my ears and she cried out, over and over. I could have spilled my seed over the soft grass, just from bringing her pleasure. It took all my focus to stop myself.

I pulled away from the sweet cleft between her legs, giving her some time to recover and trying to ignore the incessant throbbing of my cock. Her eyes were soft and unfocused; I watched her perfect breast swell and fall as she tried to catch her breath. By the Nine Realms, she was irresistible. Before she'd stopped panting, I was kissing her again.

My mouth traced her neck, feeling the delicate flutter of her pulse, the deep sigh as she pulled air into her lungs. I moved to claim her lips and found them eager. Her tongue embraced me. Encouraged by her kisses, I rolled on top of her, dismissed my own clothes, and pressed my naked chest to hers. Her skin was so hot it almost seared mine. She spread her legs beneath me, but her eyes widened and her breath stopped.

"You're afraid?" I asked.

Her brow furrowed. "I... It is supposed to hurt, is it not?"

I kissed her again, for a long time, letting her savor the taste of her own sex on my lips. Then I leaned back on my heels and traced her entrance with my fingers, teasing the nub until her breath came fast and shallow. The heat pouring off her lit my body on fire; I was so hard my cock hurt with a deep, insistent ache.

"Do you want me?" I asked.

"Oh, yes," she cried.

I pressed the head of my cock against her entrance. Damn, she was so wet and so warm I had to bite the inside of my mouth to stop myself from filling her in an instant. She whimpered, a small, animal plea of hunger and need.

"Do you still want me?" I asked again, my voice hitching.

She groaned and arched her back, wrapping her heat around me. "Yes," she gasped. "Yes!"

The world stood still as I entered her as slowly as I could. Her eyes widened when I met resistance, and I brought my hand back to the hard bead of her clit, rubbing her until her body's tight entrance relaxed and her pupils dilated once again. Her breath caught, becoming a rapid staccato of gasps and pants. Gently, I thought. Gently, gently.

And then I was inside her, fully inside her. Our bodies joined together. I moaned against her neck, my hand pressed between our bodies, still caressing the apex of her sex. The hot velvet of her body clenched around mine, and her muscles rippled beneath me. Her wide eyes rolled back in her head and a long, low cry of pleasure slid from her lips as a third climax claimed her. Every nerve in my body sang as she stiffened in my arms. Heat tingled at the base of my spine, swelling upward.

Stars, no!

I clenched my jaw, grinding my teeth together. I couldn't come this quickly, not now. Not as I claimed this splendid woman's maidenhead. I had to be slow, damn it. I had to make this perfect.

Her thick, rich scent surrounded me, and her pink-tinged skin was soft and hot beneath mine. I tried to hold perfectly still until her eyes cleared, although my throbbing cock was so stiff and ready to thrust inside her that I ached.

"Are you well?" I whispered into the curl of her ear.

"I-I-It's good," she panted. "It's—very good."

I closed my eyes, drowning in that moment, in her smell, her skin, her hair. When I opened my eyes again, she was staring at me, and our hips were moving together, slowly and gently, our rhythm matching the steady crash of the waves behind us.

I DON'T KNOW HOW LONG we made love, that first afternoon in the golden sunlight of midsummer. Time lost all meaning. All that mattered in the world was her, the scent and taste of her body, the feel of her hair brushing across my chest and her ankles crossed around my waist, the sweet ecstasy of the spot where our bodies joined. She came again and again, gasping and crying as light caught in the beads of sweat on her brow and lips, until finally I could hold back no longer.

I tried to be slow, but by the end I thrust into her hard and fast, lost to everything but her scent, her warmth, the hot embrace of her sex. And she met every stroke with moans and gasps, raising her hips to meet mine, crying her pleasure into the blue heavens.

I'd resisted my own climax for so long that, when it came, it crashed over me like Ragnarök, like the very end of the Realms. I felt like I emptied my seed into her sweet body for an eternity, gasping in sharp, jagged cries as our hips shook together.

Afterward, I wanted to collapse on top of her, to feel her soft body beneath mine just a little longer, but I was wary of crushing a woman from Midgard. They are so fragile, after all. So, I rolled to my side and let her rest her head against my arm.

She gazed at the sky with her lips curved in a soft smile. When she spoke, it was as if her voice came from far away, as though she'd forgotten how to form words and was only now remembering.

"Anya," she said. "My name. It's Anya."

"And you were right about mine," I said, intertwining our fingers above my chest.

She sighed and turned to face me with those sky-blue eyes. "Thank you, Loki, son of Laufeyiar."

Hearing my name on those lips sent another tingle of arousal up my spine, and my cock twitched. The scent of our union was still thick in the air, and yet I was ready to take her again. I glanced at the sun in the soft, blue belly of the summer sky. I'd already spent a very long time with her; she'd be missed, no doubt, if we tarried longer.

I kissed her soft lips, letting just a hint of my appetite show through. Her cheeks flushed when we pulled apart.

"Maybe I'll see you again," I whispered.

Her eyes widened. "Really? You'd come back?"

I've found it unwise to make many promises. A promise is a debt, and a debt can become a weapon used against you.

But I made a promise to Anya of Midgard, even if I didn't use those words. I kissed her soft lips, then the tips of her fingers, and I said, "I'll come back."

CHAPTER FIVE

Perhaps, looking back over the span of so many dark and painful years, I should have broken that promise. The Nine Realms know I've broken enough promises in my life. What difference would one more have made, in the end?

But Anya haunted me.

I'd close my eyes and see her full lips, the swell of her pale breasts. I'd feel her wrist in my hand, her heartbeat thrumming against my fingertips. At the time, I honestly thought our dalliance was harmless. After all, what was the worst thing sex could produce? A child? We'd already taken care of that contingency. So, it was without second thoughts that I returned to Anya's village a month of so after the day she'd given me her virtue.

It was a beautiful, clear, warm day. The sun spun golden in its nest of blue, and a fair wind gusted off the ocean, carrying the briny tang that always made me think of adventure. It was full summer by now, and the entire world seemed ripe for the picking.

I swooped down on the village in the form of a sparrow, an innocuous little disguise which could get me almost anywhere. The village swarmed with people, most of whom I ignored. My sense of smell was limited in the sparrow form, so I relied on sight, circling over groups of women as I sought out her golden hair and generous curves.

There. Finally. Anya stood at an upright loom, weaving what would probably become a sail. I perched on the roof of a longhouse and watched her nimble fingers thread the weft yarns. She worked quickly and easily, and she smiled in the full summer sun. Her long hair was pulled back into a practical sprang, but thin strands had freed themselves to float around her sparkling eyes and full lips. I watched until the urge to touch her, to pull those strands of hair away from her face and press my lips to hers, became so strong it was almost painful.

Even then, I was careful to wait until she was alone. The woman working next to her excused herself, and I flew to the ground, transforming into myself. Or at least the illusions I usually used for myself.

"Hello," I said.

She spun to face me. Her hand flew to cover her lips, and her lovely ice-blue eyes welled with tears. She threw herself into my chest, wrapping her strong arms around my neck and shoulders.

"You came back!"

She pressed her face into my neck and gasped, almost as if she wanted to inhale me, to fill her entire body with my essence. Oh, by the Nine Realms, she felt good in my arms.

But I pushed her away. We stood in the middle of her village, and we would be noticed. I didn't give two shits about any of the other people in this realm, but I knew they would not take kindly to a strange man appearing suddenly in the center of their longhouses. Especially if they found him intimately embracing the most beautiful maiden in Midgard.

"Not here," I whispered.

Her cheeks flushed with color, and she stepped backward. "Of course."

"Elsewhere, perhaps?"

Anya's eyes sparkled. "Would you meet me by the stones? Where we dry the lingonberries? I—I left you an offering there."

My lips curved into a smile. An offering. As if I'd want anything other than her.

"When?" I asked.

"Now?"

I had to bite down my moan of approval. "Yes. Now."

"Anya?" Another voice echoed through the chatter of the village, and I yanked the strands of magic to transport myself back to the loose collection of boulders where I'd seen Anya spreading lingonberries to dry in the summer sun.

To my relief, the place was empty of both lingonberries and other women. I paced nervously, watching the horizon. Of course, I knew she'd come to me, but for some reason, the knot of sexual energy in my core was paired with tension. I felt nervous.

I'd made love to Anya on the sweet summer grass last time, with just my cloak between her naked body and the ground. Suddenly, I decided that wouldn't do this time around. Closing my eyes, I reached through the aether to my own ramshackle home on Asgard, which was more of a dumping ground than a proper dwelling place. I pulled my finest fur, from an ice bear on Jötunheimr, and spread it on the thick grass.

Then I tweaked my illusions, emphasizing my smile and smooth skin, checking yet again to make sure all my scars were hidden. Pacing, I debated my outfit. Typically I wore dark leather armor on Midgard; it was strong and durable, and thick enough to stop most blades. But perhaps today called for something different? A thinner shirt, perhaps? I tried on a simple wool top, like what the men of Anya's village wore.

No. Fuck that. Why would she want me to look like a man from her village? I spun on my heels, yanking the linen shirt off and tossing it across the aether back to Asgard, then pulling my leather armor back over my chest. The ice bear fur caught my eye, and I frowned. Wouldn't that be too hot for her? It was summer, after all.

"Loki?"

I jumped. Anya had come over the hill, silent and beautiful, while I was busy frowning at the furs I'd spread between the stones. She met my eyes, then turned away with a shy smile.

"Did you find my offering?"

The offering. Shit, I hadn't even looked. I reached out, feeling the strands of magic woven through Midgard's atmosphere, searching for something out of place, something that had been recently moved.

There. Grinning, I took Anya's hand and pulled her toward the beach. Yes, someone had stacked several flat rocks above the waterline to form a little altar. I took a deep breath, scenting the air. It had been Anya. The stones still carried a hint of her sweet, feminine scent. But the altar was empty. I walked all the way around it, watching Anya's shy smile.

There must be a trick. Clever. I crouched down next to the altar and pushed on the top stone. It rocked slightly, as though it were balanced on the edges and hollow beneath. I caught Anya's eye as I reached for the top stone.

"This is nicely done," I said.

Her cheeks flamed with color. "I didn't want anyone else to take it," she said.

The top stone came off easily. I leaned forward to find a waterskin nestled between the stones. It was round, full, and heavier than I'd expected. Anya beamed as I pulled it out. I made quite a show of examining the waterskin. The leather had been tanned to perfection, then rubbed with beeswax until it gleamed. It was expertly made, probably by Anya herself.

Only when Anya's hands began to twitch with impatience did I pull the thick stopper to examine the liquid within. It smelled sweet and potent. Mead. From the scent, it must have been the best batch the village had produced.

"Do you like it?" Anya asked, her words coming out in a rushed jumble. "The stories all say you like mead."

My lip curled with distaste. I could only imagine the unpleasant rumors about me that must swirl around Midgard. "You can't always believe the stories."

Her face fell. I reached forward, running my fingers along her cheek and the swell of her pink lips.

"But I do like mead," I said, softly.

Then, to encourage her, I gave her a soft kiss. Her breath caught as our lips met. By the stars, she tasted good. I almost lost myself right there; I could have spent all day kissing her, exploring the soft contours of her lips, savoring the way her breath filled the space between us.

But I also needed to properly appreciate her sacrifice. So, after one last kiss, hardly more than brushing my lips against hers, I brought the waterskin to my mouth and drank deeply.

It was good. Perhaps not as good as the mead in Val-hall, the mead which cures both war injuries and hangovers, but by Midgard's standards this stuff was exceptional. Anya watched me with wide eyes as I wiped my mouth.

"Is it good?" she asked.

I handed her the waterskin. "Please. Try it yourself."

She raised it to her lips and took a tentative sip. It occured to me to wonder how familiar she was with the effects of mead, but her appreciative smile told me she'd had at least some experience with alcohol.

"The warriors said this batch was as good as Óðinn's mead of poetry," she told me, with another shy smile.

I took another long drink, feeling the warmth of the mead slide down my throat and spread through my body.

"How did you get a hold of it?" I asked.

The color in her cheeks deepened, until they were almost as bright and red as the lingonberries she'd been picking when we met.

"I stole it," she whispered.

My laugh was loud enough to startle birds from the grass. By all Nine fucking Realms, this woman was perfect. I brought the waterskin to my lips, drained the rest of the stolen mead, and pulled her into my arms. The magic around us buzzed and pulsed with the alcohol, the heat of Anya's body against mine sent my head spinning, and the only question in my mind was why I'd waited so long to return to her embrace.

All I wanted, out of all the treasures and mysteries of the Nine Realms, was to kiss her, to feel the soft brush of her lips against mine and taste the remnants of the sweet mead on her tongue. I had missed her, this beautiful woman who'd flirted with me so coolly. I wanted to kiss her forever.

But, once I pulled her onto my lap and brought my lips to hers, Anya's shyness vanished. She turned to face me, wrapped her legs around my waist, and sank her hands into my hair. Anya pulled my mouth to hers, kissing me with a frantic hunger. It was as if she'd been starving, dying without me. Her breath came in frantic gasps and, when I leaned away to catch my breath, she moaned as though she'd been hurt.

"Loki," she whispered. "Oh, Loki, Loki—"

The sweet, heavy scent of her sex filled the air between us, and her legs tightened around my waist. Her hips rose and fell against mine. My cock responded to her urging, stiffening against the tight press of my leather armor. I dropped my head to her neck, pulling my lips and teeth across her skin, licking the salt of her summer sweat from her neck, savoring her scent.

I'd had lovers before, but they'd rarely been virgins. Anya's desperate lust, the sweet fruit of her lost innocence, struck me as incredibly beautiful. I was half tempted to stop her, to slow her down, just to extend our enjoyment of each other. But one look at her flushed face and half-lidded eyes told me any arguments for delayed gratification would fall on deaf ears.

So I slipped my hands up her thighs, watching the way her chest heaved with whimpers of pleasure as my touch skidded across the bare skin of her thighs. When I pushed the folds of her skirt aside and brushed the wet entrance of her sex, she cried my name out loud. I realized I could probably make her come with just my fingers, both of us fully clothed, exchanging nothing more than kisses.

Ah, but what fun would that have been?

I teased her clit until her body began to shake, and then I dipped into the magic to send my leather armor into the aether. The feel of her hot skin against my suddenly naked body made my hungry cock surge. Without warning, I thrust inside her, filling her fast and hard. She cried out, digging her nails into the skin of my back. Pressing my finger to her clit, I thrust into her again, and again. She gasped, cried, clung to me.

And she fell into ecstasy.

I watched as she drowned in her orgasm. Her entire body clenched around me, and her pale eyes rolled back, revealing the whites of her sclerae. Her breath hitched, coming in strangled, sharp inhales, as the heat of her sex constricted around my cock.

Damn the Realms, she felt good! I held still, crushing her to my chest until her tremors subsided. Finally, I rolled back and, my cock still buried inside her sweet body, I lay her down on the ice bear fur. Her long hair spread across the pale fur like molten gold, and some distant part of me realized I'd never again look at an ice bear without seeing that exquisite image.

Before she had a chance to catch her breath, I began moving inside her again, my finger pressing into her swollen clit and making her squirm. I wasn't gentle, not this time, but Anya rose to meet every stroke, every thrust. She locked her ankles around my back, and her sweat-slick legs dug into my hips.

I pressed my lips against hers. This time my kiss was deep and bruising, taking all of her, claiming her as my own. She arched her back under me, forcing her mouth to mine, matching my ferocity with her own. When I tried to pull away, her teeth closed around my lower lip and her fingernails dug into my back, sending a bright lance of pain shooting through the sexual ecstasy flooding my body. I responded by slamming my hips into her, driving as deep as I could.

She exploded beneath me, writhing and screaming as her body stiffened around mine. Pressure gathered at the base of my spine as my seed rose, ready to spill inside her. I held my breath, struggling to control it. Not yet. I wasn't done yet.

I forced myself to hold still, my cock buried and aching inside her, until Anya's eyes opened again. I watched as she blinked and her pupils dilated, struggling to focus. When she turned to me, a slow, lazy smile spread over her beautiful features.

"Loki," she whispered, making my name sound like an invocation.

My hips pressed against her, rolling into her sex.

"Anya," I said. "We're not done yet."

Her eyes widened, and I started to fuck her in earnest.

I MADE HER COME TWICE more before I lost control of my own body. In the end, we fell together, my seed shooting into her as she screamed my name. I was disappointed; I'd wanted to keep going all night, to see how far I could push that beautiful body of hers, but my own lust drowned me.

I let myself collapse onto the furs beside her. It was late afternoon by this point, and the sun had fallen beyond the horizon. The distant sound of the ocean filled the air between us with a low, throbbing hum, and Anya caught her breath in a series of hitching gasps.

No. My chest clenched as I recognized those sounds.

Anya was crying.

I rolled over and pulled her to my chest, running my fingers through her sweat-dampened hair.

"Anya," I said. "Oh, damn, Anya. Did I hurt you?"

Her shoulders shook, and my stomach turned. I hadn't been gentle with her, poor woman. I'd fucked her as hard as I'd fuck Angrboða or Thor, and neither of them were human.

Shit. I was such an idiot.

"I'm sorry," I murmured, wondering if there was anything I could do to make this up to her. Gold, maybe?

Anya made a strange little sound, something halfway between a sob and a laugh. I turned to face her and opened my mouth to apologize again. Her beautiful, pale eyes welled with tears, but her lips curved into a smile.

"Loki," she whispered. "Fire-hair."

"I'm so sorry," I said.

She made that strange noise again, like a half-swallowed sob. "No. Loki, I'm happy."

Her words made no sense. "I hurt you," I insisted. "You're crying."

Anya laughed. It was unmistakably a laugh this time, and a full, deep laugh at that. "No. You came back. Loki of the Æsir came back to me." She raised a hand to trace my cheek. "You came back, and you liked my offering. I'm happy, Loki. I'm so happy."

I frowned. Tears rolled down her cheeks, but she smiled. I had no idea what to make of that particular reaction to an afternoon of lovemaking. I had a number of regular lovers, but none of them had ever cried afterward.

"I-I'm glad," I stammered. "Good. I'm glad you're happy."

She sighed and turned her head to my chest. Her body relaxed in my arms, and I curled my hand around her shoulders. A gust of wind raced across the grass, beating down the full seed heads and making

Anya's golden hair swirl across my chest. The sky darkened as the sun sank toward the horizon. I leaned down to kiss the top of her head.

An unfamiliar sense of contentment swelled in my chest. The sensation was so odd and unexpected that I felt it must have come from somewhere outside of me, perhaps sinking into my skin from Anya's breasts and thighs and lips.

"I'm happy," I whispered. "I'm happy, too."

I glanced down to see how Anya had reacted to my words.

She'd fallen asleep.

CHAPTER SIX

I could not get enough of her.

I was no innocent; I'd have lovers before. Many lovers, of many species, and of all genders. But Anya lit my blood as no one had before, and it was never enough. I'd call her away from mending fishing nets on the beach, tending the fires to smoke the herring, or pulling the eel nets from the cold waters of the estuary, her pale calves streaked with mud.

One night I even woke her in the village's dim, smoky longhouse, kissing the curve of her neck and cupping her breast until she moaned. Wrapped in an illusion, I carried her through the gloom, past the hide curtain separating the sleeping quarters, and fucked her against the wall. The hearth flames leapt with our thrusts, and I pressed my lips over hers to silence the cries when we both came.

I tried to resist her, to leave her alone. I talked my way into Freyja's bedchambers, but not even her legendary beauty satisfied me. Nothing satisfied me, nothing slaked my thirst, save Anya. I neglected my duties amongst the Æsir. I even ignored a summons from Óðinn. I told myself it was nothing, just a bit of fun, but that mortal woman began to consume me. I lived for the times when we were together, our bodies joined, her lips against mine, her ankles crossed around my waist, our sweat commingling.

Not once did she refuse me. Her eyes lit every time I approached. Breathless, she'd tell me where to wait. She would slip away from the village while I paced impatiently in our meeting place. Once she arrived, we fell upon each other. Her body sang beneath my touch, and we slid together as if we'd always been meant for one another.

Afterward, once we'd pushed ourselves to the point of exhaustion, Anya and I would collapse together, intertwined on the furs I'd pulled from Asgard or the delicate, trampled grass of late summer, and let the world spin around us. She often fell asleep in my embrace, and I would run my fingers through her thick, honey colored hair as I fought the warm pull of slumber.

Those were sweet hours, with her soft body curled against mine, but they were a form of torture, too. The illusions I wore around my body came as naturally as breathing, now, after long years of practice. But if I let myself fall asleep, my handsome form would fade, and Anya would see the hideous scars I'd gained in my life with the Æsir.

She'd see what the dwarves had done to my lips.

I had no desire to send her back to her village screaming with terror at the sight of my true self. So, I struggled to keep myself awake by watching the sky, or breathing in her warm, rich scent, or imagining what it would be like to lead my lover on a tour of the Nine Realms. Where in Asgard would most impress her, I wondered? What parts of Álfheim would I show her first?

One evening we were curled in the sand as the ocean kissed the shore, embracing and receding, embracing and receding. We'd made love all afternoon, and I was watching the light leak from the sky as the stars began to show themselves above us. The night air had grown cool; I was idly contemplating pulling a fur through the aether to wrap around Anya's generous curves when she shifted against my chest. Her breath caught in her throat and pinched into a sob. That sound pierced my heart like a barbed lance.

"Are you well?" I asked.

"Well?" Her arm tightened around my chest. "Oh, Loki! I'm blessed."

I shifted to meet her gaze, wondering if she mocked me. But her pale eyes were open, and her lips curved into a sleepy smile.

"The fire-haired god of the Æsir has seen fit to give me pleasure beyond imagining," she sighed. "Of all the women in the Nine Realms, you chose me. I'm blessed."

My chest ached, as if her words had cut something deep inside me. Blessed. Even after I'd wrapped us in an illusion, carried her home, and laid her in her family's longhouse to sleep, that word echoed inside of me, filling something dark and empty.

I spent the night in the hills above her village, watching stars drift over the longhouse that held the mortal woman who thought me capable of bringing a blessing.

SOME PART OF ME WAS always ready for her to change her mind, of course.

And so, when the day came that she did not smile to see me, I wasn't truly surprised. Instead, I felt only a dull clenching around my heart, like the tired resignation which greets the arrival of winter's first frost.

It was mid-autumn. I'd been away for almost a full month, trying to patch things up on Álfheim after Thor got drunk and made an ass of himself. I had missed Anya more than I would have believed possible, and my heart hummed with the possibility of running my fingers through her rich honeyed hair or breathing the scent of her arousal.

The day was warm enough, in the sunlight at least, but the wind off the ocean carried a chill. I planned on lighting a ring of fires to keep my lover's body warm, and I was idly considering building myself a stone hut, something small and out of the way, protected by a web of illusion. Somewhere to entertain my lady during the cold, dark months of the coming winter.

When Anya finally appeared, walking slowly toward the eel traps I'd seen her harvest months ago, I almost didn't recognize her. She strode with her head down, her face hidden by a heavy cloak. Her intricate brooch glistened in the sun and I paused, watching her closely. It was unlike Anya to walk hunched over like that, with her eyes on the ground. My Anya was confident and strong, with her eyes eternally on the horizon. Perhaps this wasn't her after all.

But no, this woman was the right height and shape. I saw a flash of golden hair dancing in the wind and, when I held still, the air carried the delicate spice of Anya's scent to me.

"Hello, Anya," I said.

She jolted upright and wiped her eyes before turning to me. "Fire-hair," she whispered.

Anya closed the distance between us and fell against my chest, but she did not smile. I wrapped my arms around her, running my hand across her cheek. It was wet. Had she been crying?

"What troubles you?" I asked.

She turned away, watching the choppy, gray ocean. "I'm with child."

Of course. How very foolish of me to be surprised. From the first time I saw her picking berries in the thick sunlight of midsummer, I knew this day was coming. We belonged to different worlds; I had nothing to offer a mortal woman with child.

Only an idiot would think otherwise.

"So, have you flashed an ankle at a young man in the village?" I asked, half in jest.

"I have," she said. "I'm to be married in a week."

This shocked me even more than the news of her pregnancy. It was the solution I'd proposed the first time we made love, but I was still shaken. Perhaps I'd wanted to pretend my mortal lover did not have another life, that she existed only for my pleasure.

The thought that she'd identified the situation and found a remedy without my involvement made me feel small and insignificant. I bit my tongue and cursed myself for a fool. Why would I be anything more than a bit of fun for her, just because my own universe had begun to revolve around our time together?

"Congratulations." I forced myself to smile.

She sighed again and buried her head in my shoulder. Her scent enveloped me, warmth and sweetness and boundless erotic pleasure.

"I wish it could be you," she whispered. "That you'd bring me one of Iðunn's golden apples and take me to be your wife in the halls of Asgard."

Shock flooded my body like icy water. I shoved Anya off my chest and turned toward the sea, away from her warmth and soft curves, as I pulled together the latent strands of magic, preparing to leave.

I should have left.

But Anya embraced me from behind, and I could not force myself to go. Not while she was touching me.

"Forgive me, Fire-hair," she said. "Forgive the foolish imagination of a girl."

My heart burned in my chest, and I ground my teeth together. "Sif was a mistake," I muttered.

"Pardon me?"

I turned to face her, taking her hands in mine. They were cold. It was the close of the day, and the wind held a sharp edge.

"Cutting Sif's hair," I said. "I did it, and it was a mistake. A stupid, costly mistake. You know I wasn't born on Asgard. I'm not an Æsir, or a Vanir. I'll never really be one of them. But if I hadn't lost my mind and cut her hair...Damn, I didn't need to make so many enemies."

Her brow furrowed. "But isn't that how Thor received Mjölnir? Because you tricked the dwarves when they replaced Sif's hair?"

"Yes, but still. He was furious with me, and many of the Æsir agreed with him." I paused, wondering how best to put my delicate situation in Asgard into words. "Iðunn's golden apples. Anya, they're how the Æsir and the Vanir stay young and beautiful. They're the most valuable thing in Asgard. If I tried to take them, if I even looked like I was thinking about taking them, they would never forgive me. No one would ever forgive me."

She sighed against my chest. By the Nine Realms, that woman felt good in my arms.

"And that's not all. Anya, if I'm ever to be accepted in the halls of Asgard, truly accepted as the oath-brother of Óðinn—"

"You need to marry one of them," Anya said.

I nodded, casting a small illusion to hide the waver in my voice and the tears biting at my eyelids. "It's... It's how the world works."

She brought her cold hand to my face, cupping my cheek. "I understand, Loki. We cannot fight the way the world works."

My illusions almost crashed at my feet when she pressed her soft lips to mine. My heart ached, and I longed for her so strongly it hurt, like a shard of glass lodged deep in my chest. I devoured her kisses, pushing her to the ground, ripping off her brooch and her cloak. When I saw her pale skin pucker in the cold wind, I lit the fires, and we were surrounded by heat and dancing flame, like a sacrifice.

We were there all night. She wanted more, always more, and I gave it to her. I pushed myself past exhaustion, fueling the fires and bringing her soft mortal body to climax again and again. The light from my fires drowned out the stars, but they could not extinguish the pale glow of dawn. I noticed it swelling in the sky over her shoulder as I held her body against mine, rubbing our hips together as slowly as I could to draw out her orgasm. The soft light of the rising sun caught in her golden hair just as she climaxed, her body tightening around me, her warmth pouring over me. I closed my eyes, wishing I could die just then, in a moment of pure ecstasy.

Anya collapsed against my chest, barely conscious, and I covered her face and neck with kisses. I tried to help her into her unbearably complicated mortal clothing, but it was too much for me; in the end, I had to settle for wrapping her in her cloak.

I carried her back to her village under the distant glow of the autumnal dawn, her head resting against my collarbone, an illusion rendering us invisible. A few people were awake, pissing outside the front door of their longhouse or rubbing their eyes at the dawn. I scowled at the young men, wondering which idiot she'd chosen for a husband.

No one was awake yet in her family's longhouse, although they were beginning to shift and yawn on the sleeping platforms. I set her down, brushing her hair from her eyes and lips, kissing the curve of her cheek as I pulled the blankets to her chin. It occurred to me I could shapeshift, become a mouse perhaps, watch her from the corners as she awoke.

But some part of me realized that would hurt even more.

CHAPTER SEVEN

I sought comfort in a variety of ill-advised places.

I traveled to Jötunheimr first, where I roamed the frozen wastelands to the north, finding the blowing snow and endless ice somewhat soothing. But a chance encounter with an ice bear reminded me of Anya's golden hair spread across a different pelt. I ripped the beast to shreds with my magic, then stumbled to Útgarðar, past the slums where I was born, and up the foreboding steps of Angrboða's great palace.

Angrboða. She was dangerously ambitious and as safe as a venomous snake, but I'd been fucking her for centuries. She was probably the closest thing to a friend someone like me could ever have.

I didn't recognize the guard on her front steps, which was the first bad sign. There was a time when I'd known all Angrboða's guards and servants, and had brought most of them to orgasm as well. It was a useful association on many levels.

This face I didn't recognize, so I fell back on something undeniable and halfway honest.

"I'm here to see the Lady Hel," I told the guard with a broad smile.

"And who in the Nine Realms do you think you are?" the guard grunted. He was uncommonly unattractive, which was a tad surprising. Angrboða usually liked the pretty ones.

"Her father," I said, widening my smile until it became something predatory.

The guard rushed away, and I followed, not waiting for an invitation. I knew my way through Angrboða's palace. After three staircases and two long, narrow corridors, I heard my daughter's voice.

"Yes, thank you for telling me," Hel was saying. "I thought we'd had a frost last night."

Someone murmured in response, their voice so low I couldn't be sure if Hel was speaking to a man or a woman.

"I know," Hel answered. "We'll just see what seedlings survive. Maybe this will teach the farmers along the river to listen to my recommendations next time."

The guard and I turned one final corner. There, standing before an open door and talking to a stooped, older woman, was my daughter Hel.

I knew what to expect; even so, seeing my only daughter was always a bit of a shock. Half of Hel's face and body was that of an ordinary young woman, her dark hair reaching to her waist, her blue dress demure and perhaps a bit staid.

And her other half was dead. Not just dead, actually. Her left half was actively decomposing, with pale yellow bones showing through tattered patches of flesh. As we approached I noticed there was even an odor, a deeply disturbing blend of rosewater and decay.

Hel's head turned at our footsteps, and she fixed me with her pale, living eye. I heard the scuff of boots over stone as the guard who'd led me this far retreated back down the hallway. Hel's face was completely devoid of expression.

"Oh," she said. "It's you."

"Daughter," I replied. "You're looking truly terrible."

Ignoring me, Hel turned back to the woman before her. "Thank you, Ganglati. I look forward to hearing from you again next week."

The older woman bowed low before my daughter and turned to leave, but not before a quick, curious glance in my direction. Once she'd vanished down the corridor, Hel rolled her head back, crossed her arms, and turned to face me. I noticed a maggot writing in the desiccated, black flesh of her dead cheek.

It was an impressive illusion. She'd been scarcely more than a child when she first begged me to teach her the art of casting an illusion to alter her appearance. I acquiesced, and this nightmarish half-dead figure was what she'd done with her newfound knowledge. Technically, it was quite a difficult spell. I could only imagine how much it must irritate her mother.

"What in the Nine Realms are you doing here?" she asked.

I shrugged. "Well, it's been a while since my last visit."

The eyebrow on the living side of her face raised. "A while? Father, it's been ten years."

That long? I searched my memory, trying to recall the last time I'd been to Jötunheimr. Ah. Yes, I'd gone directly to Angrboða's chambers then. And the time before as well. And then...well, before that I'd gone directly under Angrboða's dress. During one of her weddings, I believe.

"And, how have you been?" I asked.

Hel rolled both her bright, living eye and the clouded, sightless cataract of her dead eye. The effect was quite disconcerting. "Fine. Mother wants to marry me off."

She turned to retreat into her living quarters, and I followed.

"I'm sure that's going swimmingly," I replied. "Now are you going to offer me a drink, or shall I just stand on the threshold like a slave?"

"Look, Mother isn't here. And I know she's the one you came to visit, so there's no need for you to waste your breath on me."

I frowned. "What, did she marry again?"

"Ugh, yes. To Thiassi."

"Oh. Well, that makes sense, I suppose."

Thiassi was one of the richest lords in Jötunheim. He was also one of the most boring men in the entire Nine Realms. The only interesting thing Thiassi had ever done, aside from horde his vast fortune like a portly, ill-tempered dragon, was learn how to transform his shape into a massive eagle. The eagle's sharp beak and obnoxious scream were only a slight improvement over Thiassi's ordinary appearance. I wouldn't sit through an entire dinner with him for all the gold in his palace.

"So, she's gone to Thiassi's palace in Thiassiheim, then?" I asked.

Hel snorted. "Indeed. And she can try to marry off his daughter Skadi and see how well that works out for her."

While she spoke, something dark shifted inside Hel's ribcage. I caught a glimpse of sleek fur and the flash of black eyes.

"Is that a rat?" I asked.

A touch of color splashed across Hel's living cheek. "Oh, he's new. Do you like him?"

I bent closer. The illusion was remarkable; the rotten tatters of her dress shifted with her body, and the rat climbing her ribcage was stunningly lifelike. He might even bite me if I touched him.

"Very nicely done," I admitted.

I looked up and saw the rarest of expressions on Hel's face: an actual smile.

"It took a lot of practice," she said, almost shyly.

"I'm sure."

We both fell silent. The rat blinked at me as Hel shifted on her feet, circling her living arm protectively around her decaying ribcage. I glanced over her shoulder, quickly scanning her chambers. One small, narrow bed. One chair, pushed against a desk heaped with books and reams of parchment. And no sign of wine or mead anywhere. Clearly, my daughter did not have many visitors. Perhaps marriage would be good for her, after all.

Hel cleared her throat. "Uh, Father. I do have a question. Since you're here."

"Go on."

"It's the illusion," she began. "It's, um, when I sleep. It doesn't last. One of the servants told me so."

Her cheek flushed again, and I wondered if there was more to the story. Learning how to hold my body's handsome illusion while drunk, or during an orgasm, had been quite the challenge. Was Hel trying to master those particular tricks?

I glanced again at her disturbingly spartan chambers and permanent, deep-set frown. Probably not, I decided. If she was getting drunk or laid, she'd look happier.

"I can't maintain my illusions when I sleep either, child."

Hel sighed, clearly disappointed. "But what do you do?"

"The same thing as your mother. I don't sleep."

MUCH AS I WOULD HAVE liked to try to forget Anya by burying my cock in Angrboða, I couldn't bring myself to travel to Thiassi's palace. That man was truly insufferable. Instead, I washed up in Asgard, went to Val-hall, and spent several days drinking myself into a stupor, until Óðinn publicly accused me of nursing a broken heart.

That was close enough to the truth to make me put down the mead of Val-hall.

Once I dried out, Freyja welcomed me in her chambers, but I found surprisingly little pleasure in our lovemaking. The soft press of her ankles locked around my waist stirred painful memories, and Freyja accused me of leaving her unsatisfied. We did not part on good terms.

Finally, as curiosity and loneliness bit at me with ever-sharper teeth, I returned to Midgard. Just to look, I told myself. Just to satisfy my curiosity, to see that my woman was still well and healthy. And, perhaps, to brush my fingers across her cheek one last time.

I didn't dare appear in the center of the longhouses, partly out of my latent self-preservation instinct and partly out of fear for what I might find. Instead, I waited on the beach, halfway between the village and the stones where Anya had once spread lingonberries to dry in the sun. It was winter by this time, the very heart of winter, and ice floes moved in the waves, looking gray and shattered in the meager, flat light. I stared at the shifting ice for a long time, trying to feel the cold. Trying to feel anything.

It was almost dusk when I heard her singing.

I turned and saw Anya silhouetted against the horizon. Her cloak was wrapped tightly around her shoulders, but it didn't entirely hide the swell of her stomach. Her cheeks were flushed with cold, and her face was turned to the sea.

She saw me, and her voice stilled. Her eyes grew wide, and she brought her hand to her lips. Then she ran across the frozen grass and fell into my arms. Her embrace was so tight I had to cast another illusion to hide my tears.

"Anya," I said, "you're looking well."

She made a strange hiccupping sound, and I realized she was crying. Crying, and smiling. "Oh, Loki! Oh, how I've missed you!"

I ran my fingers over her back and her waist, admiring the swell of her pregnancy. Her eyes hardly left my face, as though she was afraid I'd vanish.

"You," I finally said, "have grown even more beautiful."

She giggled. It was such a delicious, warm sound that I had to kiss her. She responded with such hunger I almost tore off her ridiculously complicated clothes and started making love to her in the snow.

I struggled to control my lust, won, and tore myself away from her hungry lips. "And how is married life?"

Her smile wavered somewhat. "It's...not horrible."

My heart clenched. "Anya, is he good to you? Does he hurt you?"

She gasped, and I realized my hands had tightened around her shoulders, probably painfully so.

"If he's hurt you—" I growled, heat rising in my chest. Nothing would stop my rage if that man had mistreated my mortal woman.

"No, no, it's not like that. He's a good man. That's why I chose him. He just..." She gave me a shy smile. "He's no idea what he's doing. At night."

My anger ebbed and sadness flowed back into its place. To have such a glorious wife and not know how to please her...what a waste.

Her fingers lingered on my arm. "He's interested in you, you know."

I blinked. "He's what?"

"He'd like to meet you."

"You told your husband of me?"

She giggled again, and my heart gave a painful little twinge. How I'd missed that bubbling laugh!

"Well, I didn't exactly tell him the Fire-god had my maidenhead a hundred times over. But I did tell him I'd met you. And I took him to our fire-ring to prove it."

My mind spun, trying to make sense of her words. "Our fire-ring?"

Her cheeks turned an even deeper shade of red. "Where we spent our last night together. Your flames scorched the ground. The marks are still there."

"And your husband wants to meet me? After that? Does he want to kill me?"

I tried not to smile. Mortals can't harm me, much less kill me. The Æsir and the Jötunn all know exactly how and where we'll die, after all. But the thought of splitting open Anya's husband's skull did have a certain appeal.

Anya buried her head against my shoulder. "He doesn't want to kill you," she said, her voice muffled by my cloak. "He's...interested."

She said something further, but her voice was so soft I couldn't make out her words.

I touched her cheek, turning her face to meet her eyes. "What was that, beautiful?"

She looked rather adorably embarrassed. "I said, maybe you could teach him something?" The crimson blazing in her cheeks and her soft, parted lips left no doubt which skills she was referring to.

A chance to pleasure Anya while her idiot of a husband watched? Well, how was I to turn that down?

"And, if I were interested, where could I find the newly married couple?" I asked.

Her eyes lit above her smile. "The boathouse! We could meet you there tonight!"

I raised an eyebrow, and she blushed again.

"That's...where we go. I've been trying to teach him... you know. To be more like you."

My stomach churned with completely irrational jealousy, and my desire to make Anya scream with pleasure in front of her idiot of a husband solidified into an unshakable resolution.

"Tonight. I'll be there tonight."

I kissed each of her fingers, enjoying the way it made her breath catch. Then I kissed her neck, just above her collarbone, and was rewarded with the sweet scent of her arousal. She leaned her hips into mine, the small curve of her stomach pressing just above the heat of her sex, but I put my finger to her lips and pushed her back.

"Tonight," I whispered.

She nodded, her eyes shimmering. "Thank you."

I FOUND THE BOATHOUSE by scent.

There were quite a few boathouses in the town; more houses for boats than people, actually. And then it dawned on me why Anya would take her husband to a cramped, dank boathouse. They must still share a longhouse with her family, or with his family, or with an even larger collection of relations. That would have made for an awkward wedding night, I realized, but the thought brought me no pleasure.

Light from a small fire flickered beneath the door of the very furthest boathouse. I paused long enough to take in Anya's sweet, wild scent, mixed with an unfamiliar male tang. I debated opening the door, but decided that was far too common.

In a gust of wind and a swirl of flames, I materialized inside the boathouse. The interior was so crowded Anya and her husband were standing, and I appeared close enough to touch them both. She was naked, save her hair sprang, and her pale skin glistened in the firelight.

Her husband gaped at me, and I was forced to do a quick re-assessment. He was bare from the waist up and surprisingly attractive, with dark hair and a strong, young body that smelled of coal and iron; a blacksmith, then. He was clearly astonished to see me, but even in his moment of shock his eyes moved, assessing the situation. Not a dullard, then. Anya had chosen wisely, and it pained me.

Anya smiled at me, glorious in her nakedness. A fresh tang of arousal filled the boathouse, slicking the space between her legs and making my cock stiffen. "Hello, Fire-hair," she said.

"Hello, Anya," I growled.

I was sorely tempted to start fucking her now against the rough wood of the overturned ship's hulls. But someone touched my arm, and I turned. It was Anya's husband, gently tracing his fingers along my forearm.

"Loki?" he said. "Really? Loki of the Æsir?"

He caught my eye, and something in his gaze made me hesitate. I expected shock, confusion. If he even guessed at what I'd done to his new wife, I expected a useless and possibly hilarious rage.

The look in his eyes was something entirely different. I changed my plans and brought my fingers to his forearm, mimicking his touch.

"And you are...?" I asked.

"Falur," he said. His dark eyes widened, and he followed the progress of my fingers along his arm to his wrist. His pulse raced under my touch.

"Falur," I said. "Would you like to learn how to pleasure your wife?"

He gasped a little as my fingers intertwined with his. "Y—Yes."

I turned Falur to face Anya. Her cheeks were flushed, and the air was heavy with her scent. I brought Falur's hand to the delicate curve of Anya's belly.

"Lesson one," I whispered, trailing Falur's hand down her skin. "Touch her gently." I brought his hand to the apex of her sex, where I could feel the heat pouring off her body. "Touch her right here."

I brought Falur's hand to the nub of her sex. Anya moaned with pleasure, and Falur gasped.

"Very good," I whispered, my lips against his ear. "Gently, now." I led his hand in a slow circle and Anya's hips rocked against the thick muscles of his arm. "And slowly. The slower the better."

She moaned again. Falur's breath quickened. I decided the time was ripe to do something potentially foolish. I slipped my free hand around Falur's shoulders and pressed my hips into his backside, letting him feel the full length of my erection between his legs, ready to vanish if he protested.

He did not protest. He whimpered as he pressed his ass back against my hips, his head dropping into the cradle of my collarbone.

"Good," I whispered. I pressed Falur's hand against Anya's sex and slipped my free hand down the front of his chest, down the hard ridges of his muscles. I had to use my magic to free his belt, but it only took a moment before I could wrap my hand around the full length of his cock. He was moaning and mumbling incoherently now, his hips rocking against my hand, his head thrown back against my shoulder.

"Touch her like you want to be touched," I said, and my hand matched the rhythm of his fingers against Anya's sex. I licked and kissed the exposed length of his neck, enjoying his taste and the feel of his racing pulse beneath my mouth.

He came a moment later, crying out in my arms. The boathouse filling with the salty tang of his seed as it spilled over my hand. Ah, I'd forgotten how fun men are! How delightfully straightforward. I wrapped both my arms around his waist as his legs trembled against mine. He blinked and stared around the boathouse as though he'd just woken from a dream.

I didn't give him time to recover.

"On your knees," I said, pushing his shoulders. "Your wife is not yet satisfied, Falur."

He obeyed, but he shifted to face me once his knees were on the hard ground of the boathouse. His lips almost touched my pants, almost pressed against the head of my cock. By the time I realized his intentions, his hands were caressing the inside of my thighs.

"Loki," he gasped. "I've always been...curious."

I caught Anya's eye. Her eyelids were heavy, her lips parted. She was supremely turned on by all this. She smiled at me as she very deliberately brought her fingers to her own sex, mimicking what Falur had just done.

Oh, how could I resist?

My clothes vanished as I sent them back to Asgard, and my cock sprang free, almost reaching Falur's eager lips. I plunged my fingers into his hair as he turned to meet my eyes.

"Go ahead," I said.

He kissed the head of my cock delicately, almost as if he expected it to be taken from him. When he ran his tongue along the length I couldn't stifle my groan, and when he wrapped his lips around my shaft, I closed my eyes, ready to let myself be carried away by ecstasy.

Anya's fingers wrapped around mine and my eyes fluttered open, meeting her gaze. She brought my hand to her breast and I ran my thumb over her nipple as my hips rocked against her husband's lips. I groaned in an inarticulate rush of pleasure, sinking my other hand deep into the dark tangle of Falur's hair as his lips embraced my length, sucking with wild enthusiasm. Warmth tightened at the base of my spine.

"Falur," I warned, "I'm going to—"

He pulled my cock even deeper into his mouth as he moaned with pleasure. The sound traveled through my entire body. I met Anya's eyes just as she climaxed, her cheeks flushing and her eyes rolling back. Witnessing her pleasure pushed me over the edge, sending the fire of my orgasm surging through me. Falur grunted in pleasure as he devoured my seed, his hands clamped tight around my thighs.

For a moment all three of us were breathless, panting in the warm, damp closeness of the boathouse. Anya broke the silence first.

"Will we see you again, Fire-hair?" she asked. Her voice wavered, but only slightly.

I pulled Falur to his feet and kissed him deeply, for a long time, savoring the taste of my spent seed on his lips and tongue. Then I turned and kissed Anya, losing myself in the scent and warmth of the mortal woman I thought I'd lost.

Grinning, I crushed both of them to my chest. "Just try to stop me," I said.

CHAPTER EIGHT

I built the stone hut.

I chose a location that would be easy to hide, was protected from the wind but with a nice view of the ocean, and was within easy walking distance from the village. To keep from raising undo suspicion, I decided not to rely on magic to build the structure. It was harder work than I anticipated, building a shelter with actual physical labor; those stone huts looked deceptively simple. The thought that I could have built the entire thing in a matter of minutes if I'd used my magic both tormented me and filled me with an odd sense of satisfaction.

Óðinn showed up as I was finishing the roof. I wasn't sure how long he stood and watched me, his wide-brimmed hat hiding his face in shadow, the crows Hugin and Munin looming on his shoulders. When I reached for a fresh bundle of thatch and noticed him standing there as silent as a sentinel, my heart jumped and my mouth filled with a bitter copper tang.

I leapt down and greeted him, offering hospitality, as is requisite in Midgard. My mind raced. Of course, Óðinn would know about my mortal lovers; his ravens fly the Nine Realms every day, reporting back to him all details, no matter how private or precious. What he would not know was how very much these mortal lovers meant to me.

"Nice place," Óðinn said.

I nodded. It was a nice place. I was especially proud of the large window facing the sea, the one I'd warded to keep the cold out.

Once the roof was finished and the bed constructed, it would be downright cozy.

"Bit of an odd location," he continued, glancing at me from under the wide brim of his hat.

"Well, I do appreciate my privacy."

Óðinn sniffed. "And it's just around the corner from the mortals you've been fucking."

I shrugged. "There's that."

"Listen, oath-brother. The mortals. Don't get too attached."

The illusion I'd cast on my face held, and my expression did not change. "Are you threatening me?" I asked as I pulled strands of magic tight in my fist. I could bring this pile of rocks down atop Óðinn in an instant. That wouldn't hurt him, of course, but it would be a hell of a way to prove my point.

"Loki, if I threaten you, you'll know it."

He met my gaze with his one pale blue eye, and a cold shiver worked its way down my spine. I've always feared Óðinn. Respected as well as feared, yes, but fear always came first. He stared at me, and all my years fell away. I was once again nothing more than the bastard son of Laufeyiar, trying desperately to impress the All-father and gain a ticket to a better life. Then his shoulders slumped, and the moment broke.

"Mead?" I asked.

"Please."

I poured two flagons of the mead I'd stolen from Val-hall, and together we walked back outside, stretching our legs on the wooden bench I'd built, drinking Asgardian mead in the pale winter sunlight. We were silent until we had both drained our flagons.

"I'm trying to help you," Óðinn finally said. "The mortals. They live such short little lives. They're like...cute little insects. It doesn't pay to get too attached."

I snorted. "Your warning may be well-intentioned, All-father, but it's unnecessary. I don't get attached. To anything."

Óðinn raised an eyebrow above his empty socket. The expression was a bit upsetting.

"More mead?" I offered.

"You know what you should do? Try some of the warriors in Val-hall, my friend. All the fun of mortals, and you have centuries to play together."

I thought of the filthy, idiotic warriors who filled Val-hall. My lip curled.

"It's what I do," Óðinn said.

"Perhaps," I said, taking his empty flagon. "Now, allow me to refill this."

"And never dream of drinking ale, unless to both of us the draught is offered," Óðinn said, reciting the vows we made as we swore our oath of brotherhood. The oath that made me one of the Æsir of Asgard. Óðinn's pale eye twinkled. What the fuck is he up to? I wondered. I never could quite read him.

Óðinn stayed for several hours, long enough to prevent me from finishing the roof, and I still was no closer to discerning the reason for his visit by the time he left. Irritating old shithead, I thought, as I lay on my back on the frozen ground of the hut and watched the cold stars twinkle through the hole in the roof.

I FINISHED MY HUT IN just under a month, although it took me several more days to perfect the interior. The wooden platform, which I covered with feather mattresses from Val-hall, took up a full half of the building, and I filled it with soft linen sheets and warm furs. On the very top, I placed my prized ice bear fur, wondering if Anya would remember making love on that last summer. Then I rocked back and examined it critically. It looked like the perfect sleeping platform. Not that I expected to actually do much sleeping there.

I built a table and fit it to the curve in the wall. At the last minute I stole three golden plates from Val-hall and linked them to Asgard so they would fill with food every morning and evening. I placed beeswax candles in the alcoves I'd set around the bed, lit the hearth fire, and stepped back, satisfied.

It was already late at night, but I was tired of waiting. I walked across the frozen fields to town and entered the longhouse. Hearthfires flared as I walked the length of the dwelling, singing softly. *The Briar and the Rose.*

Anya's voice crept through the air moments later, quietly echoing the refrain above the snores and groans of sleeping mortals. A soft rustle sounded through the longhouse as she pushed the curtain aside from her bunk, and I heard the soft echo of her footfalls. She embraced me from behind, the tight curve of her pregnancy pressed against my spine. My heart swelled.

"Bring Falur," I whispered. "I have something to show you both."

She kissed me softly and disappeared into the gloom, returning a moment later with her husband. He wiped the sleep from his eyes and grinned like a madman when he saw me. Oh, they were glorious! I pulled them to my chest and struggled with the momentary urge to fuck them both in the middle of the longhouse.

I'd never used my magic to move a person other than myself, but the night was cold, and I wanted to impress my lovers. So, I pulled the strands of magical energy and took all three of us to the inside of the house I'd built.

Hearthfire and candlelight bathed the small, circular room in a warm golden glow. The distant thud of the breakers crashed above the gasps of both my mortal lovers.

"What is this magic?" Falur finally said.

"Just somewhere warm," I said. "Unless of course you prefer the boathouse?"

Anya walked very slowly around the room, running her hands over the stones and the furs, touching the beeswax candles in their alcoves. "It's amazing," she whispered.

For you, I thought. All for you.

"Mead?" I asked.

I'd stolen three flagons from Val-hall. They were linked to Asgard, so they would never run empty. Both Anya and Falur chose to sit on the bed, and I removed my cloak and unbuttoned my shirt before picking up my own flagon. Falur's eyes lingered on my chest.

"It occurs to me," I said slowly, running my gaze over both of their bodies, "that I've made a mistake."

Falur swallowed hard, and Anya's breath caught in her throat. I took a long drink from my flagon, drawing out the moment as the mead spread its warmth through my body. Then I set the flagon down and crawled onto the bed, into the space between them.

"I did promise to teach Falur," I said, my voice already thick with desire, "how to please his beautiful wife. But it seems we've only just begun those lessons."

I kissed them both, Anya first and then Falur. Anya's kiss was deep and hungry, while Falur seemed almost stunned. Then I pulled Anya's sleeping shrift over her head and pressed her to the mattress, covering her neck and chest with kisses. The curve of her pregnancy echoed her full breasts. Damn, but she was glorious!

When Anya lay before us, naked, bathed in the soft glow of candlelight, her legs spread and her cheeks flushed, I stepped back. Falur had already pulled his shirt off his chest. He watched his wife with his lips slightly parted and his cock straining against the soft linen of his pants.

"Kiss her," I said.

Falur leaned over Anya's chest, but I pulled him back.

"No. Kiss her here."

I guided Falur's head between Anya's thighs, then leaned down next to him.

"Kiss her like this," I said, running my lips over the downy hair curling around Anya's sex. Oh, fuck, she smelled good. I sank deeper, pressing my lips to hers, letting the heat and scent of her sweet cunt surround me. Somewhere above me, Anya moaned in pleasure.

I pulled back, gesturing to Falur. "Now. You kiss her."

With a grin, Falur sank between her legs. I found it hard to believe he'd never tasted his wife, but perhaps a crowded longhouse wasn't the best place for sexual experimentation. Or perhaps he was just humoring me.

Either way, Anya's body rippled with pleasure as Falur devoured her. I waited until they were both gasping before I sank to the mattress and pressed my body between Falur's legs.

"Very nice," I murmured, running my hands up Falur's strong thighs.

Falur groaned and lifted his hips, showing me the curve of his ass. I wondered briefly if he knew what he was asking for, offering himself to me like that.

Well, he was about to find out.

I licked my lips and ran my fingers over his back. With my other hand, I reached between Falur's legs to grasp the heat of his stiff cock. His body tensed as my fingers danced over his shaft. I leaned closer, until I was kissing the small of his back, running my lips and tongue down the curve of his spine and to the swell of his muscular ass. Then I kissed him, just as he was kissing Anya's sex. Falur flinched and stiffened, but I held his thighs, offering him no escape.

He said something, some wordless, animal cry of protest and pleasure all mixed together. I thrust my tongue between his cheeks, feeling the tight swirl of his anus. I loved the thought that I was the first person to taste Falur, his heat and sweat, his dark moans that mixed pleasure and shame. His cock throbbed in my hands, and I realized he had stopped moving. He was frozen, trapped between my mouth and Anya's hips.

"Go on," I said, pulling away far enough to slip my fingers between his cheeks. "Don't stop, Falur. Pleasure your wife."

His neck bent between Anya's legs again, and her cries echoed through the stone hut. She was close, I could tell from the rhythm of her hips and her hitching, gasping breath. She was so fucking close.

And so was Falur. I pressed against the muscles of his anus, softening them. He groaned as his body relaxed. My own cock surged when I slipped my finger inside his tight hole.

Anya screamed, and I glanced up to see her body contort with pleasure. Her back arched as her thighs closed around Falur's head. I slid a second finger inside Falur. He was gasping now, his hips thrusting against my hand, his cock pressing into my fist. I leaned against him, pressing my chest into his back.

"Falur," I whispered. "I'm going to fuck you."

He moaned, and his hips kicked up, offering himself to me. Opening to me. I spread my fingers, stretching him, before I tilted my own hips and pressed my cock between his cheeks. There was a moment of resistance, a moment of hesitation when I knew his body would register my invasion as pain, and then I was inside of him, surrounded and embraced by the heat of his strong body.

Oh, fuck. Falur felt just as good as I'd imagined. I closed my eyes and held still, thinking of nothing at all, letting myself drown in the feeling of our bodies joined together. Then he began to move against me, to press closer, as if he wanted even more.

More? I could do more.

I grabbed his hips and thrust into him, slowly at first, then faster and harder as he began to cry out, to beg for it. I would have liked to fuck him all night, but I couldn't hold out; when my climax came, it came fast and hard, swallowing me in a flood of ecstatic heat that began at my balls and drowned out all my conscious control. I shot my seed into the dark heat of Falur's body, then wrapped my fist around his cock and pumped him until he came into the bed beneath us.

Sweaty and trembling, I pulled out of Falur and reached for my flagon of mead. As my eyes slowly adjusted to the candlelight, I saw Anya sprawled across the bed, her pale eyes watching us. One of her hands cupped her breast, rolling a bright, pink nipple between her fingers. And her other hand was on her own sex, tracing the swollen bud of her clit almost lazily.

"I hope you have more for me," she said, her voice throaty and breathless.

My cock stirred at that, and I grinned. "For you? Always."

Before I fell backward into the bed and let my lovers have me again, I strengthened the wards around the hut.

Not even Óðinn's ravens would see what we chose to do in here.

I AWOKE WITH A JOLT.

Something bit at my side with a sharp, sudden stab of magically energy. Wincing, I pulled the strand of magic from my body. It was my own cantrip, sent to pierce me if I fell asleep. One of the final touches in this hut was that spell to keep me from sleeping, lest I risk letting my lovers see the horrible scars on my body. From the sound of the steady, even breathing in the darkness surrounding me, both Anya and Falur were fast asleep.

Still. Even if the darkness hid my deformation, my skin would feel rough against theirs. I shuddered at the thought and pulled my illusions tight, giving myself smooth skin and an easy smile. The kind of easy smile I'd worn without illusions before the dwarves sewed my lips shut.

Wincing at the memory, I sat and lit one of the candles in the wall. It shed a gentle light over the rumpled furs and linen sheets. Falur lay on his back, one arm above his head, the other curled in Anya's golden hair. I smiled at his position. Unless my memories deceived me, I'd been pressed against his broad, muscular chest when sleep took him.

But to sleep myself? Sloppy. And risky.

I slid from the bed, making sure an illusion kept me from disturbing the mattress. Perhaps I'd expended more energy than I thought, making love to both of them. Images of Anya's body spread beneath me, the swell of her stomach and the curve of her breasts, flashed through my memory. And then Falur, gasping with pleasure as I knelt before him and embraced the stiff curve of his cock with my lips.

Yes, that had taken a fair amount of energy.

Grinning in the darkness, I grabbed a flagon of mead from the table, drained it, and watched as it magically refilled. Anya shifted in her sleep, moaning slightly. I extinguished the candle, wanting to let my lovers sleep in peace, and I tugged the magic around my body, pulling myself to the outside of my hut without the noise and hassle of opening the door.

Cold. It was so damned cold outside that the air bit at my lungs, and the stars shone like ice crystals dancing just above my head. I drained the flagon a second time, allowing Asgard's mead to warm my stomach. The space between the sea and the sky hummed with a narrow band of gray light; morning approached. I frowned and drained the mead again, enjoying the way my body was beginning to respond to the alcohol.

The door behind me opened with a soft whoosh, and I spun. It was too dark to make out features, but those enormous shoulders could only have belonged to Falur. I immediately lit a fire on the ice-covered grass before the hut, hoping to keep him warm.

Falur's lips twitched into a half smile. "Show off," he whispered as he pulled the door shut.

He'd been wise enough to bring a fur with him, I noted. This man seemed unusually clever for a mortal from Midgard. I wondered how long it had taken him to determine the child his wife carried wasn't his.

"Mead?" I asked, twitching my fingers into the magic to pull the second flagon from inside the house.

He shook his head. "No, thanks. We can't all drink like the Æsir."

I glanced down at the flagon in my hands, which was once again refilling itself. With a flick, I sent both flagons back into the hut. This time, I reached across the Nine Realms, pulling two steaming mugs all the way from Asgard's kitchens. I pressed one of them into Falur's hands. He inhaled deeply, breathing in the steam off a fresh cup of blackberry tea.

"Nice," he said.

I found the subtle compliment ridiculously satisfying. "You're welcome."

He gave me that little half smile again. "It's true what Anya said about you."

I waited until it became obvious Falur was not going to offer more information. "And what did she say about me?"

His grin widened until it reached his dark, sparkling eyes. "She said you're like one of us, but better. That you make everything better."

I shifted against the cold stone wall. Coming from anyone else, I'd be tempted to agree with that statement. I knew my magical prowess was unrivaled, except perhaps by Óðinn himself. And my mother was a Jötunn, making me stronger, tougher, and much longer lived than the mortals on Midgard. Yet Falur's words made me uncomfortable. They felt almost like another promise I'd be obligated to keep.

"You'll need to return to the village?" I asked, trying to shift the conversation.

Falur barked a sharp laugh. "Unfortunately."

"Is life...unpleasant there?"

Falur's expression tightened. "No. Not really."

The fire crackled in the silence between us. Falur sipped his tea and watched the horizon, where the pale gray dawn was beginning to spread across the leaden waves.

"The child," Falur finally said. "Will he be better, too?"

I noticed Falur was pointedly avoiding my gaze, as though the slowly unfurling dawn across the Northern Sea had completely captured his attention.

"Your child?" I asked.

Falur's laugh was more genuine this time. "My mother says Anya's showing early. Very early, I think."

He finally turned to me, and our eyes met in the low flicker of the firelight. I remembered meeting his eyes last night, beside another fire, as he swallowed my cock. The memory sent a thrill of sensual pleasure through my body. I brought my own mug to my lips to hide my smile.

"I don't honestly know," I confessed. "Children are difficult to predict. Sometimes the offspring bear very little resemblance to their sires."

I thought of Hel, with her rat writhing inside her ribcage. Her talents with illusions were unparalleled, but she had no control over fire, and she struggled to move through the aether. Her stubborn obstinacy, however, had probably come from me.

"What about your parents?" Falur asked. "What were they like?"

The mug jumped in my hands, spilling hot liquid over my knuckles. I hissed and flicked it back to Asgard. Falur watched me with an open, curious expression, and I had to bite down my sarcastic response. The innocence of that expression meant there was at least one person in the Nine Realms who knew nothing of my bastard parentage. Or of my mother, who'd been driven insane by the magic flowing through her unborn child.

"I was...unusual," I finally said. "Unexpected."

Falur's eyes widened, and I wondered if he understood the full implications of my diplomatic response.

"The mortal children I've had have been unremarkable," I said, trying once again to divert the conversation.

It was a lie, but a mild one. I knew very little about my potential offspring; I hardly ever visited the same woman more than once or twice. A long shiver snaked up my spine, and I felt a mounting desperation to talk about something else. Anything else.

"So, Anya told you about me," I said, watching Falur from the corner of my eye. "How did that conversation go?"

Falur ran his strong hand through his dark hair. "Oh, that. Loki, I was so relieved."

"Relieved?" That was not what I'd expected.

"She took my to the fire-ring, in the early morning. Before we'd be missed. She seemed...afraid, I guess. Maybe she didn't expect me to believe her."

"But...relieved?" I pressed.

"Well, of course. It meant I wasn't to blame."

I frowned. Perhaps I'd had too much mead this morning; I wasn't following this conversation.

"You know," Falur continued, "before I married her, Anya was happy. No, not just happy. Joyful. She sang, wherever she went. And the way she smiled, like she knew something wonderful, something the rest of us could only guess at."

I nodded, remember the way Anya and I sang together. "The Briar and the Rose," I whispered, half to myself.

"Right," Falur said. "That was her favorite."

"Was?"

Falur met my gaze. "You don't miss much, do you?"

I said nothing, and he continued.

"Once we married, all that happiness, that secret joy she'd carried around inside her—" Falur lifted his hand, opened his fist, and blew air through his lips. I thought of a bubble popping, or a seed head releasing its white fluff into the wind.

"Gone," Falur said. "Like it had never existed. She stopped smiling. She cried every night, when she thought I was asleep. Once I found out she was pregnant, it all fell into place. I promised her a divorce, told her she could go to live with the man she actually loved. And she laughed."

I sucked breath over my lips and into my chest, which had become painfully tight. During all the weeks I'd knocked around the Nine Realms, bothering Hel, drinking in Val-hall, half-heartedly fucking Freyja, it never once occurred to me Anya may have been suffering in my absence.

Falur continued, oblivious to my churning thoughts. "I tried to learn how to please her. I kept asking her to show me how to touch her, to tell me what she liked. I guess I thought, if I could make love to her properly, I might be able to offer her some semblance of what she'd had before. Shit, I had no idea how wrong I was. Until she told me about you."

He laughed again. The bright sound cut through my dark reflections. Falur, I reflected, is a man who found he was cuckolded. And he responded with open arms. For both his beautiful wife, and the man who'd impregnated her.

I moved to face him. A curl of hair had fallen across his forehead, and I brushed it back. His eyes flickered over my face, then dropped to the ground as his cheeks darkened.

"You're a rare man," I said. My voice sounded odd, as though the words were coming from somewhere far away.

He opened his mouth, but I pressed my lips to his before he could protest.

Falur's body stiffened in surprise, although he did not pull away. I opened my lips, allowing him access to my mouth, and he accepted the invitation. His tongue moved over my lips softly, almost as if he were shy, despite everything we'd already shared.

We sat together for a long time, trading kisses whose subtle sweetness surprised me. For such a big, strong man, Falur was amazingly gentle. Anya, for all her feminine softness, was much more aggressive with her lust. Falur seemed content to kiss, to explore my lips and tongue, to press the rasp of his stubble against my cheeks.

I let him decide if he wanted to take things further. And, once the sky above us had lightened to indigo from the blackness of night, he dropped his hand along my chest and into my lap. His fingers ran across the tip of my throbbing cock so gently I moaned into his mouth.

"So," Falur said. "You do like this."

I tried not to laugh at his concern. Taking his hand in mine, I pressed his palm against the very solid evidence of exactly how much I was enjoying our kisses. His fingers closed around my shaft, and I leaned forward, catching his bottom lip in my teeth.

"Very much," I whispered. "I like this very, very much."

Falur's heartbeat hammered in his throat. "I thought you were d-doing it for her. For Anya."

I ran my lips along Falur's neck, savoring the salt of his sweat. "Men don't take male lovers in your village?"

"No," he stammered.

"How very boring."

I pushed the fur off his shoulders, revealing his toned arms and broad chest. I devoured his gorgeous body with my eyes, letting him see exactly how much I appreciated the view.

"I take male lovers," I said.

Falur began to tremble. It occured to me that, although we'd kissed and sucked each other, he hadn't had the chance to take me. I shed my own clothes and stood naked before him, watching his wide eyes in the firelight. I'd furnished the hut with several bottles of scented oil, and I pulled one outside now, opened it, and rubbed it slowly over my cock, between my legs, and between the split of my ass. The delicate scent of roses filled the space between us. Falur watched me with wide eyes. I wondered if he knew he licked his lips before he bent down, reaching for my cock.

I almost let him. Falur was good with his mouth, and getting even better as he stole the tricks I used on him. The thought of letting him suck me off against the heat of the fire as the swelling dawn filled the sky with light was very tempting.

But no. I pushed his shoulders back, pressing him against the stone wall of the hut. I had something different in mind for this morning.

He stammered in response, but I kissed him before his protests could take the shape of words. My kiss wasn't gentle this time; it was rough, insistent. Hungry. He responded in kind, pressing our mouths together.

Good. I wanted him hard, and hungry.

Without breaking our kiss, I wrapped my arms around his neck and lowered myself to his lap, my legs spread wide. I pressed our bodies together until the heat of his cock surged between my legs, and my cock slid against the heat and sweat of his stomach. And then I lifted my hips, guiding him between the oiled split of my ass.

Falur pulled away as he realized what I was doing.

"Shhhhh," I said. "Don't stop."

He shook his head. "No, Loki. This is—This is shameful. This is what you do to your enemies—"

I kissed him again, softly and gently. "Are you my enemy, then? Didn't I do this to you last night?"

"That's—That's different. You're so far above us. You can do what you—"

I pressed against him again, feeling his cock throb against the tight ring of my muscles. "I want this," I said. "I want you, all of you. I want you to fuck me, Falur."

He hesitated just long enough for me to think he didn't share my desire, that his beliefs about what was and was not shameful were so deeply rooted he was about to deny me the pleasure of his body. Then he thrust up, entering me with that initial shock of pain.

He froze, panting, once he was inside me. Our chests pressed together, rising and falling in unison, and the scent of roses swelled between us. I pressed my forehead to his, the feel of his cock filling me, surging through me, until the entire world narrowed to the sensation of our bodies, the rasp of his chest hair against me, the ecstacy of being filled by him.

I moved first, rising and falling in Falur's lap, my own cock surging in the oil-slicked space between our bodies. I clung to him, sinking my fingers into the muscles of his shoulders. Despite everything, all the times we'd come together last night, all the seed I'd spilled in Anya and Falur's bodies, I felt the rising tide of my own orgasm approaching. I wouldn't be able to hold out for long.

Falur's grip tightened around my waist, and his thrusts grew stronger, less rhythmic. His breath grew faster, until he was almost panting. Sweat poured off our bodies, running together down our chests, mingling with the oil and wood smoke from the fire. We slipped together, clinging to each other as if we were drowning, tossed by the storms of desire.

Falur's breath hitched, and he moaned as he shot his seed inside me. The pulse of his cock within me, the press of his hot body against mine, pushed me over the edge. I leaned back and closed my eyes as my own seed spilled across our chests. Then I collapsed against his chest, letting Falur wrap his arms around me. I was dimly aware of Falur kissing the top of my head as my mind spun through its post-orgasmic haze. An odd thought bubbled through my consciousness as I lay, panting and naked, in Falur's strong arms.

"I'm...happy," I whispered into Falur's chest.

His grip around my shoulders tightened. "So am I," he said.

CHAPTER NINE

We were all incredibly foolish that winter.

I had no real inkling of trouble. Not then, not in those golden months. The hours I spent with Falur and Anya, together in the warmth of the stone hut I'd built, were the happiest of my long life. They spent almost every night with me, and sometimes all day as well. I enjoyed both of them far more than I imagined possible; Falur's sly humor, Anya's warmth. And I found them both irresistible, especially as Anya's belly grew.

I'd never been drawn to a pregnant woman before, but on Anya the rounded, full stomach carrying my child was irresistibly erotic. I loved every part of her blossoming motherhood, from her heavy, newly sensitive breasts to the way her pale skin stretched taut over the curve of her belly. It seemed my life in the stone hut, where the walls I'd build shielded myself and my lovers from the cold of Midgard's winter, was perfectly complete, and I was able to shrug off any lingering doubts from Óðinn's words.

It did not occur to me to wonder about Anya and Falur's village. Or rather, if it did occur to me, I pushed the thought aside. I did not like to imagine my lovers' lives without me, or to dwell on the parts of their existence that did not revolve around our mutual sexual satisfaction. And my lovers seemed content to join me in that illusion.

One night, after Anya had fallen asleep, I leaned against the stone wall with a flagon of Val-hall's mead in my hand and Falur's head on my lap. The beeswax candles had burned low and dripped their wax down the stone walls. Through the window of the hut, I was watching the stars fade as dawn stretched golden fingers toward us.

"I suppose I should take you back to the village," I said, raising the flagon to my lips.

Falur laughed in a tired voice. "I wish you wouldn't."

"Is it so bad there?"

"Nah." He shook his head slowly, and his dark hair brushed my thighs. "But they hate me in the village."

"I can't imagine anyone hating you."

Falur grinned at me. His cheeks were flushed, and his eyes were glossy. He'd had quite a bit of mead that night. "Did I tell you I fell asleep at the anvil last week? I thought they were going to throw me in the ocean."

The thought of Falur falling asleep at his anvil made me grin. "Really?"

He rubbed his hands over his eyes. "They just want nails. Nails, nails, nails."

"You're not a fan of nails, then?"

"Ugh. I hate them. There's no beauty in nails, Loki. No artistry. You understand."

"Do I?" My smile widened. I looked down at him, at his beautiful, strong, muscular body, and thought how unexpected it was for a man like him to have an artistic soul.

Falur met my eyes in the dim flicker of the remaining candles. "Of course you do. Don't tell me it was an accident how the stones come together over the window."

We both turned to the window. Yes, I had been deliberate with those stones. The large window was framed by small, dark rocks that appeared to flow upward, filling in the chinks between the larger, paler rocks like dancing tendrils of flame. It started by accident, as I placed a few lines of rock which happened to be both dark and the right size but, when I recognized the pattern, I made it into a conscious design.

"You noticed." My voice was soft. Mortals on Midgard weren't known for their powers of observation.

Falur settled back on the mattress and closed his eyes. "You just aren't used to people who pay attention," he said.

A moment later he was asleep, and the light of a new day washed gently through the window, dancing over the faces of my lovers. I could have brought them back to the village, but they seemed so peaceful in the shelter of our hut. Let the villagers think they awoke early, I told myself as I watched my flagon refill. Let the villagers think they've gone for a walk together to experience the dawn.

I could have cast an illusion in the village to make it seem they were still present, that bodies occupied their spaces on the sleeping benches in the longhouse. But it did not occur to me to do such a thing.

I could have spent that morning making nails for Falur, a thousand times faster than a mortal blacksmith. I could have created an illusion to forge the nails, so the villagers would think Falur was working day and night at his anvil when in fact he was with me, his lips and tongue and hard, muscular body otherwise engaged.

Looking back, there were many things I could have done differently.

THERE WAS A SHARP RAP outside my door, and I jumped. I'd been dozing, with Anya curled next to me and Falur's hair spread over my lap. The flagon of mead in my hand had tipped, spilling its sparkling contents across the stone floor. I curled my lip at the mess, and the sharp rap came again.

I was out of bed in an instant, leaving a magical cushion for Falur's head so as not to wake him. Pulling my illusions tight, I tugged myself through the aether to spare my lovers the discomfort of having the door opened. And to keep whoever was outside from seeing the companions in my bed.

A large, jet-black raven crouched on the stones outside my door. He cocked his head and fixed me with an icy stare.

"Hugin?" I asked.

"Loki," the bird croaked in a rusty voice. "Óðinn will see you."

"You're his errand boy now?"

Hugin hopped away from me. "Fuck you. You're wanted in Asgard."

"Regarding?" I asked, but Hugin was already spreading his wings to depart.

I glanced at the hut behind me. While I didn't want to leave without warning Anya and Falur, I also didn't want to reveal how precious the contents of this hut were to me. Let Óðinn and the rest of them think I just liked the winters in Midgard.

Promising myself I'd explain the situation to Anya and Falur when I returned, I pulled myself through the aether and toward Val-hall. The magic was a bit more finicky than I'd expected, and I had enough time to regret all the mead Falur and I had shared before the rough-hewn walls of Val-hall's council room came into focus.

My eyes adjusted in time to see Óðinn's scowl of disapproval.

"Drunk again," he grunted, with a frown.

"Please. I'm barely even tipsy," I said, forcing myself to stand up straight. I was painfully aware that I may have swayed.

The door behind me opened, and I was spared from any further awkward conversation when Óðinn's son Baldr came in, smiling as always, and clearly not drunk. They called him Baldr the Beautiful, and he was the most effective negotiator in Asgard. I wondered what mess we were about to clean up when the door swung open again.

Freyja entered, a scowl etched across her lovely face. Her dark hair was mussed, her eyes were glossy, and the scent of sex hung heavy in the air around her. I sniffed delicately, wondering if I could tell whom she'd been fucking, but it was impossible. Freyja glared at me as if she knew exactly what I was doing; apparently I hadn't yet been forgiven for leaving her unsatisfied while I nursed my broken heart over Anya's marriage.

While Baldr was a masterful negotiator, always letting the other side think they'd gotten a tremendous deal even if they'd just sworn away their very souls, Freyja's emotions always ran too close to the surface for her to be an effective diplomat. But she was intimidatingly beautiful, and without question the best fuck in Asgard. I frowned as the implications sank in to my groggy consciousness. We must not be here for negotiations after all.

We were here for seduction.

"So, father, where are we off to?" Baldr asked, sounding so unreasonably cheerful that Freyja snorted in disgust.

Óðinn didn't speak. Instead, he looked around the room, fixing each of us with his single, piercing blue eye. The many flagons of mead in my gut shifted uncomfortably under his stare.

"Hunting," Óðinn said, finally. "We've been invited to go hunting. On Svartálfaheimr."

I groaned. Svartálfaheimr was the realm of the dwarves, and I just fucking hated dwarves. Ever since Brokk the dwarf sewed my lips shut while the Æsir and Vanir watched and laughed, being around dwarves made my skin crawl.

Óðinn glared at me, and I shut up. "We're hunting boar. It's a full expedition, which means we'll be there for almost a month."

"Darling," Freyja began.

Óðinn raised a hand to silence her. "I know your feelings about hunting, Freyja. Consider your objections noted."

Freyja's expression darkened considerably. I was impressed. Óðinn usually had a soft spot for Freyja and all her explosive moods.

What could possibly be more valuable to Óðinn than his nights in Freyja's arms?

"What do you need out of us?" Baldr asked.

He was always cheerful, Baldr the Beautiful. Always eager to please. It was rather sickening.

Óðinn took his time to respond, staring at each of us in turn while the tension in the room notched upward. Finally, when I was about ready to strangle him, he spoke.

"Information," Óðinn said. "That's what I need. Everything and anything you can get. Rumors. Insinuations. Hints. Pick a target - someone young enough to be stupid, important enough to know something worth knowing, and attractive enough to be cocky. Then get everything you can out of them."

Silence. Baldr nodded, although his expression was grim. Freyja crossed her hands over her chest and chewed her bottom lip. I cleared my throat.

"Loki?" Óðinn asked in a way that made it sound like he was in the middle of accomplishing something important, and I was hindering him.

"It occurs to me," I said, "that we're going to get a great deal of information. Sexual fantasies. Favorite foods. Perhaps you'll want to narrow down our search just a bit?"

Across from me, Freyja struggled to suppress a smile. Óðinn huffed in annoyance.

"Fine. Information about the elves."

Stunned silence greeted this announcement. Óðinn bunched his lips together, as though he were struggling to keep his secrets from escaping.

"There are...rumors," he said. "Apparently some of the dwarves are meeting with some of the elves. If this is just part of the conflict between the elves, it's no concern of ours. But if Svartálfaheimr and Álfheim are pursuing an alliance—"

Óðinn stopped. Yes, I had to grant, an alliance between Svartálfaheimr and Álfheim would be dangerous. Both the dwarves and the elves were tenuous allies of Asgard, mostly because none of us were strong enough to take out the others. But the dwarves and elves together would pose a significant risk to the Æsir and Vanir. My head started to ache, the first sign that last night's mead was retreating in the face of another hangover.

"Great," I said. "Wonderful. When do we leave?"

Óðinn drew himself up to his full height. "Right now. The banquet has already begun."

Freyja uttered a weak protest, but her words were lost as Óðinn grabbed our hands and pulled the three of us through the aether. A moment later the stench of Svartálfaheimr's underground passageways and tallow-burning torches hit my nostrils, and the ache beating at the inside of my skull intensified.

I turned to see Baldr clenching his jaw while Freyja ran her fingers through her hair. The air around me tingled with magic as Freyja pulled appropriate clothing from Asgard, wrapping herself in red silk with golden brocade. Lastly, she adjusted the glimmering necklace of the Brísingamen around her neck. The pale gold looked especially striking against Freyja's dark skin, although I couldn't help but wonder how it would look spread across Anya's pale neck.

Freyja turned to smile at me and Baldr, and to offer her back to Óðinn. I saw she'd taken a moment to outline her eyes with kohl and coat her lips with something red and shiny. She gave us a smile that could have coaxed the moon down from the sky.

"Gentlemen," Freyja purred. "Let's find someone stupid and cocky, shall we?"

I took her arm with a smile. I almost felt sorry for Freyja's target.

NOTHING HAPPENS QUICKLY on Svartálfaheimr.

First, we had to feast with the rest of the Æsir and Vanir, and the dwarven ruling class. Óðinn had brought a surprisingly large contingent from Asgard. I couldn't help but wonder if the presence of Thor, Týr, Freyr, and Heimdallr was to distract the dwarves from the somewhat less likely hunters like Freyja, or if the other Æsir had their own oblique information-gathering missions.

Regardless, we had to spend several days eating roast ox and toasting our hosts with the dwarves's salty, bitter beer, which led to terrible hangovers. Thor seemed in an especially foul mood on the third morning, when we were finally led to our drooling, six-legged reptilian mounts for the trip to the hunting grounds. I watched Thor cringe at the bright sunlight and wondered if Óðinn made surly "drunk again" comments to Thor as well, or if those snide remarks were a special humiliation he reserved for his oath-brother.

We spent an uncomfortable day baking in our saddles as we traversed the southern mountains of Svartálfaheimr. It was parched, dessicated territory, inhabited by poisonous reptiles, mad dwarves, and the occasional trapped demon.

The landscape made me uncomfortable. There are areas where the Nine Realms are stacked closely together, where travel between them is almost as simple as breathing; Asgard is one of those places, at least for those of us who have eaten Iðunn's apples.

But there are also places where the Realms are stretched thin, and it takes a great deal of time and energy to tug the aethers together. The mountains of Svartálfaheimr were one of the most remote and inaccessible places in the Nine Realms. It took an inordinate amount of effort just to pull more comfortable clothing from Asgard, let alone to travel away from that stupid hunting party. My chest ached under that unforgiving sun. I hadn't said goodbye to Anya and Falur. Did they think they'd been abandoned?

Did they think I wasn't planning to return?

That night, once the small army of servants assembled our personal tents and the feast hall, I wanted nothing more than to down an ocean of dwarven beer and forget I was trapped on Svartálfaheimr. But Óðinn caught my eye over the table, and I put down my flagon to assess potential targets.

The current ruler of Svartálfaheimr was Queen Vestri. She was somewhat attractive, for a dwarf. Like most of the dwarves, she tended toward short and round. What she lacked in robust facial hair, she more than made up for with her alarmingly militaristic attitude and her boundless enthusiasm for slaughtering wild boars. But it was already clear Queen Vestri was Óðinn's target. They spent the evenings drinking together at the end of the long table, trading blatant flirtations which got more and more revolting as the night progressed.

To my left, Freyja had chosen her target: The Queen's handmaiden. That was rather brilliant, I had to admit. Freyja had spent most of her time on Svartálfaheimr fighting off male advances, occasionally literally, so choosing a female target was a clever move. Besides, Freyja actually looked like she may have been enjoying herself.

No such luck for me. I spent the night nursing my beer and wishing I were on Midgard. When Þor got drunk enough to rip off his shirt and hoist his hammer Mjölnir into the air, offering a solemn oath as to how many boar he was going to kill, I decided to turn in early. I wasn't going anywhere, and neither were my potential targets.

We found boar early the next morning. Or, more accurately, the Queen's servants rose before dawn, circled through the low bushes and scrubland, and chased the boars into a nearby box canyon. Then the noble hunting party, myself included, rose to enjoy a luxurious breakfast before riding our mounts to the canyon for the slaughter.

I hung back at the mouth of the canyon, working very little to conceal my general disdain for hunting and forced outdoor adventures. Baldr stayed with me, while Freyja remained in camp. Even from the back of the group, I could hear Thor's voice roaring in triumph above the screams of dying animals.

Eventually, a few bedraggled dwarves drifted back to us. One of them was clearly a prince, given his ridiculous outfit, stupid smirk, and cloud of attendants. He was reasonably attractive, in a bland, soft way, but his voice was high pitched, whiny, and self-pitying.

"I had that boar," he said, quite loudly. "It was mine! There is clearly a problem with my spear."

He hefted the offensive spear into the air, where its perfectly clean blade sparkled in the desert sun.

"Inferior craftsmanship," the prince snorted. "I"ll see that the men who made this piece of shit hang for it!"

A cry rose in the dusty air, and the riders in front of us shuffled backward, yelling and cursing. The air suddenly pulled taut as everyone's focus shifted to the rocky ground. Baldr's mount reared and spun, and mine leapt backward. Someone shouted, a high-pitched, sustained shriek.

There was a dark blur of motion against the cliff face. I pulled a blade from the aether and moved without thought, straightening my arm to fling my dagger in the space of a single breath.

The boar was dead before it had a chance to scream. It crashed face-first into the dirt as Baldr's mount thudded back to the ground. No one spoke; Baldr's panting filled the air as he forced his mount backward in a show of dominance.

"Nice shot," Baldr finally said, once his mount had dropped its head in submission.

I flicked dirt off my sleeves in response. As I did, a spear crashed to the ground several lengths away from the boar.

"See!" the dwarven prince shouted. "See how terrible the aim is! Garbage! That spear is absolute garbage!" With that, he spun his mount and thundered off toward the camp.

"Who's that?" I asked.

One of the dwarven attendants grunted. "That would be Prince Vitri," he said, scarcely bothering to veil his contempt.

"Charmed, I'm sure," I responded.

I watched the dust trail rise up behind Prince Vitri's poor mount, then jumped to the ground to inspect the boar's lifeless body. My dagger had caught the young male in the trachea, probably killing it before the beast had a chance to realize what had happened. I wondered if the boar's spirit was now running through the dark chaos of Niflhel.

"Nice kill," the dwarf who'd identified Prince Vitri said.

"I am honored by the spirit of this beast," I replied, to comply with dwarven tradition.

A dark pool of blood was already soaking into the hungry ground beneath the carcass. I rolled the motionless beast onto its back with my foot, reclaimed my dagger, and left the unpleasant task of gutting the boar to the dwarves.

CHAPTER TEN

I expected the night's feast to be filled with Thor's booming recollections of his glorious hunt, with all the bloody details recounted in painful detail. But, to my surprise, the one recounting the bloody details was Queen Vestri. I watched with mounting fascination and disgust as she detailed throat slitting and head bashing. When she talked about ripping a still-beating heart from an enormous boar, my gaze drifted over to Óðinn, who was watching her with misty eyes.

Ugh. Was the merciless slaughter of trapped animals really what turned my oath-brother on? Or was this all part of his calculated information gathering seduction?

What was worse?

The dwarves' bitter beer shifted uncomfortably in my gut, and I stood to push my way out of the tent. The desert air was cold outside the feast tent. I breathed deeply, as if I'd just emerged from underwater. Stepping a respectable distance away from the tent to take a piss, I tilted my head back and watched the splatter of stars across the vast darkness above Svartálfaheimr. I tried not to think about how much I missed Anya and Falur, but their memory surged forward anyway, filling my conscious thought. Yes, the balance of power in the Nine Realms may have hung on my actions, but at the moment seeing Anya and Falur again seemed more important than saving the Realms.

Let the Realms burn, I thought. I want to go home.

"Loki."

I straightened my back and turned toward that voice. Prince Vitri leaned against a tent pole, watching me. He looked a bit more solemn on his own feet, with his scraggly beard covering his neck. Or perhaps he just looked a bit more noble with his mouth shut.

"Prince Vitri." I bowed low.

"I hear you're quite the trouble maker," he said. His voice was cool and aloof, as if he couldn't possibly care less how I responded.

"Perhaps," I answered.

"I don't have much time for trouble, myself. I'm prince of this realm."

"Oh?" I said, as if I'd somehow managed to miss the crown on his head, or the tangle of insignias he wore on his shoulders denoting his rank.

Vitri licked his lips. The action made me feel slightly nauseous.

"I might have some time tonight," he said. "Come to my tent when the feast is over."

With that, Vitri turned and re-entered the feast tent. I stood in the darkness, trying to remember if I'd ever heard a less appealing pick up line.

Well, shit. I had a job to do, and I'd done fuck all to pick a target in the days we'd been on Svartálfaheimr. While Óðinn hadn't exactly threatened consequences if I didn't follow through, there were a thousand ways he could make my life unpleasant if I didn't fuck my way into some useful information. Anya and Falur again surfaced in my consciousness. The scent of her hair. The feel of his calloused hands on my skin. Óðinn could make their lives miserable, if he so chose.

Shivering, I followed Vitri into the tent.

It took several hours for the feast to conclude. By the time Vitri stood to leave the banquet table at the head of the tent, Freyja had been gone for hours, Thor had passed out and was snoring loudly at the table, and Óðinn appeared to have his hand up the Queen's skirt.

Although there wasn't nearly enough beer on Svartálfaheimr to make this situation bearable, I'd been careful with the alcohol tonight. I didn't doubt my seductive talents, but I also didn't want to fuck this up.

Quietly, I slipped outside the tent to follow Vitri. And I almost stepped on Baldr, who was also leaving the feast tent.

"Where are you headed?" Baldr asked, with a conspiratorial smile.

I nodded in the direction of the Queen's encampment. "Vitri."

"Personal invitation?"

My lips pulled back in distaste. "It certainly wasn't my idea."

Baldr's smile broadened. "You're not the only one who got an invite from Vitri."

That sneaky little shit! Vitri had invited both Baldr and me to his tent on the same night? My assessment of Prince Vitri's personality ticked upward ever so slightly.

"That's cocky," I said.

"And stupid," Baldr agreed, clapping me on the back. "Let's get him drunk and milk him for all he's worth."

OUR PLAN WORKED BEAUTIFULLY.

Vitri was only too ready to drink with us, and he seemed especially keen to prove his alcohol-consuming acumen to the Æsir. He also didn't seem to notice that Baldr and I weren't draining our flagons of beer, and he didn't seem to care how drunk he was getting in front of the men he'd invited to his personal tent.

We spent several hours handing him flagons of beer, and listening to lengthy, one-sided monologues about Vitri's important awards and positions, most of which seemed to boil down to being the sixth son of the queen of Svartálfaheimr. If this was what counted as dwarven foreplay, I wasn't sure how they ever managed to reproduce.

I met Baldr's eyes across the bed. We were sitting on either side of Vitri, with our shirts open across our chests. He tilted his head slightly toward Vitri, then nodded at me. Fine. If someone had to make the first move, it might as well be me.

I raised my hand and brushed my fingertips across Vitri's thick lips. He was so startled he stopped in mid-monologue. I leaned in to kiss him at the same moment he reached for my head and pulled me forward. Our teeth met with a clash, and his lips clamped down over mine. Suddenly he wasn't so much kissing me as trying to suck my tongue out through my mouth. I pulled away, and we came apart with an audible pop.

"You like that, don't you?" he growled. "I've heard all about you Æsir. Bunch of sluts, you are."

I moved back slightly, putting myself out of range for further attacks. Baldr took advantage of the opening to run his open palm down Vitri's chest. Vitri's attention shifted to Baldr the Beautiful, allowing me to discreetly wipe my mouth on his sheets. And check to make sure my lips were still intact.

"So, handsome," Baldr said, "you certainly seem to know a lot about seduction. I wonder, have you ever slept with an elf?"

Brilliant, really. I smiled at Baldr to show my appreciation. He winked at me behind Vitri's back.

Vitri snorted a laugh. "Of course! Who hasn't screwed an elf? They're the easiest fuck in the—the—"

His back stiffened. Baldr's hand had unlaced Vitri's pants, freeing an unimpressive cock. Even by dwarven standards.

"Mmmm," Baldr purred, bending to rub his lips across Vitri's neck. "Tell me about the elves you've seduced, you irresistible prince."

I took advantage of the momentary pause to press another full flagon of mead into Vitri's hand.

"Well, that last delegation," Vitri said, his speech somewhat slurred from the beer. "I fucked, oh, at least half of them."

"Wow! And the delegation must have been here to see you," Baldr continued.

Vitri shifted and drained the flagon of mead, coughing afterward. "Me, and the Queen. Mother really valuesh my opinion."

Oh, I'm sure she does, I thought, taking the empty flagon from Vitri's hand and replacing it with a full one.

"Politics," Baldr said, as if the very thought of politics bored him.

"Yeah," Vitri agreed. His head tilted back, and his hips thrust up, straining against Baldr's grip. "Keep—keep doin' that."

Baldr gave Vitri an unsettlingly seductive smile as his hand pumped Vitri's cock. "Shall we continue talking politics?"

"That's boring shit," Vitri grunted. "Like I care if General Asador needs a place to dump a bunch of his enemies. Svartálfaheimr belongs to us, to the—the—"

Vitri's back stiffened again, and his eyes widened as he moaned loudly. For a second I thought he was going to come across Baldr's naked chest. Then he grabbed Baldr's long, blond hair and shoved his head down.

"Suck me," he growled.

Baldr did. I tried to drown my laugh in my flagon of beer. Vitri came in a heartbeat, roaring his climax for all the rest of the camp to hear. I've never understood why some men feel the need to shout at the top of their lungs as they come, but I wasn't the least bit surprised Vitri was one of those men.

Baldr took it like a champion, settling back onto the bed with a satisfied smile and running his hands gently over Vitri's thighs. I followed Baldr's lead and began to kiss Vitri's neck and shoulders, massaging his shoulders. His muscles were soft, and I guessed he had maybe another decade before his reasonably good looks were buried under a mountain of soft flab.

"Yeah," Vitri said. "Yeah. Keep doin' that."

From behind Vitri's back, I raised an eyebrow at Baldr. It didn't seem to have occured to the dear prince that Baldr or I may have wanted some satisfaction from the night. Baldr raised his hand to his mouth to cover his grin.

"Negotiating with General Asador?" I said, running my lips along the prince's ear. "I'm impressed."

Vitri grunted. "Well, I am the prince."

He raised the full flagon to his lips, drained half of it, then grimaced in distaste. The flagon fell from his hand and spilled the remaining beer across his bed. Vitri didn't seem to notice. I wrapped my arm around his chest, running my fingers down his soft abdomen.

"I bet you took them for all they're worth," I said.

He grunted again. "Yeah. Yeah, we took 'em. We'll take their enemiesh, but we're going to come out of it the richest fucking family in the Nine Realms."

Baldr met my eyes. Well, this was interesting. The elves had been squabbling for years, but it sounded like their internal conflict was about to get significantly more serious. I wrapped my hand around Vitri's soft cock and began to massage it, seeing if I could coax anything more out of him.

It worked. As I rubbed Vitri's limp cock back to life, he regaled us both with the exact details of what General Asador had promised the Queen in exchange for imprisoning elves on Svartálfaheimr. As he spoke, Baldr shifted to rub and kiss Vitri's shoulders, pointedly pushing me toward Vitri's wavering cock, which seemed almost as drunk as he was.

I did my best, caressing his limp cock, soft thighs, and hairy balls as if the prince's pleasure were the only thing that mattered to me in the entire Nine Realms. I couldn't believe Vitri was still talking, to be honest. After all the beer, and all my lavish attentions between his legs, how could this asshole still be ranting about his own greatness? When he shifted the conversation back to how his lance was to blame for his missing the greatest boar in the hunt, I decided to go down on him in the hopes he'd just shut up.

Vitri's breath caught in his throat as I wrapped my lips around the head of his cock, and I could have sighed in relief. I took him in my mouth before he could catch his breath, sucking hard as I lashed the head of his cock with my tongue. Vitri sank his hands into my hair, forcing me down. Above me, he was making a strange sort of choking gurgle. Whatever. At least he wasn't fucking talking anymore. I focused on his limp dick as if the very existence of the Nine Realms depended upon it.

Vitri made a horrible gagging noise, and hot, wet liquid splashed all over my head and back. I shot back just as Vitri puked again, this time hitting me full in the face with a jet of regurgitated beer.

The tent filled with absolute silence. I wiped my eyes and glared at Baldr, who was obviously trying very hard not to burst out laughing.

"Your fault," Vitri said, blearily. "Thish was your fault."

He raised a clumsy hand and swiped at me. Stunned, I realized he was trying to hit me. He was actually trying to fucking hit me. I ground my teeth together and struggled to tamp down the desire to pull a blade from the aether and bury it in his worthless neck.

"Oh, my prince," Baldr purred. "Shhhhhh. Lie down, darling."

Baldr pulled on Vitri's shoulders until the prince surrendered and fell back into his own bed. A moment later, his eyes rolled back in their sockets and the tent filled with his royal, very loud snores. They were only slightly less irritating than his conversation.

"That was fucking wretched," I growled, grabbing one of the prince's sheets to wipe myself off.

"Need any help?" Baldr offered. He still looked like he was about a heartbeat away from collapsing into uncontrollable laughter.

My lips pulled back in a snarl. Baldr was trying to be mildly helpful but, at the moment, I didn't think I'd ever want to touch anyone again. All I wanted to do was find a hot springs and soak myself until this fucking trip was over and I could return to Midgard in peace.

"No," I said, scrubbing at my scalp with the sheet. "We'll report tomorrow morning?"

Baldr nodded and let me leave in peace.

WE COULDN'T REPORT to Óðinn in the morning, because Óðinn's tent was empty. Baldr and I stared at each other as the tent walls buffeted in the early morning wind. I'd spent the night scrubbing myself with sand in the thin trickle of water that was the closest thing to a river Svartálfaheimr's mountains had to offer, and it hadn't done much to improve my mood.

Still, at least we'd found some excellent information. The elves were indeed working with the dwarves, but it didn't sound like an alliance was imminent. We even had names to offer Óðinn. Hopefully that would be enough to get me out of this fucking hunt, off of Svartálfaheimr, and back to my lovers on Midgard.

"You don't think he's with the queen?" Baldr asked, raising an eyebrow at the tent's empty interior.

I let my expression reflect my feelings about the queen. Baldr laughed.

"Fuck it," he said, clapping me on the shoulder. "Let's get some breakfast. We'll catch him later."

But Óðinn was difficult to catch. We finally cornered him in the afternoon, when the dwarven hunting party returned in the heat of the day to rest while the servants prepared the boars for the feast.

Óðinn waved us into his tent. My skin tingled as Óðinn cast a cantrip to distort our words in case any of the omnipresent dwarven servants were listening.

"We found something," Baldr began.

Óðinn grunted and waved his hand for Baldr to continue. He was pulling off his dusty riding gloves, and he looked irritable. I was glad Baldr was doing the talking; Óðinn was slightly less likely to strike out in rage at his favorite son.

"The Queen is in negotiations with one of the elves," Baldr reported.

"General Asador," I added.

Baldr nodded and continued. "Apparently, Asador is looking for a place to trap his enemies. And he's willing to pay for it."

Óðinn grunted again. "Yeah. I know."

I didn't think I could feel much worse after getting a facefull of Prince Vitri's vomit last night, but there it was. My stomach dropped. I felt like I'd been treading water, and Óðinn had just handed me a lead weight. The permanent smile etched across Baldr's full lips fell like a stone.

Óðinn splashed his face from a washbasin and fixed us with his single blue eye. "I need more details. How many elves does Asador hope to trap in Svartálfaheimr? Where will they be trapped? And when?"

Baldr nodded, his handsome features turning solemn and serious. I could have smacked him. He was just as irritatingly obedient as Óðinn's ravens Hugin and Munin.

"And just how long are you expecting us to—" I started, prepared to argue my way out of this stupid hunting trip.

"Shut it," Óðinn snapped. "You will both remain on Svartálfaheimr until the expedition is complete and the celebratory feasts are over. And I don't care if you have to fuck every single dwarf here. Get me some useful information!"

I ground my molars together as Baldr pushed through the tent flap behind me. Óðinn closed the distance between us and put his hand on my shoulder. "Your mortal pets aren't going anywhere, oath-brother," he said, in a voice low enough to shield his words from Baldr.

My entire body felt cold. I glanced down and realized my hands had clenched into fists. Was that a threat? And what could I do if it was?

"I'll do it," I said.

CHAPTER ELEVEN

T he hunting expedition dragged on for nearly a month. The one saving grace of the entire expedition was that Prince Vitri was overcome with a mysterious illness and retreated with his entire entourage to the Queen's underground fortress after spending two days sequestered in his tent, presumably nursing his hangover.

I did what Óðinn asked of me, riding with the hunting party during the day, drinking and fucking at night, drawing information out of princes and servants, handmaidens and ferriers. For all my efforts, I wasn't able to unearth anything especially exciting. Queen Vestri was negotiating with the elven general Asador, who had promised the Queen an unspecified amount of treasure to take an unspecified number of his enemies at some unspecified time in the future. Very little of the information I provided to Óðinn seemed satisfactory, but I didn't dwell on his black mood. I was too busy nursing my own resentments. And missing my sweet lovers on Midgard.

By the time our journey finally ended and I crossed the Realms to the hills outside Anya and Falur's village, spring had arrived on Midgard. The hills, which had been dull and ice-crusted the last time I brought my lovers to our stone hut, were now beginning to swell with green grass. The hollows still held snow, but tiny white blossoms covered the southern-facing hillsides, filling the sea air with their sweet perfume.

The inside of the hut seemed musty, so I pulled down the magical shields which kept the cold out and let the spring breeze scour the interior. I replaced the beeswax candles and, on a whim, gathered an armful of the little, white flowers, weaving them around the ledges in the stones until the hut filled with their sweet aroma. Artistry, I thought, with a smile. Falur would appreciate it. Hesitating, I bit my lower lip. What would I say to them? How could I explain my prolonged absence?

What if they were not happy to see me?

I took a deep breath of the perfumed air and contemplated returning to Asgard. Thor would no doubt be holding his own celebration tonight, recounting the epic hunting trip on Svartálfaheimr, and probably ending the night with an orgy. I knew from past experience that I'd be welcome.

But I didn't want Thor. I didn't even want an orgy with Thor. I wanted Anya and Falur, in my arms, in this stone hut. I wanted to kiss them, to taste them, to breathe them in until I felt like they were a part of me again. With a sigh, I realized I'd been pacing in a tight circle around the inside of the hut.

This was stupid. It was time to go.

I made myself invisible, and traveled through the aether to their village.

I followed the sound of a hammer, and Falur's thick, masculine scent, toward the forge. The structure was enclosed on three sides, leaving the southern end open to the elements. Falur was inside, bent over his anvil and pounding at a sliver of iron held in his tongs. He wore a loose linen shirt beneath his heavy, soot-stained, leather apron. The sleeves were pushed up high enough for me to see the bulge of his muscles. My heart thudded in my throat as I approached, still wrapped in my invisible illusions. Although the village hummed with activity, there weren't many people around the smith, perhaps because the heat of the forge was enough to make even me sweat.

Falur sighed, set his hammer down, and wiped his eyes. I glanced toward the bellows, confirmed he was alone, then licked my lips as I watched his bare arms flex. Stars, how I'd missed those arms! With another quick look behind me, I decided to drop my invisibility.

"Nails again?" I asked.

Falur looked up. His dark eyes sparkled as they met mine. "I thought you'd come back," he said.

Without waiting for an invitation, I stepped between Falur and the anvil and pressed our lips together. The heat of his body surged against my chest. He tasted like sweat and coal smoke, like iron and fire. He tasted like home.

Falur moved closer to me, letting me feel the stiffening length of his cock through his leather apron, but I pulled back. Voices surged in the distance, and the Realms only knew how this village would respond to finding their blacksmith embracing a red-haired stranger. I broke our kiss, but pressed my forehead to his.

"Stars, I missed you," I whispered.

He laughed, low and soft. "We missed you, too."

I found the strength to pull away from him. "How is Anya?"

"Glorious. Enormous. She's down by the water, with the women, if you want to see her." Falur's expression tightened, and he glanced to his feet. "She...didn't think you were coming back."

My chest tightened. "Can you bring her to the hut? Today?"

"Of course," he said, but his fingers tightened around my hand, pulling me closer. He reached into the pouch around his waist, pulled something out, and pressed it into my palm.

I turned my hand over. He'd given me a small, delicate birch leaf made of iron. It was so realistic it looked as though a living leaf had somehow been transformed into metal. I turned it over in my palm, running my fingers over the thin, delicate edge. This was the kind of thing I could make, of course, by pulling on the latent magic in Midgard, transforming it into something solid and real, like creating gold coins or jewels.

But Falur had made this himself, with his hands, with nothing more than iron and fire, hammer and tongs. His mastery of Midgard's crude methods amazed me.

"It's a wonder," I said.

Falur's eyes danced with the compliment. "It's for you," he said, closing my fingers over the metal leaf. "I wanted to give you something. So you could remember us."

"I don't need this to remember you."

Falur looked away from me, toward the ocean. An odd cascade of expressions chased themselves across the strong contours of his face. I had the strange, fleeting impression Falur didn't believe me, and it stung.

"Come to the hut," I urged. "Please. Bring Anya. I'll be waiting for you both."

"Of course," he said.

TIME SEEMED FROZEN that afternoon, as I paced across the newly green grass surrounding our hut and waited for my lovers. The hut was too cold, at first; I'd left the window wards down so the spring breeze could blow freely through the windows, but it had chilled the air. So I lit the heartfire, but I'd left the hearth stocked for winter, and the interior of the stone hut was soon roasting. I dropped the wards again; the wind off the ocean mixed with the smoke from my fire and the delicate scent of the tiny, white flowers.

Irritated, I went outside to watch the horizon. I rolled Falur's beautiful iron leaf in my fingers as I waited, running my thumb along the thin edges. It was oddly calming to hold something made by human hands. I wished I'd brought gifts for them. I could have pulled just about anything from the aether, of course. A necklace to rival Freyja's. The finest drinking horn in all of Midgard.

But how could they possibly explain those treasures to their village? I'd spent enough time on Midgard to know what a necklace like Freyja's could provoke. My lovers would have to leave any treasures I brought for them here, in the safety of our secret stone hut. And what good is a gift you can't take with you?

Finally, the wind brought me something other than the screech of gulls and the steady crash of the waves against the shore. A soft, familiar melody filled the air, faint and distant at first, but rising in strength. It was a woman's voice, singing. *The Briar and the Rose.*

I fiddled with the leather armor on my chest, creating a hidden pocket near my heart for Falur's leaf. Then I hummed the melody for a few refrains before beginning to sing myself. Anya and Falur crested the hill just as I finished the second chorus and the sun dropped toward the waves.

The golden, late afternoon light lit Anya's hair like molten gold, burnishing her face, making her features glow. Had I truly thought I'd seen beauty before that day? No, I'd been mistaken. Pregnancy had rounded her face and figure, softening her cheeks and adding color to her lips. She looked like a queen, or a goddess. She looked like she was capable of creating entire worlds, spun from her beauty alone. Freyja would have paled next to her; Baldr the Beautiful would have appeared weak and ordinary.

Even as she walked toward me, I realized what I was seeing that afternoon would forever be burned in my memory, and every beautiful thing my life held from here on out would have to compare to the sight of Anya, her body rounded and full with my child, her long, golden hair catching the afternoon sun as the scents and sounds of spring on Midgard rose between us.

Anya hesitated before me, and I reached for her, pulling her into my arms. Oh, she smelled good! I wrapped my arms around her shoulders as the swell of her belly pressed against my hips. I closed my eyes, momentarily overwhelmed.

"Fire-hair," she whispered. "You came back."

I pulled away, bringing my hand to her chin until her ice blue eyes met mine. "Of course I came back. It was just a trip to Svartálfaheimr, my darling. Not Ragnarök."

Anya glanced away, over the tumult of the ocean's waves, and her eyes flickered with a strange expression. It was, I realized with some discomfort, the same look Falur had given me when he presented me with the metal birch leaf. As if she didn't quite trust my words.

"Of course I came back," I murmured again, pressing my lips into her neck.

Anya sighed in pleasure. I felt the warmth of Falur's hard body press against my back, then withdraw. A moment later the creak of the door filled the air.

"Shall we?" Falur asked.

I hesitated. Anya's body in my arms; Falur's warmth and scent behind me. The door to our hut ajar, waiting. If I could have frozen that moment somehow, sculpted it out of iron to give to Falur and Anya as a treasure, I would have.

"Yes," I said, stepping away from Anya's embrace. "Let's."

ONCE INSIDE OUR HUT, Falur stripped his linen shirt while I lit a low, smoldering fire on the hearth. I stood and kissed Falur again, pressing against him until I could feel his teeth through my lips. Stars, I'd missed that kiss! I'd missed his taste, the feel of his tongue in my mouth, the press of his muscular arms around my waist.

He pulled back, panting, and we both turned to Anya. She stood by the door, and she hadn't yet removed so much as her hair sprang. In the firelight, her cheeks and lips seemed even fuller than I'd remembered. I left Falur to run my fingers through her hair and tilt her lips to mine, kissing her as softly as a whisper.

"Join us," I said.

Her cheeks colored, but she looked away.

"She's embarrassed," Falur said, from behind me.

I frowned, glancing backward at Falur. He shrugged. "She's worried you won't find her so comely now."

"What?" I turned back to Anya, struggling to find the words to describe the way her beauty had so overpowered me as she crossed the dells to our hut.

Anya's shoulders sank, and she gestured to her stomach. "Loki. Look at me. Beneath this dress, I'm as round and streaked as a beetle."

I raised an eyebrow. "You know, I've always found beetles surprisingly attractive."

They both laughed. I dropped to my knees, slipping my hands up Anya's dress. She was silent as Falur and I pulled her shift over her head, exposing her glorious body. Her belly had grown tremendously in the month I'd been away. Her skin pulled taut over the child I'd planted inside her and, yes, a series of bright pink stripes flared from her sex up to her protruding belly button. They reminded me of bright curls of flame, or the tendrils of black stones I'd laid around the stone hut's window.

"You're beautiful," I said, staring up at the swell of her stomach from my position on my knees.

Anya choked back her words. Tears shone in her eyes. For the first time, it struck me how horrible it would be to go through life without the benefit of illusions to wrap around your body. To be forced to show every scar, every tear, every scratch and bruise to the entire world. I ran my fingers along the curve of Anya's belly. It felt as hard as skin pulled over a drum.

"You are still the most beautiful woman in the Nine Realms," I said.

"Isn't she though?" Falur said. He wrapped his arm around her back, then leaned to kiss her neck.

I followed his lead, bending to run my fingers over the streaks her pregnancy had left on her skin, and then kissing her lower lips. She gasped at my touch; heat flashed through my body. All the nights I'd spent on Svartálfaheimr, trying to seduce and charm, and I'd never once felt this aroused. I nuzzled her sex, licking and kissing, while her thighs trembled around my cheeks.

"Lie down," Falur said. "Lie down, beautiful maiden, and let us enjoy you."

Anya moaned in response, and together we led her to the bed. Falur kissed and licked her neck, her breasts, her mouth while I traced every stripe and curve of her belly with my tongue. At one point the child inside her kicked at me, and I began to hum to it, some half-remembered lullaby from my far distant youth. Anya's body rocked with the melody, and the babe quieted, allowing Falur and me to continue with our seduction.

I brought Anya to climax once with my fingers, then again with my lips, while Falur kissed and caressed her. Only then, once she was panting and blinking at the ceiling, did I spread her legs and lower myself between them.

"Anya," I whispered. "I would make love to the most beautiful woman in the Nine Realms. If you would have me."

"Oh!" she gasped, her blue eyes focused on mine. "Oh, Loki! Yes!"

I brought her ankles to my shoulders, kissing both of them as my cock pressed against her wet heat. She gasped for breath, and I let my fingers linger on the damp swell of her clit before raising my hips to bring my cock home.

I closed my eyes as I entered her, partly to focus on the exquisite feel of her heat, her velvet embrace, and partly to slow myself down.

I wanted this to last, damn it. I wanted Anya to feel how much I'd missed her.

It was only when I opened my eyes to watch Anya's face flush with color that I noticed Falur had moved. A moment later, the scent of roses filled the smoky air, and I knew Falur had gone for the bottle of oil. I groaned in anticipation before I could stop myself, and Falur's strong arm circled my chest. I let my head roll back to rest against the hollow of Falur's neck while his fingers trailed down my back and between the split of my ass.

My hips rocked against Falur's hand, making my cock surge in the tight heat of Anya's sex. Anya's heels wrapped around my shoulders as Falur slid his fingers inside me, first one, then two. By the time his hand withdrew, I was gasping and incoherent with pleasure. The heat of his cock pressed against me, and I exhaled, opening myself.

Falur entered me, filling me with the shock and pain and intense pleasure that always came from being penetrated. I cried out as he pushed me against Anya, sinking my cock even further into the tight heat of her glorious body. I was trapped between my two lovers, with pleasure burning through every nerve in my body.

Something bubbled up from far inside me, rippling through my consciousness as Falur began to move inside me, to press me into Anya in a slow, gentle rhythm. This was beyond happiness, I slowly realized, beyond sexual pleasure, even beyond ecstacy.

This was love.

I gasped as if in pain, and Falur's arms tightened around my chest as his thrusts increased. I'd never said that word before, to anyone. I'd never had reason to. But it hit me then, as my body ricocheted between the pleasures of Anya's heat engulfing my cock and Falur moving inside me. Love. The word burned and surged inside me, like an orgasm, until I felt I was about to explode. I opened my mouth to speak the truth, to tell my lovers what they meant to me.

And I was caught by my own ecstacy. I fell into an orgasm so tremendous it seemed to go on forever, drowning my mind and destroying my body. A series of gasps and cries flew from my lips as I spent my seed, over and over, inside the beautiful woman carrying my child. The feeling was overwhelming, like drowning; I suddenly understood why Anya sometimes cried after we made love. My own eyes filled with sudden tears, as if the force of that orgasm had drawn all my emotions to the surface.

But I couldn't. I was Loki, and Loki didn't cry.

Reflexively, I pulled my illusions tighter around my body, then let myself collapse next to Anya and Falur, our sweat soaking into the sheets I'd stolen from Asgard, our panting breaths commingling with smoke from the low-burning candles, which were almost drowned in their pools of sweet-smelling wax. I could tell them now, I thought, but the intensity, the need, had subsided with that earth-shattering orgasm, and I was reluctant to break the sweet silence between us. Anya's eyes had closed, and Falur's breath was slowing, as if in sleep. There was no urgency now; we had all the time in the Realms.

The babe inside Anya's belly kicked, hard and unmistakable, against my palm. I grinned as Anya's eyes flew back open. The babe shifted under my hand, and I moved my fingers, trying to follow.

"He doesn't want to let me sleep," Anya said, with a yawn.

"He?" I asked.

"Anya's mother thinks it's a boy," Falur explained, his voice thick with sleep. "She says Anya's belly is too low to be a girl."

"I didn't think that sort of thing could be predicted," I said.

The babe kicked again, this time high and hard. I pressed my palm against the tight skin of Anya's belly, imagining I could feel a foot, or perhaps an elbow. It was like seeking a connection with another world.

Anya yawned, then looked at me with her sleep-heavy eyes. "I'm glad you came back," she murmured. "Even if it's just once more, before—"

"Before what?" I asked.

"She's right," Falur said, with a yawn of his own. "It was good to enjoy you while we still can."

"What do you mean?" I pressed.

Falur laughed softly. "I doubt we'll see you much, soon."

I didn't follow. I turned to Anya. She took my fingers in hers and moved them lower, until I felt another push from the babe.

"Once the baby comes," she explained.

"Why would that stop me?"

Both Falur and Anya laughed sleepily at that.

"Oh, Loki," Anya said. "We hardly expect to see you once I'm leaking milk like a cow, and we've neither of us slept in days, and there's a squalling babe with a full nappy."

I grinned at both of them. "Once the baby comes," I said, raising myself above Anya's body, "I will suck the milk from these glorious teats." I demonstrated, making her gasp.

"And I will kiss the exhausted father," I said, leaning over to meet Falur's hungry lips.

"And then I'll send you both to bed as I change the nappy," I finished.

They laughed again, then Falur yawned and Anya shifted in the furs. I rocked back on my heels, watching my lovers as sleep took them.

I wish it could be you, Anya had said, when she'd first revealed her pregnancy. *That you'd bring me one of Iðunn's golden apples and take me to be your wife in the halls of Asgard.*

A shock ran through me like a jolt of lightning. Iðunn's apples. Anya was right, of course. The Midgardian myths and legends call them the golden apples of youth, but Iðunn's treasured apples bring more than youth and beauty.

They tie us to Asgard. Those golden apples bind the Æsir and the Vanir, and even Jötunheimr strays like me, to the shining shores of Asgard. Eating the apples means we are welcomed at Val-hall. We can call on Heimdallr to open the Bifröst. Whoever eats one of Iðunn's apples, regardless of their birth or race, is forever afterward to be counted among the Æsir.

My heart hammered against my ribs as I watched Anya and Falur's chests rising and falling beneath the furs. I'd never heard of a Midgardian mortal eating one of Iðunn's apples, but why the hell not?

What was there to stop me trying?

I'm the trickster, after all. I've been both male and female, I am both Æsir and Jötunn. Why not marry a man and a woman? Why not bring my mortal lovers to Asgard, one on either arm, and raise my babe in that hallowed realm? And to the dark mists of Niflhel with any Æsir or Vanir who voiced protest over the choices of the All-father's oath-brother.

I scarcely dared to breathe as I edged off the sleeping platform, my mind spinning. The golden apples are the Æsir's most valuable possession, and very closely guarded.

Closely guarded by only one person. One woman.

I smiled, and the hearthfire flared.

CHAPTER TWELVE

There was no precedent for what I intended to do.

I searched Val-hall's libraries and came up empty, so I decided to err on the side of caution. One apple would not do; I'd need three. One for Anya, one for Falur, and one for the babe who would be joining us shortly.

I could have given them my apples, of course, and given them gladly. But my mother was one of the Jötunn. She'd even been a member of one of Jötunheimr's ruling families, at least until the swell of her belly revealed my presence, and she was cast out for her illegitimate pregnancy. The Jötunn are especially long-lived. I only needed the apples of youth and beauty once every thousand years or so. My lovers and my child would be long in their quiet graves by the time Iðunn freely gave me a golden apple.

Naturally, my first impulse was to steal Iðunn's apples. But I hadn't exaggerated their importance when I told Anya what they meant to the Æsir. There were no treasures in Asgard as well-guarded. Iðunn kept the apples, and Iðunn hardly ever went anywhere. She usually carried the apples with her, in an elegant ash wood box which positively hummed of magic. Iðunn wasn't above a bit of drama, and she liked to make a show of it when she opened the box to present an apple. Usually that involved gathering all the Æsir in Val-hall for a night of feasting and barely tolerable music played by her insufferable husband Bragi. Hardly ideal conditions for a heist.

I watched Iðunn closely my first night back in Val-hall. No one approached her for an apple; I wasn't that lucky. But she let the box rest on the table next to her while her fingers traced its smooth surface, almost as if she were stroking a beloved pet. I reached out for the magical currents running through the air, and felt them swirl and eddy around the box.

There had to be more to it than just a damn wooden box, of course. That pretty ash wood construction was small enough for Iðunn to carry under one arm, so it would hardly hold more than three or four blessed apples. It must have been linked to something, or somewhere. I pressed harder, tracing the magical currents around the box. Most magical items are easy enough to unravel, given time and space—

"Loki?"

My eyes flew open, and my awareness snapped back into Val-hall. Iðunn was staring directly at me, with one delicate eyebrow raised.

"My apologies," I said, immediately discarding the bands of magic as I stood to approach her. "I've lived among the Æsir and Vanir of Asgard for so long, yet your beauty still distracts me."

I noted the flush traveling up the curve of her neck and left before she could grow suspicious.

That night I stayed on Asgard, staring at the soot-blackened roof beams of my meager living quarters. I hadn't slept in this dump in an age; I tried to spend as little time on Asgard as possible. My own cabin was deliberately modest, and crammed with shit I hadn't bothered to put away, which made it altogether a rather unappealing place. I'd drunk enough mead to make the room sway and pulse around me, so the place was tolerable, if only just.

I didn't dare build something better, at least not yet. Not until I brought Anya and Falur here with me. The Nine Realms knew I didn't need to provoke any more resentment among the Æsir and Vanir who thought Óðinn had lost his mind when he invited me to live among them.

Óðinn knows, I realized grimly. Of course Óðinn would know the secret of the box, or he at least would be able to guess it. He wouldn't tolerate something in his realm that he couldn't understand or, if need be, control. But my oath-brother never gave up his secrets for free, and I'd grown wary of his price. It was frequently much higher than I was willing to pay.

"It's just a box," I muttered into the darkness as I tried to remember its exact dimensions, its color and shape, the way it had pulled at the room's magic the way a large stone will make a river bend around its flow.

Where was it now, I wondered? Where did Iðunn keep the most valuable treasure of the Æsir when she was sleeping?

My lips curved into a smile. That at least was a mystery I could solve.

THEY SAY THE WONDROUS Val-hall has five hundred and forty doors.

Actually, it has a great deal more than that. Óðinn and I built the place together, and we tied every part of Asgard into Val-hall in some way. Open one door, and you're in Thor's great palace; another, and you're on the lovely Freyja's doorstep. Some of the doors even lead outside the realm of Asgard, in case the All-father might wish to travel in secrecy.

But the door I wanted was easy to find. It was, after all, where all the Æsir and Vanir traveled at one time or another, seeking Iðunn's magical boon.

The door to the palace Iðunn shared with her husband Bragi was broad and grand, with delicate little carvings above the lintel. It was the door, I thought as I examined it in the innocuous form of a black fly, of someone who has nothing to hide. The doorknob was probably locked but, as a fly, I had no way to test that particular theory. The keyhole looked large and inviting, but I declined. It was likely there was some magic over that entrance, just in case someone tried to jam the lock.

Luckily, the gap between the door and the floor was just large enough to admit a black fly, and I flattered myself for a moment by thinking that particular detail had somehow escaped Óðinn's notice. I crawled through, letting my eyes adjust to the darkness inside. Sometimes, when the doors of Val-hall opened, what they revealed was a surprise. The Æsir and Vanir liked to play with their private spaces, using their magic to rearrange the rooms or alter the landscape.

Iðunn and Bragi's quarters were an utter disappointment. The rooms were still structured exactly how Óðinn and I had designed them, with a main hall and several private booths along the side. Iðunn, I realized, must be a woman of very little imagination.

After a bit of buzzing around in the smoky air, I found the sleeping figures of Iðunn and Bragi. I landed on the wall above them, scanning the floor and shelves for her ash wood box. It was not immediately apparent, oddly enough. At first, I'd thought perhaps it was under her arm, that she slept with the damned thing, but a closer investigation of their marital bed revealed only rumpled furs. Husband and wife, I noted, slept some distance from each other.

I scanned the shelves lining their great hall and found nothing the size of Iðunn's box. It was only when I tried to touch the latent magical currents of the room, a challenge in the fly's form, that I found the spot where magic swirled around the sleeping couple.

An enormous, dark chest squatted at the foot of Iðunn and Bragi's bed. I let myself drift down slowly, examining it through multi-faceted eyes. The lid of the box was ever so slightly ajar; I flattened my fly's body against the crack and squeezed through.

Chains. There was another box inside the first, and this one was lined with chains. I crawled slowly over their oily surface, trying to puzzle through this elaborate storage system. There was no clear lock, and no guarantee the chain-covered box would be the final barrier between a potential thief, like myself, and the golden apples.

I enjoy puzzles. I daresay I'm even good at them. But this mess of chains looked impossible. Any attempt to untie them here would cause them to rattle. I slipped back out of the larger box and flew to the ceiling, examining the room again. I could drug Bragi and Iðunn, of course, or just wait until they both got drunk enough to be insensible. But would that give me enough time? What if the chains were just the first of the challenges?

Idly, I scratched at my wing with a back leg. I could take the entire box, chains and all, to some secret place. But even if I were able to transport this mess through the aether without raising any alarms, it was doubtful if I'd be able to open the damn thing before the Æsir and Vanir came screaming for my head. And I intended to bring my husband and wife here, to raise my child on Asgard. I really couldn't afford to make any fresh enemies.

Damn.

I flew out the crack beneath the door and went back to the feast hall to do the rest of my thinking with a full flagon of mead in my hand.

IT TOOK THREE MORE days of close observation before I learned something new about Iðunn's thrice-damned ash wood box. I did not spare the time to visit my mortal lovers during those three days.

I had no way of realizing how deeply I would regret that decision.

On the third morning of my surveillance, Iðunn went to the bathhouses. Without her box. She walked with a cluster of other women, gossiping with a somewhat grim expression on her permanently somber face, her arms empty of anything but fabrics and soaps. I immediately flew to her door and slipped beneath.

Oh, by the Nine Realms! My heart raced, and the fly's shape faltered somewhat, causing me to lose elevation and almost slam into a table.

The ash wood box sat at the foot of the bed, atop the dark chest where it lay at night. It was completely unguarded.

After checking behind all the furniture and tapestries, I shifted back into my own form and took a few deep, steadying breaths. The box gleamed softly in the early morning light, almost as if it were glowing from within. Magic pulsed so strongly around it that my skin hummed as I approached.

There were no markings or adornments, nothing aside from the constant buzz of magical energy to mark it as anything special. Magic shot through my fingers as I traced the lip, and I wondered briefly how Iðunn could stand to hold the damn thing.

It had no obvious latch. In fact, it had no obvious lid. It may as well have been a solid chunk of wood. I tried to remember how exactly the thing opened when Iðunn pulled an apple from its depths. Did she touch the lid? I tried running my fingers over the lid. Nothing. I pressed the sides and, finally, lifted the thing entirely. It was heavy, with no sign of joints or hinges.

Footsteps sounded on the other side of the door. As delicately as possible, I set Iðunn's box back on the chest and shifted into a fly. I was hovering in midair when the door swung open and Iðunn entered the room, her wet hair plastered down her back. She wore a scowl like a thunderclap, and she searched the room with her thick towel clasped to her small breasts. I let myself drift idly, just like an innocent fly.

With a huff, Iðunn crossed the room. The lid of her box flew open before she was halfway to the bed. The currents of magic rippling off its lid buffeted me through the air, and I bumped into a rather insipid tapestry of Álfheim. Iðunn sank to the mattress and pulled an apple from the box, examining it closely. She pulled a second, then a third, sniffing them and running her fingers across their gleaming skin. Finally, she put them back in the box.

The lid swung closed without her touching the wood. She stood and picked up the box with a final, critical glance around the room. I sank into the tapestry, trying to blend into the dark wool the weaver had used to poorly represent the jagged mountains of Álfheim. For a heartbeat, I was certain her sharp, pale eyes rested on me. I froze.

Iðunn huffed again, turned on her heels, and left the room, her ash wood box firmly tucked under her arm.

Damn. Again.

I counted slowly to one thousand, then let myself out the window. I shifted to my sparrow shape and flew to a far group of warriors, joining them in their training exercises and making them laugh so hard they would easily claim I'd been there all day. If anyone should ask.

STEALING THE APPLES, I finally decided as I stared at my own drunkenly swaying, soot stained roof beams from my lumpy and mildewed mattress, might actually be impossible. Or, if not impossible, at least highly impractical.

I'd seen enough to be almost certain the magic of Iðunn's ash wood box was tied to her personally, opening and closing according to the dictates of her will. If it were magically sealed all the time, I reasoned, there would be no need for the chains at night. But none of us could sustain our personal magic while we slept; perhaps, in sleep, the lid of Iðunn's box yawned open. Why else would it be so closely guarded?

Waiting until I needed a golden apple was impossible. Stealing the box looked similarly impossible. But if I could get Iðunn alone, and somewhere private...

I shifted on the mattress, trying to remember everything I'd seen of Iðunn. She took her role as guardian of the apples painfully seriously. She seemed to take everything painfully seriously. That, combined with the distance between her body and husband's body in their bed, made me think she was more in need of a good fucking than most of the Æsir. And, from what I knew of her husband Bragi, a delicate and mercurial soul at the best of times, a good, hard fucking was probably long overdue.

If the magic of Iðunn's box was tied to her personally, and if I could ply her with enough mead and multiple orgasms, she may relax enough to allow me to slip open the lid of her precious box and steal three of her golden apples.

Probably.

But where in the Nine Realms could I get Iðunn drunk and fuck her senseless? Not Asgard, of course. The Æsir and Vanir would have my head if they knew what I intended to do, and Bragi would be first in line.

And not Midgard, the realm of the mortals. I trusted Anya and Falur, but I'd seen enough of that world to know bringing the apples of eternal youth anywhere near the human race would be a colossal mistake.

Not Niflhel, realm of the inglorious dead. Nothing about that dark realm spoke of seduction. And not Svartálfaheim; the dwarves hated me. Nor Álfheim. I didn't trust those pretentious Light-elves as far as I could throw them.

No, I needed somewhere private, somewhere that was none too closely affiliated with the Æsir. Somewhere I had an ally.

Somewhere I could pull a favor.

CHAPTER THIRTEEN

"You only ever visit me when you want something," Angrboða said, leaning over to pour me another glass of ice-wine.

She'd welcomed me with no hesitation, and with very little regard for her new husband Thiassi. She actually left the dinner table when I arrived, taking my hand and pulling me into her chambers while Thiassi watched with an open mouth.

Poor cuckolded ass. It was all I could do not to wink at him as we left.

"And you never visit me at all," I said.

Angrboða gave me the barest hint of a smile. "It would not be to my advantage to leave Jötunheimr."

"Would that be the delicacy of your position, my dear? Or do you simply distrust your most recent husband?"

She frowned, her brows furrowing under her raven hair. She was a beautiful woman, Angrboða. At least, her illusions were beautiful. I'd never actually seen her, just as she'd never actually seen me.

"I'll never forgive you for teaching Hel illusions," she said, neatly shifting our conversation. "She's refused to take off that hideous face for years."

I made sure my own illusion hid my smile. "That must be complicating your plans to marry her off."

Angrboða shrugged. "Only mildly. Her powers and potential are well-known. Even with her appearance, I have several suitors to choose from."

I made a noncommittal murmur as I took another sip of wine. I wasn't drinking it; I tried to never lose control of myself around Angrboða, even when we were fucking. She was not to be trusted.

Of course, neither was I.

"And I assume Hel is delighted with her options?" I asked.

Angrboða frowned. "You know how she is."

I leaned closer, chin on my hand, as though I had no idea how she was.

"She's impossible," Angrboða scowled. "Just like her father. At this rate I'll have to drug her and drag her to the marital bed."

"Oh, that sounds just lovely. Is that how you brought Thiassi to the altar?"

Angrboða rolled her eyes and leaned back, placing her impressive cleavage on full display. "Don't be an ass. Now did you come here to fuck me, or just insult me?"

"I'm quite happy to do both. Which do you prefer?"

"Such a shame when you use that talented tongue of yours for talking," she replied. Several of the buttons holding back her dress popped open, revealing the slightest hint of her dusky nipples.

Clever trick, I thought. I set down my glass and kissed her hand. "Look, gorgeous, I've come to request a favor. In addition to the fucking. And the insults."

She raised an eyebrow. "A favor? And what's in it for me?"

"Besides sensual pleasure beyond your wildest dreams?"

She laughed. "Oh, please, Loki. You're not the only one in the Nine Realms who can make me come."

That stung, but I knew better than to show it. I leaned back and grinned, spreading my legs as I tweaked my illusions to make it look like I had an enormous erection. Her eyes lingered on it, I noticed.

"All right, what do you want?" she asked.

"Just some privacy. I'd like to entertain a guest, somewhere well away from Asgard. And any prying Æsir or Vanir eyes."

She tilted her head, pouting very full, red lips. "And who is this mystery guest?"

"All in good time, beautiful. Now. As for what's in it for you."

She leaned forward, close enough that I could smell her perfume. It was a heady mixture of floral sweetness and the sting of exotic spices, a scent I always associated with raw ambition.

"I'll talk to Hel," I said. "If you give me a place, somewhere quiet, somewhere private, for three days, then I'll get Hel to marry one of her suitors."

Angrboða's eyes widened. "You'd do that?"

I had no idea if such a thing were even possible. Hel seemed to have inherited the very worst qualities from both Angrboða and me; if you asked her to turn left, she's race to the right just to spite you. But marriage would probably be good for my daughter. At any rate, it couldn't possibly make her any more dour. And, to be honest, I didn't much care whether or not I could follow through on my part of the bargain. I'd get the golden apples for my new family, and then I'd deal with the fallout.

"Of course I'd do that," I said, with a shrug. I adjusted my legs to make my erection even more prominent. At this point, with Angrboða's dress unbuttoned almost to her waist, my arousal was not entirely an illusion.

"That's the first inclination toward fatherhood you've ever shown," Angrboða said.

That stung as well, although I made sure to keep smiling. I tried to remember Hel's childhood. She had been beautiful, so heartbreakingly beautiful, even as an infant. And her magic was unbelievable. I remembered reinforcing the walls of the nursery so she couldn't bring them down, but the rest was a blur of servants and attendants, and Angrboða's shrill demands to get the hell out before someone important came to visit.

Had I ever rocked my daughter to sleep? Had I ever changed her nappy?

Had I ever changed anyone's nappy, for that matter?

Angrboða set down her glass. Her cheeks were flushed; I guessed she'd actually been drinking the ice-wine. I supposed that meant she trusted me. Or at least she trusted me within the confines of her own palace.

"Fine," she said. She stood up and extended her hand, which I took. She pulled me to my feet and reached between my legs as her clothing vanished. "Now. Make me come, Lie-smith."

I did as she said.

I could say I didn't enjoy myself, but that would be a lie.

ANGRBOÐA PROMISED ME three days of privacy in a tiny retreat near one of Jötunheimr's apple orchards. Of course, the offer came with numerous conditions, including my promise to convince Hel to marry a suitor of Angrboða's choosing. Also, Angrboða declared that my three days of privacy began immediately. On the fourth day, she casually informed me, she would instruct her guards to kill any trespassers.

That gave me precious little time to seduce Iðunn.

So I began immediately, with four flagons of mead and a long chat by the fireside. I quickly discovered Iðunn was, without a doubt, the single most boring Æsir in Asgard. She seemed to have no interests beyond guarding the apples and needlework. I learned more about needlework over those few days than any person has a right to know, and the whole time I nodded and smiled and acted as though I was hanging on every single word that fell from her pursed lips.

As the second day drew to a close, I touched Iðunn. First a small, friendly embrace as a greeting, and then a moment when my hand lingered on hers, making her stammer and blush. I waited until her female companions had left the table before asking to join her for dinner. She had already eaten, but she welcomed my company, and she didn't even seem to notice that I ate nothing. I made sure her flagon stayed full, watched the pink flush that crept across her chest and cheeks, and smiled at everything she said.

After three hours of mead and painfully one-sided, needlework-centered conversation, the torches along the walls had burned low, and Val-hall was nearly empty. I ran my fingers along Iðunn's wrist casually, as though I were doing such a thing without even noticing. Her voice faltered. I could smell her sex over the scent of the candles.

"You know, Iðunn," I said, noting her flushed cheeks, her parted lips, "I remember an apple grove on Jötunheimr, when I was a child."

"Oh?" She leaned forward. Of course apples would interest Iðunn. Hardly anything else did.

I bent closer, as though what I had to say next were a secret. "They were glorious, the apples of that orchard. So full and round, blushed with crimson, and aching to be picked."

My breath raised the flesh of her neck, and her breathing hitched. She squirmed in her chair.

"Is... that so?" she asked.

"Mmmmm, yes." I let my purr brush her skin before leaning back to refill her flagon. When I dared glace at the ash wood box on the seat next to her, I noticed the tiniest crack yawning between its heavy lid and solid body. Excitement surged in my chest, making the fire on the hearth leap toward the ceiling.

"If only you could have tasted them, my sweet Iðunn. That firm, pale flesh against your lips—"

My hand dropped below the table to brush the outside of Iðunn's thigh gently, almost as if by accident. She inhaled sharply as her body stiffened. I pulled away, bringing my hand to Iðunn's empty flagon, which I refilled from the large pitcher on our table. She was watching me with a dark, hungry expression, and her hips kept shifting, as if she were uncomfortable. My fingers lingered on hers as I handed Iðunn her flagon. She drank deeply. Her dark eyes were glossy, and her pupils dilated. The scent of her arousal hung heavy in the air between us.

"I'd love to take you there someday," I whispered, "if that's something that might interest you."

She set her flagon down with a clang. "Now," she breathed.

I leaned back, not letting my eyes slip from her flushed cheeks. "Now? Oh, I don't know. It's a bit late, isn't it?"

Something squeezed my thigh. I glanced down to see Iðunn's fingers wrapped around my leg. The dark crack between the lid and base of her wooden box had widened by a hair.

"Now," she said. "I would see these...apples." Her cheeks turned almost as dark as her eyes.

The fire on the hearth flared again. I really shouldn't have been enjoying this but, stars help me, I was.

"Well, my sweet, if you truly don't want to wait..."

She took another deep gulp from her flagon, almost as though she were fortifying herself, and then rocked unsteadily to her feet. I stood and offered her my arm.

"Oh, you may want to take your apples," I added, as if such a thought had just occurred to me. "So you can compare them, you know."

She giggled. I'd never heard Iðunn giggle before. Clearly, the mead and my dazzling smiles were working.

"Oh, I take the apples everywhere!" Iðunn gushed.

She bent to collect the ash wood box, then pressed herself against my arm. I doubted there was anyone still awake in Val-hall. Just in case, I extinguished the torches as we walked the halls. I also whispered descriptions of the succulent, round, sweet apples on

Jötunheimr, and how I loved to bury my face in them, sucking and licking their juice until it ran down my chin.

I don't think Iðunn even noticed the torches going out.

Once we were through the doors of Val-hall and outside Óðinn's wards, I pulled the strands of magic together and transported us across the Realms. We arrived on the outskirts of a small apple grove in Jötunheimr just at dusk. It was cold, of course; it was always colder in Jötunheimr.

"Just through here," I said, being very careful not to even look at the ash wood box tucked under her arm.

Iðunn smiled like a child as she followed me. Her eyes drifted to the branches pregnant with heavy fruit. They were apples, naturally. Just ordinary apples, taken from Midgard and planted in Jötunheimr aeons ago. But they were a truly lovely blend of red and gold, and I hoped they would be enough to tempt Iðunn into the apple grove. And into Angrboða's little retreat, which I'd outfitted with a roaring fire, plenty of mead, scented oil, and an enormous bed.

We'd only taken two steps when it all went wrong. I felt a gust of wind and heard the low, heavy beating of wings.

"Loki," Iðunn began. "What's that sou—"

The giant eagle descended from the sky and grabbed Iðunn's waist in his talons. Her words dissolved as the air was forced from her lungs. Fear and rage played across her delicate features, although her outraged screams were lost in a massive whoosh of air as the eagle took flight, soaring into the already darkening sky.

And then she was gone. I twisted my body into the most reliable flight-shape I had, a sparrow, although I already knew it would be useless. By the time I rose above the tangled mass of tree limbs, all I could see was the distant eagle-shape heading north, with Iðunn's limp body clasped in his talons.

I knew that thrice-damned eagle.

He could only be Thiassi, Angrboða's new husband. My sparrow-shape shuddered as the realization hit me. Angrboða betrayed me. She'd played me like a fool.

I yelled curses after Thiassi's eagle-shape, curses upon his foul marriage bed and the lying snake Angrboða, and then a series of curses upon myself for ever trusting that deceitful, venomous bitch, but all that came from my mouth was a series of sparrow's chirps. Finally, I drifted back to the ground and pulled off the sparrow-shape, wincing. Shape-shifting always hurt.

I paced in the darkness under the trees, weighing my options. Thiassi must have taken Iðunn to his palace. The palace in Thiassiheim that he now shared with Angrboða, that hideous, deceitful cunt. But at least I knew how to find that palace, and I could guess where they'd keep Iðunn. Perhaps if I were able to rescue her, somehow, I could beg three golden apples in return—

Anya screamed.

I froze as her cry shot through my mind and heart. Somewhere across the Nine Realms, my beloved Anya screamed in fear or rage, and her clarion call had echoed off the branches of the World Tree until it reached me.

I held my breath, tried even to will my heartbeat to stop, and strained to listen. The cry did not come again. I was very much alone, at night, in the dark forests of Jötunheimr.

Perhaps I imagined it?

No. Something heavy and cold settled in my chest. No, that I did not imagine. I pulled a fistful of magic around me and left Jötunheimr.

It's not easy, travel between the Realms. It's not even easy for me, and I've been traveling between the Realms since I was a child. All the direct paths from Jötunheimr to Midgard were destroyed long ago, or they're so far damaged and overrun with monsters as to be impassable. I was forced to travel from Jötunheimr to Asgard, then from Asgard to Midgard.

It did not take such a long time, perhaps.

But it was long enough.

CHAPTER FOURTEEN

I went to our stone hut first. It was empty, the coals in the hearth long dead, the sleeping furs heaped in the corner. I hesitated long enough to curse my foolishness; why would I think Anya and Falur would come here?

Next, I materialized in the center of the village. It was dusk on Midgard, with the sun sinking into the waves, and the town was oddly silent. A few people stood huddled along the cliffs, staring at the ocean. Some of them were crying.

The cold weight in my heart grew.

My footsteps echoed in the gloaming as I approached the largest longhouse, casting an illusion to make myself appear as an old crone. Someone non-threatening. Someone who would be offered hospitality.

The door creaked as I pushed it open. Men and women sat along the walls, staring at the flames of the central fire, drinking silently. In here as well, some were crying, although they did it without expression or sound. Just cold tears trickling down cold faces.

A man standing by the fire turned to stare at me.

"What brings you here, old woman, on this dark day?"

He had the countenance and bearing of a leader, with enormous golden brooches around his cloak and a muscular build that spoke of good eating. But his greeting was rude, even by Midgard's low standards, and he did not exactly meet my eyes.

"Is that how you hail your elders?" I asked.

His eyes narrowed. "There is dark magic in this village. Your arrival is ill-timed."

I could not smell them, I realized. Fear clawed at the pit of my stomach. This was where Anya and Falur slept, but I could not smell them.

"What dark magic?" I entered the room, drawing myself up tall, far taller than any old woman had a right to be.

The mortals didn't even notice.

"A couple in this town has been consorting with evil forces all winter," the man continued, ignoring me as he prodded the fire with a long stick. "It was long suspected, but we had the proof of it only this morning."

"What proof?" I demanded.

"The babe," one of the men muttered, staring at his flagon. "The babe had red hair."

I knew then.

Perhaps I'd known even earlier, to be honest. Perhaps I'd known since the moment I saw the empty furs on our bed, or set foot in the village.

Or heard my lover's scream echo across the Realms.

The longhouse blurred before me as I tore out, materializing on the cliffs above the sea and then screaming into my flight shape, my sparrow-self diving toward the cold chop of the waves.

Had the sea began to ebb, I would have lost them forever. But I was not so late, and the bodies of my family still turned and drifted in the foam at the base of the cliffs.

I dove into the water and pulled them one by one to the rocky shore, my beautiful lovers. I found Falur first and dragged him across the waves, then used all my strength and magic on the broken stones as I tried to restart his heart. Dark saltwater bubbled from his mouth, although his body remained cold. I screamed and pounded on his chest long after my rational self accepted he was gone.

Finally, I rocked back on my heels, kissed his blue lips, and pulled his eyelids closed. Then I found Anya, smoothed back her cloak and blouse, and lay her at her husband's side.

I did not expect to find the babe, but find him I did.

He did indeed have red hair.

I BURIED MY FAMILY outside our hut.

I dug the grave myself. It took a very long time, although the ground had already thawed with the coming of spring. At first, I wanted three graves, but when I stared at the three dark holes in the ground it seemed unbearably cruel to separate their cold, pale bodies. So I continued digging, until the three holes became one, and I could lay them out together and cover them with Val-Hall's fine linen sheets and my prized ice bear fur.

I watched them for a long time, in the cold white light of Midgard's moon. I watched them and tried to imagine they slept. But when the gibbous moon finally set behind the distant, jagged mountains, I took a deep breath, pulled tight the latent strands of magic in Midgard's air, and brought all the stones of our hut down on top of them.

Then I stepped back, crossed my arms, and stared at the cairn until the dust settled, all the words I'd never said to Anya and Falur cold and dead on my tongue, a slow rage smoldering in my gut. When the pale light of dawn began to spill across the stones of my family's grave, I decided it was time to go. I wiped my eyes and walked across the dew-laden grass, toward the village.

They were just waking up, the people of that town. I did not bother with my illusions. My arms and face were streaked with grave-dirt, my hair a wild wreath of flames above my head, and my lips marred with scars from when the dwarf Brokk sewed my lips shut. The villagers who saw me gasped and backed away. Some of them covered their eyes; some screamed.

Anya used to call me handsome.

But, of course, she'd never truly seen me.

I ignored the villagers and walked straight to the biggest longhouse, the one where the chief had stood prodding the fire as he rambled on about dark magic and evil forces. The longhouse was abuzz with morning activity, but it all fell silent at my arrival. They backed away as I stalked to their prized mead and grabbed the largest barrel, hoisting it to my shoulders. A few people gasped from the shadows.

When I turned to the door a tall, burly man with angry, bloodshot eyes tried to block my way. I hit him with my full strength. His face folded inward like an old linen sheet. A fine red spray filled the air as his body collapsed at my feet. No one else tried to stop me. I stepped over his body, re-adjusted the barrel of mead, and left their longhouse.

I walked slowly up the steps carved into the hillside, until I sat in the very place where I'd first asked Anya her name. Most of the villagers were now crowding the area below me, watching me from a careful distance. I nestled the barrel of mead safely in the grass, tapped it, filled my flagon, and drank it all in one long gulp. Then I wiped my mouth and took a deep breath, feeling the strands of magic tighten around my fists.

I set it all aflame.

The buildings. The boats. Even the dew-wet grass burned before me.

The people screamed, but not for long.

I stayed on the hillside, drinking their mead until I could no longer stand, and I kept the fires burning.

CHAPTER FIFTEEN

I t took me a long time to realize Loki had stopped talking.

The lights in the coffee shop were being turned off, one at a time. Loki was silent. And I was sobbing.

I pushed that last concern away and leaned forward until I could wrap my arms around Loki's shoulders. When he embraced me, I really started to ugly cry. My shoulders heaved against his chest and tears ran down my cheeks in rivers, soaking into Loki's black shirt. Loki wove his fingers through my hair and pressed his cheek against my forehead, holding me until I was finally able to control myself.

"Oh, fuck," I stammered. "Oh, shit, Loki! Oh, I'm so sorry!"

I met his eyes and, for a moment, saw he had been crying as well. Then the air swirled with his magic and he looked perfectly, unapproachably handsome once again.

"My darling," he whispered. "I'm afraid the woman who works here is about to kill us. They closed over an hour ago."

"Right."

I tried to wipe my eyes with a paper napkin. It fell apart in my hands. Loki offered me a soft handkerchief from God-knows-where as he helped me to my feet. We shuffled toward the door, leaning against each other, and I tried to give the woman behind the counter an apologetic smile. She did indeed look like she wanted to kill us.

The streets were dark and silent when we left The Holy Brew. Cold, gray fog from San Francisco bay swirled around our ankles. I leaned against my husband, and he wrapped his arm around my shoulders. It wasn't exactly cold out, but I shivered all the same.

"I did rescue Iðunn," Loki said, after we'd walked the length of the block.

I nodded, trying to pull my jumbled thoughts together. No, I'd never heard any stories about a village Loki destroyed. But I had heard of Iðunn and her apples, of Hel and Angrboða, of Thiassi's eagle shape.

A car purred past us, sliding through the fog. I glanced at Loki as the headlights flashed across his pale face. He may as well have been wearing a mask.

"Not that it mattered." The words fell like stones from his mouth. "Iðunn never forgave me. None of them ever forgave me."

We rounded the first corner of our walk home in silence. Fog swirled and drifted between our legs. I tried to think of something I could say, anything at all, but my words felt empty and meaningless. How could I possibly comfort him? My thirty-one years were completely insignificant in the face of all the long centuries of his life. I swallowed hard and pressed my body against his, wishing my touch were able to convey what I couldn't find the words to express.

A mockingbird called from the hidden branches above us, sharp and sweet, almost as if it were repeating a half-forgotten name over and over into the night. Loki glanced up; I wondered if he was able to see what the darkness hid from me.

We turned the corner between Sycamore Street and Eucalyptus Drive. The yellow glow of our porchlight shone warmly two short blocks away. I hesitated, pulling Loki to a stop.

"Loki." I turned to face him. "I...I don't think less of you."

His lips curved into a smile. I felt like he was about to speak, but his back stiffened and he turned away.

"She's crying," he said—

—And we were both suddenly standing under the porchlight on our own front stairs. The door swung open before I could reach the handle. Adelina's screams rushed out, filling the air between us.

Loki brushed past me while I blinked in the blinding light from our own living room light. Stephanie gave Loki a very warm, welcoming smile, which he completely ignored. He took Adelina from Stephanie's arms and left the room, singing softly. I didn't recognize the words, or even the language, but I knew the tune. I knew it very well, now.

The Briar and the Rose.

I paid Stephanie and listened distractedly to her painfully detailed recounting of the evening, right down to the most recent diaper change. By the time I thanked her and got her out the door, I was exhausted.

Adelina's bedroom had fallen silent. The door was open, and the sounds of soothing harp music drifted through the door from the *Baby Sleeps!* CD, which had been a total waste of money. Adelina's turtle night light cast a faint green glow over the hallway.

Loki stood with his back to me, his hands wrapped around the railing of our daughter's crib. Adelina slept before him, wrapped in her star-patterned pink swaddle. I could just see her tiny, pale face between the smooth wooden railings. Her eyes were closed, and her puckered pink bow of a mouth had opened slightly.

There had never been anything so perfect in all the world.

Unbidden, another image rose from the darkness of my mind. Steep cliffs, rising sharply above the swirling, hungry ocean. My throat tightened. I pulled my arms around my chest, as if that motion could staunch the ache in my breast. If that had been my family in the churning foam of the north Atlantic, my husband and newborn daughter—

"I would have done it, too," I said.

My own voice surprised me. It sounded hard and cold, filled with the rage of another lifetime.

Loki's shoulders straightened, and he turned to face me. His expression was dark, inscrutable. We may as well have been talking about the weather for all the emotions that look betrayed.

"Would you like to see?" he asked.

I had no idea what he was talking about, but I didn't hesitate.

"Yes."

Loki picked up Adelina so gently she didn't even stir, and my heart clenched with a fierce combination of affection and jealousy. It just didn't seem fair that he could hold her without waking her, or get her to sleep when she was in hysterics in my arms. As I watched, Loki nestled her little, swaddled body within his arms, then reached for my arm. His hands felt different, rough and uneven against my skin. For the second time that night, I wondered if he was actually all right.

And, if he wasn't, what the hell could I do about it?

The room swirled around us. A moment later, the thick, rich scent of the ocean hit me, and I blinked against the sudden glint of sunlight against a vast, undulating expanse of glittering water. It took me a moment to make sense of where we were. I was standing on a high cliff overlooking the ocean. The thick, green grass below us was dotted with tiny, dark blue flowers, and the wind racing across the ocean was cold. The sun hung low over the ocean; something about the way the light hit my eyes made me think we were very far north.

I shivered, and Loki pulled something over my shoulders. I looked down and saw he'd wrapped me in a thick, black fur of some sort. I was too grateful for the warmth to be squeamish about what sort of animal may have worn that fur before me.

"Thanks," I said, turning to Loki.

He nodded. His illusions were now perfect, even his hands, which I found oddly comforting. But the rest of his outfit was horribly out of place in the modern world; black and gold streaked leather armor that was tight across his chest and hips, with an enormous, flowing black cape, which the wind unfurled behind him like an ominous shadow. Adelina looked absurdly tiny and vulnerable in her bright pink swaddle, pressed against his armor. As I watched, Loki pulled the corner of his cape over her small, sleeping body.

Only then did the rest of our surroundings register on me. We stood on some sort of peninsula, a low point surrounded on three sides by the crashing ocean. A few brightly colored fishing boats dotted the waves beyond us and, somewhere far off in the distance, I heard the hum of cars passing on a road. Just behind Loki lay two low hills. The first was completely covered with thick grass and the same little, waving stalks of blue flowers.

But the second hill was clearly a burial mound. The rough stones lay exposed to the weather. Some distant part of my mind realized they hadn't had time, yet, to be covered with the dust that would eventually become earth, and the seeds that would turn to a carpet of grass, transforming the burial mound into a low hill.

I felt cold, despite the thick fur. We stood between the sea and two burial mounds.

"You know, this place is a bit of a geological marvel," Loki said. "By all rights, it should have crashed into the Atlantic hundreds of years ago."

He gave me a little half-smile, the kind of expression he wore when he'd done something especially clever with his magic. Like when he turned our linen closet into the entrance to an enormous, subterranean hot springs lined with thousands of candles.

"I assume the phenomenon has been thoroughly researched?" I asked, playing into his game.

Loki shrugged. "There have been a few research expeditions. Oddly enough, they seem to run into terrible luck with their instruments."

That smile returned, a bit stronger this time. I let my gaze wander from his face to the two burial mounds, lying side by side, separated by perhaps a thousand years. I didn't ask if anyone had ever suggested an archaeological expedition. Even from here, I could feel the faint thrumming hum of Loki's magic protecting this place. I could probably only see the mounds because he wanted me to see them.

The sting of tears welled behind my eyelids. Watching the green grass and the nodding blue heads of the flowers bobbing in the wind somehow made Loki's story horribly, painfully real. Perhaps Loki felt the same, because his smile vanished as he turned to the ocean. He pressed his hand to his chest and reached into the folds of his armor.

A moment later, Loki held his arm out to me. I wrapped my hand around his cold fingers, and he pressed something into my palm.

I unfurled my fingers slowly. It was a leaf. An iron leaf so old it had developed a gentle teal patina over its delicate veins and ridges. It felt impossibly ancient. My vision blurred with tears as I ran my finger along the thin edges.

"Do you..." I asked, but my voice faltered. I made a noise which was something like a laugh and something like a cry. "Do you always carry this around with you?"

Loki nodded, and the edges of his lips twitched up. "It's part of my armor, now. Along with—"

He reached into the folds near his heart a second time, then held his hand out to me again, his fingers clenched into a fist. I extended my arm, and he opened his hand to press something soft into my palm. I frowned. It was a rumpled mess of bright red fabric. A gust of wind made me hunch my shoulders against the cold before I grabbed an edge and shook out the fabric.

It was underwear. Women's underwear. What the hell?

I stared with utter disbelief at the faded red underwear fluttering happily in the wind. It wasn't particularly sexy. It looked like plain, cotton undies. Hanes plain cotton undies, the kind that came in a plastic-wrapped pack of six at Wal-Mart. In fact, it looked just like something I would wear. Or something I would have worn, back in Chicago, when I was broke and single.

"Is this...mine?"

Loki pulled the underwear from my hand and tucked in back into some secret pocket on his chest. "It was."

"You carry my underwear in your armor? What the fuck?"

His eyes darkened. "I took it from you when the clouds of Ragnarök began to gather. I wanted to die on Vígríðr holding something of yours."

"Oh." I blinked fast, trying to clear my eyes. I wasn't sure if that made the whole thing more or less creepy. "Damn. What else do you carry around in there?"

The hint of a smile pulled at the corners of his lips. "Just this."

He didn't bother trying to hide the square of pale fabric he pulled from the folds of his armor. It fluttered open in the breeze, giving me a glimpse of pale pink and soft green as I took it from his outstretched hand. The fabric felt light and insubstantial, as if it were woven of cobwebs. I smoothed it over my palm, although creases remained to show where it had been folded into a tight square.

The fabric was covered with tiny stitches, the kind of careful, even work I associated with machines. But there was something organic about this shape, something delicate and even loving which made me think it had to be handmade. I turned the fabric over in my hands, examining the colorful image from all angles.

It was a flower. Five overlapping pink petals unfurled around a blazing yellow core. The threads were so fine I could almost see the pollen-laden stamens bending against the petals. Green leaves twined protectively above and below the pink blossom.

I touched the stitching very gently with my fingertips. This looked like a wild rose, the kind which grew in thick tangles all over the beach dunes from San Diego to Seattle. It struck me as odd to make such a careful, beautiful representation of such an ordinary flower.

My gaze wandered from the embroidered flower in my hands to the burial mounds which stood between me and the churning ocean. The grass-covered mound must be Anya, Falur, and the child. But the exposed stones, the mound that had yet to weather into soil?

Loki had been married before. All the myths and legends mention his wife, Sigyn, the incantation-fetter. Sigyn the faithful. The beautiful woman who had been bound with Loki beneath the earth, when the Æsir and Vanir imprisoned him for Baldr's death. The *Eddas* made it sound like she had chosen to be with her husband, and named her the goddess of fidelity.

Loki told me a different story, one frigid Valentine's Day in Chicago, as we walked the frozen shore of Lake Michigan. Sigyn had not chosen her fate, Loki said. She'd been trapped. In the end, after centuries of torment and countless failed attempts to escape, they agreed to leave the pit together, in spirit, if not in body.

They drank the poison at the same time, Loki said, his voice low and even despite the tears streaming down his cheeks. But it had only killed her.

"Sigyn?" I asked. My voice trembled. I tried to pretend it was only the wind.

"Yes. Sigyn." His lips curved into a gentle, secret smile that made me feel like I'd swallowed broken glass.

Suddenly, I didn't want to be touching the soft fabric anymore. I held my hand out to Loki, and he pulled the beautifully embroidered rose from between my fingers, folded it carefully, and tucked in back into some secret pocket in his armor. It struck me that Falur and Sigyn had both made something beautiful for him, some artistic labor of love and talent.

For me, he'd taken dirty underwear.

"Would you like to hear the rest?" Loki asked.

His voice startled me out of my self pity. I shivered against the wind. The sun was strong and bright here, but I felt cold in a way the heavy fur cloak could do little to mitigate.

"Of course," I said.

Loki nodded, then raised a finger in the air. He shifted his cloak, revealing Adelina's fuzzy pink swaddle, and her little scrunched-up face. She was squirming against the blanket, making little chirps of frustration as her forehead furrowed in concentration. Her mouth opened and closed against Loki's arm, searching for sustenance.

"Oh, let me take her!" I said.

"Shall we go home?" Loki asked.

I shook my head, not wanting to waste time. Once Adelina woke, we had to move fast. She progressed rapidly from upset to screaming to apoplectic with rage. If we let her get that far, nothing would settle her down. I pulled Adelina from his arms and tugged my battered dress down over one shoulder to expose my milk-heavy breast, then glanced around, looking for a good place to sit.

"Here," Loki said.

He waved his hand, and the upholstered rocking chair from Adelina's nursery appeared next to me. I sank into the chair with a grateful sigh as Loki handed me the nursing pillow. I'd always thought breastfeeding was natural and, by definition, would be easy to perform. But my experience with Adelina had been anything but easy.

My full breasts were hard and aching by the time I got Adelina settled on the nursing pillow and started to line her gaping, hungry mouth up with my nipple at just the right angle. After a half dozen false starts, during which time Adelina's cries escalated alarmingly, we finally got it right. Adelina began to make satisfied little grunts, and my breasts tingled as the milk let down. I pulled the heavy fur over her body, then wrapped it around my exposed chest, shielding us from the wind.

"It must be two in the morning back home," I murmured to Loki.

Adelina wasn't anywhere close to sleeping through the night, but her schedule had at least gotten more regular. She woke up, now, at ten, midnight, two, and four in the morning, almost like clockwork.

Loki didn't respond. I turned from watching Adelina's plump little cheeks suck down milk to catch my husband's eye. But he wasn't looking at me. He was on his knees before the grass-covered burial mound.

Silently, and without turning to me, Loki spread his fingers against the earth, then bent until his forehead almost brushed the nodding bunches of bright blue flowers. His lips moved, but the wind stole his words before they could reach me.

Just as well. They weren't meant for me.

Wrapping the fur cloak tight against the cold, I turned away. Two brightly colored fishing boats bobbed on the waves below the cliffs, glinting in the bright sunshine. For a moment, I wondered if they could see us. If the fishermen glanced toward the cliffs, would they see a woman in a ridiculously overpriced rocking chair breastfeeding an infant while her husband knelt beside her, whispering to a thousand year old burial mound?

Loki touched my shoulder a moment later, making me jump.

"Let's go home," he said.

"Sure."

Adelina squirmed against my arms as the ocean fell away—

—And the familiar contours of our living room filled my vision, as warm and comfortable as an embrace. The fur around my shoulders had vanished, and Adelina gurgled contentedly from the nursing pillow. Loki picked her up, gently rested her against his shoulder, and patted her back. I heard her rich, thick burp as they vanished down the hallway, and I found myself blinking against a fresh onslaught of tears. I sank onto the couch as I listened to the sound of my husband opening the Diaper Genie, humming to Adelina, and finally closing the nursery door. A moment later the kitchen light flicked to life, and I heard Loki switch on the kettle in the kitchen.

I felt numb, as though the cold of those oceanside burial mounds had sunk into my very bones. A strange thought bubbled through my consciousness as I heard Loki open and close the kitchen cabinets. I'd never given much consideration to where I'd be buried. I had supposed I'd be cremated, with my ashes scattered in the ocean, just like Noni when she'd passed away my senior year of high school.

But now, I knew better. They might scatter something in the vast, sparkling Pacific, my children or my grandchildren or whoever was around to do such a thing. But my body would be beneath a burial mound, somewhere far north, on a peninsula which should have crashed into the ocean centuries ago.

It was not an especially comforting thought.

"How are you?" Loki asked, from behind me.

I turned and rubbed my eyes. Loki stood in the doorway, framed by the soft yellow glow of the kitchen light, holding two steaming mugs. The scent of lavender chamomile tea washed over me, followed a moment later by the acrid sting of gin. Loki must have put something a little stronger than Sleepytime Tea in his mug.

"I'm—" I shook my head as Loki handed me a mug and sank onto the couch next to me. "I'm okay. I think. You?"

He was silent for a long time. In the backlit glow of the kitchen, it was hard to tell if he still wore his illusions. His flame-red hair drifted above his face as he brought the mug to his lips and drank deeply.

"Fine," he said.

His tone was colder than the wind above the burial mounds. I put my tea down and reached for him, cupping his cheek in my palm.

He felt like ice. His eyes closed at my touch, and I pulled him into my arms. His shoulders trembled, then fell still. For a long time, there was no sound but his deep, ragged breathing.

Then, just as I'd begun to think he must have fallen asleep, his back straightened. He took my hand in his, intertwined our fingers, and looked out the window into the darkness of our backyard, as if that familiar vista held the answer to some question he'd been asking for millenia.

"I kept the fires burning," he began. "I drank, and I kept the fires burning, for a very long time."

CHAPTER SIXTEEN

I drank, and I kept the fires burning, for a very long time.

The sun rose behind a thick skrim of inky smoke, and it set wreathed in flames. I sat on that hill, and I drank the mead of the doomed village. I drank until my vision swam, until I was no longer certain if the sun were rising or setting.

And then, I slowly realized, I was no longer alone.

I blinked, struggling to focus. Two figures stood before me— No, make that one figure. One tall figure wearing a broad-brimmed hat.

Oh. Right. I groaned.

"You know," Óðinn said, after clearing his throat several times, "this village has burned for an entire week. Even after a rainstorm. Quite impressive."

I belched and made the fires behind him flare.

Óðinn sat down. "There's nothing left to burn, oath-brother. You've melted the very rocks. Nothing will grow here for a century."

I shrugged and fumbled for my flagon, bringing it to my lips. It was empty. Just my damned luck.

Óðinn cleared his throat again. "The apples," he said.

"Applesh?"

I tried to focus on turning the tap to the mead barrel. Damn thing didn't seem to work.

"I know you took Iðunn. At this point, I am the only person in Asgard who is certain you're the one behind Iðunn's absence."

He paused, and I ignored him.

"If you bring her back home, I'll make sure it stays that way," Óðinn said.

I gave up on the fucking tap, leaned closer to Óðinn, and retched all over his shoes.

Óðinn shook his head as he stood and stepped delicately away from the pool of my vomit. "Fine. Your decision."

Something dark tugged at the edge of my brain, bringing a fresh swell of rage. I struggled to my feet and blinked until there were no longer two of him swimming in my vision.

"Did you do this?" I demanded.

Óðinn laughed, but there was no joy in it. "You think I have nothing better to do than turn the mortals against each other? Oh no, oath-brother, this was not my doing. You want to cast blame on someone, you look to yourself. You were hardly subtle with them."

I collapsed back on the dirt, letting my body slump against the mead barrel.

Óðinn snorted above me. "You didn't even bother to track her cycles. That was sloppy, planting your seed in a woman when it would take root."

A horrible, strangled sound slipped from my lips before I could stop it. A moment later, I was retching again. At least I was able to hit Óðinn's feet with a second hot wash of vomit.

Óðinn sighed heavily. Disappointment radiated from him in thick waves, almost as palpable as the magic pulsing around Iðunn's ash wood box. He ignored the mess at his feet and sank to his knees in front of me, bringing his face level with mine.

"Listen, Loki. We'll bargain. You like to bargain, right? Well, we need the apples back, and you want...what? What does the Lie-smith want?"

I glared at his blurry, wavering form. "More mead," I slurred defiantly.

"Why in the Nine Realms would you take Iðunn and her apples away from Asgard? What did you have to gain from it?"

His bright blue eye burned as he stared at me. His face drifted in and out of focus in a way that made my stomach turn. I almost closed my eyes. But no, that would have been surrender.

"You stole the apples of youth and beauty, and then you came here, to the village of your little mortal pets." Óðinn paused, then clapped his hands together.

I winced at the loud crack.

"Ah, of course. You wanted mates, didn't you, Loki?" Óðinn stood and wiped his hands on his robe. "Reckless, short sighted, and driven by blind passion, as usual. You want to plant your seed in some willing bitch with round hips and nice tits? You want to raise a pack of whelps on Asgard?"

I opened my mouth to protest, but my numb lips seemed to have forgotten how to form words.

"Fine," Óðinn said. "If that's your entire plan, if Loki's grand ambition is fucking and reproducing like a damned animal, so be it. I can give that to you."

He paused. A particularly strong gust of wind swept across the peninsula, clearing away the smoke and replacing it with the thick, heavy brine of the ocean. The air began to tingle with magic.

"I'll give you a wife," Óðinn said, "and you'll return the apples."

"Wha—"

"And bring Iðunn back too, if she's still alive and not too much trouble."

Óðinn grabbed my arm and hauled me to my feet.

The world spun. I staggered forward. I would have fallen to my knees if Óðinn hadn't steadied me with his hand on my neck, squeezing my muscles a hell of a lot firmer than was strictly necessary. I winced as I tried to regain my balance and make sense of my surroundings.

Curtains. Delicately embroidered curtains framed a large, sunny window. The room was warm, and it smelled good. Like flowers and fresh bread. My stomach rolled over itself, shifting the rapidly curdling mead in a very unpleasant manner.

"Sigyn!" Óðinn's voice boomed. "I've brought your husband."

My eyes narrowed, and I noticed a woman next to the fireplace. She must have been sitting when we arrived, but now she stood with a pale hand held over her mouth. She was small and delicate, with thick tumbles of auburn hair down her back, and she wore a pale blue dress with long sleeves and a high neckline. What looked like an embroidery project had fallen in a heap at her feet.

"Loki!" Óðinn shoved me forward. I caught myself, spinning a desperate illusion so I looked somewhat respectable. "Your wife."

She didn't look frightened, even when Óðinn clasped his hand around her shoulders and pushed her toward me. When she stood in front of me, Óðinn took both our hands and linked them together. Her palms felt warm against mine.

"Say the words," he said.

The woman swallowed and met my eyes. Brave, I thought.

"Loki," she said, "I am bound to you. You are a part of me."

The air around me tingled with intention. Sigyn and Óðinn both turned to stare at me.

"You have got to be kidding me," I said.

"Loki. The words." Óðinn's voice carried the barest hint of a threat.

I struggled to control my wildly spinning thoughts. I didn't know Sigyn, not exactly, but I knew of her. She was one of the Æsir, well-born, gentle, shy, and so far above my ilk I'd hardly spoken to her. I watched her now, behind my illusions, wondering what she's done to anger Óðinn enough to be bound to me for eternity.

I supposed I'd find out.

"I am bound to you," I said, very slowly. The words felt heavy on my numb lips. "You are a part of me."

The air tingled again, and my head started to throb with the first pangs of what I knew was going to be an epically terrible hangover.

"Good!" Óðinn clapped us both on the shoulders, rocking my head back and making me wince beneath my illusion. "Sober up, oath-brother. I'll see you in a day or so. We have plans to discuss."

The air in Sigyn's chambers swirled as Óðinn vanished. And then I was alone, staring at my new bride's wide, caramel-colored eyes. I ran my fingers through my hair as I took a step back. My calves hit something hard and I dropped, landing on an upholstered stool.

"Husband. Are you well?"

My laugh sounded rusty. I'd thought sitting stone-drunk in the mud watching the ruins of that rathole village burn was just about the most uncomfortable place in all of the Nine Realms.

But this was worse.

"Shit," I muttered. "Sigyn, right?"

She nodded and sat next to me, taking one of my hands in hers. Her touch was gentle, her skin soft. I shook my head, and the throbbing behind my temples intensified.

"Tell me, Sigyn. What did you do to make Óðinn angry?"

Her eyes widened. "Me? What do you mean?"

I laughed again. It hurt. "What did you do to piss him off so much he'd shackle you to me till Ragnarök?"

She turned away to face the gently smoldering fire. Her fingers moved gently over mine. "I... asked for you."

I narrowed my eyes, wondering if I'd misheard her. "You what?"

"I asked Óðinn for your hand. Years ago."

The dull ache behind my temples intensified as I stared at her. "By all the Nine fucking Realms, why the hell would you ask for me?"

She said nothing. The flush across her cheeks and neck deepened until her skin was almost crimson. An unexpected rush of sympathy filled my mead-soaked heart. Poor woman. This had to be the worst wedding in Asgard's history. I slumped forward, cradling my pounding head in my hands.

"Sigyn," I muttered, trying to get used to the taste of her name in my mouth. "I'll make this up to you."

The fire crackled in the hearth. Her window was open, and the faint sound of birdsong drifted through the early summer air, mingled with the dull, distant thud of waves.

"I'm so sorry for your loss," Sigyn said. Her voice was low and gentle, the kind of voice people use with unruly children, or wild animals who may bite. "The man and the woman you loved. I heard what happened. You must feel terrible."

My illusions slipped, and I spread my fingers, hiding my face.

"When you need me," Sigyn said, "I'll be here."

I raised my head, staring at her through bleary eyes. She was such a small thing, this strange woman I'd just married. Slender and small. How easy it would be to hate her. To curse that lithe frame for lacking Anya's curves, or to loathe her brown eyes, which were so different from Falur's intense gaze.

And she must know this. No matter how innocent or naive she may be, Sigyn had to realize how precarious her position was in my tempestuous heart. How easily my rage and grief could turn against her, this slender stranger to whom I'd just been bound. Our eyes met in the thick, golden sunlight. She did not turn away.

My throat felt as dry as the deserts of Svartálfaheimr, and the growing hangover pounded at my temples with rhythmic insistence. I squeezed my eyes shut and took a deep breath to steady myself.

"Sigyn," I whispered. "I do not blame you. And I will not resent you."

Her little frame trembled, but she did not pull away. Brave, I thought again. An uncomfortable realization wormed its way through my aching head and battered heart. She deserved more. More than me, undoubtedly, but this woman also deserved more than just an assurance that her new husband would not hate her.

I reached for her arm, catching her wrist between my fingers. Slowly, I brought her hand to my lips, breathing her in. Her scent was delicate and floral; there was nothing to betray the strength she possessed, or the bravery she'd just displayed. Her pulse trembled beneath my lips like a butterfly's wings.

"I do need you," I whispered.

She said nothing. Through the open windows, I heard the distant thrum and roar of the ocean crashing against the shore. Birds fluttered outside, and the fire gave a little hiss as a pocket of sap locked inside one of the logs escaped as steam.

I realized she may want to make love.

Most women would, I assumed, after exchanging marital vows. My current hungover, exhausted, and emotionally numb state wasn't ideal for pleasuring a woman, especially one I'd never met, but I was prepared to do whatever was needed. Without moving, I gathered a few tendrils of magic around my body, ready to support my illusions for as long as it took to show Sigyn I could be a passable imitation of a husband.

We leaned together for a long time, my lips pressed to her wrist, her slender body trembling against mine, as I waited for her to make the first move. Perhaps I should have tried to seduce her, but I couldn't find the strength. I couldn't even force my lips to form any further words.

Finally, she pulled away. "You must be tired," she said. "Come with me."

I managed to get to my feet without staggering, and I followed her like a child, my mind hardly comprehending what I saw. Her quarters were beautiful. The scent and sounds of the ocean drifted through the open windows. I dimly realized Sigyn must have one of the most desirable houses on Asgard, perhaps even the one tucked among the rose bushes near the beach.

Before I could identify our location, she'd led me to a small bedchamber. I turned to face her, strengthening my illusion to hide my bleary eyes and wretched smell, but she ignored me. Instead, she pulled heavy curtains across the windows, plunging the room into a thick twilight. I felt myself swaying on my feet, as if I'd been awake for a thousand years. Still, I forced my lips to give my new wife a seductive smile.

"Rest," she said, walking past me to stand in the doorway. "I'll see you are not disturbed."

The door closed behind her, and I fell backward into the bed. I had just enough energy to cast the cantrips that would wake me if anyone entered the room before the blackness of sleep engulfed me.

CHAPTER SEVENTEEN

Voices. A man's and a woman's, passing a conversation between them like tossing a ball. The voices wove themselves into the images in my dreams, into the figures of Anya and Falur. I had my arms wrapped around them both, holding their sweet bodies close to mine. But the voices—

The voices were wrong. Anya didn't sound like that. No, Anya—Anya screamed.

My throat narrowed, and suddenly I couldn't breathe. My eyes snapped open as my heartbeat thundered in my ears. It felt like I'd just swallowed sand. The dimly lit room swam in and out of focus, and Anya's distant scream echoed through layers of dream and memory.

Awareness hit me square in the gut, as solid as a fist. Anya and Falur were gone. I doubled over, pulling my knees to my chest, grief rising in me like a black tide. The flames of their village burned in my mind; I struggled to push them away.

The man's voice rose. I wiped my eyes and rolled to face the door. It was Óðinn's voice. My mind registered that fact with no emotion whatsoever, just a numb sense of detachment. Idly, I wondered if anything would surprise me ever again.

"So, you just want me to sit here all day, is that it? Just waiting for him to walk through that door?" Óðinn said.

"If you please."

That soft, lilting voice must be the woman. I cast my mind out, searching again for her name.

Ah, yes. Sigyn.

I pushed myself off the bed. My legs trembled so badly I almost fell flat on my face, and my stomach voiced its empty displeasure with a series of painful cramps. Curling my lip in disgust, I pulled at the magic in the room. My grasp was weaker than I'd have liked; for one panicked moment I thought I might not even be able to weave my customary illusion.

Then the magic fell into alignment, and I was myself once again. Hungry, trembling, and filthy underneath, but at least I looked like Loki again. Only once I was at the door did it occur to me to look for a wash basin to actually clean myself. I spotted one in the far corner, half hidden by the heavy drapes.

Fuck it, I thought. I wrenched the door open.

The scent of smoked fish and roasted potatoes enveloped me. It had been so long since I'd put anything but mead into my stomach that the aroma was almost painful. Without my magic to keep me upright, I'd probably have doubled over in the doorway.

I blinked and tightened my grip on the latent magical strands. Slowly, my vision cleared. The light in this hallway was almost at the same angle it had been when Óðinn dropped me next to Sigyn's hearth fire. Had I been asleep for an entire day and night?

By the Nine Realms, had I been asleep even longer than that?

I pushed down a surge of panic and walked to the end of the hallways as though I were in my own quarters, my dimly lit and mouldering shack, instead of Sigyn's oddly pleasant little cottage. Four steps brought me to a beautiful, sunlit kitchen.

Óðinn and Sigyn both sat at a solid, wooden table, the kind of table that's functional but also holds its own quiet beauty. Óðinn's broad-brimmed hat rested on the table between them, and Sigyn wore another oddly modest dress, with long sleeves and a neckline cinched tight at the base of her throat. Freyja wouldn't be caught dead in anything that dowdy. An odd mixture of emotions flared in my chest at the sight of Óðinn and my new wife sharing a breakfast platter as though they were an old married couple.

"Good morning," I said, announcing my presence.

"Finally," Óðinn grumbled.

Sigyn gave me a polite, inscrutable smile. "Good morning, husband."

I nodded at both of them before collapsing in a chair and pulling the platter of smoked fish toward me. I only had time to swallow a half dozen mouthfuls before Óðinn flung something at my chest. Glancing down, I saw a rumpled mess of gray feathers in my lap.

Freyja's falcon cloak. Apparently this time I wouldn't even have the pleasure of trying to convince Freyja to loan me one of her most treasured possessions.

"It's time," Óðinn said.

Óðinn's lone blue eye fixed on me with an expression of oppressive disapproval. I forced myself to swallow what was in my mouth and smile at both of them.

"Is there anything else you'll need?" Óðinn asked.

Leaning back in the chair, I let my gaze drift to the ceiling as I tried to think. Anya's ice blue eyes swam into my memory, followed by a stab of pain so acute I almost cried out. Tears welled behind my eyelids, blurring my vision; I comforted myself with the knowledge that my illusions would hide everything. To Óðinn and Sigyn, I was still smiling.

Think, damn it. Think.

Thiassi had taken Iðunn. He'd worn his eagle shape, really the only trick he had, and there was only one safe place he could have taken both her and the apples. His fortress in Thiassiheim. Thiassi didn't have the imagination to hide her anywhere else.

Unless Angrboða was still directing his movements. I ground my molars together so tightly my jaw ached. Fuck Angrboða. Fuck that lying, deceitful bitch.

It made no difference, anyway. Even if Angrboða had found another place to stash Iðunn and her apples, I would find them. I had nothing but time, now. I could shadow Thiassi in the form of an insect for years. I could search every frozen, desolate patch of Jötunheimr.

The idea was strangely appealing.

In the end, I'd find Iðunn. And what would Thiassi do once I'd reclaimed her for the Æsir? Well, he'd use his one party trick, of course. The eagle shape.

I couldn't out-fight Thiassi. If I was being honest, I couldn't out-fight many people. I'd always been small, especially for a Jötunn, and I preferred the elegance of magic to the brute force of physical violence. There were some among the Æsir would could take on Thiassi and win; Thor, of course. Probably Týr. Possibly Heimdallr.

But they wouldn't want to kill Thiassi. Staining their hands with the blood of a king of Jötunheimr would open the doors to all kinds of trouble. Thiassi had alliances, lesser warlords and vassals who'd sworn fealty and would be honor-bound to avenge his outright murder. The politics of Jötunheimr were a morass of shifting alliances and desperate betrayals during the best of times. Dispose of Thiassi outright, and the entire realm might erupt in war.

Not that it mattered much to me. The thought of plunging Angrboða's realm into a bloody, horrific civil war was darkly appealing. But it didn't change the fact that I'd be hard pressed to find an Æsir warrior both strong enough to kill Thiassi and stupid enough to commit that political blunder. Even Thor knew better.

No, it would have to look like an accident.

I would be able to outrun Thiassi's eagle form, at least for a little while. And this falcon shape could certainly out-maneuver that massive eagle.

A vision began to take shape in my mind, the image of a small, dark falcon diving toward Asgard's walls, pursued by an enormous eagle. The eagle so intent upon capture that it ignores what's piled behind the wall.

I grinned, showing all my teeth. Fire, of course. Fire would end this.

"Wood," I told Óðinn. "Dry wood and wood shavings. Pile them along the inside of Asgard's walls."

Óðinn nodded, although his glacial expression had not changed. "Fine. Now go recover what you stole, Loki."

My stomach rumbled in protest as I pushed the platter of fish away, but I ignored it and came to my feet with Freyja's cloak clasped in my hands. Of course, I can take the shape of a falcon on my own; I can take the shape of anything on my own. But Freyja's falcon cloak amplifies the magic of the wearer, making a stronger, faster falcon form. In all the years I'd been borrowing her cloak, I'd never quite managed to duplicate its subtle magic.

I pulled Freyja's delicate cloak over my shoulders. As always, the gentle buzz of the cloak's magic surrounded my body like an embrace. In the past I'd found the sensation pleasant, even sensual. But this morning it was just another detail, minor and easily overlooked.

It was only after Óðinn had swung open the front door that it occurred to me to look back at Sigyn. She still sat at the table, carving a potato into infinitesimally small pieces. Our eyes met. Her smile may as well have been carved out of wood, and her dark eyes betrayed nothing.

"Be careful," she said.

I swallowed hard as the smoked fish churned in my gut. No response came to mind, so I merely nodded as I left the house.

Once outside, Óðinn summoned the Bifröst, as I'd hoped he would. There are many paths among and between the Realms, but the rainbow bridge of the Bifröst is the fastest route from Asgard to

Jötunheimr. And speed, I gathered, was of the essence. To Óðinn, at least.

Thanks to whatever wicked stars shone on my path, Heimdallr was not guarding the Bifröst. Not that I had anything in particular against him, but his self-righteous indignation always rubbed me the wrong way. I was feeling especially impatient this morning, and I couldn't guarantee I wouldn't have knocked the golden teeth out of Heimdallr's smug skull at the first snide comment about where I'd been or what I'd done. Or with whom.

"Calm down," Óðinn growled.

Surprised, I glanced down to see I'd balled my hands into two tight fists. I took a deep breath, pulling Freyja's cloak around me and letting the warmth of her falcon shape sink into me. My body tingled with Freyja's erotic magic, but I ignored the unwelcome distraction.

I planned to cross the Bifröst in my own body, because flying between the Realms was nigh impossible, then shift into the falcon's sleek form as soon as my feet hit the frozen ground of Jötunheimr. I stepped forward and shivered as the cold mist between the worlds engulfed my legs.

"Loki!" Óðinn called.

I glanced at Óðinn and raised an eyebrow, half expecting him to echo Sigyn's sentiments and tell me to be careful.

"Don't fuck this up," he said.

I turned my back on Asgard and let the mists swallow me.

IT TOOK ME THREE DAYS to find Iðunn.

Most of that time was spent crossing the frozen wastes of Jötunheimr. For whatever reason, either strategic thinking or personal vendetta, the Bifröst had dropped me on the far northern edges of Jötunheimr's great Ironwood Forest. Thiassi's castle lay directly over the jagged granite daggers of the Iron Mountains, the spine which splits the Ironwood Forest.

I could have flown around the mountains. Shit, I could have shapeshifted into one of my traveling forms, an old woman or a young, hapless warrior, and traveled through the hardscrabble cities that ring those wild lands.

Instead, I flew directly over the mountains. It wasn't that I felt especially eager to reach Thiassi, or Iðunn. The cold desolation of the high mountains just called to me, although the traveling was hard and food was scarce.

At one point in my life, I would have loved that journey. The mountains of Jötunheimr have an untamed beauty all their own, and I've always enjoyed wearing Freyja's falcon cloak. But this trip left me feeling empty, numbed from the cold and dead to the majesty unfolding below me. Even the erotic strands of magic from Freyja's cloak inspired no reaction.

My second night in the mountains, as I huddled against a granite crag and watched a glorious sunset streak the sky with its thousand shades of red and gold, I wondered if I'd ever find anything beautiful again. How could the Nine Realms hold any beauty now, when Anya and Falur were gone?

The falcon form shook as my concentration shattered. I'd flown hard all day with nothing to eat, and my treacherous body chose that moment to rebel. In half a breath, I found myself sitting naked on a sliver of granite, my knees tight to my chest, the air cold enough to freeze the breath streaking out of my nostrils.

I wrapped my head in my arms, letting the wind rip at the feathers of Freyja's cloak. There, where no one in the Nine Realms could possibly see me, I howled for the loss of my beautiful family.

CHAPTER EIGHTEEN

Thiassi's castle reflected the personality of its owner: squat, ugly, and boring. It hunched over a featureless bay a day's flight from the foothills of the Iron Mountains. The vassals who'd been forced to swear their fealty to Thiassi were mostly fishermen, aside from the poor bastards who had to harvest timber from the fringes of the Ironwood, or toil in the gold mines.

Yes, Thiassi's wealth was not due to his business acumen, or even ruthless trading and warring. He was just lucky enough to be born atop the richest gold vein in Jötunheimr, dropped on the fortune like a pile of steaming cow shit.

In the falcon shape, I spun high above his dour castle in great, lazy circles. All the gold in Jötunheimr, I thought, and that architectural monstrosity was the best he could do? The thought that Angrboða had chosen to marry him made my gut churn.

An odd sound stopped me in my circles. I tilted my falcon's head to the side. Someone was singing. A woman, with a delicate, sweet voice that was dimly familiar. Slowly, as though my actions were random and thoughtless as a beast, I dropped closer to the castle. The sound was coming from a very tall tower in the heart of the fortress. The falcon's eyes were strong enough to allow me to make out the woman in the window, even though I was still several paces away.

It was Iðunn. She was trapped in the highest tower of the castle, of course. I rolled my eyes within my falcon shape. What a fucking cliche. Yes, it would have been nigh impossible to storm that room, even with an army, but did Thiassi really have that little imagination?

I took another lazy circle around the castle. Moving closer to the tower allowed me to examine Iðunn in more detail. Her eyes were red and puffy with tears, and her hair was a damn mess, but she didn't look like she'd been damaged. The only thing I couldn't see was her ash wood box. Where the hell were the apples?

Only one way to find out.

After a quick glance around the grounds to see if anyone was tracking my progress, I dove toward the window.

Iðunn didn't even notice me. The castle walls filled my vision. They raced up to meet me as my falcon shape fell like a stone toward the highest tower. Iðunn just sat there, perched on the window sill, singing and running her fingers through her long hair.

Shit.

I couldn't make noise for fear of alerting someone to my presence, so I braced myself for an inevitable collision. At the very last minute, Iðunn looked up, saw what must have appeared to be a suicidal bird of prey barreling toward her, and screamed loudly enough to wake the dead. Iðunn flattened herself against the window frame, allowing me just enough room to crash through the open window and land heavily on the wood floor of her cell.

So much for subtlety.

I shook off the falcon's shape, pulling on my leather armor as I reclaimed my own form, and stood in front of Iðunn. Her cell was sparse but serviceable, with a straw mattress, a rough table and chairs, and a washbasin. An untouched plate of what looked like sausages and eggs sat congealing on the table. I tried not to be too obvious as I scanned the room for the apples.

Ah. There. Iðunn's wooden box was on the floor at her feet, sealed so tightly it may as well have been a solid chunk of ash.

"Loki!" Iðunn spat, her eyes narrowing.

"Hello, Iðunn."

I took a step closer to her, and she shifted away. Once, not so long ago, she'd found me attractive. Now there was nothing but hatred in her gaze. If this room had contained a knife, she probably would have tried to stab me.

"I'm here to rescue you," I said.

"Fuck you!"

"I really don't think there's time."

Iðunn growled something incomprehensible. The swell of distant, angry voices sounded through the heavy wooden door behind her.

"Come on," I said, approaching her again. "Take my hand."

She slid along the wall, away from me. "If you think I'm going anywhere with you, asshole, you're dead wrong!"

I stifled a sigh. The spell to transform Iðunn and her apples into something small and portable was fairly straightforward, but I had to touch her for it to work. And she had to be touching the apples.

The voices sounded again, louder this time. I heard the hollow thud of boots on stairs. Shit. They were coming for Iðunn. Or, more accurately, they were coming for the apples.

"I'm going to take you back to Asgard," I said, as gently as I could manage.

"Go to Niflhel!"

"Shhhh!" I hissed, glancing at the door.

"If you so much as lay a hand on me, you lying bastard, I'll scream my head off!"

I ground my teeth together. By all Nine fucking Realms, I hated references to my parenthood. And Iðunn knew it. They all knew it.

The sound of feet pounding up the staircase grew steadily louder. Mildly desperate, I decided to try a different tact. "Fine. I'm here to rescue you, but fine. If you prefer to stay with Thiassi, I'll leave you with him."

I shifted away from the door and toward the window. Iðunn's gaze followed me, dripping venom.

"You must think I'm a complete idiot to ever trust you again." Tears were starting to well up in her eyes. Never a good sign.

I shrugged, as if it meant nothing to me, and positioned myself halfway between the window and Iðunn's ashwood box.

"Maybe Thiassi will be good to you," I said. "Maybe he's got a thick, enormous, satisfying...heart."

Iðunn sniffed and turned away. Shit, shit, shit! She wasn't taking the bait. The noises coming up the staircase were so close I could almost make out their individual voices. It sounded like a lot of individual voices.

Fine. Elegance and tact be damned.

"I'm taking the apples!" I cried.

I fell to the ground, grabbing for the box. Iðunn screamed more loudly than I would have believed possible. She lunged for her wooden box, snatching it away from my hands. I caught her wrist. She glanced up for a second, her teary eyes swirling with confusion, before the magic enveloped her and she vanished in a cloud of golden dust.

Iðunn and her apples fell to the ground, transformed into a tiny hazelnut with an exceptionally thick shell. The wooden door behind me rattled. Someone screamed Iðunn's name. The bolt on the other side of the door began to slide open with a rusty shriek.

I flexed my arms and shifted into Freyja's falcon shape. With the hazelnut containing Iðunn and her apples firmly in my talons, I shot through the window. Men screamed behind me, and what looked like Iðunn's breakfast plate soared through the air well below me.

Heh. Idiots.

Now that our cover was blown and subtlety had gone out the window as surely as Iðunn's last meal, I tore for the nearest path between the Realms. I'd have precious little time. As soon as word got out Iðunn was gone, Thiassi would be after me.

The magic throbbing around Iðunn's apples made the hazelnut clasped in my talons inordinately heavy. Worse, I could feel Iðunn in there, struggling against the spell. She wouldn't overcome the magic trapping her, but it was distracting.

An enormous roar filled the air behind me, and a rush of wind buffeted my lithe falcon's body.

Fuck me. Thiassi had taken to the air in his thrice-damned eagle form. I had even less time than I'd hoped.

I squeezed my eyes shut, concentrating on the magical currents of Jötunheimr. They weren't strong enough here for me to travel directly through the aether, not with the distracting eddies swirling from Iðunn's hazelnut, but I could sense a pathway nearby. Folding my wings tight to my body, I dove toward the path and pulled the magic around us.

Cold enveloped me as I slipped between worlds, and the falcon's body was immediately rocked by a fierce crosswind. I struggled to stay upright as chill air bit through my feathers. The winds between the worlds pried at my body and tugged at Iðunn's nut as though it could tell what was hidden in there. As though it wanted to claim the apples, and leave them here forever, in the dim, cold netherworld between the Realms.

Another gust of air pushed me down hard, and I strained my wings to rise again. It took much more effort than I expected. Shit, I hated trying to fly in here. The cold winds seemed to seek out illusion, to try to rip it from existence.

A burst of frigid air hit me from the side and I rolled over, the talons holding Iðunn flipping upside-down. For a heartbeat, I lost my connection to Asgard. Trembling, I flapped my wings hard, beating against the currents as I tried to right myself.

Something roared behind me. Thiassi, damn him. The heavy beating of his wings spiked fear through my body, and my connection to Asgard was once again crystal clear. I pushed forward, my muscles burning with the effort, and slipped from the between-place into the clear blue skies of Asgard.

But where in Asgard was I?

My falcon eyes scanned the stony ground beneath me. I couldn't see the gleam of the ocean or the faint, magical glimmer of Val-Hall. I heard nothing; no screams from the warriors, no sounds of chopping wood.

Fuck me sideways. This was Asgard, but Asgard is a big realm. I had no idea where I was.

Trapped in her hazelnut, Iðunn's magic surged. The nut suddenly tripled in weight, pulling me down. A moment later, the air rolled around me as Thiassi's enormous eagle shape burst into Asgard, blotting out the sun above me. I dragged my falcon shape over the rocks, my talons scraping the ground. I had no idea where I was, or where I was going. The nut in my talons rocked again. I picked a direction and decided to run with it. With Thiassi screaming in behind me, I beat the wings of my falcon shape as hard as they could possibly go.

Thiassi's eagle shape was so enormous his wings churned the air currents, buffeting my much smaller falcon's form. I banked sharply to keep from being driven into the ground. Iðunn's nut throbbed with her magic, and my muscles burned from holding her. As I spun to regain control, my falcon's eyes caught the glimmer of light off the water. I dipped and turned toward that thin line of light on the horizon, leaving Thiassi struggling to turn fast enough to catch me.

If it had been a lake or a river, I'd have been truly screwed. I could only spin and duck for so long before Thiassi's massive talons eviscerated me. But it was the ocean, thank the stars. And, squat and heavy just beyond the shimmer of the waves, I saw the dark, enormous walls of Val-hall.

I turned fast, trying to fly as low to the thick shore grass as possible. Sheep and goats panicked before me and ran bleating in every direction. Thisassi was so close the grass bowed down before the wind swirling off his wings. Deep in the nut, Iðunn's apples throbbed with magic. My entire body burned with effort.

Someone along Asgard's ramparts raised the alarm, and voices began to shout. The air around my falcon's body exploded with screams as Thiassi, sensing it was now or never, dove toward me. His shadow engulfed me, and the wind whistled through his talons as they closed the distance between us. My muscles tensed, bracing for the impact of his claws on my throat. Any second now—

At the very last moment, I banked hard. A bolt of fresh pain shot through my body as Thiassi's talons scraped my left wing, freeing several feathers. Crimson blood sprayed through the air.

I beat on, although my flight wobbled. Thiassi couldn't turn as quickly as I, but my evasive spin meant I was now further from Asgard's walls and still far too low to clear them. Straining, I tried to climb into the air. Iðunn's nut seemed to weigh as much as all the Æsir and Vanir put together, or even the whole goddamn ocean. White spots danced across my vision. My lungs burned. Behind me, Thiassi screamed, drowning out the calls of welcome from the walls of Asgard.

Iðunn, I realized. They were screaming her name.

Not mine.

My vision danced and wavered, and a fine mist of hot blood filled the air each time I flexed the wing Thiassi had raked with his claws. But the wall. I was finally higher than the wall. And - I strained my vision to check - yes, a line of firewood was stacked along the inside.

I tucked my wings against my body just as Thiassi reached me. Agony streaked through the falcon's shape as Thiassi tore a clawfull of feathers from my tail. I clamped my eyes shut against the dizzying pain.

Fuck it. I didn't need to fly anymore.

I just needed to fall.

Tilting my beak to the ground, I fell toward Asgard like a stone. The air whistled past my ears, screaming over my injuries. My talons stretched before me, holding Iðunn's nut out like an offering as the grass and sea of Asgard reduced to a blur of color and motion.

When I passed the wall, my body tingled with the wards and warnings. Frantically, I glanced backward. Thiassi was diving behind me, his steely, pale eyes filled with rage. His outstretched talons were almost level with the top of the walls. Almost—

There!

Thiassi's claws brushed the top of the wall, and I set the wood alight. Flames exploded into the clear blue sky. Thiassi tried to correct, to bring his massive body up safely, but it was too late.

He screamed.

That scream pierced me like an arrow. It was nothing like Anya's scream, nothing like the bright, sharp call of rage and pain that had sent me racing across the Realms. And yet—

My bloody, injured falcon's body flailed against the air. I was still dropping like a stone, moving too fast, losing control. My wings refused to work. Iðunn's nut burned against my body, and my talons opened. The nut charm vanished; Iðunn fell to the ground.

Screaming. So much screaming.

"Anya," I moaned.

My falcon shape evaporated. Voices surged below me, cheering and victorious, but not for me. Never for me. The ground swelled up, filling my vision, and I hit hard. Hot, red agony flooded my vision as the arm Thiassi had torn shattered against the stones.

I didn't realize I'd been screaming until the pain made me vomit, and the screaming stopped. Shit. I looked down at my crumpled body, bloody, streaked with soot, and naked in the searing light of the flames. My left arm hung uselessly at my side, a mess of blood and shattered bone.

The sky was streaked with oily smoke, and the flames roared before me. Somewhere in the distance, people were cheering. I squinted against the light, trying to make them out. A row of warriors, their blades shimmering with the heat and light of my fire, stood watch over the flames. Not that there was any chance Thiassi would actually survive this. No, I realized, their presence was more of a show of respect. Like a funeral pyre.

And, yes, there was Iðunn, just beyond the warriors. She stood tall and beautiful against the flames, embracing the Æsir and Vanir or Asgard. Welcomed back by her family.

My gut churned as the pain in my arm blurred my vision. It was all too fucking much. The heat of the flames before me reminded me of another fire, another funeral pyre I'd kept burning for much too long.

I staggered unevenly to my feet, glaring at them all. A few of the Æsir returned my angry stares. None of them rushed forward to help me.

Alcohol. I needed alcohol. The mead of Val-hall cures war injuries. A few sips, and my arm would be restored.

But I sure as hell wouldn't stop at a few sips.

CHAPTER NINETEEN

Oh, fuck.

My eyes opened slowly, and the exposed beams of the ceiling above me pulsed and swirled in welcome. Fuck, I was drunk. Gloriously, gloriously drunk. And— I narrowed my eyes, shutting out the distracting way the room kept spinning. Yes.

Someone was sucking my cock.

Sucking it well.

Fuck. Yes. Someone was down there who knew just what I liked, and they were getting me off quite nicely. My hips rocked forward, filled with the pleasure of being drunk and a gathering tightness in my lower spine which meant I might actually come.

"Falur," I moaned.

Damn, he'd gotten good at this. Why had I waited so long to get well and properly drunk with them? I grinned, picturing the way his eyes must be burning into mine, the curve of those soft lips around the head of my cock. Those lips—

But those lips were cold. Falur's lips were cold, and seawater poured from them as I screamed and pounded on his chest.

Falur was gone.

My eyes flew open as my body stiffened. The lips pressed to my cock paused for a second, then resumed. Pleasure crept slowly through my body as my heart raced and the mead in my stomach shifted uncomfortably. Who the fuck—

"S-Sigyn?" I stammered.

"Try again."

Shit. I knew that voice. I flinched, but my body didn't respond. It was like my arms were made of stone. Stupid. Ah, fuck, I was stupid. Blinking, I rolled my head to the side, trying to force myself to concentrate.

Oh. Ropes. Silvery ropes bound my wrists, and they hummed with magic. It wasn't— I blinked again and tried desperately to focus. It wasn't complicated magic, but— My hips rose and rocked as hands joined lips, tightening around my cock.

"Fuck!" I yelled.

Grinding my teeth together, I forced myself to look down.

Angrboða lay between my legs, wearing a black dress that covered nothing. Her tits flashed as she rose, triumphant, my stiff cock clasped between her fingers.

"You crazy bitch!" I spat.

"Now, now, let's save the pillow talk for your new wife," she purred. "I'm sure she'll be thrilled to hear she was only your second guess."

Angrboða's hand tightened and rolled, making my hips ripple beneath her before I could stop myself.

"What the f-fuck are you doing?" I demanded.

Angrboða's painfully exquisite features composed themselves into the very picture of innocence. "Why, whatever do you mean?"

I flexed my arms, tugging the ropes tight. "You think I can't get out of thish? It's a f-fucking s-s-simple trap."

Angrboða gave me a coy smile. "Darling. Of course you can escape. But right now you're very drunk, you're hard as a stone, and you're about to come."

Her fingers rubbed the head of my cock. A moan slipped from my lips before I could catch it. The room spun and wavered, and my balls tightened. Oh, fuck, no. I could not be this close to coming. Not for her.

"Why?" Damn, my voice sounded fucking terrible. Almost a whimper.

Angrboða rose before me like a black-clad demon. She threw one leg around my side, and her dress engulfed my hips. A heartbeat later, the tight heat of her cunt slid over my cock.

"I need a son," she said.

Her hips rocked against mine. Stars help me, but my body responded. She'd gotten me so close to bursting with her hips and her hands that the embrace of her heat felt damn good.

"No!" I said, despite the way my hips rose to meet hers.

"I do," she panted. "The last seed you planted... didn't take. I need this, damn it."

She dug her fingers into my scalp. I tried to flinch, but she grabbed my hair, pulling it tight. A hot wave of pleasure washed over my body.

"A son," she continued. "A son with...your magic...and Thiassi's gold. A son like that... could rule...all of Jötunheimr."

Her breath was coming short and fast now. Some distant, disconnected part of my brain noted that what really got Angrboða off was the thought of ruling Jötunheimr. Not riding my cock.

"It won't work," I said, trying to lift my knees enough to buck her off. Rope bit into my ankles as I pulled. Damn all the Nine Realms, she'd tied my legs up too.

"You can't rule Jötunheimr, you dumb cunt!" I screamed.

Her hand tightened in my hair. "Shut up."

I bit down on my tongue, trying to fight the way the entire room was now sliding in and out of focus to the rhythm of Angrboða's relentless, black-clad hips.

"They'll never let a woman rule," I gasped.

Heat began to gather at the base of my spine, tingling in anticipation. I rocked my head back, hitting the ground so hard that white spots danced across my vision. Angrboða's hand pulled at my hair, keeping me from doing it again. A thin strand of pain worked its way into the pleasure, heightening and intensifying the dark ecstacy of her body.

"Regent," she panted. "For... Thiassi's son."

"It's...he won't be...not Thiassi's."

The room was positively swaying now, sinking into an alcohol-blurred haze of sex and pleasure. I tried to fight the swelling pressure rising inside me, but I may as well have tried to beat back the tide with my daggers.

"Oh, fuck me—" My words vanished as the wave of my orgasm crashed over me, inexorable and crushing as the sea. I screamed as my cock pulsed inside Angrboða, but it wasn't in pleasure.

Angrboða thrust against me as my cock throbbed, grinding her body into mine. The push of her hips began to shift the ocean of mead in stomach, until I felt the sting of bile against the back of my throat. I had enough time to think how perfect it would be if I could throw up all over her tits when she sank her fingernails into my scalp and gave a sharp, harshly victorious cry. Angrboða's orgasm closed around me, her body clenching tight, sucking my seed deep inside her. The motion of our bodies slowed, leaving me to catch my breath is short, strangled gasps.

"Oh, by all the shit-smeared Realms, Loki," Angrboða panted. "Are you fucking crying?"

I froze, grasping at the strands of magic wrapped around my body. They hummed and buzzed around me, spinning crazily. Fuck being drunk. Had I let my illusions slip? I opened my mouth to yell at her, to distract her.

"You vile, treacherous bitch! My family died because of you!"

Shit. That wasn't at all what I'd intended to say.

The stunned look of confusion that flitted across Angrboða's exquisite features told me what a horrible mistake I'd just made.

Angrboða hardly ever left Jötunheimr. She could care less about what happened on Midgard.

She hadn't known about Anya and Falur.

"Your family!" I yelled, quickly correcting myself. "Your family died because of you! Thiassi died because of you!"

Angrboða's features hardened. "Well, at least my dearly departed husband left me pregnant."

My stomach rolled, and I yanked at the ropes around my wrists. "No one is going to believe Thiassi got you pregnant."

Angrboða rocked backward, sliding off my cock. "I don't really care what they believe. Thiassi died with no son, married to me. My belly will swell a reasonable time after his death. It will be in everyone's best interest to accept the child as Thiassi's."

She shrugged as she pulled her black skirts off my prone body. "And, if this seed doesn't take, I'll just come back next month and fuck you again."

The room spun. Sour mead rose again in the back of my mouth. I gagged.

"Mind the dress, dear," Angrboða said as she rose. "It's very expensive."

I tried to hit her with my vomit, but she moved away too quickly. I thought Angrboða would leave me like that, naked, tied up, and gagging on my own regurgitated mead, but she paused in the doorway. From my position on the floor, Angrboða towered over me. The pale curve of her tits looked as enormous as the mountains I'd crossed in Jötunheimr.

"One more thing," Angrboða said, looking down at me as if I were something smeared across the bottom of her shoe. "Thiassi's daughter Skadi is raising an army. She intends to invade Asgard as retribution for her beloved, murdered father."

"Fuck off," I spat.

Angrboða's blood red lips curled into a downright predatory smile. "Óðinn can buy her off. Give her a husband as a peace treaty, and she'll leave well enough alone. She's been lusting after Baldr the Beautiful since she first grew tits."

"Fuck...off!" I yelled. The effect was probably ruined somewhat by the vomit streaking down my chest.

"Oh, and do give my very best regards to your new wife. Sigyn, was it?"

I tried to hide the shiver that ran the length of my exhausted, abused body. Sigyn's delicate features flashed across my memory. Damn it, she didn't deserve to be on Angrboða's shit list. She didn't deserve any of this.

"You know, legal paternity notwithstanding, I'm sure rumors will swirl about this child. And won't your Sigyn be just delighted to hear the whispers saying you've already fathered another child with me?" Angrboða curled her arms around her flat abdomen as though it had already begun to grow with pregnancy.

"I think I'll name him Fenris," she said.

Angrboða took the torch from the wall as she left, plunging me into darkness.

IT WOULD HAVE BEEN a mercy to pass out, to let myself forget what had just happened and drift into unconsciousness, at least for a few hours. But my body did not grant those mercies. Instead, I fought to loosen the magically enhanced ropes around my wrists and ankles and tried to ignore the way the room spun in and out of focus.

The ropes weren't complicated, just as Angrboða had said. But I was very drunk, and the brief time I'd spent passed out in this dark room hadn't done much to relieve the bone-deep exhaustion I felt after narrowly escaping from Thiassi. On top of that, I found it inordinately hard to concentrate when my mind kept insisting on replaying images of Angrboða's black-clad body writhing above me.

Slowly, as I struggled with the magic holding the knots taut, sunlight began to swell through the cracks between the planks of the little room where I'd been bound. The light shimmered all around me in dull, vertical shafts. My numbed brain finally registered the bands of light as swords, neatly stacked along their racks. Angrboða had dragged me into one of the warrior's storage sheds.

A room full of deadly weapons. Fucking perfect for that psychotic bitch.

Actually, the racks of swords lifted my spirits. At first, I'd been afraid Angrboða had taken me to Jötunheimr. But if this dusty shack actually was what it appeared to be, then I was still on Asgard.

Things were looking up.

With a low slithering, the ropes finally let go of my wrists. A second later, my ankles were also free. Groaning, I pushed myself up to sitting. My back was raw with scrapes, and probably more than a few deep splinters. My gut still churned, and my arms and legs trembled. I had to expend more energy than I expected just getting to my feet.

Staggering, I tried to remember the last time I'd actually eaten something. Incoherent, blurry flashes of the previous night came back to me. The hard faces of the Æsir and Vanir staring me down as I dragged myself toward Val-Hall. Ashes floating through the air. Thiassi's scream as my flames burst upward, catching the wings of his eagle form.

And then drinking. Lots of drinking.

I remembered falling down in the middle of Val-hall, the floorboards smacking my face. Someone pulled me back onto my feet. Was it Thor? I shook my head. It didn't matter.

Another image surfaced, one of all the Æsir and Vanir watching me, their mouths open in shock or horror. I remembered feeling quite pleased with myself, like I'd said something extremely clever. And had I punched someone? I flexed my right hand; my knuckles ached.

Great. I had punched someone.

I bit my lip and searched through the tatters of my memory. Another image floated up, this time two women with amazing tits. No, only one woman. I'd wanted to drown in that cleavage, and she'd led me out of the room. Angrboða, of course, although I'd hardly been in any state to recognize her.

Before that, damn it.

Music. Halting, obnoxious music. Ah, shit. It all came back to me in a flood, and my raw, emptied stomach churned again. Iðunn's insipid husband Bragi had already composed a ballad about her victorious return to Asgard, but he'd fucked up the beginning. Instead of starting with Iðunn and her apples, or my attempts at seduction, he told some far-fetched story about a long journey with Óðinn and that misfit Hœnir. Apparently, at some point in that imagined journey, I was abducted by Thiassi in his eagle form, and I offered Thiassi Iðunn's apples in exchange for my own worthless skin.

My head began to throb as the details of the song reverberated through my skull. Bragi had spent a very long time detailing exactly how the dull and stupid Thiassi had gotten the drop on Loki the Lie-smith, and how he'd threatened and abused me in his eagle form. The fact that none of it had actually happened didn't bother me that much. Even in my painfully inebriated state, I could sense it might be for the best if all of Asgard didn't know about Anya and Falur. No, verisimilitude wasn't the problem.

It was the way they laughed.

Every verse - and there seemed to be hundreds of them - described some new, imagined torment inflicted upon me by the eagle Thiassi. He smashed me against the side of a mountain. He dragged me through an icy mountain river. He dropped me, ass first, into the spikey top of a pine tree. The very walls of Val-hall shook with Æsir and Vanir laughter.

My memories went blurry after that. I remembered swaggering up to Bragi, silence falling across the hall as I shouted at the Æsir, hurling insults. Bragi and I swung at each other, and I went down. I remembered staring at the grit embedded in the floorboards before someone hauled me up. Thor? An image of his bearded face swirled through my memory, dull and hazy.

"I think you should go home," he'd said.

Were we outside at that point? We must have been, because I remembered the way the moonlight shone on his hair.

"Look, we're all sorry for what happened on Midgard." Thor must have been trying to whisper; it sounded instead like someone was choking him. "Why don't you go home, sober up. I'll come visit you later."

Had he tried to kiss me? I couldn't remember. At any rate, I'd pushed him away, insisting I was perfectly fine, and I was far from finished drinking. I'd shouted something about having just as much right to the mead of Asgard as any of the rest of them.

Groaning, I wiped my hands across my face. The rest of the evening was a jumble of indistinct images and flashes, aside from the swell of the enormous, pale breasts on the woman who finally dragged me out of Val-hall. Fuck, it was obvious in retrospect. How had I not known she was Angrboða?

With a sigh, I glanced down at my body. Naked, filthy, streaked with mead and vomit, with dark bands of purple bruises blossoming around my wrists and ankles. I was pathetic, and rapidly approaching sobriety. My head throbbed. At this point, all I wanted to do was soak myself in the boiling pools of Asgard's hot springs, possibly for days. Tentatively, I reached for the latent strands of magic humming through Asgard and spun my illusions, making myself look healthy and clean and well-attired.

It took more energy than I'd have liked. My gut growled in displeasure. Really, how long had it been since I'd eaten? I remembered picking the flesh from a skinny marmot somewhere in the Iron Mountains in Jötunheimr.

Fuck, was that it?

A wave of nausea swept over me, and I bit hard, gritting my teeth against the impulse to heave out my empty stomach. There was no way around it; I had to eat soon, or I'd be completely worthless.

Well, with any luck, I could slip into Val-hall without anyone noticing.

CHAPTER TWENTY

The sun was still low on the horizon when I crept from the weapon storage sheds and walked toward Val-hall. The poor warrior bastards who'd been left behind on the training grounds after the battles were just stirring awake, moaning and wondering why no one brought them mead last night so they could heal and drink with the others, but no one else was up and about. Thank the stars.

The scent of food wafting through Val-hall's wide doors made my stomach clench painfully. I grabbed the first flagon I saw, reflexively downing the entire serving of mead. The sweet alcohol burned my throat and made my gut shift unpleasantly, but it also eased the worst of the hangover pounding behind my temples. Another flagon or three would help even more, I knew from long experience. But first, food. I took a platter of brown bread, new potatoes, and boiled eggs, and vanished behind a column to devour it in the shadows. Maybe one or two more flagons of mead after this, and I'd be ready to—

"But you certainly didn't have to marry him!"

I froze in mid-bite. That was Iðunn's voice, damn it. Aside from Angrboða, I couldn't think of a single person in all Nine Realms I'd be less happy to see this particular morning.

"My dear, you know you can have the agreement annulled. Just say you haven't consummated the marriage. Or, I don't know, claim he's impotent."

Another voice murmured something indistinct. A cold sense of foreboding began to pool in my stomach, sitting uncomfortably close to the half dozen boiled eggs I'd just inhaled.

"I wanted to reach out to you as soon as I heard," Iðunn continued. "I just can't imagine how horrible this all must be for you. I mean, you did hear how drunk he got last night?"

No response from Iðunn's companion. Iðunn continued undeterred.

"I'd be surprised if he even managed to make it home." There was an ominous pause. "He did make it home, didn't he?"

"Of course. My husband is just fine."

Shit, shit, shit. That was Sigyn's voice. Lying, on my behalf. I stood frozen, a hunk of brown bread halfway to my lips, and wondered how the hell I could get out of this one, when Iðunn and Sigyn turned the corner and almost ran directly into me.

"Loki!" Iðunn spat. Her features curdled into a snarl.

I glanced down reflexively to see if she was carrying a weapon. No, her hands just held her box of apples, although the way she gripped that hunk of wood made me wonder how it would feel if she decided to bring it down on my skull.

"A fine morning to you, Iðunn," I said.

"You pathetic, lying—" Iðunn growled.

"Husband," Sigyn said, warmly. Her face broke into a wide smile that I guessed was entirely for Iðunn's benefit.

Sigyn stepped forward, putting her hand on my arm. "I believe I'm done here. Would you be willing to take us home?"

I nodded, as much in surprise as agreement.

"I do thank you for your concerns, Iðunn," Sigyn said, with that same warm smile plastered across her face. "Loki and I are quite happy together. And we're all so glad you're home."

Together Sigyn and I watched the blood drain from Iðunn's shocked face. Stars help me, I couldn't help pushing it just a bit further.

"Oh, Iðunn, there is one thing I didn't get the chance to say last night," I said.

Iðunn's eyes narrowed in suspicion.

"You're welcome," I said. "For rescuing you."

With that, I pulled the magic tight around my body. A heartbeat later, Sigyn and I were standing on the gentle slope of the beach outside her little cabin. Her eyebrows raised.

"You didn't take us inside," she said. Her voice was much softer now that it was just the two of us.

"I didn't want to presume."

She fell silent. Her hand still pressed against my arm. The air between us seemed to thicken, as thought it had taken on a weight all its own.

"Sigyn," I said, my voice halting. "About last night. I—I'm sorry."

"Don't." She spun to face me. "Please, don't. I don't want you to apologize."

"You didn't need to lie—"

"Hush," she said.

I opened my mouth, found nothing to say, and closed it again. Silence stretched between us. Sigyn's soft, caramel colored eyes moved over my face slowly, as though she were seeing me for the first time. Her expression gave no hint as to what she thought. My heart rattled in its cage as my mind spun.

Sigyn raised her hand in the space between us. When I didn't flinch, she brought her fingertips gently to my lips.

"I was there.". Her voice was so low it was almost a whisper. "When the dwarves sewed your lips shut. I saw it happen."

I couldn't stop the shudder that ran through my body. That was the price of Thor's hammer, the mighty Mjölnir. That was my punishment for cutting Sif's hair. I'd gone to the dwarves to find a replacement for Sif's golden locks, and I'd made a rash, stupid bet, promising my own head if the Æsir weren't impressed with what the dwarves made. When the dwarves won the bet, I'd looked to Óðinn for help. And he had helped me, I suppose. I just hadn't expected his help to arrive in the form of getting my own lips sewed shut.

"You hide them well," she said, "the scars on your lips."

I said nothing. Those weren't the only scars I hid.

Her hand moved to cup my cheek. "I kept thinking about you, after that day. How you had no place to go. No one to care for you."

"So, you wanted to care for me?"

My back stiffened as I tried to hide the distaste that curled my lips. What an extremely unpleasant thought.

"No!" Sigyn snapped.

She stepped away, her eyes flashing. A flush almost as dark as the plum colored, high-necked dress she wore crept into her cheeks. Her chest rose and fell quickly, as if she'd been running. The breeze rising off the ocean mingled with a different scent, the sweet tang of a woman's wet and ready sex.

Ah. Of course. Women could be so predictable.

I didn't especially feel like fucking. After what Angrboða did to me in the shed, I honestly wasn't sure I'd ever feel like fucking again. And I was filthy and exhausted, although I could count on my illusions to hide both those facts.

Angrboða's blood red lips surfaced in my memory, her self-satisfied sneer as she spat out the name of my new wife. My hand clenched into a fist. Sigyn didn't deserve that. She didn't deserve any of the shit I'd brought into her life.

But she did find me attractive. That much was obvious. At least I could give her something in return. I leaned toward Sigyn, bending to brush her lips with mine. I was already planning my next step, sweeping her into my arms and carrying her to the bed like a proper husband.

"Stop."

I froze. Sigyn stepped backward, so I'd have to cross the space between us to reach her for a kiss. The wind gusted, and the scent of her arousal swirled around me. I wondered if she knew how obvious her attraction to me was. I stepped toward her, ready to wrap my arms around her waist.

"Don't," she said. She knotted her fingers together and glanced at the ocean, the sky, her cottage, looking everywhere but at me.

"You don't want me?" I asked.

Her cheeks reddened even further, burning against her pale skin. "I want you," she said in a voice so low it may as well have been the wind.

Well, what the fuck? I stood in front of her, my illusions smiling seductively, with no idea of what to do next. She'd lied to Iðunn on my behalf. She welcomed me when Óðinn dropped me on her doorstep like garbage, she found me attractive enough to make her heart race and her sex slick, but she stepped away from my embrace?

Stars, what an odd woman she was.

Silence pulled taut between us, as vast, cold, and unbridgeable as the ocean. I'd just begun to think Sigyn would prefer it if I'd vanish when she sighed, clenched her hands into a ball, and spoke.

"I loved a man on Midgard."

Her voice was thin and halting, as though the words were being pulled from somewhere deep inside her. She took another step backward. The hem of her dark dress brushed the tangle of rose bushes behind her. I noted her use of the past tense, but dared not point it out. The moment between us seemed too fragile.

Sigyn stared at the ocean. "His name was Ragnavaldr. He was a fisherman, in Sweorice."

Silence again.

"I know Sweorice," I said, as gently as I could manage. Technically, I supposed Anya and Falur's village had fallen within Sweorice's borders.

Her chest rose and fell several times in rapid succession. "It wasn't just a...a fling. I loved him. I would have married him."

Past tense again. This time I said nothing. The early morning sun made the tears welling in her eyes sparkle, but they did not fall down her cheeks.

"He got sick. It was an infection, from a cut he got on his boat. Such a little cut, on the bottom of his foot." She laughed, although it came out as more of a strangled sob. "When his fever soared, and he started to hallucinate, I ran back to Asgard. I requested a council of the Æsir, and I...I begged. I begged Iðunn for one of her apples."

Sigyn pressed the backs of her hands against her cheeks. I remembered the glare on Iðunn's face this morning, and I could guess how well that particular request had gone over.

"They laughed at me," Sigyn whispered. "All of them. They just...laughed. By the time I made it back to Midgard, Ragnavaldr's body was cold."

My chest felt tight, as though I were experiencing Sigyn's grief myself. "I'm sorry," I said, knowing the words meant nothing.

A tremor rippled through Sigyn's small frame. "Óðinn offered me my choice of a husband. He came to me as I stood over Ragnavaldr's grave and promised I could choose any of the them, Æsir or Vanir, anyone I wanted. As if that were some sort of recompense. At the time, I swore I'd never love anyone again."

I shifted uncomfortably. My temples throbbed, and my mouth felt as dry as the sand beneath our feet. Sigyn took several deep, gulping breaths, ran her fingers through the long waves of her auburn hair, and turned to me again. A shy smile crept across her face. The expression was Realms apart from the pained cheer she'd used on Iðunn this morning.

"I didn't even think to steal the apples," she said.

I was surprised to find myself smiling back at her, as though we'd just shared some private joke.

"That didn't exactly work out well for me," I pointed out.

Her smile widened, and she stepped closer, closing the distance between us without actually touching me.

"I do want you, Loki," she said. "But not now. Please, only kiss me when you actually want to kiss me."

"And if that doesn't happen?"

Her expression hardened. I instantly regretted my words. I hadn't realized how harsh they would sound. The shared warmth of that smile evaporated; again, the distance between us seemed unbridgeable.

"It was almost one hundred years before I approached Óðinn," Sigyn said, "and told him I was ready to request my husband. But I didn't ask him to drop you in my lap. I expected there'd be some courtship, some—"

Sigyn's voice choked, and she shook her head. She pulled away from me, turning her back before I could catch her expression. Her delicate shoulders rose and fell as she opened her arms in an expansive gesture, encompassing the ocean, the beach, and the snug little cottage nestled among the wild roses.

"This is your home, now. Come here when you need a place to rest. Or to hide." She turned to face me. "And, if wife is too much, perhaps we can settle on friend?"

My shoulders dropped. Of all the things she'd said, the word *rest* was what tugged at me. "It's...more than I deserve," I said.

"It's not."

Her smile faltered as her gaze met mine. Her brown irises swam with little golden flecks, I realized. Her eyes were nothing like Anya's, which had been almost as translucent as ice. Or Falur's, so dark they were almost black.

No, Sigyn's eyes were unlike anything I'd seen before. Much like the rest of her.

"I'm going for a walk," Sigyn said. "If the bedroom door is closed when I return, I'll see you're not disturbed."

I gave her a polite nod. It didn't seem right to flee into the little house until I was alone, so I stood on the beach and watched her walk across the dunes.

The roar of the ocean filled the air, punctuated by the calls of shorebirds, and the rising sun caught in the long strands of her auburn hair and danced over the dark ripples of her long skirt. The vision of another long-haired woman walking along the beach came back to me with the force of a kick to the gut. A strong, beautiful, sensual woman who had loved me, and died for it.

At least I made it into the rose bushes, and out of Sigyn's sight, by the time I started to vomit again.

CHAPTER TWENTY ONE

I woke into darkness.

The pounding behind my temples had subsided, but my body still felt weak. Blinking, I tried to make sense of my surroundings. Something dark covered my chest and spread over my legs. A lance of panic shot through my chest, and I nearly jumped out of the bed.

No. No, it wasn't Angrboða.

Panting, with my heart hammering in my ears, I tried to swallow that sudden, irrational surge of panic. For fuck's sake, I wasn't tied up on the floor of a weapons storage shed. I was in the middle of a large, comfortable bed, covered with dark furs. Thick curtains hid the windows. Curtains I remembered pulling shut.

I reached out for the strands of magic, checking the cantrips I'd laid around the bed. They were undisturbed. Sigyn must not have even cracked the door open to check if I was still here. Trusting, maybe. Or just unconcerned. For a heartbeat I wondered which quality I'd prefer in my new wife.

Pulling my illusions tight around my body, I slipped from the bed and opened a curtain. The silent darkness beyond Sigyn's windows was thick as velvet. A thin sliver of moon hung low over the slowly undulating waves.

It was nice here, I had to admit. Much nicer than my own crumbling shack. Idly, I scratched at the back of my neck. The boiling hot spring of Asgard would be perfect right now. In the darkness, with no company, I could let go of all my illusions. The thought was so appealing I began to finger the latent magic in the house, preparing to slide through the aether and submerge myself in the water for days.

But my stomach growled in protest. First, food.

I'd only been in Sigyn's house twice, both times painfully hungover, but I'd gotten the basic layout. A luxurious bedroom. A cheerful kitchen. And a main hall with a fireplace, which was where Óðinn had first dumped me.

The bedroom door opened silently, and I padded through the darkness of the main hall. A small hearthfire flared to life when I entered the kitchen. Something rustled in the corner. I froze as my heart leapt into my mouth. Angrboða's dark skirts filled my memory, and my fingers curled into a fist. I turned slowly, ready to drive my hand through someone's face.

At first, I saw nothing. Then my eyes adjusted, and I made out the figure sprawled on the bench by the fireside.

Sigyn. She was sleeping out here.

I could have smacked myself. Of course she didn't have another bedroom. I'd have to fix that little problem before I spent another night here. I walked to the kitchen table, watching Sigyn out of the corner of my eye. Most of her body was covered with a thick, dark blanket. But the blanket had slipped off her feet. Her bare toes looked pale and delicate against the wall.

My fingers ran along the smooth surface of the kitchen table, noting the faint hum of magic. I took my time admiring the neat spell. Sigyn's understated table was covered with elegant incantations, linking it to Asgard's kitchens. It didn't feel like Óðinn's magic. In fact, it felt like nothing I'd encountered before; beautifully functional, and deceptively simple. It looked like all I had to do was place my hands against the table—

I leaned forward, resting my weight against the wooden surface. A plate of roasted pork belly topped with pickled mushrooms and leeks appeared before me, filling the room with a scent that made my mouth water. Four thick slices of rye bread appeared next, and a full flagon of mead. I waited, still leaning against the table, until a third plate appeared holding a baked apple topped with cream.

Damn. Very nice.

I leaned back, slid the rye bread onto the roast, and balanced the apple on top of everything else. I cast a longing glance at the mead, but decided it would be too difficult to carry. Once I'd picked up the plate and stepped back from the table, the mead and empty bread platter vanished, leaving the surface once again smooth and clear. Impressive. I reached for the strands of magic that always hummed through Asgard, then glanced again at Sigyn on her bench by the hearth.

Before I traveled through the aether to the hot spring, I pulled the blanket up and over her bare feet.

RAIN.

Cold rain, and lots of it. The kind that feels like someone is standing just above you, dumping a bucket directly on your head. I frowned down at my plate in the weak light of the setting crescent moon. The rye bread was clearly a lost cause. The pork roast was already soaked, the sauce running off the meat in watery streams, and the pickled mushrooms and leeks appeared to be floating. I grabbed the meat off my plate and ate it anyway, rainwater and all. Then I finished the baked apple, although the cold rainwater did nothing to improve its flavor. The rest of the meal I flicked back to Asgard.

Despite the rain, the sulfur scent of the hot spring hung heavy over the black volcanic rocks. I tried to convince myself the pouring rain was an asset. At least no one else was likely to be here, soaking in the waters.

But it was the middle of the thrice-damned night, and this was the least accessible spring in Asgard. I knew no one else was here. No one else was ever here.

Still, I glanced behind a few of the larger boulders and did a quick check of the latent magical strands for any disturbances before shrugging off my clothes. I slipped into the steaming waters, sinking in up to my chin. The incessant downpour had fucked up the hot springs, making the top layer too cold. I curled my lip in frustration, then checked behind me one last time.

No one there. I was alone.

With a sigh, I let go of my illusions. The water felt different without the buffer of my magic, both hotter on my legs and colder against my chest and shoulders. I dunked my head, scooping handfuls of sand from the bottom of the pool to rub against my scarred skin. It hurt, but I ignored the pain. Angrboða's black skirts loomed in my memory, and I scrubbed gritty handfuls of sand into my thighs and stomach until my skin felt raw and angry.

There. Good enough. I kicked off the bottom and let myself drift into the center of the pool, where the scalding waters boiled up from the fiery realm of Múspell. Cold rain ran down my face and shoulders in sheets while the heat of the springs nearly burned my legs. I was suspended like an insect encased in a chunk of amber, trapped between worlds.

Fuck this. I dunked my head again and dove, letting the heat of the spring's volcanic source wash over me. When the heat increased enough to cause actual pain, I renewed my illusions and kicked upwards, turning my face to the wash of frigid rain falling from the darkened sky.

I needed a place like this. One that was protected from the rain. Floating on my back with my eyes closed against the rain's onslaught, another memory surfaced. Thor and I had spent several intensely memorable nights on Jötunheimr with a warlord named Thrym.

Thrym's private quarters, with which Thor and I were now very well acquainted, boasted a bathroom with an enormous, sunken pool of bubbling hot water.

I kicked myself back to the shore, wiping rain from my eyes. Yes, that was exactly the kind of place I needed. It wouldn't be complicated to link a pool to this hot springs. I could use the same technique Óðinn and I had used to link the tables to Asgard to provide food. Or how I'd connected the flagons in my stone hut to Val-hall's mead.

My chest pinched as I inhaled sharply. I pressed my hands to my eyes until the pressure hurt, then tugged myself through the aether and into my own cabin in Asgard.

My cabin was dark and cold. I shook my hair dry, then lit the hearth fires. Ugh. This place looked especially pathetic after waking up in Sigyn's neat little cottage. The floor and table were heaped with shit I'd shifted here without bothering to find any of it a proper place, usually because I was too drunk to bother. It was clothing, mostly, in various states of cleanliness. Or decomposition. Wrinkling my nose, I kicked a few empty bottles out of the way.

Something sparkled in the firelight, and I bent down to examine it. It was a delicate golden diadem sprinkled with diamonds. I ran my fingers over the glimmering stones, trying to remember where the hell this had come from.

Ah. Yes. It adorned the head of a princess from Álfheim, the member of an especially lovely delegation of elves. And this diadem had been the last item of clothing I removed from her body, if I remembered correctly. I grinned. This would look good on Anya.

Would have, I correctly myself. My grin evaporated as a cold fist closed around my chest. The crown would have looked good on Anya.

I stood, tossing the useless trinket back onto the floor. Something cold splattered against the back of my neck, and I looked up, scowling. The roof was leaking. Fantastic. With a slight tug of the magical energies in the house, I repaired that leak, and the half-dozen others I found. Then I made a slow circle around the cluttered, cold, and damp single room of my quarters on Asgard.

Had I really thought to bring Anya and Falur here? This place wasn't even fit for livestock. For centuries, I'd deliberately kept it disheveled, afraid of stirring the ire of the Æsir and Vanir.

Or perhaps I just didn't want to get too comfortable on Asgard.

I rolled my shoulders with a sigh. I could fix this house up, of course. It would just take time, and energy, and the will. A vision of Sigyn's cottage swam in my vision, with its extremely comfortable bed and curtains so thick you couldn't tell if it was night or day. She'd said that was my home, now. It didn't feel quite right, but perhaps I could start there. I could make something for Sigyn, something to thank her for making me look good in front of Iðunn. And, I rationalized, I could always fix up my own place later.

With a plan in mind, I pulled myself through the aether and back to Sigyn's darkened kitchen. She was still asleep on the bench, but she'd turned onto her back. She still wore the high-necked plum dress, but it lay pressed against her body, revealing her delicate curves. Her small breasts rose and fell with her deep, even breathing. I slowly realized I was smiling as I watched her eyes flutter beneath her closed lids.

I did feel something for her, it seemed. Not love. Not the undeniable tide of lust that had pulled me to Anya, or even the spark of sexual attraction that had flared so unexpectedly between me and Falur. But something.

Sigyn shifted, and I sank into the shadows. If I worked quickly, perhaps I could surprise her when she woke.

I MADE THE SECOND BEDROOM first. That was by far the easiest. I added it to the hallway between the bedroom and kitchen, just a simple door leading to a room barely wider than the hall. I pulled a narrow, single mattress for the bed, added a few candles, and finished with a flagon linked to Val-hall's mead. My one concession to artistry was a window the size of the entire far wall.

Not bad, I thought, tilting my head at the vista. The rain that had poured over me in the hot spring had worked its way down to the beach, and it beat against the walls of Sigyn's cottage in relentless waves. The moon had set, and I could barely make out the dark, hulking shapes of the dunes, and the dimly phosophresing breakers beyond the beach.

Yes, not bad at all. I could be comfortable here, sitting on this bed, drinking mead and watching the ocean. What was it Sigyn had said to me this morning? A place to rest, or to hide. Yes. This would do.

But it wasn't the surprise I wanted to offer Sigyn.

For that, I created a door next to her bedroom. This room I made larger, almost as large as the main hall. I used rough stones for these walls, to make it feel like the hot spring, and I lined the deep pool with sand from the dunes outside her cottage. I briefly considered another enormous window, but Sigyn's long sleeved, high necked dresses made me think she may not want to be naked in front of an enormous window.

So I made the ceiling transparent instead. I glanced up to see a haze of clouds drift across the star-filled sky. The rain stopped just above my head, leaving me warm and dry.

Perfect. Fucking perfect.

The trickiest part would be linking the hot springs to this pool. I paused, pulling a flagon of mead from Val-hall to sip while I contemplated my next move. It wasn't quite as simple as making a flagon which refilled, like I'd done in the cottage I built for Anya and

Falur. I'd want the water to flow in and out at a steady rate, and the temperature should stay constant, no matter what was happening at the hot spring outside.

I drained the flagon, took a deep breath, and worked my magic. The sulfur scent of Asgard's hot spring rose to fill the air, and steam breathed into the air around me. With a grin, I lit the beeswax candles I'd places along the edge of the pool. As I'd hoped, their sweetness provided a decent counterpoint to the sulfurous stench of the water.

Good. It was very good. I pulled another flagon of mead to celebrate, and took a step back to admire the room I'd just created.

But the mead rolled over in my stomach as I stared at the glimmers of candlelight reflecting in the still, hot waters. This bath wasn't built for one person. Shit. I had made this place for three people. My vision blurred, and I tossed the flagon aside to press my palms against my eyes.

I hadn't made this for Sigyn at all. I'd made a private hot spring for my dead lovers. Something bitter rose in the back of my throat, and for a moment I contemplated tearing the whole place down, scattering stones and candles and sand across the Nine Realms.

Breathing deeply, I lowered my hands from my eyes. The sky above me was streaked with the pale, delicate filaments of dawn. It was impossibly, painfully beautiful. The very beauty of it felt like an insult, or an injustice.

No, it wasn't enough to tear down the room I'd made. I wanted to tear everything down. I wanted to burn all Nine Realms, to destroy the universe that no longer contained my beautiful family. The family I'd wanted to bring to Asgard.

I shivered despite the steamy warmth of the room. My Anya and Falur, the little babe we would have raised together. I'd never asked them if they wanted to live on Asgard, among the Æsir and Vanir's constant, tiresome plotting and shifting alliances. I never asked if they wanted to abandon their families, their entire realm, to live with me in my filthy cottage with the leaking roof.

Just like I hadn't asked Sigyn if she wanted a private hot spring off her bedroom.

I sank to the floor and let my head drop between my legs. The heat of the water and the thick scent of the candles was almost uncomfortable. The steam made me feel like I was suffocating. I'd have to tear it down, then. Build it up and tear it down. Story of my fucking life—

A sudden, explosive bang sounded through the room. I jumped, wiping my cheeks with the back of my hand. What the fuck?

It came again, a rattling boom that echoed through the entire house. This time I heard Sigyn call something in response, and I tore through the aether to materialize in the main hall, daggers in both my fists. Who in the Nine fucking Realms just woke my wife?

The boom sounded a third time. This time I recognized it; someone was banging on the door. Someone who felt like he owned the place, and was just a few steps away from breaking down the thrice-damned door.

"Óðinn?" I yelled.

Óðinn pulled open the door just as Sigyn entered the room, her dark blanket still wrapped around her shoulders.

"Sorry to interrupt," Óðinn said. He raised an eyebrow at the daggers clenched in both my fists. "It looks like you and Sigyn are getting on."

"Good morning, All-father," Sigyn said in a voice that did not sound particularly welcoming.

"Why are you here?" I said.

Óðinn fixed his lone, pale eye on me. "We've got a problem."

I narrowed my eyes. Angrboða's blood red lips flashed in my memory, grinning above the pale curve of her exposed breasts.

"Thiassi's daughter," I guessed.

Óðinn nodded. "Her name is—"

"Skadi," I finished. "She's raising an army?"

Óðinn's lips pressed into a thin white line. Not a good sign. "You'd better come with me," he said.

I turned to Sigyn. Her auburn hair drifted in a messy tangle around her sleep-blurred face. It occurred to me that, if it weren't for my intrusion into her life, she would have spent the night in her own bed. And she wouldn't have been awoken at dawn by Óðinn practically banging her door down.

There seemed to be many things I needed to say to her, not the least of which was a warning that her house now contained two additional rooms, but I wasn't sure where to begin. She met my gaze with a soft, sleepy smile.

"Be careful," Sigyn whispered.

It was the same thing she'd said before I left to rescue Iðunn. And once again, I couldn't think of an appropriate response. I nodded to her in silence and took Óðinn's hand, letting him pull me across the aether.

"SHIT," I SPAT.

Óðinn and I were huddled against the cold on a bluff overlooking Skadi's war encampment. We were disguised as two old beggar women. It was not the Realm's most comfortable disguise. And nothing about the panorama before me made me feel any better.

It had only been a handful of days since Thiassi died in the flames inside Asgard's walls, and already Skadi had managed to raise over a hundred soldiers. Worse than that, though, was the formidable size of the encampment. The existing troops took up less than a quarter of the space that had been cleared and organized in tight, military squares.

"How many legions pledged their loyalty to Thiassi?" I whispered. It didn't seem likely we'd be overheard, but something about spying on a massive military camp make me feel like whispering.

Óðinn laughed. It sounded bitter. "How much gold is in Thiassi's vault?"

I chewed on that for a while. This was bad. The Æsir and Vanir of Asgard are strong warriors but, if the armies of Jötunheimr united against us, it would be one hell of a fight. It wouldn't be a rout, but it would be a long, bloody conflict, and both sides would be decimated.

So far at least, the armies of Jötunheimr hadn't been a concern. No one wanted a war doomed to end in a stalemate of death and destruction. Neither Jötunheimr nor Asgard offered enough to the other side to be worth conquering, and neither side had a distinct advantage, nor sufficient motivation.

Thiassi's death changed everything. Revenge was a motivation, and Thiassi's gold would buy a significant advantage. I'd never met Thiassi's daughter Skadi, but any woman willing to buck Jötunheimr's oppressively sexist hierarchy and raise her own army was not to be underestimated. I thought of Angrboða again, then struggled to swallow the bile rising in the back of my throat.

"We need an in," Óðinn said. "We need to turn someone."

I scratched absently at my hair. The lice were only an illusion, but they still itched. "Who's working with her so far?"

Óðinn grunted. "That's what you'll need to find out. I suggest you disguise yourself as a whore."

I spat in distaste. Whore for a group of disgusting soldiers? "Please tell me you're kidding."

Óðinn didn't respond. I had to remind myself he actually liked soldiers. Angrboða's black dress and pale breasts rose in my memory again, and my throat felt like it was being crushed.

"We could buy Skadi off," I said, hating myself for suggesting Angrboða's idea. "We could offer her, I don't know. A husband."

Óðinn slapped at the back of his neck. "Maybe. But not now, not while she has an army and we have nothing."

He turned to face me. No matter what illusion Óðinn wore, he always had the same disconcerting, ageless blue eyes. The kind of eyes that drilled straight into you.

"Turn one of the generals," Óðinn said. "Do whatever you need to do. Find a place where she's vulnerable, where we can attack. Then we'll negotiate."

Something dark and cold rose inside me. This was it, then. Betrayal and cunning, strategies and war. This was my entire life now, stretching out from here until Ragnarök.

"Fine," I said. "I'll do it. But I'm not going as a whore."

Óðinn's laugh lingered in the chill morning air long after he himself had vanished.

CHAPTER TWENTY TWO

Darkness and water.

I swam through the water, searching for something. For my family. For the bodies of Anya and Falur, and the tiny shape of the babe. They were spinning in the dark somewhere, and if I could only reach them, if I were just fast enough—

My lungs burned. I was underwater, far underwater, and cold. I couldn't breathe. I flailed, twisting my arms and legs, but the binds around my ankles and wrists held tight. And now it wasn't the ocean but a black dress which engulfed me, drowning me.

Somewhere far above me, Angrboða laughed and laughed.

I sat bolt upright, both fists clenched around the cold hilts of my daggers, my heart hammering against my breastbone, and a sharp, metallic tang in the back of my mouth.

Where the hell was I?

It was black as death around me, and my head throbbed with the familiar dull ache of a hangover. The cantrips I always set before falling asleep hummed comfortingly beside me. Someone called in the darkness, and another, farther voice responded. A watch. A watch for a soldier's camp.

With a sigh, I re-sheathed the daggers at my waist. I was in Skadi's camp, spying for Óðinn. Not drowning. Not bound and writhing beneath Angrboða.

Shivering with the unpleasant vestiges of my nightmare, I stood and pulled back the cantrips. I'd disguised myself as a new recruit, although two weeks of training with Skadi's army had gotten me absolutely nothing. Óðinn may have been on to something with his whore suggestion, although I still couldn't quite force myself to go down that route. Even though the whores' tents seemed more comfortable than the barracks where I currently found myself.

I'd gone without sleep until tonight, when exhaustion forced me to claim the darkest corner of the barracks and try to set my most subtle protections. This wasn't Midgard, after all; many of the elite fighters in Skadi's army could sense magic, if not use it themselves. Anything more complex than my usual illusions and cantrips had the potential to set off their alarms.

Another voice called from the darkness. I held my breath, listening for the response. When it came, the answering cry was farther away than I'd expected. Was someone new arriving now, in the middle of the night?

How very interesting.

I slipped through the thick canvas doors of the tent, blinking in the darkness. Torches flickered around the perimeters of the camp. And there, in the darkness of the valley, was the distant, orange gleam of another torch. Followed by another. And another.

As I watched, a stream of torches flowed between the mountains, moving closer and closer to the barracks. The guards called and were answered with friendly greetings. I slipped between the tents, standing in the shadows, until I could see the camp's main entrance. Several horses stamped in the gloom just inside the ring of torchlight. I recognized three of Skadi's four generals.

And, riding the biggest, most formidable mount, was Thiassi's daughter Skadi. Moonlight glinted off her armor, and off the longsword hanging at her side. I'd only glimpsed her before; she didn't deign to come near the raw recruits, and I could hardly blame her for that. I'd thought briefly about attempting to pass as a male escort and gain entrance to her tent, but nothing about Skadi's strict military operation or grim demeanor made me think she'd be interested in a little wartime dalliance.

A horse whinnied from the mountains and was answered by Skadi's stallion. Her dark mount pranced a bit, until she pulled him under control. One of the mares in the approaching battalion must be in heat. I grinned to myself in the shadows. Horses were just as predictable as the rest of us.

It didn't take long for the approaching troops to come within the flickering glow of the torches. A crier came first, galloping the last few feet to approach Skadi and her generals. He was hardly more than a boy, and he slid off his mount to bow low at the iron-clad feet of Skadi's war stallion.

"My Lord," the boy panted. "Thrym of the Iron Wastes swears his fealty, and presents his men unto your service."

The boy stood, blinking in the torchlight. Skadi did not acknowledge him; her eyes were fixed on the column of approaching soldiers.

"It's about damn time," grunted Hryery, one of the older generals under Skadi's command. "Send him up!"

My heart rose to my throat. Holding my breath, I stepped further into the shadows. I knew Thrym. I knew him quite intimately, actually. But I'd have to ascertain where his loyalties lay before I dared to approach him.

The boy, whose face had now turned quite pale, struggled to re-mount his horse. Even I could see his legs trembling. Once he'd finally regained his seat, he did not look back before he vanished into the darkness.

There was a slight flicker of motion among the river of torches along the valley, and the indistinct murmur of voices. Then another set of hooves thundered toward us. A moment later I saw Thrym, wearing his full armor, astride a great blood bay warhorse.

I almost sighed in appreciation. I first met Thrym when he stole Mjölnir, Thor's magical hammer. I'd expected to fight him, perhaps even kill him, but the evening had ended in a much more satisfactory manner. Since then I'd paid several visits to Thrym, almost all for the pure pleasure of his strong, hard warrior's body and his downright decadent living quarters. He was a generous and surprising lover, and he'd been one of my favorites, before Anya caught my eye on Midgard.

Even now, with Asgard's fate hanging in the balance, the sight of Thrym's bare arms and stubble-covered jaw lit a fire somewhere deep inside me. That warmth spread until I felt my cheeks flush beneath my illusions, although it took me a moment longer to recognize it for what it was.

Ah. Apparently I could still feel lust.

I frowned in the darkness, trying to push away both the distraction of my sudden arousal and the gnawing sense I'd just betrayed the memory of Anya and Falur. A few steps in front of me, Thrym reined in his steed, raised his fist to his forehead, and bowed very slightly.

"My Lord Skadi," he rumbled. "We have come."

Skadi sniffed dismissively. "It took you that long to cross the wastes, Thrym?"

Thrym's dark eyes narrowed in the torchlight. "Winter approaches, Lord Skadi. I could not force my men to leave in the middle of their harvests. But, once the troops were gathered, we made due haste. As you can see, we traveled through the night to reach your camp."

"Am I supposed to be impressed?" Skadi sneered. "Apparently you care more for harvesting corn than you care for avenging my father, your sworn ally."

Thrym pulled back his shoulders. Even for a Jötunn, he was enormous. He made the stallion beneath him look like a pony.

"Make no mistake," Thrym growled. "I am here because you left me no option, woman. Threatening to burn my lands may have forced my hand, but it did not gain you an ally. And I daresay I'm not the only one of your generals who feels this way."

Thrym glared at the four men standing beside Skadi. The horses shifted awkwardly, stamping the hard packed ground. Thrym's stallion whirled and vanished into the darkness, and the slow progression of torches resumed its progress toward the camp.

"Insolent shit—" Skadi began, but I slipped away before I could hear the rest of her rant.

I'd learned enough already.

I WAITED FOUR DAYS. Enough time for Thrym and his troops to settle into Skadi's encampment, but not enough time for the generals to make any major tactical decisions. Then I waited until the sun had sunk behind the hills, and the thin crescent moon began to shine on the hard rock slopes of the mountains which loomed above the camp.

It was cold enough to turn my breath into a cloud of frost before my lips, which I'd painted extravagantly for the occasion. I shivered beneath the skimpy dress I'd wrapped around my curvaceous female illusion and hoped Thrym had a good fire going in his tent. I was shaped like a woman tonight, and a very attractive woman at that. I'd been invisible for most of my approach in order to avoid breaking the arms of any especially grabby soldiers, but now it was time to announce my presence.

As a whore. I stifled a sigh. Somewhere across the Nine Realms, I was certain Óðinn was laughing at me.

The guards standing outside Thrym's private tent were literally speechless when I stepped into the flickering circle of lamplight. Always a good sign.

"Gentlemen," I purred. "I'm here for the general."

The taller guard blinked a few times, then stammered something unintelligible. Ah, being a woman was such fun. I'd almost forgotten the effect a nice pair of tits has on most men.

Without waiting for a reply, I sashayed through the heavy folds of the tent's door. The low rumble of conversation followed me, but a subtle refraction charm kept me from making out the exact words. My eyes slowly adjusted to the gloom, and I saw three men seated at a low table before a guttering fire. Two of them stared at me with gaping jaws. Thrym, however, was already halfway to his feet with his sword drawn. His dark eyes narrowed. For the first time, it occurred to me that I could be in quite a spot of trouble if Thrym didn't recognize me.

"Leave us," Thrym growled, gesturing with his blade to the men seated around his table.

They stumbled awkwardly to their feet, still stealing glances at me. I thrust out a hip and pouted while Thrym made quite a show of sheathing his sword.

"It's about time," Thrym said, meeting my eye as the two men slinked past us.

"Lucky bastard," one of them whispered.

"How much d'you think she's worth?" the other replied.

Thrym crossed the floor and wrapped his massive arms around me, hiding his lips in my hair. My skin prickled at the sudden contact.

"Loki?" he whispered.

I sighed with relief. "Of course."

His hands tightened around my waist. "They'll be watching. Make an illusion."

Nodding slightly, I pulled the strands of magic in the tent taut around our bodies, then braced myself against the inevitable lance of pain that came whenever I made a complicated illusion. A moment later another couple stepped toward the bed, the beautiful woman already slipping her dress down to her ankles.

I felt for another strand of magic, preparing to teleport us outside the tent, but Thrym grabbed my wrist and pinned it to my back.

"Don't," he hissed. "There's nowhere safe."

I pulled back enough to meet his eyes. His face was lined and hard; he seemed to have aged decades in the handful of years since I'd last seen him.

"Just make us invisible," he whispered. "Magic inside the tent's fine. They'll just think I'm using a few spells to supplement my endurance. But outside's too risky. This damn place is the most heavily warded valley in Jötunheimr. Skadi trusts no one."

"Wise of her," I said, pulling the strands of magic tight enough to render us invisible.

The ghost of a smile passed across Thrym's face, and he sank to the cushions on the floor. "We're hidden?" he whispered.

"We are. Anyone watching will only see them," I said, nodding at the illusion couple now kissing passionately at the foot of Thrym's bed.

"Then I'll tell you there's nothing wise about Skadi," Thrym said, with a heavy sigh. "What she wants to do will destroy both Realms. She's mad with rage and grief, and she's using her father's gold to buy off my soldier's lives."

I sat on the rug next to Thrym. On the bed behind him, my female illusion was sinking to her knees to unbuckle the Thrym illusion's massive belt. The tent flap rustled softly, suggesting Thrym was right. His guards were indeed watching my little show.

"You don't think Skadi's forces could take on the Æsir?" I asked.

Thrym shrugged. "Anyone could take on the Æsir, I suppose. But no one could beat them. Óðinn's made sure of that. The Nine

Realms are balanced, because anyone attacking Óðinn's forces would be destroyed."

"Skadi knows this?" I pressed.

"Yes. She knows. But she doesn't care. She's assembled enough men to pose a threat. Even if her armies were defeated, which they probably would be, Asgard would be in ruins." He paused, glancing at the closed tent door before continuing. "And I honestly think that's all she wants. She wants to hurt Asgard, even if it costs every life under her service."

I pressed my fingers to my lips. Angrboða's words surfaced in my mind, and I hated myself for it.

"What if Óðinn bargained with her?" I asked.

Thrym laughed weakly. "I don't think she can be bought, if that's what you're here for. She's the richest woman in Jötunheimr, now that her father's dead."

"A husband?" I asked, lamely.

Thrym's snorted response was so loud I strengthened the illusions around us, making sure we were inaudible as well as invisible. "No, Loki, I don't think sex can fix this one. Besides, who'd be the sacrificial lamb for that one? I can't imagine any of the Æsir leaping to their feet to become Skadi's hen-pecked husband."

I glanced across the tent. My female illusions had freed Thrym's enormous cock, and was sucking on it with apparent delight. The illusion of Thrym had his hand wrapped around her skull as he groaned with pleasure.

"What if she was cornered?" I said. "What if Óðinn's armies managed to surprise her while she was vulnerable?"

Thrym caught my eye. "You're saying you need someone to betray her?"

In the silence that followed, I could hear the pounding of my own heart. The illusions behind us groaned and sighed with carnal pleasure and, from somewhere outside the tent, I heard a faint, sensual moan from one of the guards. Well, at least they were distracted.

I reached for Thrym, closing my fingers around his hand. "What's the alternative? Having your men die on her battlefield?"

Thrym pulled away from my touch and ran his fingers through his hair, tugging the graying strands so hard it almost hurt to watch. "Or watch them die here, executed for my treason? That's a lovely alternative you've offered."

Damn. I clenched my fist, watching Thrym's tight lips and stiff back and cursing my own lack of forethought. If I'd done this right, I'd have a plan to present to him. But of course I hadn't done it right, and now I'd have to make something up as I went along.

"I'm not going to abandon you," I insisted.

Thrym raised a weary eyebrow. He looked like he'd already given up on this conversation.

"I have a place," I lied. "Off of this realm, away from Jötunheimr. Somewhere warm. You can be, uh—"

I cast about frantically in my mind, trying to grasp onto something that would appeal to Thrym. The first image that surfaced was the row of sleek, dark wine bottles we'd shared during my last visit to his fortress. When I'd awoken the next morning, they had surrounded Thrym's bed like guards standing at attention.

"A vintner," I said. "Buying and selling wine. You'll get to use some of your other talents, the ones that don't involve killing and maiming."

Thrym's eyes widened for a heartbeat, then narrowed into what was almost a glare. I had the impression a door had opened, briefly, and then slammed shut.

"I can't bring everyone," I said, glancing toward the tent flaps. I knew Thrym preferred men to women; it was possible he had a few lovers in his regiment. "If you have, say, a few special men in your care..."

He growled. "That's poor form. I don't mix business and pleasure, Loki."

"Well, still. The offer stands. I should be able to hold the gate for a dozen men, plus that many horses."

Thrym's laugh sounded rusty. "And how would I get a dozen men, plus horses, out from under Skadi's nose? Even if I agree to this suicidal plan, which I most certainly have not."

Behind him, the female illusion on the bed screamed in ecstasy. A moment later, Thrym's illusion roared his own climax. I tugged on the magic, getting the illusions ready for another performance.

"You'll be moving already," I whispered. "That's what we need to know. When, and where, Skadi is moving. We'll scout the route, find a place where we could ambush her. If we have the element of surprise, and we surround her troops, Óðinn will get her to negotiate."

"Or Óðinn will give the order to attack and mow us down like summer wheat."

I huffed. That did sound exactly like Óðinn.

"Even if we had the element of surprise, it would be a tough fight," I said. "I don't think Óðinn's willing to take on the combined forces of Jötunheimr. Not if there's a way we can negotiate with Skadi. But we can't even bring her to the table until we have her armies pinned. And for that, Master Thrym of the Iron Wastes, we need you."

Thrym sighed heavily and leaned back against a tent pole. Behind him, the naked illusions were once again embracing on the bed, trading deep, passionate kisses. I heard panting and a wet, rhythmic slapping from beyond the tent flaps; it sounded like at least one of the guards was thoroughly enjoying my show.

"You think," Thrym finally said. "You don't actually know what Óðinn plans to do."

"No one knows what Óðinn plans to do," I admitted. "But, if you tell me when and where this army is moving, I will get you out of here. I promise."

Thrym's dark eyes bore into me, then shifted to trace the lines of his tent upward to the smoke hole. I followed his gaze. There, through the shifting gusts of woodsmoke, icy stars glittered in Jötunheimr's sky.

"I've heard what your word is worth," he said.

That stung. I exhaled slowly, trying to unclench my fists. "Thrym, have I ever let you down?"

The corners of his lips twitched, as though he were fighting the urge to grin. "You've never made me any promises, Lie-smith."

Well, shit. The masturbating guard on the other side of the tent let out a long groan. A moment later his feet shuffled past where I was sitting. Damn it. Time was running short, and I had nothing else to offer Thrym. Nothing but...

I leaned forward, pressing my palm against Thrym's massive chest. "Thrym," I whispered as I spread my fingers wide. At the rasp of his chest hair against my palm, a flicker of arousal sparked to life somewhere deep inside me. I wasn't dreading this. For the first time since Thiassi pulled Iðunn from my side in the dark apple orchard on Jötunheimr, the thought of sex actually pleased me.

"Stop it," Thrym growled, pushing my hand aside.

I rocked back, blinking in surprise. Thrym's face softened somewhat.

"Any other time and place, Loki, and I'd fuck you so hard you'd be limping for a week. But here—" He glanced at the tent wall again, and the hard lines around his lips and eyes reappeared.

He was scared, I realized, with an unpleasant jolt. I'd never seen the mighty Thrym frightened.

Thrym shook his head and ran his massive hand through his hair, tugging again. He laughed to himself in a resigned sort of way that sounded like air leaking from a bellows. "You're an unlikely savior, Loki, but I suppose you're all I've got. If I'm going to die on a battlefield either way—"

"You're not going to die," I insisted. "I've got a place for you."

My half-assed idea to offer sanctuary to Thrym on some other realm crystallized into an absolute necessity. Somehow, I was going to make that happen.

Thrym waved his hand dismissively. "If I betray Skadi, then perhaps you're right. Perhaps there is a chance this war could be averted, and Jötunheimr and Asgard won't burn."

I froze, afraid to speak. Thrym leaned closer to me.

"I'll do it." His voice was flat and resigned. "If it saves just one life, I suppose my betrayal will be worth the cost."

He didn't believe me. The realization made me feel cold. Thrym hadn't, for one second, believed I had a place to shelter him from Skadi's wrath.

I didn't have a place, of course, but still. His lack of faith galled me.

"You'd better go," Thrym said, tipping his head toward the illusions on his bed.

His tent was now heavy with the scent of sex, a nice touch of verisimilitude which was probably wasted on my current audience. I ran my fingers through the strands of magic, making both illusions scream in pleasure again, first the woman and then Thrym. As they fell panting to Thrym's enormous bed, I stood and extended my hand to Thrym. He took it and, surprisingly, did not let go as we walked the few steps to the edge of his bed.

"It would be easiest if you sit down," I whispered, although my illusions were still wrapped around us, rendering us both invisible.

Thrym hesitated. Then, instead of sitting, he wrapped his arms around me and pulled me to his chest for a crushing kiss. My entire body stiffened in shock, and I barely had time to open my mouth to his before he pulled away.

"Loki." He ran his fingers along my cheek, his dark eyes gleaming strangely in the torchlight. "I wish the circumstances were different. But, all the same, I'm glad it was you."

He sank to the bed, and I staggered backward, stunned by the force of his unexpected tenderness. Glad it was *me*? I'd always assumed he preferred Thor. Everyone preferred Thor.

My chest tightened as if my rib cage were caught in a vise. I felt something fierce and volatile slip loose inside me, a maelstrom of rage and grief and aching loneliness that rose inside my chest like a black tide, pressing against my throat, choking my breath.

"I won't let you down," I whispered.

I closed my eyes so I wouldn't have to see the expression on his face and tightened my illusions like a shell around my body, trying to bring myself back under control. A moment later, I slipped into the illusion of the beautiful woman, who was now gloriously naked. She walked through Thrym's tent without a backward glance, her skin glistening with sweat and her thighs streaked with Thrym's seed.

"Three days," Thrym called from the bed behind me. "Come back in three days."

I nodded, waving my delicate fingers above my head in a gesture that could have been taken as agreement.

CHAPTER TWENTY THREE

I took a deep breath of the evening air and listened to the soft, mournful cries of a collared dove hiding somewhere in the bushes behind me. Before me, the sun was setting across the hills, covering the verdant landscape with a golden haze. I hadn't planned to return to Midgard but, upon leaving Thrym's tent and reviewing my scanty options, I decided this was the best place in the Nine Realms for a fugitive warrior. Most of the Jötunn dismiss Midgard entirely as an uncivilized, useless Realm. With any luck, Skadi would share those prejudices and wouldn't think to look for Thrym here.

Besides, Midgard's Roman Empire had excellent wine.

Behind me, wooden trellises marched in straight lines across the curving landscape, laden with heavy grapevines. I'd passed quite a few vineyards on my journey today, but the one before me was different. The others had been prosperous, with neatly trimmed vines and freshly repaired trellises. The field in front of me, however, was clearly slipping into disrepair. Grass grew thick between the rows, and the trellises had collapsed in several places, spilling their dark grapes across the ground.

Perfect.

By sunrise the next morning, I'd shared a few bottles of very good wine with the widow who owned the crumbling vineyard. I'd heard her lengthy tale of woe, chiefly involving ungrateful children and vengeful in-laws. And then I'd paid double her asking price for the entire vineyard, with her modest domus and all the furniture inside it included, even though the rear half of the house seemed to be sinking into the earth.

I left her in a frenzy of preparation, summoning her slaves to begin packing her belongings. She'd offered to sell me most of the slaves as well, all but her personal servants, but I declined. I was looking for something different.

Actually, I was looking for someone different.

Thrym was clever and ruthless, and he'd probably make an excellent businessman. But he wouldn't speak a word of the language, and I doubted he knew much about cultivating grapes. Most of the agricultural skills he could hire out; I could literally pull money from thin air in Midgard, and I'd leave him rich as a king.

Still, he'd need someone to ease his transition. Money only went so far, especially among the tribal barbarians of this backward realm. I wasn't about to save Thrym from Skadi's clutches only to have his throat slit by Midgardian mortals angered by the sudden appearance of a wealthy barbarian who couldn't even speak their languages.

The Empire's famous roads were mostly empty this early in the morning, although I did pass an old man leading an even older donkey, and a few beggars lounged beside the spur road leading to the temples. I tossed them a few coins.

"May the gods favor you!" one cried at me.

I grinned. I'd met most of the Empire's gods, and I daresay they did not favor me.

By mid-morning I was in the civilized city of Lucca. I transformed my appearance several times, spread a few rumors about the imminent arrival of a barbarian whose wealth was legend and who had just acquired a vineyard outside of town, and then settled in at a pleasantly disreputable dive to drink wine and listen to the local rumors. By the time the sun sank toward the western hills, I'd found my man.

He was causing quite the stir in Lucca. I'd heard stories about several disreputable types, freemen driven to extremes by debt or plain old poor judgement, but none of them had an air of scandal. No, those penniless and desperate men and women were just sad, boring stories, the type found the world over.

But the stories swirling around Marcus Salonius Quintilius were of a different sort. The rumors agreed he'd been a legionary and not originally from Lucca. He was also a freeman of some social standing, although not enough to protect him when the scandal broke.

Like all the best scandals, it seemed to involve sex, heartbreak, and tragedy. I heard half a dozen wildly differing accounts, from which I pieced together a much less salacious timeline. Marcus Salonius, I gathered, had fallen in love with a man. On its face, there was nothing wrong with this fact. Except that both men were freemen, and sexual relations were supposed to exist only between freemen and slaves. Or women, who were hardly more than slaves in the minds of most legionaries.

Falur's words echoed in my mind as I reconstructed the story of Marcus Quintilius from naughty rumors and whispered innuendos. For all the distance separating the Roman Empire from Sweorice, both cultures seemed to share alarmingly primitive attitudes toward sex. This is what you do to your enemies, Falur had said, as I wrapped my legs around his waist and lowered myself to him. As if making love were a punishment. The familiar cold fist of grief tightened around my chest, although perhaps its hold was not quite so fierce as it had been weeks ago.

I put down my mug of watery, salted wine.

"What does he want, then?" I asked the man next to me, who'd been reveling in his story about how Marcus Salonius had been discovered in the throes of passion with another freeman and multiple goats.

The man stopped in mid-sentence, blinking at me. I had long enough to regret buying him so much wine before he cleared his throat.

"Eh? What does who want?"

"Marcus Salonius," I said. "The legionary. What's he doing in Lucca?"

Another man at our long communal table snorted in disgust. "Trying to avoid selling himself into slavery, that's what."

"Pervert," someone spat. "You watch him. He never takes off his cloak. Ten to one there's scars from a flogging across his shoulders. What he did, he's lucky to have his life."

"Well, that won't pay for bread," another man added, to a solid round of laughter.

I stayed for several more minutes, smiling under the illusions of a well-dressed but utterly forgettable traveler. He wasn't from here, this Marcus. He was smart enough not to go back to his family, and clever enough to talk his way out of an execution.

Tossing several coins on the table, I excused myself and left the bar. The night air had grown chill, and the tight streets of Lucca filled with a fog rising from the Serchio River. The moon was almost full, giving the fog a luminous cast and making the entire city gleam like silver.

This part of Midgard was nothing like Sweorice, I told myself as I followed the gently sloping streets downward, letting my mind drift in a haze of bad wine. Yet something about the chill night air made my throat tighten all the same. I realized I'd pulled Falur's leaf from my pocket and was turning it over in my palm, running my fingers along its sharp, delicate edge. When I reached the docks along the river, I kissed the leaf before returning it to my pocket. Immediately, I missed its smooth weight between my fingers.

He was sleeping behind a collection of empty barrels, the infamous Marcus Salonius. There were a number of unconscious figures scattered around the docks, some being investigated by rats, and most of them were almost obliterated by the haze of alcohol rising from their prone bodies. Marcus was the only one wearing a cloak. He was also the only one who, when I nudged him with my foot, spun to face me with a blade in his hand.

"Marcus Salonius Quintilius?" I asked.

"Who the hell are you?" he spat.

I'd expected him to be drunk. I sure as hell would have been drunk under those circumstances. But Marcus sounded sober, and he moved with the fluid, practiced motions of a fighter. His dark eyes glittered malevolently as he appraised me.

"I want to know what happened to you," I said. "And then I've got a job for you."

"Fuck you."

I shrugged. "Very well. If you've got a better offer, I'll leave you to it."

He let me take almost a dozen steps before he called out.

"Wait!"

I turned to see him sheathing his dagger and dusting off his tunic. He was silent as I rejoined him.

"What's the job?" he asked.

"Does it matter?"

The fog around us shifted. I saw his shoulders fall. "No," Marcus admitted. "It doesn't matter."

Something about his abject tone tugged at me. I reached for him and closed my hand around his shoulder. He didn't pull away. When he met my eyes, something bright and hot flashed between us.

"What do you need to know?" he asked.

I sighed. Honestly, the spark that had just passed between us told me everything I needed to know about Marcus Salonius Quintilius.

"Nothing," I said. "I need a bodyguard, of sorts."

He eyed me again, this time as if he were assessing my vulnerabilities.

"Not for me," I snapped. "For a barbarian. Someone who's very wealthy, and he's moving to the Empire to start over fresh. He's coming from very far away. He'll know nothing about life here. You'll need to teach him everything."

Marcus crossed his arms over his chest and rocked back. "Why are you asking me?"

The fog lifted for a moment, and the moon shone down upon us, bathing Marcus in cold, white light. I tilted my head and looked him over. He stood on the balls of his feet, ready to spring to action. His body was hard and well trained, if a bit scrawny, and I was willing to bet those dark eyes didn't miss much.

And he was handsome. Not beautiful like Baldr, but attractive in a rough, rugged sort of way. He looked like the type of man you'd want by your side at the end of the world, someone you could count on to start a fire or butcher a deer or find his way through the forest at night.

He looked like he could be Thrym's equal. Thank the Nine fucking Realms.

"I'll move you to the domus immediately," I said, clearly not answering his question. "You'll be responsible for taking charge of the place until the barbarian arrives. It's in a sad state, I'll be honest. Both the house and the vineyards. They're going to take a lot of work."

Marcus's eyes narrowed again, and his hand dropped almost imperceptibly toward his belt. Going for his knife, I guessed. I held my hands up, wide and open, in a gesture of innocence.

"That's the offer," I said. "Take it or leave it."

He didn't move. His hand still hovered above his belt.

"Or, you can stab me," I added. "But that'll piss me the fuck off, and I'll rescind the offer."

His hand moved away from his belt. "You're drunk."

"Is that a yes or a no?"

For the first time since I'd met him, Marcus's face wrinkled in frustration. He rocked back, out of reach, and ran his hands through his hair.

"Is this a joke?" he finally said.

I tipped my head to the sky and exhaled. All the wine I'd drunk today was beginning to catch up with me, and I just wanted to find somewhere quiet and dark to collapse. For years, preferably.

But there wasn't time. Thrym told me to come back in three days. That was tomorrow night, for fuck's sake. I had the vineyard and the house, but they would be useless without someone to explain the intricacies of life in the Roman Empire.

And I couldn't stay on Midgard. Skadi was going to be furious; I couldn't risk her tracking me to Thrym. Not to mention Óðinn, who would probably advise me to slit Thrym's throat myself and be done with the entire affair.

"Fine. If you won't take the job, I'll pick someone else." I wrapped my cape around my shoulders with as much dignity as I could manage. "Good luck finding your next meal."

"No!" he said. "No. I'll... I'll take it."

I let the air out of my lungs in a huff. "Thank the fucking stars. Let's go. We've got a long walk ahead of us."

WE REACHED THE CRUMBLING domus just as the sky was beginning to fade from black to gray. It was dark and looked abandoned, the old widow and her contingent of slaves having set out for the coast the day before. The front door was locked, but I shattered the chain with a sharp burst of magic. The long walk from Lucca had made me first sober, and then hungover, and I was in no mood to fuss with chains and locks.

Marcus had been mostly silent on the journey, after voicing several concerns about the dubious wisdom of walking the Empire's roads at night, by ourselves. I'd ignored those, and the two of us had settled into a more or less companionable silence.

I swung the doors open and tugged on the strands of magic to light the oil lamps nestled in the walls. They all flared to life as one. Behind me, Marcus gasped. I turned to see him stepping backward.

"Oh, come on," I grumbled. "I don't have time to do things the ordinary way."

A cascade of emotions chased themselves across the hard lines of Marcus's face. Finally his features settled into an expression of grim resolution, and he stepped across the lintel. He seemed mildly surprised the experience didn't kill him.

"Go find something to eat," I said. "Your stomach growled the whole way here."

"So did yours," he answered.

I hid my smile beneath my illusions. The kind of man who can snap back at someone who'd just blown an iron lock to bits and lit a half dozen oil lamps by magic was the kind of man who could handle Thrym.

While Marcus took a lamp to inspect the dormer's larder, I pulled together enough magic to create a pile of coins and wrap them in a rough sack. It should be enough to start on repairs to the house, at least, if not hire workers for the vineyard.

That done, I drew up a few legal documents, giving ownership of the property to Thrym, in the express care of Marcus Salonius Quintilius. Those took a fair amount of concentration to generate; the Empire was particularly fussy about legal documents.

"What's this?" Marcus asked.

He'd appeared with the lamp balanced on a trap holding a few wedges of hard cheese scattered around a bottle of wine. I took the wine gratefully, planning on drinking just enough to ease the hangover hammering at the inside of my skull. The day was young, and I still had to face Thrym, gather information, and betray Skadi's troop movements to Óðinn.

"See for yourself," I said, pulling the cork from the bottle.

Marcus read carefully as I drank the wine. I watched his lips move as he formed the words, whispering to himself. When he was finished, he leaned against the wall and chewed a hunk of dried cheese in silence.

"What's the catch?" he finally asked.

I put down the wine and took a piece of hard cheese. "Thrym won't speak the language," I said.

"What language? Latin? Greek?"

"Not those."

Marcus shifted against the wall. "I spent some time in Germania. I know a little Gothic, and some Celt."

"No. I mean, he won't speak any of your languages."

Marcus's eyes widened. "Oh. Is he a—"

"He's in danger," I said, cutting Marcus off. "Or, he will be. There are many lives at stake, somewhere very far from the human world. Thrym is going to do something dangerous to save them, and then he's going to hide out here."

Marcus processed this silently. "For how long?"

"Well, at least as long as you're going to live."

Perhaps not the best thing to say. But Marcus took it well, and the only sign of his fear was the way his shoulders hunched up, as if he were getting ready to punch someone.

"Is he going to kill me, then?" Marcus asked.

I sighed and eyed the half empty wine bottle with a pang of regret. "No. No, he's not going to kill anyone. But, if he's left on his own, he's going to blunder into something idiotic and get himself in even more trouble. I need you to teach him, Marcus. And be patient with him. He's about to lose everything."

Marcus frowned. "I'm a soldier. I'm not a teacher."

The open window behind Marcus was slowly filling with light as the sun crept toward Midgard's horizon. It would be late afternoon on Jötunheimr. Fuck me, I had to go.

"He's a soldier, too," I said, which was only a slight exaggeration. Warlord was the better term, but that wouldn't translate so well. "You'll be fine."

Marcus held up a finger. "One more thing. Last night, you said you needed to know what happened to me. I didn't tell you. And yet you have all this—" he waved a hand over the legal documents, "ready to go."

"I changed my mind. I don't need to know."

He raised an eyebrow. "Or you already know."

Really, I didn't know the details of Marcus's story. But it hadn't been too difficult to put the pieces together. He'd clearly had some sort of romance with another soldier, another freeman, and they'd gotten caught. There was only one part of the story I couldn't guess.

"Did you love him?" I asked.

Marcus's face crumpled like a sail dropping to the floor of a ship. A moment later, he hid his head in his hands, and his shoulders shook.

"Nevermind," I said, brushing off my armor. "I don't need to know."

"Octavius. His name is Octavius." Marcus's voice was muffled by his hands, but his words were clear enough. "And yes. I loved him. Everything I did, I did to protect him. I told them I'd prostituted myself, that I'd gotten him drunk. I told them anything I could to make sure I'd be the only one getting publicly flogged."

Marcus's shoulders tightened, and he coughed to clear his throat. "I don't regret my ignominiosa missio. At least I was able to protect Octavius. His future was always brighter than mine, anyway."

Oh, fuck me sideways. My chest tightened, and my own eyes stung at this outpouring of emotion. The raw wound Anya and Falur's deaths had scratched across my heart was like an open window, leaving me vulnerable to all the suffering in the Nine Realms. I felt like I'd just lost them again, as if all the sorrow in Midgard now flowed through me.

I clasped my hand over Marcus's arm. "I'm sorry."

Marcus nodded, then stiffened his back and blinked several times. I pretended not to see the tears; tears were considered seriously unmanly in the Empire, of course.

"Are you Bacchus?" Marcus suddenly asked.

I was startled enough to laugh. "Him? Oh, shit, no."

"Mercury?"

"Closer," I said, with a grin. I liked the person who called himself Mercury, or Hermes, although our paths rarely crossed.

"Hades?"

"Oh, please! I have a sense of humor."

Marcus frowned at that. I decided to cut him off before he could throw any truly offensive names at me.

"Check the bag," I said.

Marcus started, then bent over the small table where I'd placed the legal documents and the bag of money. His lips pressed together as he ran his hands through the piles of coin inside the bag. The muted sound of their heavy edges clinking together filled the room. It was noticeably lighter now, and the birds had begun to sing in earnest outside the window. Dawn was approaching on Midgard. Night would be falling on Jötunheimr.

"I'm leaving now," I continued. "It might be some time until the barbarian arrives, or it might be tomorrow. Is that enough money for you to get started on what needs to be done?"

Marcus's dark eyes met mine again, but this time his expression was impossible to read. "And if I take this money, and run as far as I can from this place?"

I sighed in frustration. I could feel the time slipping away, almost as if it were strands of magic stretching thin across the back of my hands. I was tempted to tell Marcus that I'd track him down and dismember him very slowly if he betrayed me, but I remembered the way he had collapsed when he talked about Octavius.

"You won't," I said.

Marcus just nodded, his lips still a tight, white line in his chiseled face.

"I'm leaving. I'll drop copies of these contracts in the appropriate places. You, get to work."

With that, I tugged myself through the aether and let the domus dissolve around me. Marcus's wide eyes and pale, shocked expression were the last thing I saw on Midgard.

CHAPTER TWENTY FOUR

I had to walk several miles to reach Skadi's army. She'd strengthened the wards around her encampment, and I was afraid traveling through the aether would trip them off and alert her to my presence. That would end very badly, for me and for Asgard.

By the time I finally reached the rows of tents, full darkness had fallen across the camp. Fires burned at the crossroads, and the camp hummed with an unusual level of activity. I noticed the horses first. Lots of horses. More horses than the soldiers would need to stay encamped.

I remained invisible until I was almost in front of Thrym's tent. The same group of guards stood at attention outside his door, but their expressions seemed even grimmer than before, reflecting the general mood I'd observed in the camp. Conversations were subdued, and the men hadn't smiled at one another. I'd counted twelve different soldiers sharpening their swords with a look of dejected determination.

Well, perhaps I could put a smile on the guard's faces, at least. With a tug of the magical energies, I transformed into the curvaceous brunette, this time wearing a skin-tight dress the color of the sky just before dawn. I adjusted my skirt before stepping into the circle of firelight.

"Gentlemen," I purred, running a hand through the long, thick curls of my illusion. "Remember me?"

Their eyes widened, but they didn't smile. Shit, that was a very bad sign. I had enough time to wonder just how deeply screwed we were before the taller guard pulled back the tent flap and barked something to Thrym.

"Send her in," Thrym answered, from the darkness.

I pulled a dagger from the aether and pressed the handle into my palm, hiding the blade up my sleeve. If Skadi were waiting for me in that tent, I'd go out with a bang. I thrust my tits out, pursed my lips, and entered the darkness of Thrym's tent.

My heart hammered in my throat as my eyes struggled to make sense of the gloom. Thrym hadn't lit any lamps, although the remnants of a fire smoldered silently in the center of the tent. I could make out Thrym's looming form sitting on the bed, and I swept the corners of the tent for another body. Someone who was about the get my blade in their jugular.

"You're late," Thrym growled.

I raised an eyebrow and thrust out my hip. "I am exactly on time."

Thrym rose. The darkness inside the tent slowly lifted as my eyes adjusted to the low light. It looked like we were alone. Thrym's tent was more sparsely furnished than last time; I could have sworn he had more chests and furs, and a few more pillows heaped in the corners.

Thrym paced the perimeter of the tent, pausing to peg the tent door closed. I heard the guards shifting outside. There were still plenty of cracks in the heavy canvas, in case they wanted to peek. As we all knew.

Once the door was secure, Thrym approached me. He stopped just in front of me, so close our chests almost touched. I could smell him, the thick, rich, male scent of a warrior in his prime. Oh, damn. Thrym's rough sexuality was irresistible, especially as a woman. I felt a rush of precipitous arousal, true sexual arousal, with no illusions.

"I wasn't sure you'd come back," Thrym whispered.

I licked my lips, suddenly finding it very difficult to concentrate.

"Make the illusions," Thrym hissed. His breath felt very warm against the bare skin of my chest and shoulders.

I nodded, trying to swallow my vague sense of disappointment that Thrym wanted illusions to do the fucking. A moment later the air tingled as I made Thrym and myself invisible, and an illusion couple stepped over the flickering embers and embraced before the foot of the bed.

"Are we invisible?" Thrym whispered.

"Yes."

"Good." He grabbed my arms, not gently, and pulled me to the darkest corner of his tent. "You need to leave. Now."

"I—what?"

"Leave. Skadi is moving her army tomorrow afternoon. We're to attack the Bifröst just outside Útgarðar."

I tried to respond, but my mouth felt dry. That was a surprisingly good plan. The chaotic urban warren of Útgarðar would make an excellent stronghold, and the Bifröst stretched wide open between Asgard and Jötunheimr in that part of the Nine Realms. If Skadi could hold the Bifröst, she could inflict serious damage on the Æsir and Vanir. It was still unlikely she could actually win. She'd be attacking the Æsir and Vanir warriors in their stronghold, and depending on their Bifröst to move her troops.

They would all die. But they'd take a lot of us with them.

"Oh," I finally managed to stammer. That explained the grim expressions in the camp, the defeated, mechanistic blade-sharpening and stoic refusal to smile. This was a suicide mission, and the soldiers knew it.

Thrym's grip around my arm tightened. "She'll be most vulnerable when she crosses the Körmt River. That's why we're fording it at night, just above the Ironwood forest."

"At night," I echoed. His plan was beginning to make sense.

"If someone were to surprise Skadi there, with half her army on one bank and half on another..." Thrym whispered.

"You'll cross tomorrow night?"

He nodded. "Go. Now." He tilted his head at the illusions. The woman was now straddling illusion-Thrym's massive waist, lowering herself very slowly onto his thick cock. "Leave them. You can do that, right?"

I bristled at the implication of doubt in my magical abilities. "Of course."

"Then go. Make your report."

He released my arms, but did not turn to look at me.

"I'll meet you in the mountains," I said. "I'll be on a white horse. I'll ride beside you for a few minutes, then you follow me."

Thrym gave no indication he'd heard me. After an extended, awkward silence, I slipped from the tent. Thrym's two guards had their faces pressed together in a loud, sloppy kiss, and their hands down each other's pants. Good for them, I thought, as I moved, invisible, into the darkness between the tents.

"SHE'S CROSSING THE Körmt River," I said, pausing for dramatic effect. This was the first time I'd ever presented information to Óðinn's war council, and I was determined to make the most of it.

"Tomorrow night," I continued. "That's when she's going to be most vulnerable."

"Then that's when we'll attack!" Thor announced, slamming his hammer Mjölnir against the table. The oak of the table shuddered rather alarmingly.

Óðinn clicked his tongue against the roof of his mouth and raised two fingers in the air. Thor fell silent, scowling.

"Other opinions?" Óðinn asked.

Týr laced his fingers before his chin. "How exactly did you come by this information, Lie-smith?" he asked.

"One of her generals betrayed her."

Týr's cool expression was unchanged. "And why would he do that?"

"Skadi's army is in no rush to die," I said. "They know their cause is hopeless."

"Who was it?" Heimdallr asked.

I raised an eyebrow at him. "A gentleman never asks, Heimdallr."

"His name is Thrym," Óðinn said.

For a heartbeat, my eyes met Thor's. His ruddy cheeks darkened slightly. The two of us had spent many nights together in Thrym's fortress, drinking and fucking each other senseless. As far as I knew, none of the other Æsir were aware of those particular adventures.

"Thrym?" Baldr asked. "Isn't he the one who stole Mjölnir? I thought he was dead."

Thor's blush deepened. He looked like he was trying to shrink into his seat.

"Not dead," I said, briskly. "Just severely reprimanded over the whole Mjölnir incident. At any rate, it doesn't matter where the information comes from. What matters is what we do with it. And here's what I suggest."

I paused, waiting for Óðinn to cut me off. When he said nothing, I pressed ahead, trying to stifle the wave of nausea that came from remembering Angrboða's words.

"We wait for Skadi on both sides of the Körmt River. When half her army is across, we make our presence known."

"We can't attack!" Thor interrupted. "I mean, that many soldiers... You know, it wouldn't be strategic, exactly."

I made sure my illusions hid my smile. It was sweet, really, to see how Thor shifted from mindless violence to negotiations once he learned Thrym was part of Skadi's army. Perhaps Thor actually cared for Thrym. I'd have to give them a nice little reunion on Midgard once this mess had blown over.

"Right," I agreed. "Even with her army split by the Körmt, both sides would be looking at heavy losses. Honestly, a full-on attack isn't worth the risk. But, once we have her army pinned, I think we can get Skadi to negotiate."

The room was silent. I stared back at their grim expressions and unblinking, cold eyes. Presenting to Óðinn's war council was not exactly as fun as I'd hoped it would be.

"Why?" Óðinn asked.

"Excuse me?" I sputtered.

Óðinn's pale blue eye burned into me. "Why would Skadi agree to negotiations? Even with her army split, as you said, she still poses a significant threat. Why would she suddenly lay down her arms to talk?"

I swallowed hard. "Two reasons. First, because she doesn't want a battle on the banks of the Körmt. She wants her army to attack Asgard, not to be decimated in the forests of Jötunheimr. And second, because we can give her what she wants."

Silence again. I could almost feel it pressing against my chest like a cold stone.

"So, what does she want?" Týr asked in his soft, cold voice.

"She wants to make sure her father is remembered," I said. "That's why she wants Asgard to burn, as a memorial for Thiassi. So, we give her a memorial. Óðinn can name some stars after him, or something. And second—"

I paused again, my gaze resting on Baldr. He shifted uncomfortably. His handsome face had already folded into a frown. Subtle, I thought. Let's be subtle with this one.

"She wants a husband," I said, careful not to name any particular individuals.

The room erupted in laughter. Good. Laughter meant they weren't afraid. My shoulders relaxed, and I let myself feel a glimmer of hope.

"A husband?" Thor roared, wiping tears of laughter from his eyes. "To that crazy Xanthippe?"

"Please tell us you're joking," Týr said. He had not laughed, I noticed. Then again, Týr wasn't married.

"It's a good plan," Óðinn said.

The room fell silent again. All the men who were already married, like Thor, were beaming. The bachelors looked increasingly nervous, especially poor Baldr. I supposed there were downsides to being the most beautiful man in the Nine Realms.

"We can buy her off with a minimum of damage," Óðinn continued. "We'll do it."

"Wait!" Baldr cried. His exceptionally gorgeous features were a shade paler than usual. "Who's going to marry—"

Heimdallr cut in. "Loki kidnapped Iðunn and got us into this mess in the first place. I say Loki marries her."

There was a round of murmurs, almost all of them affirmative. I leaned back in my chair and crossed my arms behind my head.

"Oh, trust me, I'd love to marry the war-crazed, vengeance driven princess," I said, once the chatter died down. "But I happen to be married already."

Stunned silence greeted this remark. Their expressions ran the gamut from outright disbelief on Heimdallr's face to slightly hurt surprise on Thor's. Odd. I'd assumed all of Asgard knew about my marriage after Iðunn confronted Sigyn in Val-hall. Perhaps news of this kind travels faster among women than men.

Óðinn sighed heavily. "Yes, Loki married Sigyn. But don't worry, the process of choosing Skadi's husband will be fair and—"

"Sigyn?" Thor interrupted, a wide smile breaking across his face. "Little Sigyn, the brunette?"

Óðinn scowled. "There's only one Sigyn in Asgard, son."

Thor's laugh boomed from the rafters, filling the entire room. "Loki married Sigyn? She's the most boring woman in the Nine Realms!"

Týr narrowed his eyes. "Why would Sigyn marry you?"

"This is a real marriage?" Heimdallr said, leaning forward ominously. "Binding? And consummated?"

I felt like something cold had just trickled down the back of my neck. Skadi was the last person in the Nine Realms I'd want to marry, but Heimdallr had a point. Sigyn and I had not exactly consummated our bizzare marriage.

"Yes, of course. Consummated, and thoroughly enjoyed," I lied, with a lecherous smile.

"That's everything, then," Óðinn announced. "We'll surround the ford over the Körmt. Bring your best fighters. Heimdallr and Freyr, you take the Ironwood side of the river. Thor, Týr, and Loki, with me."

The room filled with the clatter of stools scuttering across the stone floor as everyone came to their feet. I bit my lip; I still had obligations to fulfill. If Skadi realized she'd been betrayed before I got Thrym off of Jötunheimr, her fury would destroy him.

"I'll meet you there, All-father," I said.

Óðinn shrugged. "Fine. Don't be too drunk."

I pulled at the strands of magic, preparing to cross the aether to Jötunheimr. Heimdallr's voice followed me as I vanished.

"Are you sure you want to bring Loki, All-father? He's nothing but—"

The room dissolved around me before I could hear the end of Heimdallr's insult.

JÖTUNHEIMR WAS COLD.

I pulled my dark fur more tightly around my shoulders. There was a reason people rarely traveled at night through this realm; it was fucking miserable. I contemplated making the illusion horse beneath me shift, just to restore circulation to my legs, but dismissed the idea almost as soon as it had formed. Someone in Skadi's troop might be sensitive to magic, and I didn't want to give my position away before I saw Thrym.

The moon was little more than a sliver of silver light, hanging above the dark mountains which hemmed either side of the pass. I'd chosen this spot because the road was rough here, which would force Skadi's army to move slowly. Hopefully everyone would be too cold and distracted by the rough path to notice Thrym and his men slipping away.

Hopefully Thrym would come.

A shape came into focus toward the end of the line. I could have shouted with relief. Even in the moon's pale half-light, I recognized Thrym's massive shoulders. I shed my invisibility and made the white horse illusion stamp beneath me. A few soldiers turned toward me, but none seemed suspicious. They looked envious, if anything, and I didn't blame them. This path would have been even more miserable on foot.

I hated to admit it, since the plan had come from Óðinn and Angrboða, but this was brilliant. These frozen, demoralized troops wouldn't be able to rally, even if Asgard's forces decided to attack.

The thought sent a fresh shiver up my spine. Were Asgard's forces going to attack? I wouldn't put it past Óðinn to add a fresh layer of betrayal on top of a perfectly satisfactory battle plan.

"You came."

Thrym's voice was hardly more than a whisper as he led his horse into step beside mine.

I decided not to dignify that remark with a response. We walked together as the path narrowed and the shadows deepened. There was a tiny spur of a trail here, hardly more than a deer track through a thick stand of scrubby, frost-bitten oak. I tugged at a delicate strand of magic, changing the color of my horse from white to a more subtle dark gray.

"Here," I said, making the word sound like a cough.

With that, I pulled off the trail. The horse vanished as I stepped into the darkness beneath the oaks. Thrym came a moment later, dismounting silently. I waited in the shadows, watching the space behind him.

"Where are the others?" I finally asked. I'd told Thrym he could bring a dozen men, plus their horses. I guess I'd imagined he would want to pack up his entire tent and carry it to his new home.

"I face my fate alone," Thrym said.

Oh, I could have slapped him! Of all the stupid, stubborn, dramatic things to say. My mind flickered briefly back to Marcus Salonius Quintilius. I could picture him saying almost the exact same thing. The darkness hid my smile as I pulled open a portal through the aether. Poor Thrym, soon to be abandoned on Midgard with a heap of money and a very handsome ex-soldier who just happened to prefer men.

With a shimmer, the portal opened before us, a narrow and gleaming crack in the fabric of the Realms.

"In," I hissed, glancing behind us to make sure we weren't followed.

Thrym's horse nickered nervously, and he reached up, rubbing the giant bay stallion's nose and whispering something soft and comforting. A moment later they walked through the portal together, Thrym's arm over the stallion's thick neck. I followed, pulling the entrance closed behind us.

"We have to walk the pathways," I explained, still whispering, although there was now no chance Skadi's army would overhear us. Other things dwelled on the paths between the worlds, and it paid to move as quietly as possible. "We'll cross through three different Realms. Just in case we're being tracked."

Thrym just nodded. His expression was slightly more visible in the hazy half-light of the between places, but I almost wished it wasn't. He looked like a man headed to his own execution.

"Right, then," I said. "Múspell first. Stay close."

CHAPTER TWENTY FIVE

Time was difficult to measure on the paths, but it couldn't have been more than an hour before I felt heat wafting through the crack which led to Múspell. Thrym stayed close, one arm around the neck of his stallion, and one hand almost touching mine. I reached out for that hand only once, spreading my fingers until they brushed his. But Thrym flinched and pulled away as if I'd burned him, so I tucked my fingers into my pocket instead.

Magic swirled and pulsed on the paths, pulling at my clothes, my hair, and my illusions with soft, cold fingers. I tried to push away the distraction while I focused on opening the door to Múspell wide enough to allow the three of us. Bleak, white-hot sunlight fell onto the paths. I felt the magic recoil around me.

"Through here," I said. "Go on."

Thrym sighed almost inaudibly. Then he pulled himself forward, his shoulders bent as if he carried something very heavy on his back. I followed just behind him, making sure the portal didn't snap closed on the poor horse.

Múspell, Surtr's Realm of fire, was unpleasant during the best of circumstances. Thrym and I had appeared in the middle of the day, and in one of the hotter regions. A parched wind that felt like air escaping from an oven threw fistfuls of grit into our faces.

"Cover your mouth," I yelled, pulling two black scarves from my pocket.

Thrym stared at it as if he didn't recognize the function of the smooth fabric. Then, oddly, he started to cover his eyes.

"No!" I yelled. "Your mouth! This—" I gestured at the swirling sand "—it's hell on your lungs."

I tied my scarf around my neck, pulling it up to cover my mouth and nose. I wished I did have something to cover my eyes; instead, I cupped my hands to shade my vision and squinted into the storm.

"At least this will cover our tracks," I yelled. Thrym didn't respond, and I realized he probably couldn't hear me over the storm.

I'd hoped to travel farther in Múspell, but I was worried about the horse. And Thrym. He still wore his heavy armor and, although his steps didn't falter, he had to be at serious risk of heat exhaustion. Trusting the sandstorm to obscure any trace of our magical energies, I tore open another portal. Its cool, gray surface shimmered like a mirage. Impatiently, I pointed at Thrym to enter.

He just stared at me. The storm had turned his eyes red and angry, and the thick, black grit of Múspell had already settled in all the cracks of his armor. His cheeks and beard were streaked with sweat and grime, and he stared at me with an expression of utter incredulity.

What the fuck? He'd just seen me open a portal. Maybe it was heat exhaustion. I glanced at the horse, wondering if I could get the beast to drag Thrym if he lost consciousness.

Just as I decided the fierce-looking warhorse would probably kick my in the intestines if I stepped any closer, Thrym lurched into motion. Stumbling against the rocks and sand, he pulled his horse through the portal. I followed, closing the entrance as elegantly as I could.

After the roar of Múspell's sandstorm, the misty silence of the pathways felt deafening. I wiped grit from my eyes, trying to clear my vision. Beside me, Thrym pulled the scarf from his face and stared at it again, as if he were an explorer who'd stumbled upon some ancient relic and was trying to puzzle out its purpose.

"Fuck Múspell," I finally said, after spitting several times to clear the dirt from my mouth.

Thrym just nodded. He let the scarf fall from his hands. I bent to pick it up.

"No trace," I whispered. "We can't leave any sign of our—"

I was interrupted by a truly colossal fart. Behind me, Thrym's warhorse spread his legs and unloaded a massive pile of steaming shit into the swirling fog of the paths. Thrym snorted something that may have been a suppressed laugh.

"Seriously?" I said, to the horse. It glared at me malevolently.

I tore open another portal, shifted the refuse to Múspell, and wiped my hands across my pants. Thrym grabbed my shoulders as I started forward.

"Óðinn would have left me in Múspell," he said. His voice sounded gritty and thick, as if his throat was still clogged with sand from the storm.

And Thrym was almost right. Óðinn would have slit his throat first, then dumped his lifeless body in Múspell. I could almost hear Óðinn's voice, whispering among the mists of the between places. There'd be fewer questions if Thrym were dead. Fewer complications.

"I know," I said.

Thrym's red-rimmed eyes blinked rapidly. "Thank—"

"Don't," I said. "We're not out yet."

WE CROSSED SVARTÁLFAHEIMR next, entering in the high mountains. It was the dead of night, and the stars shone like knife-holes in the heavens. We had to walk through deep, fresh snow, which made me feel painfully exposed. With Thrym's dark armor against the star-lit white snowfields, we might as well have screamed our presence to all the Nine Realms. From the corner of my eye, I saw something black take flight from the crest of the ridge.

"Fuck," I whispered, through chattering teeth.

I couldn't be certain it had been a raven. Even if it had been a raven, I couldn't be certain it was Hugin or Munin, Óðinn's spies. Still, my pulse raced and my muscles tightened, as if in anticipation for a battle.

Deciding to cut our excursion through Svartálfaheimr short, I ripped open a portal against the bleak, snow-smeared face of a cliff. It wasn't a natural opening to the paths; the magic strained and tugged against me. But I was stronger and, with a grunt, I slit the face of the realm and exposed the places behind. Thrym and his horse followed me while I tried to patch the damage as best as I could. The strain on the magical energies would last, but no one should be able to discern who made the hole.

At least, that's what I hoped.

"Where to now?" Thrym asked.

He sounded almost jovial. I guessed that realizing he wasn't going to die abandoned among the demons and flames of Múspell had done wonders for his mood.

"This way," I bluffed.

My plan, insofar as I had a plan at all, had been to hop from Múspell to Svartálfaheimr to Asgard, and then finally to the sunny vineyards of Midgard. But it didn't feel like we were remotely close to any paths leading to Asgard. I raised my hand slightly, letting the currents of magical energy swirl around my fingers. Svartálfaheimr's distinct energies were everywhere. I tried to tune them out, to listen for something more subtle.

Múspell. To our left, a path ran back to the dry heat and sand of Múspell. It was probably the path we'd taken, still glowing with magic activated by our recent passage. That was no good either. I didn't dare walk that particular path again; it would be like leaving a signpost for Skadi.

Something cool brushed the palm of my hand, and I took a step to the right. The cold increased.

It was Niflhel, the chaotic realm of the inglorious dead. Anyone in the Nine Realms who did not die in battle traveled to Niflhel before passing into the final darkness.

I froze. My heart hammered wildly in my chest, and my mouth had gone dry. Everything seemed to slow until it was locked in place. My body. My heartbeat. The swirling, gray mists of the between places. Even the breath in my throat caught and remained, trapped halfway between my lungs and the freedom of the world outside.

The dead. Those who had not fallen in battle.

Anya and Falur. Even the little babe. They would be in Niflhel.

That thought exploded across the inside of my skull. By all the living creatures in all Nine Realms, how had I not realized this before? My own loves, my precious little family. Of course they would be in Niflhel.

And I'd been to Niflhel. Once. It was a horrible, dangerous place, completely uncharted and nigh uncontained. Óðinn and I had traveled there together, not long after we'd sworn the oath of blood-brotherhood, when I still would have done anything to prove myself to the rest of the Æsir. Óðinn had thought Niflhel could be claimed, made into one of his protectorates.

What we found was a screaming horror. The landscape was defined by an enormous river, surrounded on one side by mountains and on the other with a wild tangle of ancient forest. Worst of all, the entire realm was threaded through with pockets of oblivion. Óðinn called it the darkness, and it lay like shadows across the realm. They were portals to another realm, those dark places, but they only went one way: toward oblivion.

The inglorious dead wandered through the forest, stunned and usually incoherent. Occasionally we met someone lucid enough to realize they were dead, but mostly people sobbed, or screamed, or just stared blankly ahead, as if they were waiting for their fate to claim them.

There didn't seem to be nearly enough of the dead, however, and I surmised most of them fled into the darkness almost as soon as they arrived in Niflhel. And, even after spending only a few days in that realm, the darkness began to call to me as well. It was a subtle tug, like the pull of a comfortable bed after a very long day.

And the darkness was everywhere. The entire realm was like a thrice-damned sponge, riddled with those dark portals and waiting to claim the souls. There seemed to be a portal resting at the bottom of every valley, behind every tree, beneath every stone. There were a million ways to vanish forever from Niflhel, and precious few pathways back home. In the end, Óðinn and I had to combine our magic to rip a hole in the fabric of the land of the inglorious dead and clammer back to Asgard.

"That's a miserable shit-hole of a realm," I said to Óðinn, once we'd wiped the mud from Niflhel's dark and twisted forest off our boots.

Óðinn had shrugged. "It's not so bad. All it needs is the right ruler to set it straight."

He'd looked directly at me then, piercing my illusions with his sharp blue eye.

"Not a chance," I'd said. "You want someone to rule Niflhel, you find yourself another sucker."

That was ages ago, and Niflhel remained ungoverned, wild, and locked away from the other Realms. It had even become a bit of a joke around Asgard, as in, "You'd better shape up, if you don't want to end up ruling Niflhel."

Still. In the absolute silence of the pathways, I let myself take a long, slow breath.

Would Niflhel be so bad if I were there with my family?

My chest ached, as if a great fist clenched my ribcage. I bit my lip, trying to clear my mind from the messy swirl of emotions. Niflhel was a morass, for one thing. There were no roads, no cities. It might take me a lifetime to find my lovers.

And why would they linger in the realm of the dead? I'd felt the pull of the darkness, even after only a few days. It called to you from Niflhel, seductive and beckoning. After long enough in Nfilhel, you began to long for the darkness. It began to feel like the next step, the right and proper thing to do.

Anya and Falur were both strong and brave. They wouldn't be afraid to face what came after death. No, they would probably embrace it. They might go together, hand in hand, perhaps with the babe nestled at Anya's breast.

I'd seen the dead entering the darkness, when Óðinn and I were beginning to get frantic about finding a way out of Niflhel. They smiled. All of them smiled. I'd seen a small child run in, almost skipping, followed by a woman who closed her eyes in ecstasy as the darkness rose to meet her, slipping around her waist like the arms of a lover.

The iron tang of blood filled my mouth. I realized I'd bitten my own lip. The mists wavered around me as my eyes filled with tears.

No, it wasn't just my tears. The mists were parting. They were responding to my desires, the unspoken urges of my battered heart. A portal took shape, dark and even. The winding trunks of black trees began to swim in my vision.

"Through here?" Thrym asked from behind me.

"No!" I snapped, jumping back.

The portal remained open, temping and easy. Fuck, of course it was easy to get to the Realm of the dead. It was the easiest thing in the worlds. The hard part was coming out.

And I wouldn't come out. I knew it with the same fierce certainty that I'd known I loved Anya and Falur on our blissful last night together. If I entered Niflhel, I'd be there forever. I'd stay, wandering between those dark trees, searching for my lost lovers, until Ragnarök. Or until I slipped into the darkness myself.

But that's not what I promised Thrym.

Behind me, Thrym's warhorse snorted as if he knew what I was thinking and disapproved. I closed my eyes and brought my hands up, pulling the portal to Niflhel closed. It took more effort than I'd expected; as much as my mind wanted to close that rift, my heart throbbed in protest. By the time I'd closed the portal, I was panting with effort, my body slick with sweat.

"What was that?" Thrym whispered.

I spat, but it did nothing to clear the bitter tang from my mouth. "Niflhel."

A moment later, Thrym's hand closed around my shoulder. His strong arms wrapped around me, holding me up as his warhorse stamped in impatience. I let myself fall against his broad chest as my body trembled with cold and exhaustion.

"Thank you," he whispered into my hair.

Tears slid down my cheeks. I made sure my illusions hid them.

CHAPTER TWENTY SIX

W̶e crossed through Álfheim instead, the intoxicating Realm of the Elves. Thrym sighed as soon as we stepped from the portal and onto the soft, thick grass between the trees. It was twilight. The sky was a delicate blush of lavender, and thick shadows pooled beneath the trees, but I took no pleasure in the surroundings. My nerves sang as if on fire as I tried to listen to every strand of magical energy in the realm. This was the most beautiful realm, but also the most dangerous. The Elves were merciless, and we were quite blatantly trespassing.

"Where—" Thrym began, in a tone of hushed wonder.

"Shhhhh!" I hissed. "Álfheim."

Thrym's eyes widened, and he glanced from side to side as if waking from a dream. "So it's real, then?"

I huffed impatiently. That sense of time slipping away was building again, as if each moment we spent wandering the Realms was being ripped from my skin. Óðinn's armies would be in position now. Skadi's forces would be approaching the Körmt River.

And they were expecting me.

"Yes, of course it's real," I snapped. "It's all fucking real. You've just walked through thrice-damned Múspell, you idiot."

Thrym shrugged, still gazing at the velvet twilight with wide eyes. "I never doubted Múspell. I always believed the nasty stories. But this..."

His voice trailed off as he swept his hand at the trees, the nodding flowers tucked in the grass, and the distant murmur of a gentle stream. Beside him, the warhorse nickered appreciatively.

"It's not a nice place," I whispered. "Move quietly, and quickly."

Thrym's mouth tightened, and he did as I said. The knot of irritation that had formed as an instinctive response to his child-like wonder began to slowly dissipate. What kind of a person believes all the nasty stories and suspects the pleasant ones?

I glanced over my back to see Thrym following closely, his hand wrapped around the pommel of his sword. His gaze traveled back and forth along the trees, watching his surroundings with a warrior's calm attention. He'd spared only a moment for Álfheim's seductive beauty.

My chest ached. I wished I could give him Álfheim, with the peace and beauty of its long nights and sunny days. I wished I had something better to offer Thrym than Midgard's Roman Empire, where he would always be an outsider. A barbarian.

We stopped at the edge of the trees and looked out on a vast field filled with the heavy scent of wildflowers. The skin of Álfheim was thinner here. I pressed my fingers between the strands of magic, coaxing a portal to open for us, almost as if I were pleasuring a lover. The magic parted easily, and the edges of the portal yawned open.

"This is the last time," I whispered.

Thrym nodded. He did not look back as he left Álfheim. I closed the portal behind us, shutting out the glimmer of starlight and the calls of the evening birds.

Once we were sealed inside the pathways, a wave of cold exhaustion hit my body, leaving me breathless and unsteady. My head swam as if I were drunk, and I staggered forward for a few lurching steps. Clenching a fistful of magical energy kept me from falling to my knees, but only just.

"Loki?" Thrym's voice sounded hushed and strange in the odd, flat air of the pathways.

I waved a hand, dismissing his concerns. "Just...catching my breath."

Stars. I pressed my hands to my eyes until white spots danced across my vision. My stomach rumbled, low and loud. I'd gone too long without eating again, and I couldn't recall the last time I'd slept.

No matter. I'd get us to Midgard first. Álfheim and Midgard lay close to each other, although the paths between them were rarely used. The Elves considered Midgard a primitive backwater, and the mortals of Midgard lacked the magical awareness to make use of the paths.

Still, the paths existed, even if they'd grown a bit dim. Thrym's breath echoed around us as I led us down a darker, colder route. The fog pressed against us, tugging at our clothing and hair. Behind me, the horse snorted and stamped.

"Hang on to him," I said. "If that horse bolts—"

"I know." Thrym's voice was iron.

The essence of Midgard swirled around us. Above me, in the distance, I could smell the northern oceans. The scent carried the sting of painful memories, and I turned away. To my left was the sound of wind in the treetops and the scream of a hawk. And to my right, finally, the scent of sun-warmed earth and stone.

I raised my hands and began sifting through the strands of magic. Midgard was a big place, and I didn't have the time to dump us just anywhere. Óðinn's grim visage flickered through my memory. I'll meet you, I'd said. And I would.

There. My smallest finger hit the right strand, and I pulled it out, coaxing and pleading. It widened slowly, until the final portal gleamed before us. The thick, golden sunlight of a late afternoon streamed through, making the cold fog inside the pathways swirl in agitation.

"Here?" Thrym asked.

I nodded in response, feeling too drained to bother with words. Thrym and his horse walked past me, and I slipped out after them, closing the portal behind us with trembling fingers.

"Where is this?" Thrym asked, once I'd finished.

I blinked, wiped my eyes, and blinked again. The sun lay low on the horizon, making it hard to see clearly. Everything felt too bright, and too strong. An odd image surfaced in my memory. The little room I'd added to Sigyn's house, with its narrow bed, its window the size of the far wall, and the magically refilling flagon of Val-hall's mead. I longed for that little room with an intensity so fierce it almost hurt.

"Midgard," I said. My voice sounded thin, as though it had been stretched too far, across too many Realms.

Thrym cocked an eyebrow at me. "This? Midgard?"

Our surroundings slowly swam into focus. We'd materialized just by the road, which was thankfully empty, on a little rise overlooking the vineyards. One particular vineyard, in fact. One whose trellises lay on the ground, and whose half-dead, neglected grapevines spilled their bounty over the hard earth.

I coughed to clear my throat. "It's Midgard," I said. "Welcome to the Roman Empire."

Thrym snorted as if he still didn't believe me. "They have roads in Midgard?"

Narrowing my eyes against the sun, I could just make out the silhouette of the domus I'd bought for Thrym. Another round of dry coughs shook my chest, and I bent over until it passed. When I stood, Thrym was watching me with an odd blend of expressions on his grime-streaked face.

"Múspell," I rasped. "The sandstorm."

That wasn't true, and Thrym damn well knew it. But he had enough tact to remain silent.

"Come on. This is your place, now," I said, staggering to the road.

THE LITTLE DOMUS HUMMED with activity. Three men stood on the roof, replacing tiles, and the scent of roasting meat drifted through the air. I stopped a man repairing one of the window shutters and asked for Marcus. He looked at me, then at Thrym and the massive warhorse, and his eyes widened noticeably. He gave a stiff, formal bow before running off.

"Are you going to explain any of this," Thrym asked, "or do I have to puzzle it out on my own?"

Marcus appeared at the door before I could answer. He glanced at me before turning to Thrym and the blood bay stallion at his side. The horse alone would stand out on Midgard. It was far larger than ordinary Roman ponies, and it would probably live four times as long. Marcus's expression did not waver, but the corner of his eye twitched.

I turned to Thrym, who wore an almost identical expression of grim evaluation. They were appraising each other, I realized, as if they'd met on the battlefield. Calculating strengths and weaknesses.

"Thrym," I said, stepping into the charged space between them. "This is Marcus Salonius Quintilius, formerly of the Roman Army. He's a freeman and a citizen, hired to help you restore this place and bring it to glory. Also, to teach you the languages and the customs of the Empire."

Clearing my throat, I turned to Marcus and switched to Latin. "Marcus, this is Thrym, son of Thrasir, formerly of Jötunheimr. Teach him well."

I stepped back. Thrym and Marcus locked eyes, watching each other silently and intently. The muscles in Thrym's right hand twitched, as if he wanted to grab his sword, and a vein in Marcus's neck began to pulse wildly. Idly, I wondered how long it would take for the tension between them to ignite into either violence or incredibly hot sex.

Thrym's horse broke the silence with a long, exhausted sigh. Thrym rubbed the beast's forehead before turning back to Marcus.

"My steed needs food, and water," Thrym said. He spoke slowly and very loudly, as if mere volume could make up for the language barrier between them.

Marcus nodded, then turned to the man who'd been fixing the shutters when we arrived but was now watching the scene was naked fascination.

"His horse must be tired," Marcus said. "Take it to the stables."

The man leapt forward, reaching for the reins. Thrym unclenched his fist very slowly.

"Please," Marcus said, finally giving a welcoming bow and sweeping his hand toward the interior of the domus. "Do come in. The servants are almost finished with dinner."

Thrym, after watching his horse disappear around the back of the house, took a step forward. He couldn't understand Marcus's words, but the welcoming gesture was clear enough. With a sigh, I began to pull Midgard's magic around me, preparing to travel through the aether alone.

A hand on my shoulder stopped me. Startled, I looked into Thrym's dark eyes.

"Loki," he whispered. He raised a hand to brush my cheek, touching me with such surprising tenderness my vision blurred with tears. "I don't know how to thank you."

"Don't," I rasped. "It's hardly Álfheim."

His eyes softened. "You saved my life. You'll save the lives of all those men under my command. Please, stay with me. Just for the night."

Oh, I ached for it! My exhausted body longed to be touched, to be held. But I shook my head.

"I've got places to be," I stammered.

Before I could say anything more, Thrym pulled my chest to his and pressed his mouth against mine. He kissed me hard, for a long time, taking what pleasure he wanted from my lips and tongue. My body softened against his, melting like ice in the sunlight. But when he pulled away, Óðinn's pale gaze loomed in my mind.

"I can't," I whispered. "I've got an army to defeat."

Thrym smiled. "Come back," he said. "Check in on me."

"Of course. I'll even bring Thor."

Thrym's grin widened, and he gave me one last crushing embrace before releasing me completely. Behind him, I saw Marcus watching us, his mouth a round, dark O of shock.

Two months, I thought, as I pulled myself through the aether. Two months until Thrym is kissing Marcus like that.

"YOU'RE LATE," ÓÐINN growled.

"Well, at least I'm not drunk," I snapped back.

Jötunheimr was freezing, and I was exhausted. I'd traveled from Midgard to Asgard to Jötunheimr, just in case I was being tracked, and I hadn't had time to stop for food along the way.

But my bad mood was born of more than just fatigue and hunger. I felt good when I left Midgard, imagining Marcus and Thrym beginning the slow process of learning how to speak each other's languages. I felt as though I'd done something important; I'd saved some part of the Nine Realms, and been fairly clever in the process.

I wanted to share this little victory with someone. It would have made sense to tell Anya and Falur, of course, as we lay together in the warmth of our stone hut. But now that hut was just a jumble of rocks in a wind-swept, forsaken corner of Midgard. I pictured myself kneeling before the burial mound, my shoulders hunched against the wind off the ocean, whispering my story to the barren rocks. That thought made me feel as if the frigid winds of Jötunheimr had cut a direct path through my chest.

I bit my lip, trying to bring my focus back to the present moment, and the present realm. Thor, Týr, Óðinn, and I stood in the road, hidden in shadows at the point where it began to slope upward from the cold darkness of the Körmt River. Before us, Skadi's army was crossing the Körmt, mostly silently and with much difficulty. They'd commandeered a small ferry, but it wasn't large enough to hold the horses, so her troops had to unpack their gear and then coax the animals to swim.

From our perspective, it looked like a nightmare. A few torches on either side of the crossing flickered below us, illuminating shifting, nervous animals. The occasional sharp curse or long, high-pitched whinny filled the night air.

"She's got about half the troops across," Thor grunted.

I turned to examine his profile in the starlight. Thor would be happy to hear about Thrym, of course, but he wasn't exactly the audience I wanted. Thor's entire life was filled with stupidly heroic acts, so he didn't find the stupid heroism of others particularly impressive.

"Almost," Óðinn whispered.

I glanced to the hills surrounding either side of the Körmt. Our armies were there, waiting. Heimdallr and Freyr commanded legions of Óðinn's warriors from Val-hall. They had crept silently through the forests until they stood at attention, filling the woods around the Körmt. Every soldier held an unlit torch, and behind the soldiers stood a second line of torches held aloft by tall wooden stakes.

All waiting.

There was a loud splash, the high, piercing shriek of an animal, and a loud curse. Voices filled the night as figures swarmed over the wooden ferry, which had begun to tilt alarmingly.

"Now," Óðinn said. "Loki, do it."

I drew in a deep breath, more for dramatic effect than anything else. I'd held these particular magical strands tight in my palm since the moment I materialized on Jötunheimr. Each strand pulled taut, stretching thin through the cold air, until it touched down on one unlit torch.

"Boom," I whispered as I flexed my energy.

Several thousand torches flared to life. Trees, bushes, and rocks jumped into sudden illumination, and the flaming points of light sparkled off the dark, smooth waters. For a moment, it looked like the hills surrounding the Körmt River had spontaneously burst into flame.

Below us, horses screamed and bolted, although the noise of their thundering hooves was drowned out by the shouts and curses of the soldiers. The entire world undulated as confusion, then panic, rippled through Skadi's armies.

Into the chaos, two massive ravens descended. They screamed like men, in sharp, high voices, as they circled the head of the army. Torches flared to life within Skadi's army and, in their wavering light, I saw hands raised to the sky, pointing at the ravens.

"Skadi," Hugin the raven cried, his voice amplified by Óðinn's magic. "Óðinn will parley."

Any response to Hugin's words was drowned out by the rush of voices rising from Skadi's fragmented army. Hugin and Munin rose into the night sky slowly, as if they had all the time in the world. Several hastily fired arrows flew between them to land back among Skadi's troops.

We waited. The four of us moved from the shadows to stand in an obvious line, outside of arrow or spear range but still clearly visible. The torches I'd just lit burned all around us, and Óðinn's war tent luffed in the wind behind us. The tent seemed like overkill to me, but then again, I'd never been particularly military-minded.

After so long that I'd begun to shiver beneath my illusions, a single rider appeared on the road between us and Skadi's army. He carried Thiassi's banner, an unimaginative image of his ugly castle against a field of dark blue. The rider was young, and he looked nervous, although he stopped so far away from us that it was difficult to make out the nuances of his expression.

"Skadi will see you," he called. "Follow me!"

"Good!" Óðinn barked. "We come."

I raised an eyebrow at Óðinn. Walking into Skadi's camp seemed like a risk. Thor must have felt the same, because he pulled Mjölnir from the loop on his belt and tightened his grip on its handle. Óðinn leaned heavily against his spear Gungnir as we walked, making him seem weak and vulnerable. It wasn't a bad ploy. Magic tingled around him as we approached the camp, and I guessed he was making himself look even older.

Skadi's soldiers had settled somewhat by the time we entered their ranks, led by the banner-bearing horse and his young, nervous rider. Blank, angry faces followed our progress. A lot of faces. I ran my fingers through the magic in the air, trying to identify weaknesses. I found no easy passage to Asgard, but I did feel the heat of Múspell against my palm. Fleeing to Múspell would be better than death, I supposed, if it came to a fight. I'd have to drag Óðinn, Thor, and Týr with me.

The horse stopped suddenly. Beside me, Óðinn sighed heavily and leaned against his spear. A small white tent glowed before us. It looked hastily erected, with a noticeable sag in the roofline, but I was still surprised she'd had time to put anything up at all. Clearly, Skadi was trying to impress us.

We entered the tent in single file. A fire crackled in the center, sending smoke through a soot-stained hole in the sagging fabric of the roof. Skadi stood on the far side of the fire, in full armor, her arms crossed over her chest and a scowl like a thundercloud on her face.

Two guards stood at arms behind her and an older man shifted on his feet next to her, his face almost as pale as the tent's walls. He seemed familiar somehow, but I dismissed the dim whisper of recognition to focus on Skadi.

I'd never been this close to her. I wasn't expecting her to be attractive, but she was, in a fierce, warlord sort of way. She was clearly her father's daughter, but the large nose and fat lips which seemed so unattractive on Thiassi somehow looked alluring on her. The firelight made her armor glow, almost as if she were lit from within.

Óðinn coughed like an old man before he bowed low before her. The hand gripping his spear trembled, and I felt a grudging flicker of admiration for the old weasel. How do you throw a ruthless warlord off her game? Show up as a weak old man.

"Skadi, daughter of Thiassi, leader of the armies of Jötunheimr. I thank you for your willingness to parley."

Skadi's eyebrows wrinkled and moved closer together. I doubted this was the greeting she'd expected from Óðinn the All-father, and it looked like she didn't quite know what to make of the surprise.

"We are here," Óðinn continued, "to make amends for a great wrong. The death of your noble sire Thiassi was a tragedy across every hill and valley, every mountain and desert, in all the Nine great Realms."

I managed to suppress my eye roll. Skadi's lips still pressed together in an angry frown, but her right eye twitched at his words.

"I have, within my humble power, the opportunity to offer you recompense, as well as to ensure that your father, the great Thiassi, is never forgotten." Óðinn's voice dropped almost to a whisper.

Skadi's legs stiffened, and she shook her head slightly, as if casting off an enchantment. She gestured toward the fire.

"Hryery," she growled. "Step forward. Tell these men what you found."

The old man next to Skadi shuffled forward. In a flash, I remembered where I'd last seen him. It was the night Thrym arrived at the encampment, when I'd hidden in the shadows of a barracks tent. He was one of Skadi's generals.

Hryery trembled in the firelight. He glanced back at Skadi, swallowed hard, and then turned to us.

"I, uh. I found one of t-the generals—" His voice trembled, and it took him a moment to regain control. Odd. He'd seemed much more competent the night Thrym had arrived. What in the Nine Realms was wrong with him now?

"One of our generals is m-m-missing," he stammered.

"Oh?" Óðinn asked, sounding only mildly interested.

Skadi spat into the fire, which hissed and flickered in disapproval. "Only six men knew of our plans before tonight. And now, only five of them remain. Hryery?"

The older man flinched as if he'd been hit, then turned to face Skadi with wide, wild eyes. "M-My Lady?"

"Who was responsible for Thrym?"

Hryery's head dropped. "I was."

Skadi moved so quickly I hardly had time to make sense of her actions. Her arm swept across her front, there was a metallic hiss, and something hot and wet splattered across my face, stinging my eyes. The thick, iron tang of blood filled the air. I wiped my eyes in time to see Hryery's decapitated body, still standing, begin a slow and graceful descent to the packed earth beneath the tent. His spurting carotid artery sprayed the interior of the tent with a fine, red mist.

Óðinn stepped delicately to one side, allowing Hryery's corpse to crash to the ground beside him. Skadi stepped over the body, pulled a cloth from inside her breastplate, and meticulously cleaned her sword. We watched in absolute silence as she wiped the blood and grime from her blade, then resheathed the gleaming weapon. Finally, she raised her eyes to Óðinn.

"I am not your dear, Óðinn, son of Bor. And I am not so easily bribed."

Óðinn's hand tightened around the shaft of his spear. It was no longer shaking, I noticed. When he spoke, the old man's cringing vulnerability had vanished.

"Skadi. We have your armies surrounded. My troops outnumber yours two to one, and your men are exhausted and demoralized."

Skadi's expression remained unchanged, but her right eye twitched again.

"Out of respect for your father," Óðinn said, "I came here tonight to offer you an alternative to ignoble defeat. Or do you want to be remembered as the woman who led the armies of Jötunheimr to their doom?"

Skadi's lips twisted into a scowl. "I was betrayed! You cock-sucking sons of whores got to Thrym!"

"Perhaps," Óðinn said. "Or perhaps I have other ways, and Thrym had the sense to abandon a sinking ship. Rats do that, you know."

For the first time since we entered the tent, another expression flickered across Skadi's scowling visage. Curiosity?

"What, exactly, are you prepared to offer?" Skadi said.

"The stars," Óðinn replied. "I shall name two of the best and brightest stars after your father, the great Thiassi. Across all the Nine Realms, he shall never be forgotten."

Skadi snorted and spat again. The fire hissed. "Not enough."

"I've only just begun," Óðinn said. "Second, we humbly offer you one of our own."

That strange expression returned, a sort of open and incredulous fascination, before Skadi regained control and resumed her typical scowl. "A hostage?"

Óðinn shrugged. "If you like. I was thinking a husband."

Skadi's thick lips pressed together until they almost vanished beneath her glare. "Who?"

"Your choice. Anyone who's unmarried."

Her eyes widened. She glanced around the blood-stained interior of her tent as if she'd somehow missed the entrance of Baldr the Beautiful. Her dark eyes found me, and I felt something cold and heavy take root in my gut. My fingers clenched the strands of magic, but they'd been warded. It would take considerable effort to pull myself out of here.

"It's still not enough," Skadi said.

Her voice had changed. What had just been iron and blood was now soft, almost sweet. It reminded me of the low hiss a snake makes, and I had the sudden, unshakable sense things had just gotten much, much worse.

"Name your price," Óðinn said.

Skadi's arm streaked across her body a second time. Her blade hissed as it fled from her sheath. Something cold pressed into the base of my throat. Involuntarily, I made the fires surge. Their orange light streaked the cold, gleaming length of Skadi's sword as she held it against my neck.

"Loki the Lie-smith," Skadi purred. "Bastard son of that crazy bitch Laufeyiar. You lured my father to his death."

I took a step backward. Skadi's blade followed me. When I swallowed, the press of cold steel against the base of my throat deepened. It dawned on me, with sudden, hopeless clarity, that I could have stayed in Midgard. I'd be wrapped in Thrym's arms by now, well-fed and well-fucked. Possibly setting my cantrips and allowing myself to fall asleep in Thrym's strong arms.

Skadi turned to Óðinn. "A life for a life seems fair, All-father."

Óðinn said nothing. I'd rather hoped he would disagree. Skadi's dark eyes swung back to me, glittering with excitement.

"I want Loki dead," she said.

"Fine," Óðinn answered.

"What!" I yelped.

Thor cleared his throat. Loudly. "Loki's probably worth more to us alive, father."

Skadi snorted.

"I think Thor might be right," Týr added, in his soft voice.

"Thank you!" I said.

I tried to ease myself away from the point of Skadi's blade. It was no use; she followed my movements with perfect ease.

Out of the corner of my eye, I saw Óðinn raise a finger. "One moment, Skadi, if you don't mind."

She didn't answer immediately. A trickle of cold sweat made its way down the back of my neck. I tried not to breathe too deeply, lest the sword find purchase against my larynx. An unpleasant smell began to emanate from the corpse on the floor.

Without warning, Skadi shifted again, sheathing her sword. I fought to retain control of my illusions to hide the fact that I'd started to tremble badly.

"One. Single. Moment," she said, giving Óðinn a smile of pure malice. "And, All-father, you try to betray me, I swear to the Nine Realms I'll find a way to hurt you. Very, very badly."

Óðinn ignored her as she stalked out of the tent. Her soldiers followed, very obviously not looking at the decapitated, lifeless body sprawled between us.

"What the ever-loving fuck!" I growled once they'd left. "After all the mountains of shit I've climbed for you, you worthless, motherfucking—"

Óðinn lunged forward, moving much more quickly than his old man illusions would have suggested. He grabbed the neckline of my armor in his fist and shook me, snapping my head backward.

"Shut up!" he spat. "You arrogant, selfish, impulsive bastard! You kidnapped Iðunn, Loki! You, not me! You failed to bring her back unnoticed, you drew Thiassi to our very gates. You brought this upon my people, Lie-smith!"

With a shove, he released me. I staggered backward, swaying as if he'd struck me. He might as well have struck me. I blinked slowly and wiped my mouth on the back of my hand.

"My people?" I replied. "What happened to 'our people,' Oath-brother?"

Óðinn snorted, then spat on the floor between us. "Just how long do you expect me to keep cleaning up after you?"

"Father," Thor interrupted. "I really don't think it's a good idea to let Skadi—"

I raised my hand, gesturing for Thor to shut up. My mind spun. I didn't necessarily fear death, but I didn't want to die this way. Not as retribution for Thiassi. Not as Óðinn's puppet.

Closing my eyes, I cast my mind out, searching desperately for some way out of this. Óðinn's stern face surfaced in my memories, wavering in the thin sunlight of northern Midgard. *We'll bargain,* Óðinn had said, when he came to drag me from my drunken self-pity above the burning ashes of Anya and Falur's village. *What does the Lie-smith want?*

That was it. That was my answer. What did the All-father want? What could I give Óðinn to prove I was worth more alive than dead? I winced inside my illusions. Hadn't I already given Óðinn everything? I'd traveled the Nine Realms by his side. I'd retrieved Thor's hammer from Thrym, I'd gotten the Æsir the beautiful wall which ringed Asgard. I even attempted to steal Freyja's necklace for Óðinn, although Heimdallr stopped me.

The ragged edge of desperation in my chest grew stronger. I clutched at the magical energy swirling across my palms. It would take a lot of effort, but I could probably rip open the aether right now. I could flee, just like I'd traveled the paths with Thrym. Another image surfaced in my desperate mind. The round portal to Niflhel, with its dark, twisted trees, and the subtle tug of the darkness beyond.

Just like that, my answer slid into place. It was so fucking obvious I couldn't believe I hadn't thought of it before.

"Niflhel," I gasped as I opened my eyes. "I'll get you Niflhel. Ruled, organized, and answering to you."

Óðinn's face contorted in a deep frown. "You would make a terrible ruler, Loki."

"Not me," I said. "I—I know someone. I know someone who could rule Niflhel. And she'll remain loyal to you."

Óðinn's frown softened, and he raised the eyebrow above his empty eye socket. "Perhaps you do, Lie-smith."

Before I could respond, Óðinn spun and pulled back the tent's entrance flap. "My honored Skadi," he said, with another bow. "We're ready to continue our parley."

Skadi stalked back into the tent, looking very much like a cat who'd just killed a mouse in the larder. She resumed her position beside the fire, crossing her arms over the gleaming breastplate of her armor.

"Well?" Skadi asked.

"I accept your conditions," Óðinn said.

"Excuse me?" I interrupted.

Óðinn raised a finger again. "However. Although I've never had the pleasure of meeting you, honorable Skadi, daughter of the much-lamented Thiassi, I assume you've heard of me, as I've most certainly heard of you."

An awkward silence fell in the tent. Everyone tried not to look down, where the blood from Hryery's headless corpse had turned the ground at our feet to thick, foul-smelling mud.

"I've heard of you," Skadi finally admitted.

"Well. Good. Then I assume you've heard I can't resist an opportunity to add a small caveat to any of my agreements."

Silence again. Skadi's frown grew so deep I felt I could have hidden a dagger in the furrow between her eyes.

"Fine," she spat.

"Excellent. Thank you for indulging an old man in his eccentricities. Here are my conditions, which I believe you'll find quite reasonable. First, you may choose your husband from among any of the Æsir or the Vanir on Asgard. But. You must choose your husband under my conditions."

Óðinn couldn't resist a shit-eating grin, while Skadi just looked confused. She glanced down at the floor, then back up at Óðinn as if she had missed something. Beside me, Thor and Týr looked almost as lost as Skadi.

Skadi shook her head again. "Fine," she said again. "I accept. I'll choose your son Baldr, no matter the conditions."

Ah. So Angrboða had been right after all; Skadi lusted after Baldr. The thought made me feel sick to my stomach.

"Good. Now, my second condition is somewhat similar. I'm afraid, at my age, the imagination suffers somewhat—"

"Just get on with it!" Skadi snapped. "Are you going to kill that shit-eating bastard Loki for me, or shall I do it myself?"

"You can do it yourself," Óðinn said.

I flinched, and just barely restrained myself from saying something. Beside me, Thor began shaking his head frantically. Under other circumstances, I may have found his urgency touching.

"If," Óðinn said, "and only if, at your wedding feast, Loki cannot make you laugh."

Skadi snorted. "You think that piece of shit can make me laugh? Me? I'm in mourning for my father, you flea-bitten son of a cheap whore."

Óðinn didn't respond. I guessed he'd been called worse. In fact, I was planning on calling him worse, as soon as I got him alone.

"Those are our terms," Óðinn said. "Agree to them, travel with us back to Asgard, and we call off our troops. Or don't agree, and let the Nine Realms know your leadership led to the fall of Jötunheimr."

Silence. From beyond the thin walls of Skadi's tent, I heard the nervous whinny of a horse, the distant hum of voices, and the scrape of stone against metal as someone in Skadi's army decided now was an opportune time to sharpen their sword. Skadi's right eye twitched again, and her fingers tightened around the metal bracers on her arms.

"I will travel with you to Asgard," Skadi finally said. It sounded like each word had been wrenched from her lips.

Óðinn bowed low before her. "Very good. My dear sons Thor and Týr will escort you, and any men you wish to bring."

Now that the decision was made, Skadi seemed unsure of how to proceed. She turned toward the door, hesitated, then glanced again at Óðinn as if she expected him to pull a dagger from his belt. When he did nothing but smile blandly, Skadi frowned again, then spun to the door. Týr followed her. Thor hesitated at the tent's entrance and glanced at me with a worried frown knotting his features. I had no idea how to respond, so I grinned at him. Between my fingers, the latent magical energy of Jötunheimr hummed as I pressed through the wards to pull a blade into my palm.

Once they left, I spun toward Óðinn with my fist clenched around the handle of the dagger. But he was too damned fast; he raised his arm and caught me under the chin, paralyzing me with a sudden burst of magical energy. His fist closed around my throat as I struggled against his grip, casting wildly for the magical strands in the atmosphere. It was useless; Óðinn had already dampened them.

Gritting my teeth together, I sent the blade back into the aether and raised my hands, fingers spread, palms open.

"I thought you said Skadi wouldn't kill me," I hissed, keeping my voice low.

"You thick skulled shit-for-brains," Óðinn whispered. His fist tightened around my windpipe just long enough for me to think he was actually going to strangle me. "You're not going to die."

His grip loosened, and I fell free with a gasp.

"Oh, really?" I gasped. "Because that's exactly what it looked like from here."

Óðinn examined his glove closely, as if touching me had stained the fingers. "Stop whining. You'll make Skadi laugh."

"Her? That psychotic bitch just decapitated her own general in front of us. Does she strike you as a woman who has an especially strong sense of humor?"

Óðinn fixed me with his pale eye. "You'll make her laugh," he repeated. "And I want you there when she chooses her husband. I want you to keep the lights low."

"What?"

Óðinn ignored me and turned toward the tent door. I grabbed his shoulder and spun him around before he could leave.

"Are you completely out of your ancient, battle-scarred mind? You're trying to trick her? You're not going to give her Baldr?"

Óðinn's expression may as well have been carved from wood, but his lone eye twinkled. "I'm going to give her exactly what she just agreed to. And you are going to give me someone to rule Niflhel."

"Fuck you!" I spat.

If Óðinn was planning on cheating Skadi out of her marriage to Baldr, that did not bode well for my plans to make the snake laugh during her wedding feast.

Óðinn's hand was back around my neck before I could react. "You piece of shit," he growled. "I tried to be reasonable. I tried to warn you. And, when you ignored my council yet again, I tried to give you what you wanted. But this time you went too far. We could have died, Loki. We could have all died ingloriously, of old age for fuck's sake, when you stole Iðunn's apples. And for what?

Just because you liked sticking your cock in some meat bags from Midgard?"

Óðinn's face was so close to mine that his hot breath swept over me like the winds of Múspell. My mind screamed in protest. I hadn't wanted the apples of immortality for Anya and Falur because of sex. Yes, I'd chosen badly when I kidnapped Iðunn, but their lives had meant more to me than all of the Æsir and Vanir combined.

Óðinn wouldn't understand, I realized as I stared into the darkness of his empty eye socket. He'd plucked his own eye from his skull in exchange for wisdom, because with wisdom comes power.

He would never understand what it meant to love someone.

"Fuck. You." I whispered.

Óðinn let me go, turned toward the tent flap, then spun back with speed born of centuries on the battlefield. I barely saw him raise his hand before my head rocked back and my vision exploded with white starbursts. I forced my lips together to keep from crying out, although my mouth filled with the tang of blood and my cheek screamed in pain where he'd just hit me.

"Don't try it again," Óðinn said. "Or I really will kill you. And I'll be expecting the future ruler of Niflhel to meet with me on Asgard. Tonight."

With that, he pulled open the tent flap and left. I winced and rubbed my jaw as I thought about where I needed to go next.

I'd almost rather stay in Skadi's bloody tent with the headless corpse.

CHAPTER TWENTY SEVEN

The quick meal I'd devoured on Asgard shifted precipitously in my gut as the dark spires of the castle took shape in front of me. I swallowed hard, trying to keep the bread and meat from coming back up. My arms and legs trembled, and I felt painfully awake and alert, despite the fact that I hadn't slept in days. The dark cloud of Angrboða's dress surfaced in my memory, and I felt cold, as if I were being dragged back down to the ground.

No. I ground my teeth together, fighting the wave of bile in the back of my throat. There was no way Angrboða would be here. If she wanted to have any chance at ruling in Thiassi's place, she'd have to stay in his castle until the child—

That did it. Despite my best efforts, my dinner came back up. I bent over, splattering the cold rocks of Jötunheimr with the only meal I'd eaten in days. Fuck my life.

Straightening up, I wiped my hand across my lips and contemplated Angrboða's castle. I had resisted the mead of Asgard as I cut through Val-hall to grab something to eat, and right now, I seriously regretted that decision. Then again, there probably wasn't enough mead in all the Nine Realms to make me feel comfortable here.

I didn't bother with the guards this time; the fewer people who saw me, the better. Instead, I shifted into the shape of a fly and flew to the top floor. The castle was warded, of course, but my magic was stronger, although it still hurt like hell to cross those wards. I flew through an open window, winced as the fly illusion contracted in pain all around me, and clung to the wall until I could see through the red haze of pain.

My head finally cleared, and a moment later I recognized the hallway where I'd landed. In fact, I wasn't far from my goal. With a final wince, I shook off the fly illusion and became myself again. Then I strode through the halls of Angrboða's castle as if I had every right to be in her private living quarters in the hours before dawn.

The door to the room I wanted was closed. I took a deep breath and sniffed the air to confirm the occupant was inside. Alone. A thin yellow glimmer of candlelight flickered beneath her door. I raised my fist to knock, then hesitated. Would she call the guards?

Did I have any other choice?

I cleared my throat several times and knocked.

"Hel?"

There was a rustling from inside the door, and the candle flame flickered. Then the sound of footsteps. A moment later the door creaked open. The dead side of my daughter's face came into view.

"Father? What are you—"

"May I come in?" I interrupted.

She hesitated. Her skeletal face gave no indication of what she was thinking, but her feet shifted against the stone floor. Finally, she pulled the door wide open and waved me in. I entered, closing her door behind me. It had a bar over the deadbolt, I noticed. She would be able to lock it from the inside.

"Isn't that a bit dangerous?" I said, gesturing at the door.

Hel said nothing. Her half-dead face regarded me with absolutely no expression.

"I mean, what if your room caught fire?" I continued.

"Then I suppose I'd die in the flames," Hel said. "What are you doing here?"

I glanced around her sparse room. It held the same uncomfortable looking single bed, the same overflowing desk, the same disappointing lack of food or beverage. Above the desk, a small window showed the unforgiving stars of Jötunheimr.

"You could add a ladder to that window," I said, "to give yourself another exit."

Hel rolled her eyes so dramatically I could almost hear them rotate in their sockets. "Father. It's two hours before sunrise. Did you really come here to discuss fire safety?"

I wandered over to her desk, where a small abacus with delicate white and black beads nestled atop several leather bound books. A fresh roll of parchment covered the lower half of her desk. A regiment of numbers marched across the surface, the ink still gleaming wet in the light from the candle.

"What are you doing?" I asked.

"Running some figures."

"On what?"

The living side of Hel's face tightened in a frown. "Why do you want to know?"

"Humor me."

"Fine. Wool. We lease seventy-three smallholdings to families who raise sheep. But the wet spring was bad for calving. I'm trying to estimate how far behind those families are going to be come the Reaping. That way, I'll know what they're going to need to make it through the winer."

I frowned at the list of neat, black numbers which meant absolutely nothing to me. "Do you have a particular interest in wool, then?"

Hel's lips tightened further. "No. But somebody has to run this place."

"And that's you? You run this place?"

"Of course."

My grip on my illusions tightened. I'd guessed that was the case, given what I knew about my painfully serious daughter and

Angrboða's total lack of interest in actually running an estate, but damn, it was still nice to be right.

"How would you like to run something bigger?" I asked. "On your own? Without anyone trying to marry you off?"

Hel's living eye narrowed. The rat in her ribcage scratched as it shifted to stare at me with hard black eyes.

"Are you fighting with Mother again?" she asked.

I flinched under my illusions. "Óðinn has an offer for you. He wants to make you a queen, the queen of your own realm. With no need to marry, unless you choose—"

"Niflhel," she said, her voice flat and expressionless.

What the fuck? There was no way she could have known that, unless—

"Did he beat me here?" I asked.

Hel raised her eyebrow in what must have been an expression she picked up from me. I hadn't realized how condescending it looked from the outside.

"Óðinn wants power," Hel said. "He wants to either rule the Nine Realms, or have the leaders of the Realms under his influence. You're his oath-brother, so it's reasonable to assume you're helping him with this."

I opened my mouth to disagree, but Hel spoke over me.

"Plus, you just caused the death of my step-father Thiassi, so it's safe to assume you and Mother are at each other's throats again. Skadi is marching to war against the Æsir, but you're here, meaning Óðinn must have found some way to buy her off. Probably by offering her Baldr."

I blinked. "Is there anything you don't know?"

Hel ignored me. "Óðinn rules Asgard. With Skadi taken care of, the balance of power on Jötunheimr will be restored." She held up her hand, ticking off two fingers. "Surtr rules Múspell, and that's not going to change until Ragnarök. We've got the dwarves on

Svartálfaheimr, the elves on Álfheim, and Midgard is a worthless mess." She ticked off four more fingers.

"Óðinn isn't about to threaten the peace treaty with the Vanir by looking at Vanaheimr, and the mist world is uninhabitable." She held up eight fingers, five living and three skeletal. "Thus, if Óðinn is about to offer me a realm, it has to be Niflhel."

"Huh," I said. A wave of exhaustion hit me with the force of the tide and, for a moment, I thought I might stagger to Hel's bed and collapse. I pulled my illusions tighter, until they bit into my skin. The feeling passed, slowly.

Oddly enough, a strange sense of pride rose as my exhaustion ebbed. I didn't often think of Hel as being anything to do with me, perhaps because Angrboða had fought so hard to keep me away from my daughter, lest my reputation tarnish the beautiful child Hel had once been, or perhaps because Hel herself grew into such a prickly and difficult woman. But hearing her solve the mystery of Óðinn's motivations as if they were a child's puzzle box gave me an odd, unfamiliar sense of satisfaction.

This was my daughter, this capable, brilliant, strong-willed woman. She was able to weave one of the best illusions in the Nine Realms, and to out-think Óðinn the All-father.

"You'd make a very good Queen," I said.

Hel turned away, but not before I saw the blush that rose in her living cheek. Her exposed breastbone rose and fell rapidly several times, and I realized she might be struggling with some emotional depths I couldn't sense.

"If that's what you want," I added. "The decision is yours. Niflhel is a damned mess, and it's going to take centuries of work to bring it to hand."

My life may have happened to hang on her decision, but I saw no reason to point that out. I didn't want my daughter to take this role out of compulsion.

Hel took a deep breath, then turned to me with blazing eyes. "Are you using me to hurt Mother?"

I took a step back before I realized what I was doing. Angrboða's black dress filled my vision, suffocating me. Beneath my illusions, I pressed my eyes shut, trying to banish the image.

"I am not," I finally said. "Yes, I'm angry at her. She did something I found...unpleasant."

Hel's eyes widened.

"But that's not why I'm asking you," I finished.

"So why are you asking me?"

"Because Óðinn wants Niflhel," I said, honestly. "And I thought you may want this opportunity."

She tilted her head, eyeing me with her strange, pale gaze. I swallowed hard. Another uncomfortable thought rose in the place of my sudden flush of paternal pride. I'd gone ten years without visiting my daughter. I hadn't truly known Hel was running Angrboða's estate, and I could only guess at the murky complex of motivations behind her decision to transform herself into a monster.

Damnit. I'd been a shitty father to Hel.

"Look," I said, "on Jötunheimr, you're bound by the rules of the Jötunn. You'll never rule anything, unless it's in your husband's name, or your son's. Even then, you could be stripped of everything with a single word. You have no rights, no legal standing. You can't even own property."

Hel flinched. This entire castle was in the name of Angrboða's dead fifth husband Bragofi, the sucker she married before Thiassi, and Hel knew better than anyone her entire estate was just one legal battle away from being seized. So far, Angrboða had managed to sweet talk, bribe, or fuck her way into holding on to Bragofi's land and palace. But, now that Angrboða's attention had shifted to Thiassi's far richer holdings, Hel's ability to control the estate was tenuous.

"If you take the offer, you can rule Niflhel," I said. "And no one can take that away from you."

"Except for Óðinn," Hel muttered.

I sighed. She had me there. Óðinn could take anything he wanted, from anyone he wanted. Hel turned away again, showing me the white expanse of her exposed shoulder blade beneath the rotting tatters of her dress. It was a damned impressive spell, that hideous illusion. Whatever other reasons may have driven her to create it, Hel's animated corpse body was almost certainly designed to keep people away.

My chest constricted in a strange way as I remembered Hel before I'd taught her how to weave an illusion over her body. Even then, she'd been fierce and distant. She'd also been so gorgeous it almost hurt to look at her. Hel had managed to combine the best of my features with the best of her mother's, creating a distinctive, feminine beauty that rivaled any of the Vanir or Æsir.

A beauty that was now, by the looks of it, gone forever. If she barred her door at night when she slept, there would be no chance of another servant stumbling upon her with her guard down. For some reason I couldn't quite identify, the thought made me feel deflated, as though I'd made a mistake. Perhaps I should have helped Angrboða marry her off?

Hel's back stiffened, and she swept her hair from her face as she turned back to me. Her ghastly illusion even extended to her hair, hiding her natural red-gold curls beneath a pallor of limp, mousy brown.

"What are you smiling about?" she snapped.

Had I been smiling? I ran my hand over my face. Yes, I was indeed smiling, both with my illusions and with what lay beneath.

"I was just thinking how many women in the Nine Realms use an illusion to make themselves more attractive," I said. "And yet, look at what you do with yours."

Hel's face puckered as if she'd tasted sour milk. "If you start in on why women should make themselves beautiful to find a husband, I'm going to call for the guards."

My smile widened, although it did little to ease the ache in my chest. "Why don't you want to marry?"

Hel arched her eyebrow again. "That's none of your fucking business."

I shrugged. "Fine. What should I tell Óðinn?"

Hel opened her mouth, closed it, then bit the living half of her lip. For a moment, I could almost see the child she once was hiding beneath her hideous illusions. Then her living eye narrowed.

"Do I really need to explain why I wouldn't want to trade Mother's overbearing demands for the overbearing demands of some fat, rich lord who could beat me within an inch of my life, for any reason, without facing any repercussions?"

It was horribly inappropriate, but I snorted a laugh. The tightness in my chest loosened a tiny fraction. My offer to Angrboða to force Hel to marry had been a mistake, but offering my daughter the keys to Niflhel felt right.

"No," I said. "You don't need to explain anything, daughter."

"I'll do it," Hel said.

"Oh?"

I'd expected her to need some time for deliberations, but she surprised me again by taking my hand delicately into the fold of her living arm.

"I'll come with you," she said. "There are some arrangements I'll need to make that I should explain to Óðinn directly. What?"

I realized I was smiling again, grinning like an idiot actually, as I held my daughter's arm against my body.

"You're going to be very good at this," I said.

That delicate flush crept back over her living cheek. It must be leaking through her illusions, I thought, because Hel would hate to know she was giving her feelings away.

"I know," she said.

ÓÐINN ACCEPTED HEL as an equal, which surprised the shit out of me. He came down from his throne and sat at a table with her, calling up a huge number of incredibly boring maps and sheets of equally tedious figures. I stood in the shadows, yawning with increasing desperation, as they fell into a deep and thoughtful conversation about possible economic output and regulations. I was almost asleep on my feet when Óðinn snapped my name.

"Yes?" I snorted, jolting myself awake.

"Get out of here," Óðinn said, waving his hand at the door. "We've got confidential matters to discuss."

I glanced at Hel, who had her back turned toward me as she poured over a sheaf of crumbling paper.

"Your daughter is safe," Óðinn said.

"How very reassuring," I snapped, letting the acidity of my anger drip through my words.

Hel glanced up, then waved the bones of her skeletal hand at me. "I'm fine. Go on." She turned to Óðinn. "You'll have someone bring me to Jötunheimr to collect what I need before we survey Niflhel?"

"Of course," Óðinn answered. "But let's discuss what you're going to need."

As I watched the two of them, my daughter and my oath-brother, bent over the table like old friends, I weighed the risks. Would Óðinn hurt Hel? Unlikely. He wanted his mark on Niflhel, and she would make an excellent ruler. But the thought of putting her in danger—

I frowned at the swirl of my own thoughts. I'd thought I lost everything when I lost Anya and Falur. But now here I was, risking myself to bring Thrym to safety on Midgard and seething at the thought of someone hurting my very capable, and honestly terrifying, adult daughter. What in the Nine Realms had happened to me?

Hel glanced up and met my gaze with her piercing blue eyes. "What the fuck are you still doing here?" she snapped. "And why are you smiling again?"

"You've got such an elegant way with words," I said.

"Go!" She yelled.

Stifling another yawn, I went.

I WOKE TO BRIGHT SUNLIGHT and the distant sound of waves throwing themselves upon the shore. It took several minutes of blinking at the ceiling to remember where I was, and why I felt so comfortable.

Of course. This was Sigyn's house, and I'd woken up in the little room I built for myself. As I returned to consciousness, I vaguely remembered pulling myself here after introducing Óðinn to Hel and almost passing out during their incredibly tedious conversation about civilizing Niflhel.

With a yawn, I rolled over onto my side. Oh. By the fucking Realms, I'd woken up hard enough to pound nails with my cock. I grinned without thinking. It had been a while, hadn't it? Longer than I'd ever gone without a lover. I dropped a hand to cup the curve of my cock, then moaned at the touch. Yes, clearly it had been too long. I closed my eyes and again regretted my decision to leave Thrym so quickly. I could conjure an illusion of Thrym here, on the end of my bed, for me to watch while I pleasured myself.

My stomach groaned loudly, interrupting my fantasy. I ran my fingers through Asgard's magical energy, which always seemed as eager and responsive as a lover. But the latent magical strands felt distant and fuzzy this morning. My stomach protested again, this time adding a painful cramp to its vocal objections.

Right. It had also been a long time since I'd eaten anything. With a final caress, I let go of my erection and tried not to picture Thrym's naked chest.

The room wavered when I came to my feet. As if I needed another reminder my body wanted food. I pulled my illusions together, hiding the erection that was stubbornly ignoring my attempts to think about something other than how good it would feel to have someone's lips wrapped around my shaft right now.

No matter. I had to look at least somewhat presentable, for Sigyn's sake. The sun streaming through my window was low, rich, and golden; it must have been late afternoon. Of what day, I couldn't be sure.

Would Sigyn be here?

I cleared my throat several times, very loudly, before opening my bedroom door. The hallway beyond was still and silent. The doorway to Sigyn's bedchamber was shut, as was the doorway to the indoor hot spring I'd created. It occurred to me that Sigyn may be in the hot spring. An image of her small body, fully naked and embraced by the swirling warm water, surfaced in my mind. I shoved it aside. Sigyn may technically be my wife, but we were hardly close enough for me to go barging in on her unannounced. I decided it would be best to ignore that entire side of the house.

The main hall, where I'd first seen Sigyn sitting by the fire, was empty and still. Its windows were open, and the embers on the hearth were cold; the room smelled of the ocean, and of the wild beach roses which grew along the dunes. That only left the kitchen, which was also clean, silent, and empty. I stood in the doorway, frowning at the neat little room. I should have been glad for the solitude. The last thing I wanted was to have to explain myself. Right?

Fuck, I must be hungry. I wasn't even making sense in my own head. I rubbed my hand over my eyes and sat down at the kitchen table. A golden plate appeared, filled with poached salmon on a bed of wilted greens, sliced carrots, and thick, brown bread. I ate slowly, giving my stomach time to adjust as I idly admired the neat magic tying this table to the kitchens of Val-hall. It was a spell I could replicate, given enough time, but it wouldn't be easy.

The table was just like the rest of this house. Deceptively clever, perfectly done, and entirely comfortable.

A flagon of mead appeared after the meal, alongside a steaming mug of blackberry tea. I hesitated, then took only the tea. When I stood, my empty plate and the flagon of mead both vanished. The door to the beach outside was ajar, revealing thick, afternoon light sparkling off the slowly undulating waves.

"Nowhere to go but out," I whispered to myself.

Another scent drifted through the soft, warm air as I stepped outside the house. The scent of a woman's sun-warmed skin, and of her long, auburn hair. I inhaled deeply, feeling far better than I should after nothing more than rest, a meal, and blackberry tea.

Sigyn was sitting on the dunes in a long, high-necked green dress, her body bathed in sunlight, a book open on her lap. As I watched, a strand of hair fluttered across her cheek, and she lifted her hand to push it back, exposing the curve of her pale neck.

Stars, she was beautiful. How had I not noticed that before? A strange warmth slowly seeped into my body, perhaps from the late afternoon sun, perhaps from the mug of tea in my hand. Trying to stay silent, I reached for the nearest rosebush. That wild, unruly tangle of thorns was covered with rumpled pink blossoms, and the air was heavy with their sweet scent. I pulled on the magical strands to pluck the largest flower I could see, then sent it sailing through the air. It floated across the dunes as Sigyn turned a page and hesitated above her head. I tugged on the magic, and the flower drifted down to land atop Sigyn's open book.

"Oh!" Sigyn gasped. She turned around.

The smile she gave me looked like the sun breaking through the clouds, like the first warm day at the end of winter. An odd shiver moved through me as her gold-flecked eyes met mine. I'd never expected to see a smile like that on Asgard, from one of the Æsir.

"Loki!" She closed the book and cupped the rose blossom in her palm. "Did you sleep here?"

"I hope I wasn't an inconvenience?" I said as I sat down next to her.

She shook her head, sending several of her auburn curls flying. "Oh, of course not. I thought I sensed you here. Were you in that tiny little room?"

Her delicate features knotted in confusion, and I smiled.

"Where else would I sleep?"

A delicate flush of pink crept up Sigyn's neck. She turned toward the ocean. "I didn't think that room was for you. It's so —"

"It's fine," I insisted. "What more do you need when you're asleep?"

She laughed, a high, silver laugh which seemed to make the air grow warmer. "I think that entire room is smaller than Óðinn's bed."

My chest pinched at that, and I couldn't stop myself asking. "What do you know about Óðinn's bed?"

"I fought beside him," she said, turning to face me. The pink flush had reached her cheeks. "In the war with the Vanir. We used to be...very close."

That meant lovers, I guessed. But the knot in my chest loosened all the same. The Vanir war was ancient history. That bloody conflict, which had almost destroyed both the Æsir and the Vanir, had defined the world of my childhood, but Óðinn's peace treaty had held for hundreds of years. I whistled, long and low.

"You're that old?" I asked, then immediately regretted my words.

Sigyn just laughed again. It was a sweet sound, especially in that rose-scented air. "Yes. I'm that old."

I stared at her, and she turned back to the ocean. I was prepared to apologize for that comment, or to have to offer some recompense. Freyja probably would have held something like that against me for months. But Sigyn didn't even seem offended.

"Were you a Valkyrie?" I asked.

She nodded as she pushed another strand of hair behind her ear. "A long time ago. I've had enough of war, now."

So she'd been a warrior, a Valkyrie, and Óðinn's lover. She'd fought in the biggest war the Nine Realms had ever seen while I was still a child scrapping for food in the slums of Útgarðar. How in the thrice-damned Realms could Thor possibly think she was boring?

"Thor was very wrong about you," I said.

"Thor? Stars, I should hope so." She gave me another smile, this time shy and secret, before turning back to her book.

I waited for her to press me for information, or at least to ask me what Thor had said. But Sigyn seemed content to sit beside me in the rich silence and turn the pages of her book. I watched her while she read. She had thick eyelashes which cast shadows across the curve of her cheeks.

For a moment I wondered how Óðinn had possibly given her up, but the answer came almost immediately. A woman who was content with silence was not a good match for the forever-striving All-father. His current wife, Frigg, wasn't happy unless she was hosting a party. And Sigyn's beautiful, little house was most certainly not made for parties. I frowned as something fell into place.

"The magic on the kitchen table, that binding of two places. Didn't they call you the incantation-fetter?"

Sigyn closed her book and turned to me, her smile like clouds lifting after a storm. "I'm impressed."

Her lips were really quite lovely. I almost wanted to bend over and touch them. Kiss me when you want to kiss me, she'd told me the morning after I rescued Iðunn. Like an idiot, I'd thought I would never want to kiss anyone again. But, as I watched her lips part in a sweet smile, I found myself wondering how they would taste. Would Sigyn's kisses be soft and sweet, the kind that always leave you wanting more?

"I don't use my magic as fetters anymore," she said. "Not with people, at least. It was too..."

"Draining?" I offered, as her voice faltered.

"Yes. It took a lot out of me to fetter another person."

"Of course it did," I said. "Working a spell on someone else pushes your magic against theirs, unless you're collaborating. It's incredibly dangerous."

"Well, it was a war." A cloud passed over her delicate features, and I decided to change the subject.

"What was he like?" I asked. "The man you loved on Midgard. Ragnavaldr?"

That soft smile returned as she turned to gaze at her lap, where the flower I'd picked for her lay cupped in her palm. She ran her fingers over its soft pink petals.

"He was like you, I suppose," she said, her voice as soft as the flower petals. "Not as clever, perhaps. Funny. Charming." She paused, then glanced at me with a shy grin. "He had red hair too."

"Lucky guy," I said, without thinking.

Her cheeks colored, but her eyes darkened. "Perhaps. The older I get, the more I fear I was actually in love with the way he saw me. He thought I was so powerful, so wise. If I'd told him I hung the stars across the skies of the Nine Realms, he would have believed me."

She sighed, still staring at the pollen-laden stamens of the rose nestled in her lap. "He thought I was a goddess, of course. And now, all these years later, I worry that's what I really loved. The reflection of myself in his eyes."

Sigyn fell silent. I stared at her. The Æsir didn't talk like this. Every conversation I'd ever had on Asgard had been some sort of negotiation, pitting my needs and desires against the needs and desires of all the rest of them.

"Why are you telling me this?" I asked. "What do you want from me?"

"Want from you?" She laughed again, that clear, golden laugh which danced off the crashing surf below us. Her lips, I realized, were almost the same shade of delicate pink as the rose in her lap.

"I remember when you came to Asgard," she said. "Óðinn made such a production of it. Calling us all together, presenting you as the one who would help him build Val-hall. And then you extinguished all the fires, and re-lit them at once."

"I remember."

She laughed again, but softer this time, and her gaze slid back over the ocean. My chest gave a funny tug at that; I'd enjoyed watching the soft furl of her lips as she smiled at me. "You were so beautiful. So young. You made everyone laugh. I thought, oh, stars, they're going to eat that poor boy alive."

She fell silent, and her thumb caressed the rose blossom in her lap. "But you stayed. You got smarter. You grew harder. I used to watch for you, you know, when you came back to Val-hall."

Silence again. I shifted on the sand, casting back through the dim and distant memories of those first years in Asgard. Sigyn had watched for me? I had no recollection of that. All the women of Asgard had seemed so unapproachable, so beautifully aloof. Until I seduced Freyja, I hadn't even bothered to distinguish them from one another.

Sigyn sighed. "Then that horrible dwarf Brokk sewed your lips." She shivered, and the sand beneath me felt colder. "And they laughed. Just like they'd laughed at me, when I begged for one of Iðunn's apples to save Ragnavaldr."

Her voice dropped, and she closed her eyes. "I hated them, Loki. In that moment, I hated them all. You and Óðinn built Val-hall together, and look how they repaid you. That night, my mind finally realized what my heart had decided ages ago, perhaps even that first night you arrived." She paused, and the world seemed to stand still around us, waiting.

"I realized I would rather stand with you than with them," she finished, opening her eyes to the undulating expanse of the sunlit sea.

I whistled, long and low. "All that time? And you never said two words to me in the interim?"

Sigyn's soft lips curved into a shy smile. "I didn't want to just be your lover. I thought I'd wait for Óðinn to approach you, to make my intentions clear." Her eyes flickered back to her lap, and she pulled her lower lip between her teeth. "Obviously, that was a mistake."

I frowned. How would I have responded if a beautiful Æsir woman had approached me and asked for my hand in marriage?

I'd have thought she was insane, of course. I would have fucked her and discarded her, then gone to any lengths to uncover her ulterior motives. And I would have been doubly suspicious if Óðinn approached me with an offer of marriage to a beautiful woman of high standing, a former Valkyrie with elegant magical talents.

"It wasn't a mistake," I said.

Her eyes met mine and flashed in the bright sunlight. Beneath the high neckline of her dress, I saw her breastbone rise and fall several times in quick succession.

"Thank you," I said. "For everything. For telling me this."

"Of course." Sigyn rolled her shoulders in a graceful arc, mimicking the motion of the waves behind her. "We're bound to each other, now. I don't want to hide who I am. If you don't like me, it's best we find out soon, instead of dancing around it for decades."

"I like you."

I realized the words were true as they fell from my lips. I still wasn't sure what she could possibly like about me, but I enjoyed her company. She made me feel comfortable.

Sigyn pulled her hair back and took a deep, jittery breath. "Óðinn seemed upset when you left. Did you manage to resolve whatever it was with that woman? Skadi?"

I lay down on the sand beside her and sighed in contentment, happy to let her shift the conversation into shallower waters. "Yes. No worries. I saved the Nine Realms."

Sigyn's smile broadened. Another scent drifted through the air between us, swirling with the fragrance of the roses and the salt of the ocean. The sweet tang of her arousal. Damn. My own cock stirred in response, although I made sure my illusions gave nothing away.

"Not entirely by myself," I clarified. "But... mostly by myself."

Sigyn shifted on the sand, then set her book and the rose blossom aside to lay down next to me. She tucked her arm beneath her head and smiled.

"So, how did Loki manage to save the Nine Realms this time?" she asked.

I grinned. Oh, fuck, this felt good. It was so damned pleasant to be here, lying on the warm sand, well-rested and with a full stomach, talking with someone who actually wanted to listen while the purr of sexual interest hummed in the back of my mind, suggesting that things may get even more satisfying. I loved this feeling; it was something I thought I'd lost forever.

The breeze gusted between us, carrying the heady, warm scent of Sigyn's body, and her hair billowed around her face. I reached for her without thinking, brushing a tangle of curls from her cheek and tucking them behind her ear. Her caramel eyes widened and her lips parted as I touched the soft skin of her ear. Those lips. They were soft and full, and flushed a delicate rose pink. I ran my thumb over her mouth as softly as I could and felt the gasped intake of her breath against my skin.

The details of my trip to Jötunheimr may have to wait, I realized. The need to taste Sigyn's lips was suddenly overwhelming.

But first, I had to tell her how much I wanted her, and how good it felt to want someone again. How thrice-damned, fucking wonderful it felt to be here, now, with her.

"Sigyn—" I whispered.

A man coughed behind me.

I jumped against the warm sand. Sigyn's face flushed with color, then closed like a slammed door.

"Loki," Óðinn's voice cut into the space between me and my wife.

Stars damn it! I balled my hands into fists and clenched my teeth as my thoughts crashed and shattered. I'd had so many things I wanted to tell Sigyn. Now the moment was ruined.

"It's time," Óðinn said. "Skadi is going to pick her husband. You need to be there."

I forced myself to my feet and ran my hand across my face. "You asshole," I said to Óðinn.

He ignored me. "You're welcome to come as well," he said, turning to Sigyn.

Sigyn picked up her book without looking at him. "No, thank you."

I glanced at my wife, who was now sitting on the dunes and pointedly ignoring both of us. The only sign she'd just been lying on the dunes next to me with her lips against my hand was a trail of sand clinging to the side of her dress. I wanted to brush it off, to feel the warmth and curve of her body beneath that fabric. And then I wanted to take the dress off, to see what she'd look like with beach sand pressed against her naked body.

Had I really thought I'd never feel this way again, that I'd never be able to enjoy another lover? Anya would have gasped wide-eyed at that; Falur would have laughed at me. My chest tightened. Sigyn had given me a place to rest, or to hide. And, just for a moment, as we lay together on the sand in the afternoon sunlight, she'd made me feel like myself again. I dropped to one knee beside her.

"Thank you," I whispered.

Sigyn nodded. Her brow furrowed as a strange cascade of emotions tumbled through her gold-flecked eyes. "Be careful," she answered.

I smiled at that. Here we were, married for only a handful of months, and we'd already established a ritual.

"I will," I replied.

CHAPTER TWENTY EIGHT

The mood in Val-hall was hardly festive.

The long tables of the feast hall were laden with food and fragrant garlands of flowers, barrels of mead lined the walls, and the torches flickered merrily, but most of the men's faces were grim and determined. Baldr looked especially mournful, I observed as I followed Óðinn to the front of the hall. Not that I blamed him.

Skadi stood on the dais, flanked by two of her guards. She was still wearing armor, and her arms were crossed over her chest. In fact, she looked exactly like she'd looked in the tent on Jötunheimr, although I assumed she'd at least taken a prenuptial bath. At least, I hoped so, for poor Baldr's sake.

I took my place next to Thor. He, for one, wasn't looking too dour. Then again, he'd been married to Sif for an age, so it wasn't his head on the chopping block. I cleared my throat a few times to get his attention

"What kind of a blushing bride wears armor to her wedding?" I whispered to Thor.

"She looks like a real firecracker in bed, that's for sure," he muttered under his breath.

I glanced at Skadi again. With her gleaming armor, multiple swords, and fierce scowl, she looked like the very opposite of sex.

"Do you think she'll take off all her armor for Baldr?" I whispered. "Or just the crotch plate?"

Thor snorted loudly as he tried to disguise his laugh. Skadi shot us both a look that would have sent small children scurrying for safety under their beds. Apparently, she really did intend to kill me. At the moment, it seemed like it would be easier to drag the entire army of Asgard through the mists for an eternity than to make that stone cold warrior bitch laugh.

But I had to. Sigyn was waiting for me. I watched Skadi glower as Óðinn clapped his hands and called for attention. What the hell kind of jokes would a woman like that enjoy? Puns?

"My friends," Óðinn announced, looking for all the Realms as if he were actually enjoying himself. And, who knew, perhaps he was. "We are here to celebrate an historic occasion. The wise and beautiful Skadi—"

Óðinn gestured to Skadi, whose expression turned even more sour.

"Has generously agreed to preserve the peace between our two Realms," Óðinn continued. "And what better way to honor the establishment of a peace accord than with a celebration of love?"

Óðinn beamed at us. Several of the unmarried Æsir shifted uncomfortably against the stone floor.

"Skadi will now choose her husband from among the unmarried men of Asgard, Æsir and Vanir alike."

Skadi's eyes darted upward and pinned Baldr, although he'd done his best to hide in the far shadows of the feast hall. My heart went out to the poor guy. I'd always assumed Óðinn would marry Baldr off to someone for political gain, but this seemed like an especially shitty pairing. Unless Óðinn actually was planning to trick Skadi and give her someone else as a husband, which would really put her in a laughing mood.

Óðinn clapped again, drawing the attention of everyone in the room. "If I could have all the bachelors up here, please. Yes, come on up, don't be shy. Freyr, that includes you."

The unmarried men of Asgard shuffled past me, looking for all intents and purposes like they were headed to their own execution.

There were more than I'd expected; I often felt like the only single man in Val-hall, but I now saw how wrong I'd been. Týr and Heimdallr stood next to Freyja's twin brother Freyr, who sadly was not half as good in the sack as his gorgeous sister. Freyr's father Njörðr was beside Baldr, who wasn't looking nearly as beautiful as usual. Baldr's brothers Hermod and Höðr flanked him, and even Thor's teenaged sons Magni and Modi joined the throng of bachelors.

Óðinn caught my eye in the shuffle, and I gave him a slight nod. I'd been tamping down the lamps and fires since he first clapped his hands, trying to be subtle while still decreasing the light. It seemed to be working. Freyr and Njörðr were Vanir, with their dark skin and hair, while the rest of the men were Æsir and light-skinned. But now, with the dark shadows flickering across their grim faces, the Æsir and Vanir were almost indistinguishable. Still, you'd have to be blind to miss Baldr the Beautiful. He was right in the middle of the crowd, for fuck's sake, shining like the sun at midday. What in the Nine Realms was Óðinn getting at?

"Thank you, thank you," Óðinn said, calling the attention in the room back to him.

I glanced at Skadi. Her arms were still folded across the gleaming breastplate of her armor, but her eyes were softer now that they rested on Baldr.

"Now," Óðinn said to the men huddled together in the front of the hall, "if I could just get you to remove your shoes."

The men shuffled into a somewhat organized line, then bent to unlace their shoes. Once they were barefoot, Óðinn tugged an enormous sail through the aether and suspended it before the row of bachelors. Shuffling and a few coughs filtered through the room as the men lined up. I also distinctly heard someone say, "Damn that bastard Loki, huh?"

That sounded like Njörðr's voice. Well, fuck you, too, I thought, grinding my teeth together. Óðinn slipped behind the sail and issued a few instructions, telling the men to sit and be quiet. Then he reappeared and opened his arms wide, smiling magnanimously.

"I am so deeply indebted to the glorious and fearsome, Skadi," Óðinn began, "for allowing an old man to indulge his requests. And what better way to seal our peace treaty than by the sacrament of marriage, from which issues new life?"

I coughed to hide my contemptuous laugh. Since when had Óðinn showed any particular respect for the sacrament of marriage? And most of his children, Thor included, had been born far outside of wedlock. Duplicitous asshole.

"But a lasting marriage must be based on more than pure animal lust, for that attraction fades so quickly."

Several coughs joined mine after that comment. Óðinn ignored us all.

"Pick your husband, then, Skadi the Fearsome, based on his humble features. His essential, dependable qualities." Óðinn paused, then gestured toward the woven sail suspended across Val-hall's floor. A row of bare feet stuck out of the end of the thick, white fabric. I lowered the light once more, subtly, lengthening and softening the shadows.

"His feet," Óðinn said, with a flourish.

A few people laughed at this, hesitantly, as if it were a joke they didn't quite get. Skadi's lips tightened and she glanced down, as if checking her own armor-clad feet. She was silent just long enough for me to wonder what in the Nine Realms we'd do if she balked. Then she straightened her back, spat on the floor, and glared at Óðinn.

"Fine," Skadi said. "Old man, I accepted your terms back on Jötunheimr."

Óðinn's pale eye glinted in the dim light. "And you will abide by your decision? And accept your chosen husband?"

Skadi snorted. "Of course. I know who I want. I can pick Baldr out by his feet, if I have to."

Óðinn and Skadi stared at each other. For a moment, I half expected Skadi to pull out her sword and try gutting the old man. But she stepped away from the wall and slowly approached the row of bare feet along the floor.

I felt cold as I watched her prowl the length of the sail, sizing up the row of bare feet like a beast of prey. I could only imagine how it felt on the other side of the sail, among the bachelors sitting on the hard floor and watching her shadow cross the pale fabric.

And I would have been there, I realized with a shudder. If Óðinn hadn't dragged me away from that barrel of mead and thrust me into Sigyn's hall, I'd be sitting on the floor with Baldr and Freyr and the rest of them, hoping against hope the warrior woman from Jötunheimr wouldn't choose me for a husband. I tightened my illusions to hide the smile curving my lips. It seemed I owed Sigyn another debt of gratitude.

Before us, Skadi stopped pacing. She stood in front of the fourth man from the left, exactly where Baldr had been standing. I couldn't see her face, but the lines of her body were tight, as though she were coiled to strike. She bend down, with one hand extended, and Óðinn cleared his throat so loudly the sound filled the entire hall.

"Sight alone," Óðinn said. "Don't touch."

Skadi's back stiffened, and the muscles in her neck tensed. She paced the length of the sail again, coming to rest at the same place. Skadi's face wrinkled in grim determination. The dimly lit row of feet before her looked damn near identical to me; I couldn't even tell which were Æsir and which were Vanir. But Skadi appeared to have made her decision.

"Him," she said, pointing at the fourth man from the left. "These are the most lovely feet in Asgard. They could only belong to Baldr the Beautiful."

Óðinn's pale eye gleamed. Shit, I thought. Shit, shit, shit—

The sail dropped into the laps of the men sitting on the floor. I made the lamps flare, filling the hall with their bold illumination. Skadi's raised finger trembled. She was pointing at the dark, weathered face of Njörðr the Vanir, who had raised his two children Freyja and Freyr on Asgard. He tried to smile at Skadi, but his expression faltered, and he looked instead like he may have been choking.

I glanced at Skadi. The disgust and rage playing across her face were so fearsome I almost stepped back. Despite Njörðr's earlier comment about my parentage, my heart went out to him. I couldn't imagine being on the receiving end of that scowl. If Sigyn had looked at me like that before our strange marriage, I probably would have gone straight back to Midgard to drink myself to death.

"Óðinn, you cock-sucking, mother-fucking—" Skadi began.

"My lady," Óðinn said, using a voice loud enough to drown out her protests. "Choose your words carefully. This is the beginning of your marriage."

Skadi's hand dropped to the pommel of the sword strapped to her right thigh. "You tricked me."

Njörðr stood and reached across the crumpled sail on the floor to clasp Skadi's wrist. "My lady. I know this wasn't what either of us expected, but perhaps we can still find some joy in each other."

Oh. I clenched my fist at my side. That's what I should have told Sigyn after Óðinn dumped me in her lovely little house. That's exactly what a proper husband should say.

What had I said again, just after Óðinn bound us together? My words immediately came back to me, as the stupidest and most inappropriate things always do. *Shit,* I'd told my new wife. *Sigyn, right?* I winced under my illusions. Skadi's hand froze over her sword, and the silence in the hall seemed to thicken like smoke.

"Say the words," Óðinn commanded.

Njörðr's neck tensed as he swallowed. "My lady Skadi. I am bound to you. You are a part of me."

"Skadi," Óðinn said, his voice just as forceful.

Skadi drew herself up to her full, formidable height. She was taller than Njörðr, and almost as tall as Óðinn.

"I will accept this," Skadi spat. "But you will pay dearly for your treachery, you shit-slicked asshole of an Æsir." She made a fist around Njörðr's hand. "I'm bound to you. You're a part of me," she mumbled, rushing the words out.

Still, the air tingled with the magic of those vows. I felt another stab of sympathy for Njörðr. Had I honestly thought I'd had the worst wedding in the Nine Realms? Oh, by the fucking stars, this was so much more painful than the quiet exchange of vows Sigyn and I shared in her hall.

"Wonderful" Óðinn said. "And now, let us celebrate the union—"

"Stop!" Skadi yanked away from Njörðr and turned to the room, her flaming eyes wrathful. She stalked past the row of bachelors, fixing the entire crowd with her scowl as she tightened her fist around the pommel of her sword. The Æsir drew back.

Then she saw me. Skadi gave a grin of pure malice. Reflexively, I pulled at the magical energy, getting ready for a quick exit.

"Loki Laufeyiarson. The bastard," she purred. "Loki the Lie-smith. Loki, the source of all the Æsir's troubles. Óðinn tricked me out of my husband, but I think taking your head will be even sweeter than getting to fuck Baldr the Beautiful."

She pulled her sword from its sheath. A sharp, metallic rasp filled the air.

"After all the trouble you've caused, I think the Æsir might even thank me for this," Skadi said, inching closer to my neck. The crowd parted to let her through.

"My lady Skadi," I said, flashing her my most charming smile. "Perhaps the rush of your nuptials has affected your memory."

She blinked, probably trying to figure out if she was being insulted.

"You made a deal with Óðinn," I said, still smiling. I also took a few small steps away from the gleaming point of her blade.

Skadi frowned, and her blade wavered. Óðinn stepped forward, pushing Skadi's sword aside as if it were a child's plaything.

"How true!" Óðinn said, as if he were also just remembering some obscure, long-ago arrangement. "But please, Skadi, let's save this talk of beheading for after the feast. After all, we have a wedding to celebrate!"

Skadi's eyebrows knit together as she glared at me. "You're supposed to make me laugh."

I gave her a slight bow, hoping to throw her off. "It would be my deepest honor."

Skadi snorted in a very unladylike way, and something wet hit me in the face. Spit. Skadi the Fearsome had just spit on me. I ground my teeth together. My daggers were so close here on Asgard. I might even have a chance to reach Skadi's throat before her sword found my heart.

"I'll never laugh for you," Skadi growled. "You killed my father, you gutless bastard. If you and your psychotic whore of a mother had both died in childbirth, all Nine Realms would have celebrated."

"You're as eloquent as you are beautiful," I replied.

Skadi blinked again. Óðinn took advantage of her hesitation to wrap his arms around her shoulders and lead her to the long table in the front of the hall, where the feast was waiting.

I AM A FUNNY MOTHERFUCKER.

There's no need for false modesty here; I could make a stone laugh. Humor and sex are my two favorite weapons, and I have to say, I'm a stars-damned expert in both. Plus, Skadi seemed to be loosening up as the night progressed. I hung back at first, acting like there was nowhere else I'd rather be but careful not to draw too much attention to myself, while Skadi, seated between a beaming Óðinn and a rather less happy looking Njörðr, actually ate the feast. And drank the mead.

Damn, did she drink. She seemed to be trying to give Thor a run for his money as she drained flagon after flagon of Val-hall's mead, adding in unfavorable comparisons to Jötunheimr's spirits but drinking them all the same.

I sidled my way through the crowd, telling stories, making people laugh and downing flagons of mead to loosen up. When I finally reached the bridal table, I had a serious buzz on and was just hitting my stride. I continued without casting a single glance at Skadi. My story about disguising Thor as a bride to recover his hammer from Thrym was always a huge hit at weddings. I told it perfectly, without skipping a beat, although of course I couldn't tell the whole story.

Still, even though I left out the orgy at the end, the story of Thor the Beautiful had the entire bridal table in tears. Óðinn roared with laughter, and even poor Njörðr, who was being completely ignored as his new bride drank herself to oblivion and cast wide, longing glances at Baldr, managed to laugh at the key parts.

But not Skadi. That bitch just downed her mead and ignored me. When the story finally ended, with a nice touch about Thor tripping over the remains of his bridal veil, Skadi lowered her flagon and fixed me with those fierce, dark eyes.

"Your head is mine, asshole," she hissed.

Damn. I tried a few jokes after that, but the mood was effectively dead. Just as I was thinking about transforming myself into a series of ridiculous animals, Óðinn caught my eye. He tilted his head toward the side, then excused himself politely. I finished my current set of jokes, an especially filthy series, and left in a burst of shocked laughter from everyone except Skadi.

It took me a few minutes to find Óðinn, and not just because I was closing in on this side of drunk. The fucker had gone outside. He was standing on the porch, holding a rope in his fist.

"What the—" I began.

"Drop your pants," Óðinn said.

I blinked, trying to get my bearings. Óðinn was the one person in all of Asgard who'd never once expressed an interest in fucking me. This seemed like a highly inappropriate time and place to begin.

"Isn't this just a bit public?" I said, waving my hand at the open doors to Val-hall. Torchlight and laughter drifted out into the chill, dark night.

"Damn it, Loki," Óðinn grunted. He tugged on the rope in his fist, and something bleated behind him.

I glanced down. There was a small, white goat tied to the rope. The little beast looked at me through dewy, liquid eyes. Óðinn had tied the rope around the goat's beard, which must have hurt like a motherfucker.

"You sadistic ass," I said. "Why the fuck..."

My voice trailed off. A horrible, horrible plan was beginning to coalesce in my mind, a plan that had to do with tying goats to very sensitive parts.

"Drop your thrice-damned pants," Óðinn growled.

"Oh, no," I said. "No, no, no, and go fuck yourself, and no."

Óðinn's glare was merciless. "Do you value that pretty little head of yours, you shit? You want to keep it?"

"You could have just given her Baldr!"

"Baldr's spoken for."

"Oh, fuck me sideways, Óðinn! Skadi spoke for Baldr! And she'd be a hell of a lot more likely to laugh if she knew she was going home with Baldr the Beautiful tonight!"

"Baldr's marrying Nanna," Óðinn snapped.

"What?"

I frowned, wondering if I'd heard him correctly. Nanna was an uptight prig who acted like everyone on Asgard was beneath her. I'd gotten the distinct sense she didn't care much for men, or marriage, or even sex.

"Nanna's father is planning to depose me," Óðinn said. "When he makes his move, I'll marry Baldr to Nanna, and Baldr will castrate his new father-in-law's rebellion from the inside."

"Shit."

I ran my fingers through my hair. Just when I thought I'd gotten to the bottom of Óðinn's scheming, it turned out there was a sketchy basement of plans and counter-plans I hadn't even suspected.

"Does Baldr know this?" I asked.

"Of course not. Don't be naive. And don't think of telling him, either. He wouldn't believe you for a second."

"You shady old fuck. Using your own son for political gain."

Óðinn frowned at me. Disappointment radiated off him in waves. "I use all the tools at my disposal to ensure the safety of this realm. I thought you of all people would understand."

"Shit." I glanced at the goat with a rope tied around its beard. "Was that supposed to be a pep talk?"

"Just drop your pants and make the bitch laugh, Loki."

I swallowed hard. "I'm not nearly drunk enough for this."

Óðinn waved his hand, and the latent magic trembled as he pulled a flagon through the aether. He handed it to me with silent disapproval, and I drained the whole thing.

"Still not drunk enough," I declared, tossing the flagon into the darkness off Val-hall's porch.

With a sigh, Óðinn handed me another flagon. I drained that one as well, then waved my hand at him in a universal keep-them-coming sign.

"If you pass out," Óðinn growled, "she'll kill you. You know that, don't you?"

I ignored him, took the third flagon, and drained it. My stomach lurched precariously, as it always did when I'd just had a huge amount of alcohol in a very short period of time. I closed my eyes until the urge to vomit had passed, then opened them again. Óðinn was glaring at me, with a rope clenched in his fist. A rope that led to a cute little goat.

What were we talking about again?

"Drop your pants," Óðinn said.

Oh. Shit. Right. I fumbled with my belt, couldn't figure it out, and just ripped my pants off and sent them flying through the aether. The motion left me staggering, but I caught myself on the side of Val-hall. Óðinn snorted in disgust.

"You think you can tie this?" he said, pressing the rope into my palm.

I stared at it. My mind absolutely refused to understand Óðinn's words. Instead, I thought about how nice it would be to have another flagon of mead, and then maybe go lie down somewhere.

"Your damned balls got us into this mess, Loki," Óðinn declared. "And now your damned balls will get us out. It's poetry. Bragi will have a field day with this one."

My stomach lurched again, more violently this time. I squeezed my eyes shut.

"Bragi's poetry makes me want to puke," I ground out through clenched teeth.

Óðinn's hand clapped my shoulders. "They'll be talking about this for a thousand years," he said.

When I opened my eyes, Óðinn was gone. I was standing alone, half naked, on the porch of Val-hall, with a goat tied to a rope.

And the rope tied to my balls.

Just like that, we had a new contender for the worst day of my fucking life.

CHAPTER TWENTY NINE

I staggered into Val-hall, my arms spread wide, spouting some ridiculous story about how I had to take my goat to the pasture but my arms were full, and where could I tie it? Everyone in Val-hall turned to stare at me, their eyes wide and their mouths gaping. And then they all started yelling.

The goat, of course, freaked the fuck out once everyone started making noise. The little beast ran squealing across Val-hall, pulling me with it, staggering and cursing and thinking maybe one less flagon of mead would have been a better idea.

Holy fuck, did they laugh.

Thor laughed. Óðinn laughed. Njörðr, new winner of the Worst Wedding in Asgard prize, laughed so hard he actually cried.

And Skadi laughed.

Granted, Skadi put up a good fight. She didn't actually laugh until I collapsed at her feet, curled in the fetal position, my balls on fucking fire and the goat screaming at the end of its tether.

But laugh she did. Once she broke down, Skadi just roared with laughter, the kind of laughter you try to stop but it just doubles up instead. She laughed so hard I wouldn't be surprised if she pissed herself inside that gleaming bridal armor.

I didn't wait to see. Once the metallic shrill of Skadi's laughter reached me, I cut the rope off the goat and crawled away. I grabbed a few flagons of mead as I limped out the door, planning on drinking myself into oblivion and hoping against all hope the alcohol would erase tonight's memories.

At least Sigyn didn't see that, I thought, as I lurched into the nearest shed and tipped a flagon to my lips.

EVERYTHING HURT.

I hovered on the edge of consciousness, trying to cling to the blackness of sleep and ignore the screaming protests of my body. My face was cold and wet, and my balls throbbed with slow, deep agony. My stomach felt like a pit of acid, and my head ached so much it felt like it might have been split open.

I brought my hand slowly up to my forehead, just to be sure. The lower half of my face was wet and sticky. Blood? I cracked open an eye and examined my fingertips in the gloom. No, just vomit.

Groaning, I rolled over and patted myself down. I was covered in filth and probably stank to the high heavens, but I was intact. Even my swollen balls seemed more or less in one piece. I forced myself to sit up as the room around me swam into focus.

Shit!

The dull edges of swords nestled into their racks pulsated around me. I leapt to my feet, blades in both my hands. Had I really crawled into the same fucking shed where Angrboða had assaulted me? I staggered toward the door, ripped it open, and ran a few paces before collapsing in the dew covered grass. My heartbeat thundered in my ears.

Fuck. Me.

I was truly an idiot. I tilted my head back and stared at the gray skies above Asgard. Almost dawn, if I had to guess. I wiped my hand across my lips and reached for the magic, pulling my regular illusions around me. Damn, but I felt like shit. I needed the mead of Val-hall to cure my hangover and, if I were particularly lucky, ease the throb between my legs. Óðinn's mead cured both war wounds and hangovers, which was how the dead warriors of Val-hall could feast all night and fight all day. But sometimes the magical alcohol was a bit picky about what counted as a war wound. Whether or not it would cure the injuries of tying a goat to your balls was anyone's guess.

Staggering to my feet, I glanced backward at the row of weapon sheds. There was no way of knowing, really, which one Angrboða had dragged me into. I suppressed a shiver. It didn't really matter; I'd like to burn them all down.

But not with this fucking headache. I spat, wiped my mouth again, and set off for Val-hall. With any luck, everyone else would be too drunk to remember what happened last night.

"LOKI!"

Thor's booming voice greeted me as soon as I stepped through the doors of Val-hall. I winced. Thor pushed himself to his feet and came stomping toward me, grinning like an idiot.

"You in one piece this morning?" he asked, rather obviously looking at my crotch.

Someone laughed from deep inside the gloom of the feast hall, and I shot what I dearly hoped was a dirty look in their direction.

"No thanks to you," I growled.

Thor clapped me on the back. "Stars, that was fucking funny. You should have seen yourself!"

I pulled away, cringing. Did he have to be so damned loud, all the damned time?

"And how was the rest of your night?" I asked as I grabbed a flagon of mead off the closest table.

Thor snorted another laugh. "Skadi puked. You must've missed it."

I took a long pull from the flagon, letting Val-hall's mead warm my body before responding. "She what?"

"She thought she could drink like an Æsir. Ended up puking all over the table, and all over Njörðr. She ruined the desserts, too," Thor added, in a wistful tone.

I finished my flagon and winced. The mead had taken the edge off my hangover, but my head still ached and my stomach felt like it was trying to crawl out through my throat.

"Damn," I said.

"Njörðr and Freyr had to drag her out," Thor said.

I shook my head and picked a boiled potato off the table in front of me. Thor bent close to me, until his beard brushed my neck.

"You know I wouldn't have let Skadi hurt you, right?" he whispered.

I closed my eyes as I chewed the potato. Did I believe Thor? I wasn't certain. He was my lover, sure, and sometimes he even came dangerously close to being what I might consider a friend. But he was also Óðinn's son.

"Thrym is on Midgard," I whispered in response.

Thor sighed with what sounded like relief. He pressed another flagon into my hand, and I drained it slowly, letting my stomach adjust to this new assault.

"He's in the Roman Empire," I said.

Thor's brow knotted in confusion. Right. Thor shared the Æsir's prejudice against Midgard. He probably wouldn't know the Roman Empire from Sweorice.

"He's safe," I said. "I left him with a fuck ton of money and a sexy soldier who needed rescuing."

"Thank you."

Was it just the dim light, or were Thor's eyes actually getting misty? His hand lingered on my shoulder, clasping then unclasping.

"If you want to go find a place..." Thor said, his voice low and thick against my skin. "I can take care of you."

I grinned. The mead was finally working. My headache still throbbed, but the full assault had subsided, and my sorry balls felt almost normal again. I flexed my hands, tweaking my illusion. I was still tired, hungry, and filthy, but I no longer felt like I'd just risen regretfully from the dead.

And Thor the Thunderer had offered to take care of me. How fucking strange was that? Last night I'd thought Thor would be in the front row when Skadi removed my head from my shoulders, and now here he was, acting like a nursemaid. It was equal parts touching and nauseating. Was Thor really that grateful I'd saved Thrym?

I pushed Thor's hand away, gently. "Thanks, but not this morning."

Sweetly unexpected as the offer was, I didn't want to be with Thor right now. I didn't particularly want to be with anyone right now. I just wanted to be somewhere quiet, and warm, where I could pull myself together.

Just like that, I knew exactly where I wanted to be.

I pressed a quick kiss to Thor's cheek, then pulled myself through the aether.

CANDLES FLARED TO LIFE in the steam-thick darkness. Water lapped against the sandy edges of the deep pool I'd made in Sigyn's house, and the last of the night's stars shone brightly through the transparent ceiling I'd created. I glanced around the room, checking to make sure I was alone, although I didn't actually expect Sigyn to be in the hot springs at this ungodly hour.

No one else was here. Good. With a sigh of relief, I let go of my illusions and slipped beneath the steaming water. I scrubbed myself with sand for a long time, until I felt like every part of my body had been renewed. Then I pulled a plate from Val-hall, and ate a pile of potatoes and sausages while my feet trailed through the water.

It was odd for me to feel this comfortable, I thought as I sent the plate back and pulled a mug of tea through the aether. I let myself slip back into the water, the warm currents supporting my body as steam swirled aimlessly above me, alternately obscuring and revealing the fading stars. I really had built this pool for three people. And, in the steamy half light of the candles, I could almost imagine Anya and Falur here with me.

Kicking my feet down to the bottom, I snorted a laugh at myself. If Anya and Falur were still alive, we'd be the parents of an infant. We wouldn't exactly have time for floating in a hot spring. Still, my heart felt strangely light as I remembered the delicate contours of their faces, my beautiful mortal lovers. For a moment, scarcely more time than it had taken to draw a breath, I really had felt like Anya and Falur were near me again.

My chest tightened as tears surfaced in my eyes. It will never stop hurting, I realized. I'm going to live with their loss forever, like a tree that's been struck by lightning and spends the remaining aeons of its life with a black scar running down the length of its trunk. My fingers tugged at the magic, and I pulled Falur's metal leaf into my palm.

"You'll live with me," I whispered into the steam. "You'll live inside me until Ragnarök. I swear it."

I pressed my lips to the metal and imagined I could see my lovers smiling back at me.

A creak sounded through the steam, and the room filled with light. I glanced up and found Sigyn's neat figure in the doorway, the steam swirling all around her. The candles flickered as she closed the door behind her. In one smooth motion, Sigyn reached up to unclasp her hair. She shook her head, and her auburn curls fell in a cascade across her back.

Damn.

Usually hot water saps my sexual energy but, despite having spent all morning in this pool, the sight of Sigyn's long hair falling loose across her back lit something inside me. My cock stirred under the water, and I could almost feel my blood draining downward. Stars, it had been a long time since I'd had a lover.

Sigyn turned to the wall and pulled off her robe. I held my breath. Her body was more curvaceous than I would have guessed. She turned toward the water, and her skin glowed in the candlelight. Her small breasts were pert, with dark nipples, although the skin above them was strangely dimpled—

Fucking creepy, I realized, with a jolt. What kind of an asshole ogles a naked woman who doesn't even know he's there?

"Hello, Sigyn," I said.

She yelped and spun toward the door, grabbing her robe and pressing it over her body. "Loki!" she gasped. "I didn't see you!"

I pulled myself through the water until I could rest my head on the rocks just in front of her. "Good morning," I said.

"Sorry," she stammered. "I'll leave you to it."

Sigyn was holding her robe in a very strange way. I could still see those beautiful breasts, and the surprisingly generous curve of her ass. All her most interesting features were gloriously uncovered, while the robe was bunched over her sternum and side.

"You don't have to leave," I said.

She pulled her lower lip into her mouth, hesitating. The sweet scent of her arousal drifted toward me. Stars, it seemed even stronger this time. It must drive her crazy, getting so turned on with no relief.

Well, no relief from me, at least.

My cock pressed into the sand lining the hot spring, insistent and aching. Suddenly, I wanted her to know the effect she had on me, that the pull of arousal and desire between us was no longer one-sided.

With a splash, I lifted myself out of the water. I didn't need to glance down to know my cock was as hard as the rocks around us, and straining forward as if it could reach Sigyn's wet sex all by itself. Sigyn's caramel eyes widened as she stared openly at my naked, dripping wet body. Her gaze dropped, and her cheeks reddened. The scent of her sex surged through the air between us.

She liked what she saw, then. The thought made me inordinately happy.

"I'd like it if you stay," I said.

Now that I was standing before her, I could see rough, uneven patches of skin radiating from beneath her robe in tight, red lines. What was she trying to hide? A scar, perhaps? I tilted my head, trying to see around her robe. Her fists tightened, clenching the fabric closer to her body.

"I—I'm not—" she said, swallowing hard.

"I thought you didn't want to hide who you are," I said. It wasn't fair, and I knew it wasn't fair, but I couldn't stop myself.

Sigyn flinched, then closed her eyes. An expression of such horrible pain flickered across her face that, for a moment, I thought she may have just stabbed herself. Then she took a deep breath and let the robe drop to the floor in a soft heap.

I gasped. I'd thought she may have been hiding a scar. But this was so much worse than I could have imagined. There was thick knot of scar tissue the shape of a starburst, or an explosion, just below her right breast. It was the size of my fist, and it looked like something had shattered the lower half of her chest at some point. I let my eyes drop and found another, larger knot of scars along the curve of her left side. It looked like a spear had ripped her apart.

By the Realms. Lots of the Vanir and Æsir had scars, but I'd never seen anything like this. The damage must have been horrific.

"How did you survive?" My voice came out in a hushed whisper.

"With an incantation fetter." She tried to smile, but her lips trembled.

I whistled into the steam. "You cast a spell on yourself? After this?"

Sigyn nodded, dropping her eyes. "All I had to do was stop the bleeding."

"All?"

I followed the curve of her hips, tracing the scar tissue with my eyes. I wanted to touch those lines, if only to convince myself they were real, but the way she was trembling made me think that would be a bad idea.

It must have been a sword in her side, I decided, and a spear through her chest. But whoever made that slit through her abdomen must have pulled on the weapon, dragging their blade, rending flesh and blood. She must have been split open like a gutted fish.

All she had to do was stop the bleeding? Shit. That was like saying all I had to do last night was make Skadi laugh.

"I—I'm s-sorry," she said. Her breath caught in her throat. "You probably wanted a beautiful wife."

Oh, fuck. A horrible, horrible idea occurred to me. Quite possibly the worst idea I'd ever had. I touched her chin, just enough to tilt her head until she met my gaze. Her wide, caramel-colored eyes brimmed with tears. I could feel the heat of her naked body, but I didn't dare touch her. Not yet.

Before I could change my mind, I felt for the tendrils of magic humming across my body.

And I dropped the illusions that hid my scarred lips.

Sigyn gasped. I closed my eyes. This was bad enough without seeing the expression on her face. She would be disgusted, of course. And she would pity me, which felt even worse than disgust. You can't respect someone you pity. You can't desire someone you pity.

The air between us swirled with steam and breath. Sigyn was silent, but I could well imagine what she saw. Twelve angry red puncture wounds, six above my upper lip and six below my lower lip. And thick, white bands where the tether had crossed my lips so tightly it cut my skin, forever ruining my smile.

I had been an idiot. I should never have made such a rash wager with the dwarves Brokk and Eitri. More than that, I should never have trusted Óðinn and the Æsir to get me out of the deal.

They had laughed. All of the Æsir and Vanir, as far as I could tell, had laughed as Brokk used his awl to punch the holes in my lips. I'd screamed in pain and rage, at least until the thick leather pulled my lips together. And everyone laughed.

Before then, I'd been beautiful. I hadn't been innocent, of course. No one with my childhood could ever claim innocence. But I'd been handsome, truly handsome, even without my illusions.

And I'd been stupid. Naive and hopeful. I had actually thought Óðinn's oath of blood-brotherhood meant I really was one of the Æsir.

These scars on my lips changed everything. I had gone home once Brokk finished his bloody work and cut the tether by myself, even though the pain was so bad I almost lost consciousness. Then I pulled down the elegant palace I'd been building for myself in Asgard. In its place, I made the squat, ugly one room hovel I'd call home for the next thousand years. And I stayed there, working on my illusions as my lips slowly healed, until I looked like myself again. Until I could smile and drink and fuck, and no one would ever know what lay beneath my beautiful visage.

"I'm sorry," I said. My voice was tight; I had to clear my throat before I could go on. "You probably wanted a beautiful husband."

And that statement didn't even come close to touching the many ways I'd already failed her as a husband.

"Oh!" Sigyn cried.

I finally opened my eyes, bracing myself for the inevitable revulsion I'd see in my new wife's eyes. The steam-filled room slowly took shape. Sigyn stood before me, her face open as a flower, but it took me a long time to make sense of her expression. It was so far from what I'd expected. Sigyn's eyes shimmered with tears, but she was smiling. For a heartbeat I was reminded of Anya; the memory brought both pain and a strange sense of comfort.

"But, you are beautiful," she said. Her voice came out as a rasp, hardly more than a whisper.

I smiled at the gentle lie.

"May I touch you?" she asked.

The breath caught in my throat as I tried to answer. That bitch Angrboða had tied me up to use me as a stud, but my own wife asked permission before touching me.

"Please," I said.

I closed my eyes again as she reached for me. Her hand cupped my cheek, then hesitated. Sigyn's touch was soft, almost shy, but without my illusions my skin was painfully sensitive. I felt raw, exposed. Vulnerable. My cock had been out all over the Nine Realms, but I couldn't remember the last time I'd felt this naked.

I heard the soft rush of Sigyn's breath over her lips, and her hand moved. Slowly, with infinite tenderness, her fingertips brushed my mangled lips. I trembled. Her touch burned against my scars, setting every nerve in my body on edge. Stars, I felt like I'd never been touched before.

Her scent swirled in the air between us, rich and thick. She must have been dripping wet. I could almost taste the sweet nectar of her sex in the thick steam between us. My jaw tightened, holding in the moan building in my throat. To be this close to a naked woman, to be this stiff and hard at the thought of her body, and to have her touching my raw skin, my actual self, without illusions. It was almost torture.

Sigyn's hand withdrew, and I opened my eyes again. Her lips parted. Her eyes seemed darker. The space between us thrummed with energy.

"May I kiss you?" she asked.

Her voice had grown thicker, deeper. She was trembling too, I realized. The curls of her hair drifted in the steamy air, shivering in time with her body. I had the sudden, overwhelming urge to wrap her in my arms, to crush her to my chest, to hold that glorious body until the trembling passed.

"I don't think I'll be able to stop at a kiss," I answered. My voice, too, was deeper and thicker.

"Good," she said.

I'm not certain who moved first. Our bodies crashed together in the heat and steam of that place, as the candles flickered around us and the stars burned overhead. That first, incendiary kiss was not at all what I'd been expecting. I imagined quiet, kind Sigyn would be the type to kiss for hours, to tease and play and blush and giggle.

But we came together like a thunderstorm, like wildfire. She kissed me hard and deep from the very beginning, as though she'd been starving for years and needed to devour me. Sigyn forced my lips open, thrust inside me, and I groaned into her mouth. Oh, fuck, she tasted good.

I met her ferocity with my own desperate need and hunger. I plundered her sweet mouth, tasting her, claiming her. When we pulled apart, I caught her lower lip between my teeth and brought her back, needing more. And she answered by thrusting her hands into my hair, pulling me toward her.

My lips hummed with the intensity of our kisses. Sigyn's hands dropped lower, digging her nails into my shoulder blades as if she thought she'd be swept away. She was gasping for breath, making little, animal moans into my mouth. My cock wept against the soft heat of her belly, and I wrapped my arms around her waist, lifting her.

Sigyn responded by raising her leg to embrace me. She tilted her hips, and the heat of her wet sex pressed against the head of my cock. Oh, stars! I hesitated just a moment, the intense need to sink myself into her wrestling with the need to be certain she actually wanted me.

"Loki!" Sigyn gasped against my neck. "Please, Loki!"

I lifted her in my arms, and thrust into the tight heat of her body. The Nine Realms stood still as the velvet pleasure of Sigyn's sex engulfed me. She felt so stars-damned good! I wanted time to stop, I wanted Ragnarök to crash around us, so I could stay forever in that embrace.

Sigyn's legs tightened around my waist, and she pressed her hips against me, moving me deeper. I groaned in ecstacy and spun her around, shoving her back against the smooth, polished wood of the door I'd stolen from Val-hall.

It wasn't making love, what I did to my wife against that door. It wasn't the sweet, tender dance of a devoted couple.

No, this was fucking, pure, hard, animal fucking. She writhed beneath me, crying and gasping, begging me to come at her harder.

And I complied, driving myself between her hips until the door shuddered and some dim, distant part of my mind worried the very walls around us would collapse. I thrust up and into her with everything I had, leaving nothing back, as though I could actually drive myself into Sigyn's body and become a part of her.

"Fuck," I growled, my face pressed to the sweat and heat of her neck. "Oh, fuck, Sigyn!"

It wasn't what I'd intended to say, but my mind was too far gone for sweet nothings. I just wanted her. No, I needed her, I needed to bury myself in her, to drown myself in the blinding ecstacy of sex, of a lover's legs wrapped around my waist and a lover's gasping breaths against my neck. Heat tingled in the base of my spine, swelling upward. I could already tell this orgasm would be enormous.

"Fuck, yes," I panted, clinging to her body as if I'd been shipwrecked.

Sigyn came like a thunderclap.

I wasn't expecting her to come at all, so the ferocity of her orgasm took me completely by surprise. She screamed as her nails sank into the skin of my back. Her legs kicked out behind me as her entire body closed, growing even tighter and hotter, embracing my cock.

Her climax pushed me over the edge. As Sigyn shuddered and tightened around me, my own pleasure crested, and I crashed into her, emptying my seed in endless, long spasms that obliterated mind and body.

Slowly, my consciousness drifted back into my body. I was pressing Sigyn's hips and chest against the door, our sweat-soaked bodies leaning together as we gasped for breath. And she was whispering something low and soft, just barely loud enough for me to hear.

"Yes," she panted against my chest. "Yes, yes, yes."

I grabbed her chin and tilted her head up just enough for me to see her eyes. They were unfocused, brimming with tears. By the Nine Realms, I vowed to myself, I am going to fuck those tears away. Bending down, I kissed her hard, pressing her shoulder blades into the door. She gasped, then softened against me. I staggered back, with Sigyn's legs still wrapped around my waist, and flung the door open. Stepping over the soft heap of her discarded robe, I carried her down the hall to her own bedroom, our lips pressed together in a fiercely desperate kiss. By the time I threw her down across her mattress, my cock was hard again.

And she rose to meet me.

I FUCKED MY WIFE ALL day.

We paused to eat, of course, and we spent some time recovering in each other's arms. Slowly, with a hesitation I found damned adorable, Sigyn told me what she liked. I discovered her scars were intensely sensitive, and that trailing a fingertip along the raised, pink tissue where a Vanir sword had nearly ended her life was enough to make her breath catch and her heartbeat stutter. I made her come as I kissed the sunburst of scars on her chest with my hand between her legs. I tasted every inch of her body, learning the shape and texture of her skin, the sound of her cries, the press of her legs against my cheeks as she crashed into oblivion.

In return, she asked me about my pleasure, my preferences. It was strangely touching. For all the lovers I'd enjoyed across all Nine Realms, I'd never once had a conversation about what I wanted. The words came slowly, and they left me feeling strangely naked in my wife's company. It was an odd sensation. As the day drew to a close, I felt as enervated as if I'd spent all day building something with my body.

The light slowly leaked from the room as the sun set across Asgard. We'd made a mess of Sigyn's bedchamber; plates and mugs lay scattered across the floor, her blankets were in a tangled heap at the foot of her bed, and the sheets we'd managed to destroy lay balled up against the door. The room stank of sweat and sex, despite the occasional gust of salt-laden air floating in through her open windows.

From those windows I'd watched the sun sink across the ocean, turning the waves to molten gold. Now the horizon glowed with a thin band of pink, the very last light of the day. I turned to kiss the top of Sigyn's head. She lay against my chest, her form curled around my body, her breathing deep and even.

My eyelids felt heavy. The exhaustion of all that I'd done since that horrible trip to Svartálfaheimr settled over me like a thick woolen blanket. In the fading light, the white lines of Sigyn's jagged scars looked even more vivid. Even though I'd spent all day kissing and licking those scars, they were still somehow hard to believe. She should have died.

The thought made my throat close up, as though the air were leaking from the room. All the Nine Realms would have been poorer for it, had Sigyn perished in the Vanir war. I tightened my arm around her shoulders, and she sighed in her sleep, nestling closer to me. I kissed her again as my eyes closed. I thought of setting my cantrips, but decided against it. Nothing to hide.

With my wife held tight to my chest, I let sleep take me.

CHAPTER THIRTY

My mug of Sleepytime tea had gone ice cold in my hands.
I stared at Loki long after he'd stopped talking, trying to think of something I could possibly say. When my mind pulled a complete blank, I looked down at the mug of cold chamomile tea clasped in my hands as if it held the answers. All I saw was the crumpled white tea bag which had sunk to the bottom over the course of Loki's horrific story.

"Shit," I finally choked. "So it's all true?"

Of course I knew about Skadi's marriage to Njörðr. I'd written a damn essay on the symbolism of feet, and how the myth denigrates women warriors. But I'd treated it as a fucking myth, not an historical record.

"Or it's all a lie," Loki responded.

Something of his usual fire sparked in his pale eyes, and I felt marginally better. With a yawn, Loki stood, stretched, and took the cold mug from my hands. A moment later the kitchen light came back on, and I heard him open a cabinet. The liquor cabinet, I guessed.

"Pour me one, too," I called.

I'd already had more than my share of wine and champagne on our date, but fuck it. I needed this drink as much as he did.

"My pleasure," he said.

The cabinet door closed, and something fell into place. Vintner. A vintner, in Rome.

"Shit!" I said again. "The wine collection, tonight. That office above the restaurant. Was that— Does that place belong to Thrym?"

The light turned off, and Loki reappeared beside the couch. He handed me a tall glass clinking with ice cubes. I frowned. He'd even added a slice of lime. It had to be almost four in the morning, and my husband had just finished telling me the worst fucking story of my life. And then he'd sliced a lime for my gin and tonic like it was no big deal.

"It does indeed," Loki said. "I haven't seen him in an age. I figured the security camera footage would be a lovely way for us to re-connect."

I took a huge gulp of my gin and tonic as I tried to process that statement.

There was a Jötunn, one of the frost giants of Norse legend, living in San Francisco. I'd left my underwear in his office. And he would soon be watching my husband fuck me, on his desk. With a champagne bottle.

I had to take another gulp of my gin and tonic. The slice of lime hit me in the nose. Flinching, I put the drink down and wiped lime juice and gin from my face. Loki was watching me, his head tilted to the side, an odd sort of half smile on his soft lips. His illusion lips, I thought.

"You know, you remind me of her a bit," he said.

"Who?" I asked, although that answer was painfully obvious. Of course I didn't remind him of the buxom blonde Norse sex goddess.

Loki just smiled. "It's meant as a compliment. I grew to love Sigyn very deeply."

I swallowed around the tightness in my throat. Loki swirled his glass, and the delicate clink of ice cubes danced through the air. He raised the glass to his lips, drained it, turned to the window, and smiled into the darkness of our backyard.

"Although, in all the years we lived together, I could never figure out why she asked for me," he said, with that same strange half smile on his lips.

I put down my glass and reached for his arm. Loki's gaze flickered over me before turning back to the window. My husband, I thought, watching the profile of his soft lips, the shadows that pooled at the base of his throat. My husband, who was so handsome people stopped talking in mid-sentence just to stare as he walked past. My husband, the cleverest of the gods of Asgard, who once risked everything he had to find the apples of immortality. Not out of malice or to seek personal gain, but to give them to a human man and woman. Because he fell in love. Because he wanted to build a family.

Loki drew a deep breath, his chest rising against my arm, and a strange gratitude rose in my breast, erasing my earlier bitterness. Sigyn was no mystery to me. I was thankful for her, I realized. I was glad someone had been there for Loki, in the long centuries before I was born.

I reached for his cheek, pressing my palm against his cool skin, feeling for the scars I knew he hid beneath his illusions. He turned to smile at me, but his eyes were still distant. He might as well still be on the coast, standing next to those burial mounds. For a moment, I wondered how to bring him back to me.

But the answer was obvious.

I pulled his face to mine and kissed him. For a heartbeat he didn't respond, and my lips pressed against his smooth, beautiful face as if I were kissing a marble statue. Then his lips parted, slowly, almost reluctantly.

His mouth tasted like Hendrick's gin, that strange blend of floral sweetness and the sting of alcohol. As usual, I guessed Loki's gin and tonic had actually been a gin and gin, garnished with ice. He opened for me, letting me press my lips to his and slip my tongue inside his cool mouth. Feeling him. Claiming him.

Loki's hand moved up my back, and his lips danced against mine. He sank his hand into my hair, pulling my head toward him. I closed my eyes, blocking out the yellow glow of the lamp in the corner, the entire living room. All I wanted to feel was him, the cool brush of his skin against mine, the ripple of his muscles beneath my fingertips.

Without thinking, I shifted on the couch, pressing my chest against his. Then I kicked off my shoes and threw my legs across his lap. His eyes widened, but I didn't give him time to respond. Before he could speak, I was on him, straddling his legs and kissing him as though my life depended on it, our tongues and lips embracing as we traded breaths. His cock stiffened against my stomach as we kissed, and something tightened deep inside me. Had I really thought my sex life was over?

Damn, I'd never been so happy to be proven wrong.

I dug my hips into his, and Loki groaned against me. He grabbed a fistful of my dress, yanking it up. It slipped over my thighs and up my back. Loki grabbed my hips, sinking his fingers into my skin. It briefly occured to me there was no way I should be this turned on, not after hearing that story.

And then I realized I didn't fucking care. Loki was my husband, my own personal Norse sex god. Mine, damn it. I needed this, and I suspected he did too. I broke our kiss and leaned back, panting.

"There's a problem," I gasped.

Loki's brow furrowed and his eyes darkened. "What?"

I grinned like an idiot and wiggled my hips against the heat of his cock. "Your pants."

"You don't like my pants? I thought they were rather flattering."

At that point, I honestly couldn't have said exactly what Loki had been wearing when we'd left the house for our dinner date. Fuck, that felt like an entire lifetime ago. I leaned forward, catching his bottom lip between my teeth and pulling him in for another kiss. Through the thin fabric of his pants, his cock pulsed against the heat of my sex.

"I hate the pants," I growled, grinding against him. "Hate them."

His pale cheeks had flushed, and his eyes seemed unfocused. His breath was coming faster.

"Fine," Loki said. "If they're so offensive to you—"

His pants vanished, and the heat of my thighs met his cool skin.

"Ohhhhh, fuck!" I cried, tilting my hips to meet his cock.

Loki closed his eyes, tightened his grip on my waist, and thrust up, entering me in a burst of pleasure so intense it was almost pain. I had a moment of disbelief as I felt the tight heat of an orgasm building. Could I possibly be so ready to come, so soon?

Oh, God, yes.

I ground my hips into him, riding my husband for all he was worth, as he clung to my waist and tilted his head back, his breath coming in fast little gasps. I watched him as I pushed closer and closer to my climax. The hard lines of his muscular chest, the sharp angles of his face. The dark shadows pooling at the base of his throat, just beneath the flutter of his pulse. The sharp, quick gasps of his breathing. The line of his jawbone, his high, elegant cheekbones. The shadows his eyelashes cast over his pale face as he closed his eyes, and cried out—

His cock stiffened inside me, pulsing with his seed, and my body responded by pushing me over the edge. My legs tightened involuntarily around his thighs, and I tried not to scream, I tried—

"Oh, Loki!" I screamed, then collapsed against his chest.

The orgasm shuddered through me, coming in waves, overwhelming me completely. Loki kissed the top of my head as my mind spun and drifted somewhere in the aether.

Adelina's sharp cry split the air. Loki's body tensed beneath me. I blinked and swallowed, trying to recover my ability to form words.

"Shit," I mumbled. "I woke her up. Sorry."

Loki's hand tightened around my back. "No, my love. It's just four in the morning."

Blearily, I shifted off his lap. He helped me pull my dress over my head, then covered me with a blanket. I tried to keep my eyes open as he left the room, and failed miserably. The next thing I knew, Loki was kneeling beside me, fiddling with the clasp on my bra as Adelina squalled. I reached up to help, and he slipped Adelina into my arms.

My breasts tingled as she nuzzled next to me, her pink, open mouth gaping as she searched for my nipple. Usually I had a bitch of a time breastfeeding while I'm lying down but, by some miracle, she latched on after only two false starts. I sighed as my milk started to flow, and Adelina began to grunt and gulp happily. My eyelids sank as the room dissolved in a warm, soft blur.

I woke to the sound of an epically large burp. The room was dark, and I was wrapped in a blanket on the couch. Through the windows, I could just see the first blush of pink in the sky above our backyard.

Loki stood silhouetted against the windows with Adelina resting against his shoulder. He was gently patting her back. I smiled in the darkness. He must have taken her from my breast without me even noticing.

Damn, I'd had no idea Loki would be such a good father.

Adelina grunted. I saw the dark silhouette of her tiny head against the predawn sky. Loki kissed her and began to sway from side to side. Very softly, I heard him humming. *The Briar and the Rose*, of course. Tears pricked behind my heavy eyelids, but I didn't make a sound. I didn't want to interrupt.

After the second chorus, Adelina sighed heavily. Her head crashed back against Loki's shoulder, and his humming ceased. He still swayed from side to side, his long, lean body looking improbably strong against the gray sky. I let my eyes close again.

"This time," Loki whispered.

My eyes flew open, but he had turned away from me. His hand pressed against the glass, as though he could almost reach out and touch what he wanted. Adelina's soft, raspy breathing filled the room. Suddenly, the sound of my own heartbeat seemed very loud. I had enough time to wonder if I'd imagined those words before Loki spoke again, his voice a low whisper in the darkness.

"This time. The apples."

EXCERPT FROM HEL'S LOVER[1]

"Wait. Ganglati, we have a visitor."

The voices fell silent, replaced by the soft rustle of clothing and scuff of shoes against stone. I blinked as a light swung into the hallway.

"Yes?" It a man, tall and thin, with a prominent nose and full lips. He held a lantern.

I raised my hands in front of my chest to show I had no weapons and gave him a broad, easy smile. "I beg your pardon, good sir. I'm seeking the Lady Hel."

His face scarcely moved, but I sensed a strange interplay of repressed expressions. Amusement, perhaps?

"Let him enter." The woman's voice spoke from behind him.

"Very well," he said, bowing to the side.

I thanked him and walked through the door. The room was sparsely furnished, with a low hearthfire and a large table. A severe black chair dominated the far end of the room.

On the chair sat a skeleton.

A moving skeleton.

I pressed my lips together and held my back stiff, fighting the urge to scream. My hands moved to my hip, feeling for the greatsword I'd carried most of my life. It was not comforting to remember I was completely unarmed.

---

1. https://www.amazon.com/Death-Beauty-Fantasy-Inspired-Mythology-ebook/dp/B071L88ZH7/ref=asap_bc?ie=UTF8

An enormous blue eyeball jerked in the skeleton's head as it examined a ream of parchment on the table, its bony fingers flicking through the pages. The skeleton's lower jaw moved, and the woman's rich voice echoed across the room.

"One moment."

The room was silent as she turned the parchment with a dry rustle. After flipping over the last page, she sighed and turned toward me. Only my decades of warrior's training with Óðinn kept me from running.

She wasn't a skeleton.

She was *half* a skeleton.

The right side of her face and body was a young woman with pale skin and dark hair, wearing a utilitarian brown dress. And the left side of her body was a corpse. As I stared, something sleek and dark shifted inside her exposed rib cage, disrupting the tatters of her dress. I was suddenly very grateful I'd not eaten anything at that feast.

"You've found me," the skeleton woman said. "What do you want?"

I swallowed hard against the bile rising in my throat. "Gracious Lady, my name is—"

"Stop." The bones of her fingers clattered as she waved her hand in the air. "Stop it. I know who you are, Baldr Óðinnsen. And I can guess why you're here."

"Oh, really?" I gave her my most winning smile.

It was met with a flat stare from both her living and her dead eyes. "Let me guess. You've come to offer me your heroic assistance, anything I desire, in exchange for one tiny, little favor."

I tried to widen my smile. "Perhaps, dear Lady."

She snorted. "Stop. Please, by the Nine Realms. It's just Hel. And am I on the right track, Baldr?"

"You are most perceptive," I admitted.

"So you've come to request a boon. And what did you have in mind as an exchange, son of Óðinn? Were you going to offer to ride out against my enemies? To defend my borders? To act as my champion in single combat?"

I bowed so low I was almost even with her feet, one clad in a simple sandal and one made of bone. With, if I wasn't mistaken, a single maggot in the ankle. I tried to concentrate on the foot with the sandal.

"I would consider it my honor and my duty, my...uh. Hel."

She laughed. Her voice rang out, bouncing off the walls and growing in strength. I frowned as I stood. Her attendants were laughing too. The tall, thin man at least had the dignity to attempt to cover his mouth, but the young women were laughing openly.

"I...I'm not sure I understand," I said.

Hel wiped her living eye with her skeletal hand. "Oh, you fool. We're dead! What borders do we have to defend, Baldr Óðinnsen? Niflhel echoes the world above, and it belongs to only us! What enemies do the dead have?"

She stood. The effect was quite disconcerting; I could see her femur rotating in her pelvis.

"And why would I need a champion? Who would dare to attack me?"

I swallowed, thinking fast. "Let me teach you."

Her living face raised an eyebrow. "You? Teach me?"

"Of course! What do the rest of the Nine Realms have that Niflhel lacks? Just knowledge, my Lady—I mean, Hel."

She turned, examining me with the skeletal eye. I suppressed a shiver.

"You think I lack knowledge?" Her voice was hard as steel.

I forced myself to smile. "Don't we all have something to learn?"

Several of her attendants laughed, but I ignored them and focused all my attention on Hel. She'd turned so all I could see was her decaying skeletal visage. With no face or skin, it was impossible to read her expression. I had no way of knowing if my smile, or my unbuttoned shirt, was having any effect.

I had the sinking feeling it wasn't.

Hel faced me again and a cold, thin smile crept across her living lips. "Very well, Baldr, son of Óðinn. I'll offer you a deal."

A low murmur spread through the crowd of attendants. It did nothing to make me feel more comfortable.

"You teach me something I don't already know," she said, "and I'll grant you one boon. Anything you ask."

There was a gasp at that, quickly hushed. I frowned.

"You'll have three days," Hel said. "Beginning at sunrise. Now, Eriksen, please show our new guest to his quarters."

My mind spun as the tall, thin man led me from the room.

What in the Nine Realms had I just agreed to do?

Find Hel's Lover here[2]!

2. https://www.amazon.com/gp/product/B071L88ZH7

THANK YOU!

You're amazing!

Thank you so much for reading and supporting independent artists. Without your support, I wouldn't be writing!

Now that you've finished *The Trickster's Song*, please do consider leaving a review on Goodreads[1] or Amazon[2]. Reviews make or break the careers of independent authors like me, and I promise I really do read every single one! :)

Join Samantha's mailing list for your free copy of The Trickster's Honeymoon[3]

---

1.   https://www.goodreads.com/book/show/41215796-the-trickster-s-song

2.   https://www.amazon.com/dp/B07GL3HS7T/

3. https://dl.bookfunnel.com/nxonrreiwu

www.ingramcontent.com/pod-product-compliance
Lightning Source LLC
Chambersburg PA
CBHW022207030726
47494CB00021B/1753

* 9 7 8 0 9 9 7 6 8 9 8 9 1 *